Dedication.

This book is dedicated to my family. Without their support and tolerance this would not have been possible. Thank you to my beautiful wife, Tina. My research and illustration staff, my daughter's Krysta and Madison. To my son Aidan, the creator of the Aladusuch spell. To my mom Dorothy, my sisters Allyson, Jo-an and Andrea. And to my brother Glynn whose promised work is in progress. To my dad, Villard Karyl Wright and my father and mother-in-law, Victor and MaryAnn, may they rest in peace.

Original cover art by.

Krysta Wright

Index

Introduction

In this, the exciting conclusion of this Harry Potter saga, safety of the students of Hogwarts is once again threatened as an ancient threat reemerges in the form of perhaps the deadliest Dark Lord of all time, Alucard. But Justice, who feels he was born for but one purpose, to defend his coven from any impending evil, is up for the challenge. With a very unique set of skills, he prepares the staff and students to survive an inevitable attack. His charms leave Hermione torn between her feelings for Harry and her newfound feelings for Mr. Cain.

Several new students and staff members lend a hand in defending the castle and Justice ends up paying the ultimate price to ensure his new friends' safety.

Lucius and Draco lay burned and blistered in a darkened room. Draco was whimpering when the door burst open. A hooded figure swept into the room. It was large like a Dementor, and it hovered over them. "Ah, Lucius Malfoy, we finally meet face to face, and you look like this. I must say, this is by far the most courageous thing you have ever done. To come here, to my lair, after having entertained in my home in my absence. Were you comfortable there?"

"My Lord…It's true, you have returned."

"YOU DARE INTERRUPT ME!!! AFTER YOUR TRECHURY" The hooded figure barked.

Malfoy cowered. "I watched from afar as you and your ***Voldemort*** waged your own feeble attempt at war with my wizard community. Pathetic! He dared call himself a Dark Lord. One half-blood was able to defeat him, ***how***? I'll tell you. He was selfish. He was afraid and that fear caused him to be sloppy, trying to protect bits of his soul in horcruxes. When Slytherin and Westerfield came to see me, I told them it was an idiotic course. Placing faith in others, ***idiotic***! There can be only one true Dark Lord and his name is Alucard!" The figure pulled back its hood exposing a polished skull, white eyes and canine-like fangs. "My children came to me, awakened me from my slumber to report your defiance. eighteen years I'd slept awaiting the arrival of the blood sacrifice who would restore my youth, and someone orchestrates an attack on its coven. Had I not shown up to put an end to the foolishness the

Ranger would have killed them all. Tell me, who among you chose this target?" No one made a sound. "WHO???" The lamps in the room burned white hot and illuminated the two dozen wounded witches and wizards in the room. "Know this, only one of you will leave this room under your own power. It matters not to me who it is. One of you found the chronicle professing the name of the blood sacrifice and tried to kill it to keep me from rejuvenating. You dared attempt to frame me by abducting members of the Ministry on the anniversary of my coming out party? Perhaps you should have made sure I was dead before testing my patience. In any event, the sacrifice still lives, so I don't need any of you to survive." With a single wave of his hand a dozen other hooded figures, including Dementors, swooped in and began biting the wounded and collecting their souls.

"My Lord, I sought you out to offer my assistance in the retaking your rightful place as the head of the Death Eaters. Draco and I have returned to pledge our allegiance. Please spare him." Lucius pleaded. The figure extended its bony decaying hand and lifted Draco into the air. The figure clinched its fist and Draco's throat compressed. He drew him near to look him over. Draco was terrified and fought looking at him.

"Ahhh, the love of a father for his son, very touching. I wonder…Draco, this plan to attack the American coven, was it yours, or your father's?" He paused, "LOOK AT ME?" he commanded. His eyes began to glow red until flame erupted in his sockets. Draco trembled from fear.

"I know one of you put Barty up to it. Was it you Lucius? You can tell me. You may be spineless, but you have

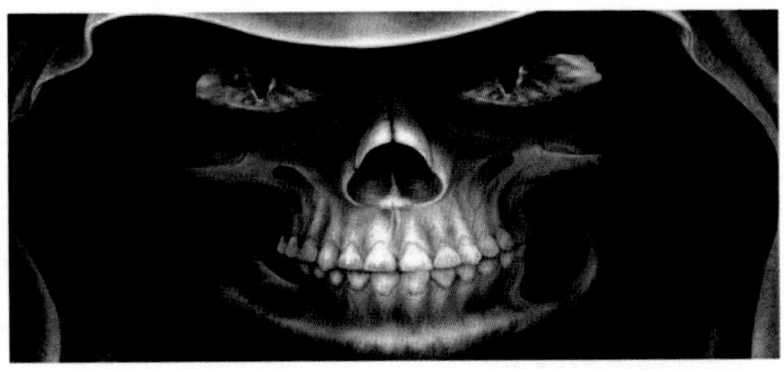

shown a moderate intelligence." He leaned in close to Lucius, the smell of fresh blood from his wounds filled Alucard's nostrils. Lucius trembled with fear. "Or perhaps you, Draco? From what I've read, the apple didn't fall far from the tree. And before you speak, know this, if your father did not plan the attack, I will not kill him. You have my word." He released Draco and after gasping to catch his breath he struggled to get the words out.

"You just said only one of us is leaving here alive. I don't want to die."

"So be it." With another wave of his hand the others burst into flames. Lucius looked at Draco then closed his eyes.

"It was my idea, my Lord." he stated. "I saw the prophecy." Draco turned away. He couldn't look his father in the eye.

"The choice is made then." Alucard raised his hand. Draco winced and turned away, making no attempt to bargain for his father's life. Alucard paused. He spared him for the moment. "How does it feel, Lucius? To have spawned such a sniveling coward. So willing to let you die in his place. Were it one of my children I'd have torn his heart out and eaten it as a snack." He leaned into Draco, "I know it was you. When you found the chronicle in Snape's affects you had no idea what it was. You orchestrated the murder of the other potential successors. What was your plan? Have your henchmen kill the others then kill them, including your own father? It almost brings a tear to my eye. There may be a place for you yet." He reached out and touched Draco. Draco began to shake. Lucius began to cry. He knew Alucard had likely hit the nail on the head. Draco had been fighting his father every step of the way since they acquired the Hallow. He was young and hot headed and driven by revenge. He was determined to beat Harry. He also harbored a secret. He was motivated to get Hermione, a secret he could never share with his father. He was a pureblood wizard, and she was a mudblood. They could never be together. "I must say, I am a bit disappointed your father hasn't taught you proper history. You thought you could kill me then resurrect Voldemort and it would secure you a place in his regime. You thought he'd be grateful. You are indeed a Malfoy, down to the same terrified expression. You bring shame to pureblood status." Draco moaned. "On the other hand," He looked around the room at all the dead bodies. "Your ambition may yet prove to be an asset. You cannot be trusted," He paused, "I like that. With the proper guidance, you may prove to be useful, and I ***am*** in need a few new recruits." He pulled Draco close to him and a long, forked tongue flicked out." You know these people. You can get close to them. You can bring them to me. You obviously have no regard for life, which I find commendable, and I do so detest the unnecessary spilling of pure blood; there is so little of it left. You see Lucius, there is a bright spot you can cling to, your son as my protégé. From utter disappointment to the apprentice of the greatest Dark Lord of all time. You may yet have done something valuable and for that I have a treat for you." He paused and both Malfoys took this as a sign he was considering using them as his servants. He turned away from them and when he turned back, he removed the hood and there, standing before them was Narcissa."

If I chose you, Lucius, you could have it all." Again, Lucius began to cry. He was speechless. He used what energy he could muster to reach for her. "***However***, since I don't need two of you to do one job…" He reared up and swooped over to Lucius and covered him with his cloak. Lucius screamed out in agony then, seconds later, he stopped moving and collapsed to the ground, white as a sheet. Draco screamed and cried, "You said..."

"I lied. Like you, ***I*** cannot be trusted."

Alucard returned to his skeletal form and floated over to Draco. He extended his hand from the cloak. It was no longer skeletal and decaying, it was a firm skin covered hand with razor sharp talons. "Give me your arm Draco." Draco was frightened and with good reason. Alucard had just killed his father. "Don't make me ask twice!" Draco reluctantly stuck his arm out. Immediately Alucard could see the residue of Draco's dark mark. He grabbed the arm and sunk his teeth into it. Draco winced and had a hard time looking but got through it. When Alucard released him, his burns were healed. "I have seen your heart Draco, black though it may be. Tell me of this fair maiden for whom you hold a torch." The smell of Hermione's blood filled his nostrils as they walked together.

Chapter 25 – Peeves' confession

GAME ONE

Ron was up early. There was nervousness, but mostly he wanted to avoid Harry. He had no idea Harry had spent the night in the hospital wing. He'd slept heavily after his collapse. The team scheduled a brief final walkthrough on the pitch after breakfast. Charista chose to let Hermione sleep. She'd slept well through the night, but with the break of dawn she found herself tossing and turning. Charista let Justice know of the events of the previous evening. He had stayed awake all night after feeling the surge of energy from the hooded figure. He assured her that Harry'd be alright. Harry was a loner. His normal mind set as a Seeker was that it was all up to him, and he'd play that way. It was what made him so good. Ron, however, in Justice's opinion, was a people person, a follower not a leader. If he and Harry didn't patch things up before the Quaffle went up they were going to have a problem. He was going to let his game be affected by his emotional state. He communicated to her to have Cam and Freddy hang near the Keep, to help. Hermione opened her eyes and when she looked across the room, she saw a figure hovering and watching her. It pulled the hood back then floated toward her. She quickly grabbed her wand, but when she turned back it was gone. She looked all around, even under the bed but found no one. She dressed quickly and went to find the others. When she pulled the door open Demetria was standing there. Hermione asked a favor. She whispered into her ear then handed her a quill and some parchment. She touched her and Demetria began to draw.

When she finished, she asked, "Who is it?"

"I don't know. It was an image from a nightmare I had."

She went to Gabrielle and asked where the library was. Gabrielle led the way.

The players went to the field for final instructions. Wood watched Harry closely. He was prepared to sit him if he didn't feel Harry was fit to play. As they separated, an argument broke out in the corner. "What's wrong with you?" Harry barked.

"*Me*? I'm not the one who acts like the world owes him something. Voldemort is dead, you're not the chosen one anymore, you're just another orphan who's not gonna have anywhere to go in six months." Ron reminded him.

"You're just mad that Hermione's with me, not you."

"Don't flatter yourself mate, Hermione is with Justice. She just doesn't want to hurt you before the tournament."

"Guys!" Charista said, "Enough! Neither of you are thinking clearly and neither of you are going to be ready for this game. I'm tempted to ask Wood to pull both of you to give us a chance."

Harry turned to walk away and Charista reached out for him. She touched his shoulder and images began to flash through her mind. They weren't making any sense. The last one had Harry walking toward her looking very angry and at less than a full step away from her he opened his mouth and exposed a huge pair of fangs. He jerked away from her just as Oliver reentered the room. "I have the starting lineup for the match. I want the starters on the field in five minutes. The rest of you get in the air and get in some sprints to work up a sweat. I may call on you at any time, so look sharp. Harry, you've been cleared to play by the doctor, how do you feel?"

"I'm ready to go."

Chapter 25 – Peeves' confession

"Okay." He posted the list and the players gathered around. Harry turned to Wood.

"You may want to keep an eye on Ron. He's distracted."

"I'll be keeping a close eye on both of you." The Chasers for the first match were Blaise, Seamus and Emmerick. The Beaters were Freddy and Cormac. Ron was the Keeper and Harry was the Seeker. Wood had considered Harry's suggestions. As Ron walked out of the room he was heard saying, "Looks like we don't have anything to worry about, the chosen one is gonna save us again."

Charista and Jade were shocked they weren't going to start the match. She relayed the line up to Justice.

"Should I come see what's going on?"

"No, you know you're not allowed. You need to start to focus on the Triwizard tryouts. I'm not sure Harry will be physically or mentally ready for the strain. How are things there?"

"All quiet so far. Have you noticed anything else there?"

"No, it's beautiful here. They are in the process of finishing the installation of silver perimeter fencing."

"Silver?" he repeated, "Did Hermione notice that too?"

"I think so."

"Any thoughts?"

"Yeah, they must have money to burn."

"Tell me about it. Is Hermione around?"

"No, after breakfast she left with one of the Beauxbatons girls. I think she mentioned the library."

"I need to talk to her. Can you get a message to her?"

"Perhaps later, the match is about to start."

"Right, well good luck and be ready. With that line up. I'm thinking you guys are gonna need some late game heroics from the M.V.P. You'll get your shot."

"I was born ready. Gotta go."

"Good luck."

"Oh, Justice, there's someone here that says she knows you. Her name is Rochelle Maynard. She was in the vision we extracted from you. Do you remember her?" She waited for a reply but heard nothing. "Justice?" He was gone. She shrugged her shoulders and headed off.

'The library, okay Jean, guide me'. He walked in and looked around, isle after isle. 'Talk to me Jean'. He closed his eyes and started to move through the room. He turned at the end of an isle and when he opened his eyes there was a hooded figure standing before him. "Who are you?" he asked. The figure raised its hands, one was normal and clean with long, sharp, pointed nails. The other was bony and skeletal. Justice fired a curse at it that passed right through it. The figure spoke.

"I feel your fear!" It cast a spell that Justice blocked. But the spell was a fake. The image was in his mind and yet he still felt it in his chest. He fell to the ground before realizing the hooded figure had disappeared. He looked around in every direction and got to his feet as he heard a voice behind him. He spun and pointed his wand.

"Hey! It's me. Marcus. What's going on? You okay?"

"Yeah, I'm fine." He stood up. "Where have you been?"

"I've been here, what do you mean?" Justice walked over to him and sniffed his clothes. The scent was familiar, but he couldn't place it. "What are you doing? Get away from me!" Marcus pushed him back then turned and stormed out. Justice started to follow him, but when he stuck his head out of the library, he saw Mallory approaching. Marcus bumped her as he stomped by and didn't acknowledge her.

Chapter 25 – Peeves' confession

"Hey!" Mallory commented, but she too let him go.

"Are you alright?" Justice asked her.

"What's his problem?"

"Not sure yet. Have you got a minute?"

"Sure, what's up?"

"You know magical history, where would I likely find information on past Dark wizards?" She led him to the restricted section, and they began to search.

Hermione sat at the table opposite Gabrielle flipping through that day's Daily Prophet and said, "I need to find something that will likely be in the restricted section. I'll need a distraction."

"Leave it to me." Gabrielle left the table and began flirting with the young man behind the counter.

Hermione slipped, undetected to the restricted isles and began to scan through the titles. She lifted her hand to make a selection and simultaneously Justice reached out blindly for a book in the Hogwarts library. They both extracted the same book. 'Dark Wizards Through the Ages'.

The books fell open to a page headed, 'Alucard'. Hermione looked at the picture.

It was a hooded figure, taken from a distance, but the pose clearly resembled the hooded figure they both thought they'd seen earlier. They began to read about him and soon learned that he was equally, if not worse than Voldemort, but when Peeves entered the room, the real story began to come out.

PEEVES

"I knew someone had opened the book."

"Who are you?" Justice asked.

"He's Peeves and I'm Myrtle." Myrtle flirted. She swooped down and sat beside Justice. Peeves, on the other hand seemed far more interested in Mallory.

"How did you know I opened the book?"

"All spirits here in the castle can feel when that book is opened. Most of us are here because of someone in that book." Peeves replied.

"And who's responsible for you being here?" Mallory asked.

"Tom Riddle set the beast loose in the castle that killed me." Myrtle blurted.

"And you?" Justice asked Peeves.

"Alucard is my killer. I still have the scar to prove it." He pulled back what was his shirts collar and exposed two small puncture wounds in his chest.

Chapter 25 – Peeves' confession

"What happened?" Mallory asked.

"Mallory Featherstone, is it not?"

"Yes. How did you know?"

"Why so curious about the book?" Peeves snapped.

"Because he may be back." Justice retorted.

"***What***?" Peeves was normally carefree and nonchalant, but this news gave him pause. He began to mumble to himself. 'It's been so long, there's no way…He won't recognize me…I won't be able to recognize him…This can't be, after all these years.'

"What are you going on about?"

"What makes you think he's returned?"

"People are going missing. Members of the Ministry are being targeted." Justice stated. "The signs are clear."

"It's just like before." Peeves whispered. "The Prophecy." he mumbled.

"What was that?" Mallory asked. Peeves ignored her.

"If there's anything you can tell me to help me fight him…" Justice began.

"Fight him?" Peeves echoed, "You can't fight him. If it's him, whomever he targets will die. You've never dealt with such a powerful wizard. He'll stop at nothing, he fears nothing."

"We have to try. We're not just going to stand by and wait for him to attack. If you know things about him, they may help us prepare, or at least defend ourselves." she said.

"If you know of a weakness, I have the skills to fight him. I can kill him." Justice stated calmly.

"Kill him?" Peeves gave him a long look. "Wizards have been trying for a thousand years. You couldn't even hurt him."

"Then I guess that's it. Thanks anyway." Justice turned

to Mallory, "He can't help. He's dead and he's more scared than either of us."

"Scared? I don't get scared. You have no idea of his power. His heart is black. He has no soul of his own. He killed me and I was his best friend. You and your ***seventh-year skills*** don't stand a chance."

"I get it. He was your best friend. You don't want to be disloyal to your friend." Justice paused, "He, on the other hand, didn't feel that killing you was crossing the line."

"Maybe he doesn't really know anything worthwhile. We'll just keep looking."

"What you want to know you won't find in any of these books, but my firsthand knowledge is of great value. What do you offer?"

"That depends on the information." Justice replied.

"Not good enough. We make a deal, or my lips are sealed."

"What do you want?" Mallory asked.

Chapter 25 – Peeves' confession

"You can learn from her." Peeves taunted as he swooped in close to her. "I don't want much, a mere trinket really. It's just an old knobby stick. It's of no use to you."

"What are you talking about?"

"Where is it?" Justice asked.

"Where is what?" Mallory asked.

"He knows where the wand is." Justice pointed out.

"I overheard the professor talking one evening. I thought he was having a conversation with someone, but he was alone. He was writing out some sort of document and muttering your name. He kept repeating that you should have it, but that it may be too much of a burden on you. It needed to be destroyed, but he wasn't strong enough. He hid it instead."

"Where is it Peeves, it's very important?" Justice demanded.

"What's it worth to you?" Peeves started to float away.

"*Aladusuch!*" Justice shouted and Peeves was trapped in a transparent globe. He began pounding at the inner wall of the containment.

"LET ME OUT!" he shouted. Myrtle laughed hysterically. "How are you doing this?"

"Tell us what you know."

"Or what?"

Justice pointed his wand and a raging flame appeared beneath the globe. "I'm not sure yet."

"I'll show you." Peeves reasoned.

"Peeves, I'm going to let you out. No more games. We need your help. That stick, as you call it, is of great importance to Alucard. You're a poltergeist, you have heightened senses. You must have felt the energy surges recently. You know what they mean. There's a dark force out there. It may not be Alucard, but whatever it is, it's coming, and soon. I've been feeling it more and more often. I'm here to fight. It's my purpose, my destiny. Tell us what you know about him and if it helps us defeat him, with Mallory's permission, you can have the wand then." Justice looked at Mallory and she shrugged her shoulders.

"I don't have the wand and haven't been told anything about it being given to me. If the information helps us win, it sounds like an acceptable deal to me. If we lose, I guess we won't have a need for it anyway." Mallory reasoned.

Peeves thought it over. Justice released him from his enclosure. "You do have an extraordinary skill set." Justice nodded his head. Peeves floated down and looked into his eyes. "You've been touched too, haven't you?"

Justice leaned in and quietly said, "If you believe I have, you know what I'm capable of and you know I have nothing to lose. Tell us what you know."

Peeves began talking. "I knew him as a boy. We grew up in the same neighborhood. He was a sickly kid for years and the other kids would tease him constantly. We weren't sure he was going to physically be able to attend school, but he was an exceptional wizard. He was so thrilled when he got his acceptance letter to Durmstrang. He was alright at first, but he took a downward turn and almost died in our second year. I saw him on his death bed and yet, just days later he was up and spryer than ever and he returned to school as healthy as a horse. I asked him about it, and he told me he'd made a deal with Death. I figured he was joking. He was different after that, and it wasn't long before students started turning up dead. I didn't notice at first that each one was someone who had teased him. Then others went missing and were never found. He'd disappear for days at a time. Then he'd just turn up out of the blue, clothes torn, dirty. He began to stay indoors all the time. He said he'd developed an allergy to the sun."

"What kind of student was he?"

"He studied everything he could find, every type of magic. We grew apart. The following year I transferred to Hogwarts to study under my hero, Salazar Slytherin, and to be closer to the beautiful Helga Hufflepuff. He wouldn't leave me alone though. He began writing me, asking me questions about Hogwarts."

"What kind of questions?" Mallory asked.

"Who was attending, who was on the staff, how to get in and out. The school was only about fifty years old, but already there were students and staff creating ways in and out."

"Like the Chamber of Secrets?" Justice paused a moment.

"You're aware of that one, are you?" Peeves paused and he suddenly pulled back and seemed hesitant. "You are an odd warlock Mr. Cain. Your skills are remarkably similar to some very famous, or should I say infamous, historical figures. Is that your ambition Mr. Cain, to become a legend?"

"We're not talking about me. This is about Alucard, remember? You were telling us about his obsession with you." The lights in the room flickered. "Perhaps I shouldn't be telling you this."

"No, I think you should." Justice stared into Peeves' eyes and produced another energy ball.

"Right."

"Why was he asking you, a new student at Hogwarts, about secret entry ways?" Mallory asked.

"I had always been considered a bit of a trickster, although I can't for the death of me figure out why. He knew I had created a passage from Nurmengard to the school and one out of Durmstrang that we used regularly to get out during the school year until the headmaster found out about it. He was certain I'd do the same here."

"And was he right?"

"Well…yes." Peeves pouted. "Do you want to hear this or not?" Justice raised his hands and stepped back. Peeves continued. "One day he showed up, here in the castle. He began causing trouble and I was being blamed. He left letters and diagrams in my belongings. He posted threats around the campus that incriminated me, and I was suspended. He visited often."

"How was he not detected? This was an entire school of witches and wizards, some of the top minds of our community." Mallory questioned.

"Things were different then. Wizard on wizard crime was in its infancy. Most magic was designed to conceal us or defend us from muggles. No one wanted to believe pureblood wizards had anything to fear from other pureblood wizards. Everything bad that happened was blamed on the half-bloods and mudbloods. Slytherin made sure to point that out every time. What is your blood status Mr. Cain?"

"Stop changing the subject."

"You didn't answer the question." Mallory reminded.

"He didn't have to register then so he came and went as he pleased."

"Register?" Mallory questioned, "He was able to transfigure?"

"He was an animagus." Justice stated.

"He's a shape shifter." Peeves corrected.

"What did he shift into?"

"Whatever, or whomever, he wanted to."

"***Whomever***?"

Chapter 25 – Peeves' confession

"He can be anything or anyone. He's the most talented wizard I've ever known next to Dumbledore. You have no idea what he's capable of. He's very persuasive."

"What happened after he got you suspended?" Mallory asked.

"He cornered me one day after I'd been reinstated. We quarreled. He wanted me to help him gather first years. Muggleborns, half-bloods, he wanted to herd them together for slaughter. He wanted me to help him kill. He had never fully respected me so he never suspected that I could read his mind. I used Legilimens on him and found out his secret. How he was able to overcome his illness and recover so completely. How he became stronger than any witch or wizard of the time. Why his heart turned as black as night." He paused.

"So, what was it?" Mallory prodded.

"He had indeed been cursed by Death himself, but at a cost."

"And what was that?" asked Mallory, thoroughly engulfed in the story.

"In exchange for eternal life he was sworn to provide Death with human souls, one million souls to be exact. Three souls for every day he walked the earth. He can't be stopped." Peeves' voice tailed off as he began to feel that his information was in vain. He was convincing himself that Alucard was, in fact, invincible.

Mallory stepped over to Justice. She whispered in his ear, "As fascinating as this is, we still don't know he has anything to do with what's happening now. You saw the Malfoy's. Why don't you think they're the ones behind all this?"

"The younger one is too aggressive. He doesn't think like a Dark Lord. He's being driven by something else. As for the father, he was too easy to defeat. Neither of them is behind this energy surge, they're just pawns." Justice clarified.

"What else did you learn when you read his mind?" Mallory asked.

"He's pure evil. There is no redeeming virtue in him." Peeves paused. "So, there's no reasoning with him."

"Then what?" Justice urged.

"He bit me." Peeves began to float in a circle. "My life ended in an instant." He was a poltergeist, a ghost, no blood, no beating heart, no emotions, yet he appeared visibly shaken.

"Again, I ask, how do we know for sure he's back?" asked Mallory

Peeves glared at her then darted with blazing speed through the library. Papers blew everywhere and a copy of the day's Daily Prophet settled before them. The headline was the start of the Intramural Tournament, but a small article on the back page spoke of a disappearance of another top Ministry official under suspicious circumstances. Just as they finished reading, a huge book slammed down on the table before them and opened to a page. The book was an archive of newspaper clippings and in the same corner of the page, of a newspaper dated the same exact month and day, nearly a thousand years earlier, was an article that read nearly word for word, the same report. "It's him alright. The energy is unmistakable."

"Peeves, I know Alucard is a shapeshifter, but if he was close to you, like in the same room, would you be able to tell it's him?" Justice asked as he shifted his eyes to Mallory.

"Without a doubt." Peeves replied. Justice took that to mean Mallory was no longer a suspect. Then Peeves added. "It's him. The energy is the same. I feel it right now. He's close." Peeves looked at Justice then at Mallory. Justice looked at Mallory again and she was looking at Justice.

Chapter 25 – Peeves' confession

Hermione had found that same article in the archives and realized the correlation between it and the story in the current paper. She folded the paper and checked her watch. The match had started, but she'd have time to catch some of it. On her way out, she noticed a row of computers. She planned to return. She passed Gabrielle and Gabrielle abruptly said her goodbyes to the young man and left.

"This obviously is no coincidence. So now that we are sure of whom we're dealing with I really need to know e verything about him. I have the skills; I just need the correct strategy to stop him once and for all. Can you tell me what I need to know? What weakness does he have that I can exploit?" Justice encouraged.

"I've told you what I know of the legend."

"I need to know what's not in the books. You do want him stopped, right?"

Peeves still wasn't fully convinced but did realize that Justice was the one warlock with a chance against Alucard, so he continued. "He's been around for about a thousand years, no one knows for sure his exact age. He's caused plagues and released viruses. He's responsible for disasters thought by muggles to be natural. His body ages fifteen years for every hundred he survives. He had an eleven hundred soul yearly quota, that if not reached caused him to lose use of a physical attribute. He's been blind for periods, deaf, mute, paralyzed on one side. He's even had an arm removed at one point. To this day, one of his severed hands remains on display at Borgin and Burkes. But the payment of a wizard soul gave him back what he'd lost, and payment of a pureblood wizard soul gives him a new power, thus making him the worst known threat to both civilians and the wizard community. No one is safe.

The unstoppable, irreversible aging of his body is taking its toll. He was falling behind and needed a plan. He began having children, the idea being that as they grew, they would bring victims to him to get him back on track. Death has a sense of humor. He always produces a boy and a girl. When the children were old enough, they went to school and the attacks began shortly thereafter. The first such event was at Durmstrang. Having been students there ourselves he already knew how to get in. Next was here at Hogwarts. Seventy-nine students and seventeen faculty members were taken. All three of the largest, oldest schools suffered attacks that first year, but his numbers were still low between the wizard opposition and the muggle authorities.

So, he learned a new trick. He learned how to attack without killing. He'd bite his victims and take the soul but leave the victim in a trans-like state. Undead, they could continue to walk the earth and do his bidding. Each soul they collected counted toward his debt. His numbers got back to where they needed to be, but he continued to age and tire. He made himself known, turning himself in to the Ministry at the age of one hundred and fifty. He claimed he was too old to be a threat and was retiring from being a Dark Lord. He had, however, as you know, studied all types of magic, Elf, Goblin, Dark, practical. While in Azkaban he studied muggles and wand lore. He corrected his imperfections and became stronger than ever. He used the time like a vacation. You asked about his weaknesses, he has no known weaknesses anymore."

"There's got to be something, no matter how small." Mallory suggested.

"He does have an allergy to silver and his aging

continues, but the souls continue to be collected by his foot soldiers. They are an army."

"Then I guess I'll have to deal with them too." Justice stated.

"Peeves, what happens when he reaches one million souls?"

"Legend tells that once he reaches his total his youth will be restored; he will truly become immortal, and his powers will be without equal. There *is* a second prophecy that is rumored to state that Death doesn't intend for Alucard to satisfy his debt and will come for him before he reaches the goal. Alucard, himself, must take the last soul. He grew tired of waiting in Azkaban, so he escaped, and another pair of his children were born shortly after that. That's all I know."

Justice looked at Mallory, "It's really not much to go on, but it'll have to do." He turned to Peeves, "Alright, lead the way to the wand."

"You're going?"

"Of course. Why?"

"I just thought you were restricted to the grounds."

"It's not here at the castle?" Mallory asked.

"No."

"I don't care." Justice snapped, "Let's go."

"I care. Justice, if you're seen leaving the castle…"

"I won't be." he replied and immediately turned invisible.

Mallory stepped between the door and where Justice last stood. "I can't let you go. I'll go. I'll get the wand and bring it back here then we'll plan the next step."

"No, it's too dangerous out there. You heard him, he could be anywhere, anyone. This is my job. I can't let you go."

"You're not ***letting*** me do anything. I want to go. You

know I'm not afraid."

He reappeared, sighed, leaned into her then said, "I don't trust our tour guide. Something's not right."

"Do you trust ***me***?"

"Of course. That's not the point."

"The point is we need this. I'm going and that's that. I'll be back before you know it."

He sighed. "Alright but take Marcus with you. He has pre-visions; he can warn you of unforeseen obstacles."

"He and I aren't exactly on speaking terms, remember?"

"He'll do his job. I mean it, he can help." He turned to Peeves. "Don't give me a reason to hunt you down."

"You can trust me." Peeves replied.

"Why did my level of trust just drop when you said that?"

"Justice, I'll be fine. We've got to go." She turned to leave. He reached for her.

"Mallory."

She turned around and he pulled her to him. "Don't take this the wrong way. Close your eyes." He leaned in and she did as he requested. He kissed her. He pulled back from her and again, he saw images of both her and Hermione and they looked eerily similar.

Chapter 25 – Peeves' confession

What was happening? He closed his eyes for a moment, but when he opened them again, he could feel Hermione before him. He could smell her vanilla perfume. He began to lean into her again but stopped when she spoke. "How should I take it?" she asked with a grin.

He blinked and everything appeared in black and white.

First her saw Hermione. Then Mallory.

He turned away and stepped over to a mirror and saw Harry's image.

Anthony Wright

He closed his eyes tightly as Mallory asked if he was feeling okay? He opened them and finally saw his own reflection.

His vision cleared. Color was restored and he responded. "Yeah, I'm fine." He quickly turned his attention to Peeves, but the little poltergeist appeared just as confused by his reaction. He turned back to Mallory.

"What did I do to deserve that?" she asked playfully.

"You'll thank me later." he grinned. At the time, she had no idea what he meant. She would find out soon enough.

"I'll thank you now." she said as she fanned herself. "I guess you've gotten over your shyness around me?" Her hair seemed to lighten as he looked at her.

"Be careful." He took her hand.

"You know I will." She let his hand go, bit her lip slightly then turned to Peeves, "Peeves, we'll leave at Midnight, okay? Meet me at the end of the bridge."

Chapter 25 – Peeves' confession

"I'll be there." He turned to leave.

"Peeves," Justice called to him. "Before you go, tell me about those ways into Durmstrang."

A hooded figure stood in a clearing not far from the Durmstrang campus. It whispered, "*Imperio*!" Jade turned from where she stood and looked in the direction of the whisper.

Hermione and Gabrielle made it to the pitch to see the score board reading:

Durmstrang 148 - Hogwarts 36

Ron had only stopped three of seventeen shots and there was a stoppage in play as they were tending to Seamus who'd suffered an injury. It appeared to be a broken leg. As the players huddled up Ron and Harry had to be separated. The team had lost its composure.

"Ron, Harry, you're both out. Jade, Robyn, you're up. Charista, you're in for Seamus. Normally we can't substitute for an injured player, but the tournament rules are different. Jade, don't let anything get by you." Wood also replaced an exhausted Cormac with Cam. The players took to the air amid giggles from the Durmstrang players. They were a burly, all male team and Hogwarts now had three women in the pitch together. There wasn't much time left. The Quaffle went up and Charista beat everyone to it. She raced toward the hoops and passed off to Blaise. He avoided a hit from the Durmstrang Beaters and passed it back to Charista who scored. **148-46**. Jade blocked two shots before Charista went on the attack again scoring quickly, **148-60**. The boys joined in the renewed burst of energy, and each scored a goal as Jade continued to shut down the opposing Chasers. **148-86**. Harry watched Charista in awe.

Viktor was furious, but time was running out. He knew, due to the time remaining, Hogwarts' only chance was catching the Snitch. He called his team together and emphatically instructed them to keep Robyn away from the Snitch. "Let them score! Stop the Seeker! That's only way they can win given time! Let's go!"

Wood used the time to give a last set of instructions to

his team and to make one last set of substitutions. He took Freddy out and put Reggie in. The size and strength of the Durmstrang team was taking its toll on Freddy who had played the entire match. "Reggie, you're fresh, you are to be Robyn's personal protector. If she catches sight of the Snitch, you plow the road for her. They know catching the Snitch is the only way we can win with the time that's left. They're gonna send everyone at her."

"Got it." stated Reggie confidently drawing a smile from Robyn.

"Blaise, Emmerick. You both played well. Vasco, Stormy, you're in."

Play resumed with just over a minute remaining. Charista got the Quaffle to Stormy and she scored immediately. Jade blocked another attempt, but the focus was on Robyn. She scanned the sky and finally saw the Snitch. She bolted for it and Reggie did as instructed. He flew interference for her as the clock wound down. The two Durmstrang Beaters closed in, and Robyn braced for an impact. Reggie flew in beneath her and when the Beaters angled toward her, she pulled back and Reggie slid into her place. When they hit, he yanked upward on his broom and Robyn dipped below them. The Durmstrang Seeker was stuck above the tangled mass of players giving Robyn a clear shot. She stretched, **Six, Five, Four**. Everyone held his breath as Vasco scored another goal. **Three, two**...she felt the wings on her fingertips. **One**, she lunged. The clock expired. She clasped her fingers around it.

"NO CAPTURE! NO CAPTURE! TIME HAD EXPIRED. DURMSTRANG WINS, 148-108."

Krum let out a sigh that could be heard in the stands. The players shook hands and congratulated one another on an exciting tournament opening match. Hermione walked up and Harry looked at her. "Charista, you were wonderful." he said to her while still facing Hermione. "Where were ***you***?"

His tone startled her. "I had some research to do."

"I thought you were here to support us, the team. You just can't allow yourself to relax for one minute, can you?"

"Leave her alone!" demanded Ron.

"Both of you, in the team meeting room, now!" commanded Wood. "The rest of you, get something to eat and get some rest. The next match is in four hours."

"I'm going to shower." stated Jade.

Hagrid stepped over to Harry. "Harry, what's goin' on? You ought not snap at Ermione that way. Its uncalled fer."

"Stay out of it, Hagrid!" Harry stormed off. Harry brushed by him but didn't touch him.

"Stay out of it?" Hagrid asked.

"I told you, he's mental, that one." Ron chipped in.

Demetria pointed out to Hagrid his nose was bleeding. Hagrid dabbed at it a couple times, but it just kept getting worse. Hagrid looked in the direction Harry had gone and just managed to say his name before he passed out.

"HAGREED!" cried Madame Maxime as she rushed to his aid. "What appened ere?" It took three of Beauxbatons staff, all using Liberacorpus to lift and move him. Wood was stunned. No one had seen Harry do anything to him, but if he stood accused, he'd certainly be suspended for the remainder of the tournament. Everyone tried to get their bearings. Justice felt a shudder in his spine. He couldn't see the hooded figure following Jade, but he knew something was amiss. He concentrated and asked Charista what was happening.

'Not sure, I'll get right back to you. Hermione may have found some information'. Charista stepped over to Hermione.

Chapter 26 – Opening match

"What'd you find?"

"I think I may know who the Ministry thinks is behind the abductions."

"Who?" Demetria asked.

"When did you get here?" Charista asked.

"HOGWARTS TEAM MEMBERS! LET'S GO!" shouted Wood. The rest of the team hurried off. Charista lagged behind with Hermione and they discussed Alucard.

"Are you sure it's him?" Charista asked.

"The signs sure point that way. He's close to reaching his goal and he'll have to show himself to take the last soul. Until then he could be anywhere, or anyone. I think Madame Maxime knows the legend and that's why the fencing is silver."

"We need to stay together in groups for safety."

"There's more." Hermione pointed out.

"What do you mean?"

"The date of the Triwizard Tournament is the anniversary of the first attack. I did the math and based on the number of people who are expected to attend the tournament, I think he's going to be there to try to collect the rest of the souls. It'll be a massacre."

"You've got to tell Justice."

"How?"

Charista took off her glove and touched Hermione's face. Hermione wiped a small trickle of blood from Charista's nose. "Now you can talk to him." she said.

"Really?"

"Charista! Why aren't you resting?" shouted Wood.

"Sorry Wood. Gotta go." she smiled and headed off.

Hermione headed off to find a quiet place. Wood reentered the common room. "I don't know what's goin on with you Potter, but you've got some explainin' to do."

"Me?" Harry rolled his eyes and turned away.

"That's it? Nothin' to say for yourself?" Harry gave no response. "Alright Harry, you leave me no choice. You're benched for the remainder of first round."

"BENCHED!" shouted Harry.

"You'll be placed on the physically unable to perform list." Wood continued. No sooner had the words come out there was a knock on the door. Wood figured it was Madame Maxime coming to discuss Harry's actions. He opened the door. Harry grabbed his scar and winced.

He had his back to Ron who had walked over to talk to him. "What's wrong with you Harry? This isn't you mate. Even I don't want you to be benched, we need you." Ron placed his hand on Harry's shoulder.

Suddenly they were both startled by Wood flying across the room and slamming into the wall. As he fell to the ground Harry and Ron turned to see a hooded figure entering the room. Before they could retrieve their wands, it cast a spell that formed a barrier between the two of them. Ron was sealed in a transparent cell of some kind and could only watch as the hooded figure moved closer to Harry. Harry scar was burning. The figure cast another spell that knocked Harry off his feet. The figure hovered over him. Harry found his glasses and put them back on. He looked at the figure.

"You?" he said before the figure covered him with its cloak.

It whispered in his ear, and he went white as a sheet. "Give this to the one w h o occupies your thoughts." Then it placed something in his hand.

"HARRRRYYYY!!!" Ron shouted, powerless to help.

Moments later Ron's barrier disappeared. The figure

Chapter 26 - Opening match

raised its wand and Ron was knocked off his feet and hit his head. The figure disappeared in a cloud of smoke. Ron struggled to his feet and stumbled over to Harry. He crouched down over him as Wood slowly came to and the door swung open. This time it ***was*** Madame Maxime followed by Pius Thicknesse and Ron, still groggy, cast a curse toward the door before he realized who it was. His spell missed.

"***Expelliarmus!***" cast Gabrielle knocking Ron's wand from his hand. "What did you do to Arry!" she questioned.

"Wait, you don't think...I didn't..."

"SILENCE!" shouted the Headmistress. "Take his wand!" she commanded. "First, you two are zeen fighting, then Hagreed iz urt and now you attack Wood and Arry."

"Attacked, no. It wasn't me. At least I don't think I..." He was confused. "There was someone else, a man... with a cloak..."

"You are banished from zee competition and will be sent back to Ogwarts tonight!" His wand was taken, and he was escorted to a waiting station for his ride back home. Wood and Harry were both taken to the hospital wing.

Hermione found a quiet place and checked to make sure

no one was around. "Justice? Can you hear me?" she asked softly.

"Jean? I'm glad you're okay. I heard some strange things have been happening there like the incident with Harry. Is everyone okay and accounted for?"

"We're all fine, but something is off with Harry."

"Do you think you're in danger?"

"From Harry? No. He'd never hurt me on purpose. What happened yesterday was a reflex and I was just standing too close. He didn't mean it."

"You're sure?"

"Yes." She paused. "Wait, can you hear everything I think?"

"Right now, yes. When we're not linked, no."

"Can you tell what I'm thinking?"

"No, my ability isn't as sophisticated as Charista's. Mine is more like a radio. I have to focus to tune in to you and you have to want to link up."

"I see." She breathed a sigh of relief.

"How does your arm feel today?"

"It's fine. It was just a scratch."

'Then why is it still bleeding?' Justice thought to himself.

"Did you say something?"

"No." He hesitated. "I was in the library earlier and you led me to the information on Alucard."

"***I*** led you too it?"

"It's a long story. All signs are pointing to him being back and he's coming for Harry, that's what I've been feeling."

"Why would he want Harry?"

"He's still the chosen one. He may be the key. Perhaps he still has a piece of the last Dark Lord to attempt a rise to

Chapter 26 - Opening match

power inside him. I don't know for sure, but he's back and he's not far away."

"I found something about Alucard as well. I think I know where and when he'll show himself." she lowered her voice as she heard people coming.

"Where? When?"

"I've got to go. Someone's coming. We'll speak later."

"Be careful. And keep an eye on Jade."

"I will."

"Hermione? Is that you?" asked Demetria.

"Yes, it's me. I just needed a little air."

"Is someone with you?" Jade asked, looking around.

"No. I'm here alone."

Jade didn't seem convinced, but let it go. "We're gonna get something to eat before the second match."

"Wanna come?" asked Demetria.

"Sure."

Anthony Wright
Chapter 27 – The promise

"You look happier than I've seen you in a long while, maybe ever, no offense. What is it?" Mallory asked.

"Now that we've confirmed it's him, I have the advantage. Knowing your opponent is halfway to being able to defeat him."

"We need to let McGonagall know?"

"Not yet. Her plate is full enough as it is. There's a lot of evidence, but what if we're wrong? Crisp will have her for lunch. We still need to deal with that guy."

"I can take care of him."

"Once we get the wand, I have to check something out."

"What is it?"

"Something's not right at the tournament."

"At Beauxbatons? You know you can't leave Hogwarts."

"I should leave now. I have to make sure she's," he caught himself, "they're safe. I have to make sure they're not in danger." He looked at her and just saw her.

"They're fine, Hagrid's with them."

He just looked into her eyes. "***I*** have to do this. I really feel its where I need to be right now. I need your help. Please." He paused, "I'll only be gone a few hours. Can you cover for me?" "I don't know Justice."

"I'll hurry back. I promise."

Chapter 27 – The promise

"You report to me the moment you get back."

"I owe you one." He kissed her on the cheek then turned to head toward the forest. As he ran by the potion's lab, he wrinkled his brow then stopped and turned back. He fond Neville working away. "Hey Neville, how's it coming?"

"Slow. It's a complicated potion."

"If anyone can do it, you can. I really need it."

"I'm trying."

"Let me know as soon as it's ready."

Justice continued out to the forest but felt a little dizzy just as he found the car. He programmed in his destination and off he went.

Hermione entered the dining hall and was immediately approached by Gabrielle. "Ermione, I am so sorry!"

"For what?"

"Ron." She paused. "You don't know?"

"Know what? What's wrong with Ron?"

"He attacked Arry and Wood. He's been banned from zee tournament."

"Where is he now?" She jumped up from her seat.

"He is gone. He was sent back to Ogwarts."

"Is Harry alright? Where is he?"

"Zee ospital."

"Take me to him, please." She followed Gabrielle from the room. The others were shocked by the news. Charista wanted to tell Justice, but she knew he'd try to come. Little did she know he was already on his way. When Hermione reached the hospital wing, she stopped to say hello to Hagrid. He indicated he was feeling better and didn't believe Harry had anything to do with his injury. She made her way to Harry. The nurse tending to him told her he'd been given a sedative to help him sleep, so not to visit too long.

"Harry, can you hear me?" she whispered.

Without opening his eyes, he responded. "I hear you." he whispered and reached out his hand to her.

"How are you feeling?" she whispered.

"Sleepy." he mumbled.

"That's the medicine. Harry, what happened?"

"I…" He dozed off for a second then continued, "I don't remember."

"Is it true? Did Ron attack you?"

"Ron." he repeated. She sighed. The drugs were taking affect. She wasn't going to find out anything until he awoke later. She started to step away, but when she let his hand go, he woke up one more time, but still didn't open his eyes.

"This is for ..." He extended his other hand and grasped in it was the beautiful antique necklace. She looked closely at it.

"Harry, this is lovely. Where did you get it?"

"I…I love…you." He placed it in her hand.

A tear formed at her eye. "Get some rest. I'll come back." She was but a few steps from the bed when he whispered Charista's name. She turned back, "What did you say?" He was asleep again. She glanced around but Charista didn't appear.

She made it to the stadium in time to see the Hogwarts team flying in formations that looked more like choreographed ballet than Quidditch. They had more speed as a team than even Beauxbatons had anticipated. With Robyn as the Seeker, Charista, Demetria and Stormy as the Chasers, Reggie and Cam as the Beaters and Jade as Keeper, they were leading **196 to 54** and time was running out. They were faster to the Quaffle than their counterparts and more aggressive on the chase. They were moments away from their first victory when they made a tactical error. Demetria secured the Quaffle and raced down the side of the pitch. She passed to Stormy who moved to the center of the field then passed to a streaking Charista, who had already scored eleven goals.

If they could score one more time, they could ensure victory even if Beauxbatons were to catch the Snitch. Robyn caught sight of the little golden object and went after it. The Beauxbatons Seeker hadn't seen it, but Robyn's move alerted her to its position, and she too dove after it. It was admittedly hard to tell which event happened first, but just as Charista took a shot, the Beauxbatons Seeker beat Robyn to the Snitch and caught it as the clock expired.

The Hogwarts players argued that the Quaffle had left Charista's hand before the time expired which should have allowed the goal to count. Meaning that even if the official's attention was on the Snitch being caught the score should still have been **206 to 204** in favor of Hogwarts at worst. Perhaps home field advantage had reared its head, but the goal was waved off and the final score read:

Beauxbatons 204 – Hogwarts 196

It was a controversial loss, but would go down as loss, nonetheless. The players halfheartedly congratulated their hosts. They were exhausted and were glad their games were done for the day. None of them expected to start the tournament 0-2. What was even worse was that by night's end they would be two wins behind one of the other teams with only four games to play, but they'd played both games down to the wire and were confident they would find their way into the win column soon.

"You guys played amazing considering having lost two players for the remainder of the tournament. You should feel proud." Hermione suggested.

"Thanks. I'm gonna go change then we can go get some dinner, okay?" Charista proposed. "Is everything alright?"

"Yes, of course. I'll wait for you here."

"Everyone is in position my Lord." Draco whispered. Alucard sat in a throne chair at the head of a table in a darkened room. He wore a mask with the face of a skeleton on it. His hands were large and well-manicured. His body was nearly completely restored.

"What is the status of the cloak?"

"We've made contact with Potter at Beauxbatons. He didn't have it with him, but we know where it is. We took a hair sample to create a Polyjuice Potion and…"

"How soon will it be attained?" he cut across Draco.

"It's in Gringotts Bank. I sent Death Eaters to snatch the goblin who would have access to the vault it's being kept in. If that doesn't work, I also know where Bill Weasley is. He used to work at Gringotts, now he teaches at Hogwarts. Between the two of them we'll get into Potter's vault."

"If it's in Gringotts you should know Polyjuice Potion

won't work. When the time comes, Potter will retrieve the cloak for me himself."

"As for the wand…"

"Do not concern yourself with the wand."

"But my Lord, we know Dumbledore had it in his possession before he died. I'll get a message to Crabbe and Goyle to have them search the castle."

"I said not to waste your time. I have already made arrangements to acquire the wand as we speak. Time is of the essence. I'm close to my goal, but by my calculations, I will need every student in attendance for the Triwizard Tournament to reach my goal." He took a sip from a goblet filled with a thick red liquid. "Nothing can stand in the way."

"What about the American, my Lord? Have you made a decision about him?"

"You seek revenge do you, for the way he dispatched you and your father?"

"I would be honored to be the one to kill him for us."

"Patience my young apprentice. Patience. As I grow stronger, I can sense him, and I can feel his weakness growing. His downfall will be his heart. It will fool him into believing he can save them all as it did that night in America. It nearly got him killed then, it will cost him everything this time." he stated. He opened his hand and in it was the Resurrection Stone. Peeves floated in through the wall. "Ah, Peeves, my loyal friend. We were just speaking of you. I was wondering when you were going to come visit me." He paused. "Did you bring my belongings?"

"I've not yet acquired them. I'm being watched."

"Really?" Alucard replied sarcastically.

"The girl, the meddlesome one, she discovered the book's hiding place and she's taken it."

"I see, and the wand? I distinctly remember you telling me you would have it before nightfall. That was weeks ago."

"Dumbledore took it outside the grounds. I know if I can get his heir outside the gates, she'll sense its exact location."

"***You*** know?" he asked in a calm tone that raised everyone's suspicions. "Let me tell you what ***I*** know. You appear to have exceeded your usefulness."

"My Lord, there is something you should know."

"Yes, Peeves?"

"The American... His skills, I've never seen a young wizard with such a variety of specialties and control over them. He reminds me of..."

"Of me?"

"Of Fiona."

"She's dead! I killed her at the peak of her power. She was no match. This...Illusionist, will suffer the same fate, but only after I take everything, he cares for from him. Then I will unleash my full fury on the muggle infestation. Once I rid the world of these retched creatures all will bow to the one true and only Dark Lord. All purebloods will join me or perish. I will restore magical order once and for all time."

"Your skills were once the most formidable in our world."

"What's your point?"

"In your advanced condition..."

"Chose your words carefully..."

"Are you sure you're ready for him? He's not alone. Potter still exists as well."

"Not that it's any of your concern, but it's not my condition that will be an issue should he ever muster the courage to face me. As, for Potter, events have been put into motion that will have Mr. Potter looking to renegotiate his allegiance. Just tell us where and when you are meeting the young professor."

"Midnight, at the end of the bridge."

"Relax Peeves, you say he has heightened senses and yet he hasn't detected us living right here under his nose in the Chamber of Secrets this whole time. He is the chief protector of his coven, charged with protecting the Elders from extinction and yet he sends his professor into the arms of the enemy. Perhaps he is not the threat you make him out to be. No, my little friend, you leave Mr. Cain to me. I've got a surprise for him that's to die for."

"They say he's never lost." Peeves blurted.

"Then perhaps it's time to show him what loss feels like."

"I'll do it." Draco interjected. Alucard grew angry with Draco's interruptions. His appearance changed back into that of a skeleton. With a wave of his hand, Draco was hurled across the room and slammed into the wall. He held his finger to his lips.

"That was the last time you will speak without being addressed!" He walked over to Draco on his human legs and reached out his hand. Draco cowered and scrambled away. Alucard clinched his fist and Draco was yanked up and pressed against the wall. "The American would cut your throat without batting an eye. I said we should show him loss, he fears not for his own safety. His weakness is his heart. We'll take those close to him and make them suffer. That will be his punishment, their agony. He's prepared to die. It's the way he was brought up. The question will be, is he prepared to watch the ones he loves die in his place?"

Beauxbatons speed was too much for Durmstrang as their match ended in a lopsided **148 to 50** score. The first match of the second day would feature Beauxbatons and Hogwarts. Hermione sat with the team as they ate dinner.

"You haven't touched your dinner." Charista pointed out.

"I'm not hungry."

"Harry's going to be fine. He's just resting. Go see him."

"No. I don't think he wants to see me."

"What are you talking about?" Charista asked.

Gabrielle walked over. "Ow is Arry doing?"

"He's still in the hospital wing, he's getting some rest." Hermione replied. She paused then asked. "Gabrielle, the computers in the library, can anyone use them?"

"You must have zee password."

"Do you have it?"

"I can get it."

"Could you, please."

"But it is only good until midnight." She glanced around and said, "I'll be right back."

"What do you have in mind?" Charista asked her.

"Nothing yet, I just have a hunch."

"You always do." Charista smiled trying to get a feel for what was bothering her. "Do you need a distraction?"

"No, I don't want to get you in any trouble. You need your rest. If you were to get caught out of bed after curfew you might

Chapter 27 – The promise

get suspended too, and without you…"

"Alright, but if you run into any trouble, you know what to do."

"Thanks." She got the access password from Gabrielle then waited until everyone was in bed. She carefully made her way to the library. She entered quietly and headed toward the row of computers. Suddenly she realized she wasn't alone. She hid behind a counter. She heard footsteps drawing nearer then they stopped. Her heart raced. She glanced left and right then a hand reached down just above her, narrowly missing grabbing a hank of her hair. She silently scooted down as the hand felt around and finally grasped a brown paper bag with the leftovers of the librarian's after dinner snack. She held her breath until the person left the room and she heard the door close. She hurried over to the computers and logged in. She searched Alucard and skimmed through some of the information. Another name was mentioned several times, so she typed it in: FIONA TATTENGER.

An article came up that she printed. She then accessed Tobin's Spirit Guide and began to flip through the pages. She felt an energy growing and could hear sounds within the walls. Within moments ghosts began to fill the room.

Several hovered around. She reached for her wand but didn't threaten them.

"Who are all of you?"

"We're students." replied one of the spirits.

"We used to be students." corrected another. "We died here at the school and the circumstances of our death have kept us here as we await passage."

"What circumstances?" Hermione asked.

"We were bitten by a Dark Wizard."

"He drained our blood."

"We would have become his undead servants, but he collected our souls."

"We need our souls back to pass to our final resting place. It's the only way for us to achieve peace."

"But if he collected them, how can you get them back?"

"There are ways. He who collected them must die then the souls will be released."

"Or he, or someone else who's been touched can set them free."

"I tried to explain that to him before he killed me, but he wouldn't listen." said one of the specters that was dressed in robes as it floated to the forefront.

"And you are?"

"Professor Paramore. I was the Defense Against the Dark Arts teacher here. I sensed the darkness in him from the start. He'd been touched, I could tell."

"Touched? Touched by what?"

"Death himself." replied the professor. "Once you've been touched, you're given a choice. Go peacefully, accepting your fate or serve him."

"What exactly does that mean?"

"Once you've been touched, the only thing keeping you alive is fulfilling you're promised commitment."

"If a person's been touched, what type of symptoms would they exhibit?"

"A lack of fear. They're already dead, so they have

nothing left to be afraid of."

"They'd be a great ally in a fight. They would lead in a battle or fight a battle all by themselves. As part of their deal, they're given heightened senses and powerful gifts of magic."

"If it wasn't for the darkness."

"The darkness?" she asked.

"A person who's been touched cannot be trusted. They're like a timebomb. They're all the same."

"How so?"

"They start off nice. They've been given a second chance. How many of us get to come back from death? They're helpful and thoughtful. It's so sad. They think they can atone for their sins in life by being generous in pre-death, but eventually they realize they're on a death row count down. They turn bitter and lash out at people. As much as they would want to be with someone, they avoid getting close because it's just too painful for them."

"Finally, they decide to take as many people with them as they can."

Hermione's mind was running wild. She looked a little teary eyed, so the ghost backed off. She tried to change the subject. "The one who collected the souls? Do you know why he did it?"

"I was one of the last he took from the first attack. He simply told me he needed them for a debt he owed the Reaper. He said he needed them more than we did."

"Where might the souls be kept?"

"A prophecy sphere perhaps or an amulet. It wouldn't need to be big, and he'd definitely keep it near him."

"You mentioned that you need your souls to be allowed to go to your final resting place. If the wizard who has these souls repays his debt and gives them to the Reaper, what will happen to them?"

"Death will consume them like a scrap of Yorkshire pudding, and we will cease to be."

"And if the wizard is defeated?"

"We would be forever in the conqueror's debt and would seek to repay that person in any way he or she chose?"

"Do you know his name, the wizard who imprisoned you?"

"Oh yes. He wanted us to know who did this to us. His name is Al..."

They heard someone approaching. She logged off and shut off the computer. She hid near the door. Her breathing sped up as she struggled to suppress thoughts of Charista. She glanced over a stack of books on a cart and could see a silhouette of a large, hooded figure. She pulled her wand and steadied herself. She heard the door handle jiggle, but not open. Suddenly it stopped. She inched closer to the door and yanked it open.

There, in the hall was a wolverine patronus. It swung its head side to side twice and turned to go down a passageway. She looked up and down the hall. There didn't appear to be anyone else around. She followed the animal and was led outside of the building. It took her behind a gazebo in the courtyard and that's where it disappeared into Justice's wand. He approached her and hugged her. "Are you alright?" he asked since she seemed apprehensive.

"I'm fine. Surprised though, how did you get here?"

"I drove. I had to come see if things were safe here."

"Did you transform in the hallway?"

"No. I never went inside."

"How did you know where I was?"

"The scent of your blood."

Chapter 27 – The promise

"Excuse me? What blood?"

"Your arm, it's bleeding again."

She glanced down and could see a fresh spot had formed beneath her dressing. She hadn't even noticed. "Your senses are that powerful?" she asked. He nodded.

"You don't seem happy to see me."

"No, I am. I just know what you risked coming here."

"You're worth it." He smiled. "I thought maybe we could take a drive to help take our minds off all that's going on. I need to tell you something. Something is going on with me..."

"I don't know." She appeared to be trembling.

"Or not. I'm sorry if I'm crowding you, I..."

"It's not that. I've just been so confused. A ride sounds nice. I've found out a lot more." They went to the car, and he opened the door for her. Once they were both in, the car flew off. "Where are we going?" she asked.

"Where would you like to go?"

Jade watched the car ascending into the night sky from her window. Her eyes were solid white, and she saw the car despite it having the invisibility mechanism engaged.

"What's it like in America?"

"That's a good question. I spent most of my life in the coven. I didn't really get to experience much. Maybe after all this is over, we can go back and visit some places."

"What do you remember about your childhood? Tell me your earliest memory."

"It's hard to say. I didn't remember most of what you and Charista saw in my past. I do remember being alone. I remember being angry a lot."

"Tell me if any of this sounds familiar. You're not afraid of anything."

"We talked about that; I do feel fear."

"But you never run from it."

"I was taught to face my fears."

"You're good in a fight."

"My win percentage is pretty good so far."

"You have heightened senses and extraordinary powers. You're nice, almost excessively. You have a loyalty to your coven that's almost as if you feel you owe them your life."

"It's part of being an Alpha."

"Justice, have you ever been close to death?"

"I've had my share of serious injuries."

"I saw you step in front of a curse to stop a fight and come away without a scratch. I saw you blow into your hand and fix your broken bones. I saw Harry curse you so hard it put you in the hospital and yet…"

"And yet, here I sit."

"I have to ask."

"Feel free, I won't lie to you."

"Jade says this battle you believe is coming is going to leave you dead."

"You can't listen to Jade. She has her own agenda."

"Others say that even if you win, the cost of victory will still be your life."

"What others?"

"Twice you've asked about my arm, and it's started bleeding?"

"Your arm was bleeding before I asked about it. There's a question you still want to ask, what is it?" He spoke in a low tone that suggested he was just as ready to answer her question as she was ready for it to be answered.

"Do you have a deal with someone who's forcing you to confront this enemy?"

He paused a moment, "Yes." she closed her eyes, "And

no. It's probably not what you think."

She looked him in the eyes. "I knew it. Perhaps it's better if you don't explain."

"I want to, I just can't be specific. I made a promise. I was made an Alpha because of my abilities. I was approached by someone who was being blackmailed in a way. They told me of their situation, and I made a pact with them like your unbreakable vow. I swore to protect them."

"With an unbreakable vow, if the other person dies, you die."

"All the more reason for me not to lose a fight."

"What if you're in over your head this time? What if your opponent is better than you?"

"It hasn't happened yet, so I can't answer that."

"Are you just waiting to die?"

"Aren't we all?" he chucked.

"You know what I mean. This isn't a laughing matter."

"Jean, I'm not going anywhere. When my time is up, I'll accept my fate."

"How can you say that when you're putting yourself in a situation where your time being up may be determined by someone else and not fate?"

"Knowing you has made my life acceptable. You've put me at ease. You've made my life better. I'm content now."

"And what about me? We've only just met. I don't want to lose you. My heart couldn't take it." She turned away.

"Jean?"

"Do you care for me? I mean ***really*** care for me?"

"More than almost anything."

"Then make me a promise, because you always keep your word."

"Jean, you know I'd do anything for you. But I have a

commitment to the coven. When the time comes, I'll have to fight," he paused, "***Or***, I can give up being an Alpha. I'd be stripped of my powers and my memory, but even starting from scratch, I know I'd want to be close to you. If you ask me to, I'd do that for you."

"I don't want you to break your commitment for me. Protecting your people is far more important than my feelings."

"To whom?"

"You're not just an Alpha, you're the Alpha One. You do what you have to do, but promise me this, if you feel yourself losing, if defeat is inevitable, promise me you'll run rather than die."

"That's not the way it works."

"Justice, I need you to promise me, or we have to stop seeing one another right now. I care too much for you to watch you sacrifice yourself."

He gazed into her eyes. "Sing with me."

"What?"

"Sing with me then I'll make the promise."

"Sing what?" she asked as she wiped away a tear.

"I don't know, let's see." He turned on the radio and found some jazz. "Too sad." He continued. He found some classical. "No words." He kept going.

"Wait, go back." she requested. He did. "I know his one."

"Seriously? I have to promise after this?" He grinned as the music played. Then he turned to her and began to sing.

"I got chills, they're multiplin' and I'm losin' control
cause the power your supplyin', it's electrifyin'"

She responded.

Chapter 27 – The promise

"You better shape up, cause I need a man, and my heart is set on you,
You better shape up, you better understand, to my heart you must be true
Nothing left, nothing left for me to do
You're the one that I want
(You're the one that I want) ooh ooh ooh, honey
The one that I want (You're the one that I want)
ooh ooh ooh, honey
The one that I want (You're the one that I want)
ooh ooh ooh, honey
The one I need (the one I need)
Oh yes indeed. (yes indeed)

They sang the duet back and forth and when done he promised. "Where are we?" she asked.

He glanced around and there were snowcapped mountains with pitch black night sky and hundreds of stars. They could see each other's breath.

"I have no idea."

"It's beautiful here."

She noticed him staring at her. "Yes, it is." he said. She blushed and rubbed her hands on her arms to warm herself up. "We should probably head back." he suggested. She put her hands in her pockets and felt something. She pulled her hand out slowly and she had the necklace Harry had given her. She tried to return it to her pocket before he noticed, but she sneezed and when she lifted her hands to cover her mouth, he saw it.

"Beautiful necklace."

"Thanks." She didn't offer an explanation and he didn't press for one.

"Would you like me to put it on you?"

She wasn't sure what to say. "Oh, okay."

He took the necklace and felt a shock. "Ouch! Static shock. You really are electrifying." She smiled then turned and lifted her hair. As he hooked it on her he noticed she already had a necklace on. "I never noticed you wearing this much jewelry."

"The Headmistress gave me this one."

"And the other?" She started to answer but sneezed again. "Bless you." He reached out and picked a lose fiber from the car seat. He rolled it into a tiny ball in the palm of his hand then continued to rub his hands together and when he separated them there was a full wool jacket. He handed it to her, and she slipped it on.

"Thank you, I hope I'm not coming down with something."

"Let's get you to some place warmer." He programmed the G.P.S. to make a return trip to Beauxbatons and off they went. After punching the buttons, he felt a sharp pain in his fingertips. He flexed them a couple times.

"Are you alright?" she asked before sneezing again.

"I'm fine, but I'm worried about you."

"I'll be okay. It's just a few sneezes." she said then sneezed twice more. "I have some more information you may be able to use." She handed him the article she'd printed.

He began reading through it. "Did you read this?" She nodded. "It's about Fiona Tattenger, the Dark Lady who was in power when Alucard was making his push." He continued to read. "The Headmistress was just talking about her." He began paraphrasing. "It says here that she was at the height of her reign when Alucard began recruiting followers. He didn't respect her boundaries and eventually their paths crossed. In a short, but epic battle, he defeated her and took over as the leader of the Death Eaters. Fiona was devastated by the loss. Not so much by being displaced as the leader, but in being double crossed by her closest companions and she vowed revenge on them. Her sister and brother were the only ones to stand by her and fight against Alucard. She went into hiding to heal and train and plot her next attack. Unfortunately for her, despite learning new magic, she began to weaken while he grew stronger.

Her anger clouded her judgment and they attacked again. This time the result was worse than before as the battle claimed the lives of both of her siblings and nearly killed her. The battle left her severely disfigured. She disappeared from the wizard community taking her many nieces and nephews with her. She was no longer able to perform magic herself, but she trained the children. Each of them became powerful dark witches and wizards and they came together to fight him again. However, by the time they were ready Alucard had an army, and he sent his minions to find and eliminate them. After four more of them were killed in his name the rest scattered and passed their magic to their children." He turned to her. "I wonder if any of her relatives are still alive?"

"I know one is." She sneezed.

"Bless you."

"Thanks. Her great-great-great Grandniece Nicole is in Azkaban."

"Can you find out more about her? If she fought him, or

has a relative who did and lived, she may know how to help me beat him."

"I will, but…"

"But what?" he questioned but realized she had paused to sneeze again.

"Bless you."

"Thanks. Even if she has information that can help, you can't talk to her, she's in the prison. There's no way you can get to her to speak with her."

"There's always a way." They arrived back at Beauxbatons. "Jean, please go to the hospital wing to get something for that sneezing."

"I will."

He leaned toward her and just as he got close, she sneezed, and head butted him. "Oh, I am so sorry." she apologized.

He laughed, "It's okay. Are you alright?" She began to laugh as she rubbed her forehead. He tried again and this time it was a sharp pain in his forearm that forced him back.

"What is it?"

"Not sure. I've gotta go. Please keep me posted on your cold and on the team's progress in the tournament."

"I will. Goodnight."

"Good morning." he replied and kissed her on the back of her hand. He touched her hand and she turned invisible. "It'll wear off in ten minutes." She got out of the car.

"Thanks." She made it back to her room. Charista was waiting up for her. "What are you still doing awake?"

"I was waiting for you. How'd it go?"

"Great." She paused. "Charista, since you're awake," she sat beside her on her bed and cast ***Muffliato***, "What did you mean when you said Justice and I were bound?"

Chapter 27 – The promise

"Well, long story short, there's an ancient tradition among witches and warlocks. Your ancestors used to pair a witch and warlock. The idea was that one would teach the other what they didn't know. It was supposed to make them both stronger. Half the time they ended up killing each other, but every now and again they got it right and put a pair together and something greater than both resulted. They called it being bound to one another because they were literally bound in chains. They stopped that part several centuries ago, but when they'd match two practitioners, ***if*** they were the right two, they could still feel the chains. You make him stronger. If you don't kill one another, he'll never hurt you and he'll never let anything bad happen to you.

"Somehow I can tell that's true." she replied with a smile.

"Get some sleep."

She closed her eyes and recalled watching him fly off. She silently climbed into bed and no sooner had she pulled the blanket over herself, she heard a voice.

"Restless evening out?"

"Go to sleep Jade." she said then sneezed.

"Keep your germs on that side of the room."

Hermione rolled over and ignored the comment. Despite her best efforts she couldn't help but at least consider if Justice could be Alucard. All he could do. Alucard is a shapeshifter. She searched every resource at her disposal to find anything that could put her at ease. None was forthcoming. The info she'd gotten from Professor Paramore now gave her yet another possibility to ponder. Had Justice been touched by death? At first, she was looking at that as a much more acceptable option, but then remembered it meant he was just staying alive until he fulfilled his commitment, then he would die. Was that what Jade was referring to? It was all exhausting.

The pain Justice had felt was a sign and he knew exactly what it meant. When he'd kissed Mallory, he transferred powers to her. The pain he felt meant she was in trouble, but she was protected. The pain she was experiencing wasn't hurting her, it was hurting him.

She'd gotten ready to leave to meet Peeves and when she opened her door Marcus was standing in the hall.

"Well, well, Mr. Reece. Come to apologize for bumping into me? It's after curfew. What can I do for you?"

"You can't go with Peeves. It's a set up."

"What do you mean?"

"May I come in and talk to you? Justice sent me." She let him in, and he explained he'd had pre-vision of her being ambushed by Death Eaters. The door closed behind them.

Chapter 28 – The truth be told

Justice arrived back at the castle under cover of darkness. He left the keys in the car and quickly made his way to Mallory's room. He knocked on the door and got no response. He tried the handle, and the door was unlocked. He pulled his wand and entered the room cautiously. The room was dark, but he could see clearly. There was someone sitting in a chair in the room near an end table. The person reached out to flip on the light and Justice reacted by having his wand transform into a white-hot sword and he extended it toward the figure's head.

"I don't know if I'm comforted by you showing up here or not." stated McGonagall calmly. The sword disappeared and he apologized to her. "Why exactly are you here, Mr. Cain?"

"I came to check on Ms. Featherstone. I had a bad feeling. Where is she?"

"So, upon getting no response at the door you chose to enter her room anyway? This isn't helping your case Mr. Cain."

"I know, I just needed to make sure she was alright."

"Mr. Cain, you're out of your room after hours in a section of the castle restricted to students. You entered someone's private room without being invited in. I know you've been off the grounds. Shall I continue?"

"No Ma'am."

"You see my predicament. You make it increasingly difficult to defend your actions. There are abductions occurring at an alarming rate and on the day one of my teachers indicates, without warning, that she's leaving...A professor has been killed."

"Leaving?" He paused, "Wait, you don't think I had anything to do with her disappearing, do you?"

"I don't know what to think. What ***do you*** think has come of Ms. Featherstone?"

"Not sure. I felt something and came to check it out. It could be nothing. Are you saying she's gone?"

"If there's one thing I've learned about you Mr. Cain, if you had a feeling. It wasn't nothing."

"Thank you."

"Not so fast. I still don't know what to make of all this." She looked into his eyes then sighed, "But I know who might."

"Who's that?"

"We'll get to that in a moment. We need to talk first, just the two of us. What's going on Mr. Cain? I have a feeling you know a great deal more than you're letting on."

"No, with all due respect, I've let on plenty, and no one seems to be listening. New evidence shows that Alucard is back, he's close. Closer even than you think and he's approaching full strength. I don't know for sure how powerful he'll be at that point, but I'm gonna fight him and I'm going to kill him, and I'd really appreciate it if anyone knows how to make that easier for me, that they'd speak up. There are still a ton of loose ends that need to be tied together. I don't have proof yet, but I have a feeling and my instincts have always been pretty good."

"Well, I wasn't born seventy-seven years ago yesterday. I have fairly good instincts as well. I think there are some people you need to meet. I'll make the arrangements, as for now, you look like you can use some sleep. Go to your house, I'll send for you tomorrow. I'm sure Miss Granger told you about Mr. Weasley." she watched his reaction. "Don't look so surprised Mr. Cain, I can smell the vanilla cookies too."

He smiled, "Goodnight, Headmistress."

"Goodnight, Mr. Cain."

As he opened the door, he turned invisible. He was, in fact, more tired than he realized. He didn't know when he fell asleep, but he woke up to Professor Hunt sitting beside him. He glanced around, "What's up?"

"We need to talk."

"About what?"

"I need to know you haven't forgotten your commitment to the coven?"

He just looked at her. "Do you have to ask?"

"You've grown quite close to some of them. I just want to make sure your focus is where it needs to be."

"The Headmistress…"

"That's what I mean." Dani cut across him. "You don't know her."

"We can trust her."

"You're sure about that, sure enough to put us all at risk?"

"You don't want to trust her, fine. Trust me."

"I'm trying Justice, I'm really trying." He got up to go brush his teeth. He tried to reach Mallory telepathically with no success and now was feeling things must have gone terribly wrong. "Someone's here to see you." she told him. He hoped it was Mallory, but it was just Neville.

"Hey Neville, give me a minute."

"Sure."

"I can't start the day until I've brushed my teeth. Morning ritual."

"Morning? It's nearly noon."

"What?" He was shocked. He rarely slept at all and never slept late but did feel particularly sluggish.

"You must have been really tired. You don't know about the tournament then. Hogwarts won both of their matches today. If Durmstrang beats Beauxbatons in the late match we'll all be tied for first place."

"That's great." He turned to Professor Hunt, "Are we done?"

"We'll continue this later."

"Thanks. I'll come to your office after dinner."

"I'll let the Elders know." She turned to go.

"Bye Professor." said Neville.

"Mr. Longbottom." she acknowledged.

Neville stepped closer to Justice. "I did it."

"The antidote?" he asked as Neville handed him a vial.

"I think so. I don't have anyone to test it on, but the theory…"

"I trust your theory. How many people should it work on?"

Chapter 28 – The truth be told

"I'm guessing of course."

"Your guesses are statistical fact in my book. What do you think?"

"Maybe five."

"Great, I'll let you know when we need it."

"I-I don't think I should hold it. Something might happen."

"Neville, I trust you."

"I don't trust me." He handed Justice the vial. "Oh yeah, McGonagall wants to see you."

"In her office?"

"No, she said to meet her at the Room of Requirement."

"Thanks."

"What's that?" Neville asked.

"What?"

Neville grabbed Justice's arm. Justice yanked away and formed a fist with the other hand. "Sorry, sorry. Reflex." He extended his arm and Neville showed him a needle mark.

"Did Crisp order another blood sample?"

"No, this means Mallory is in trouble. Alive, but in trouble."

"In trouble, I don't understand."

"I'll explain later, give me your hand." Neville extended his hand. Justice put his finger to his temple and gently pulled out a silvery stringy ribbon. He placed it in Neville's hand and pressed his hand to Neville's. "Now, keep trying to reach Mallory. Our timetable just changed. I also need a favor. I need you to get something for me. Have you ever heard of an Artic Tern?"

"The bird?"

"Yeah, I need one." He handed him some money. "Get one and put it in the Owlrey."

"Why?" Justice didn't answer. "What about Ms. Featherstone? What do I..., how?"

"Just talk to her." Justice turned to leave.

"What if she answers, what do I do?"

"Come get me." Justice kept trying Mallory as he made his way to meet McGonagall.

Harry walked into the team's meeting room to find them still celebrating. Charista was the first to notice him. She ran to him, "We did it, Harry. Welcome back." She hugged him and he held her for a moment. She noticed and pulled away.

"Thanks, it's good to be here. Great job guys." Harry said to the team.

"Harry!" they shouted. They gathered around him.

"You'd have been so proud of us. We blew by Durmstrang with a speed line up. We tired them out. I scored nine times." Charista smiled. "Robyn caught the Snitch and we set a scoring record, **486 to 42**.

"Beauxbatons was much tougher today." Reggie told him. "Jade was brilliant. We put in the big guys and wore them down. With Jade in the Keep we can't lose because the other team can't score."

"That's sweet." Jade replied.

"Unfortunately, we couldn't score either." Demetria added.

"We didn't have our scorers in, we stuck to our game plan." said Stormy.

"We just made them work harder than they planned to." said McLaggin.

"There were no goals for the first two thirds of the match. We were leading **26 to 8** when they finally scored a goal."

"Time was running out, so I let them score." Jade

defended. "Then Rochelle Maynard saw the Snitch and signaled to their seeker."

"She'd have gotten it too, if it wasn't for Robyn." Stormy added.

"What did she do?" Harry asked.

"She cut her off and ended up crashing into the wall." Cam explained.

"She's a little banged up, but she'll be alright. Her broom, however," Freddy got cut off.

"It's destroyed and the tournament rules won't allow her to use a replacement. We don't have a Seeker." Wood paused, "Unless you're up to it."

"You'll let me play?"

"Haven't got much of a choice now do I?"

The room erupted with cheers. Harry waded through his teammates to Wood. "Oliver, I..."

"Look Potter, I'm still foggy on exactly what happened yesterday, but I can't say for sure you did anything to me in that room. So, let's put it behind us and go win this tournament."

"Yes sir." replied Harry, "And thank you."

"Just don't let me down and thanks for the suggestions."

"You're welcome and I'll try not to." Harry smiled then looked around the room. "Where's Hermione?"

"She's not here. She's sick so she slept in." said Emmerick.

"Sick? Is she okay?"

"She sneezed a lot in her sleep." said Robyn.

"Thanks." Harry headed for the door.

"Listen up everyone. I want you all in the stands watching the late match. After they finish, we're gonna have a walk through on the field, so get some supper and be ready." Wood told them.

Harry stepped out into the hall and approaching was Hagrid. Harry hurried over to him. "Hagrid, how are you?"

"I'm right as rain."

"Hagrid, I'm sorry. I don't know…"

"Don't you go thinkin' on it one bit longer. I know it wasn't yer doin."

"Well, thanks anyway." Harry hurried off.

Just as Justice reached the entrance to the Room of Requirement, he heard a faint voice. He stopped in his tracks.

"Mallory?"

"Justice? Is that you?"

"Oh, thank God you're awake. Can you tell me where you are?"

"I, I don't know. I'm okay. They drugged me, but it didn't seem to take so they knocked me out. Now I'm blindfolded and chained."

"Have they hurt you?" He asked feeling himself growing angry.

Chapter 28 – The truth be told

"No, actually aside from feeling tired, I feel fine."

"Good, it's working."

"What's working? How are we doing this?"

"You won't feel any pain. I just need you to focus on anything, no matter how small, so I can come get you. Also, don't speak out loud. Once we link up you can just use telepathy, I'll hear you."

"The kiss. You transferred…"

"Yes, I didn't trust Peeves."

"Now I'm disappointed."

"Stop it." He paused, "Mallory, I am so sorry."

"Justice, it's not your fault. They gave me something, because I still have a bit of an aftertaste in my mouth and I can't remember anything clearly about being taken, but for some reason I don't think it had anything to do with Peeves."

"I'll need to know everything that's going on. The instant we can figure out where you are, I'll be there. Has anyone spoken to you about anything?"

"Not yet." She paused, "I think someone's coming."

"Mallory, don't be a hero. They can't hurt you. Let me take care of them, you just guide me to you."

"Okay."

"JUSTICE!!!" Neville shouted as he ran up the hallway. "I heard…"

"Shhh!!!" Justice put his finger to his lips. "I know."

Neville almost crashed into McGonagall as they arrived at the same moment.

"Where's the fire Mr. Longbottom?" she asked.

"Sorry Headmistress. I was looking for Justice."

"I got it Neville, thanks. Keep trying, okay."

"But…"

"I got it. Keep trying."

"Oh, okay." He finally understood. "Bye." He ran off.

"Sorry about that." Justice said to her.

"*Muffliato*." uttered McGonagall. "Mr. Cain, before we enter, I need to let you know, these people are your allies. There is a brain trust here that should be able to answer all of your questions, but…" She hesitated. "Not everyone here is convinced of your beliefs, so I need you to keep an open mind. Don't challenge these people. You may need their help later."

"Respect, Got it."

"Another thing. The Oracle, she's not left this Chamber in over five decades, so choose your words carefully. She won't be used to many of today's more colorful terms."

Together they approached the solid wall that was the entrance to the room. Justice took her arm. "Hang on." He pulled his wand. "*Aladusuch!*" A wall of smoke appeared up the hall from them blocking visibility. The door to the room formed and he pulled it open for her. They went inside then behind them the wall solidified again. The smoke cleared and Mr. Crisp was standing in the hall waving his hand and squinting to try to see where they went.

Justice looked around at what looked like Santa's workshop. Dozens of elves, goblins and people working repairing artifacts. "We had a fire in here this summer. Many priceless, irreplaceable items were lost, even more were damaged. They're restoring what they can." The two of them continued through a door into a room amid what appeared to be a heated debate. Everyone stopped talking and looked at Justice.

"It's him. It's true." said one of the people.

"Everyone, this is Justice Cain. This is the gentleman I told you all about." She turned to him.

"Justice, this is the Order of the Phoenix." He nodded. Everyone found a seat. No one said a word to Justice, but they did begin to whisper to one another. Justice looked at McGonagall. "We're not staying. We'll be back to speak with the Order later, there are more people I want to introduce you to." They continued to another room. She stopped to speak with one of them as he went ahead. There were several people in the room, all with masks and cloaks. Justice pulled his wand.

"*Expelliarmus!*" said one of the hooded figures.

His wand flew across the room. Just as the figure caught the wand Justice raised his hands and the figure was slammed against the wall. Justice rushed over and retrieved his wand from the person's outstretched hand. He then turned to see the others in the room approaching him. He raised his wand, and all the others were pressed against the wall as well.

"Justice! Let them go, now!" McGonagall demanded.

"You know these people?"

"Yes, these are the Questers."

Justice released them all, "Sorry, sorry everybody, reflex." He put his wand away and was startled when he turned around and saw McGonagall in a mask. He leaned into her and asked. "What's with the masks?"

"Maintaining anonymity is essential to the members. Given the nature of what we search for it would be easier if no one could attempt to influence another member to bring two of the items together." He could tell it was her speaking even though her voice sounded like someone much older and male. There was a fireplace in the corner. "This way Mr. Cain." she gestured for him to follow her and told him to repeat after her. "The Panel!"

He followed and arrived in a long tunnel with a single door at its end. McGonagall was in her normal appearance again. "The people in this room are among our oldest and most knowledgeable historians. You will only speak when spoken to. Once allowed, you will ask a single word question and any member of the panel with information will respond. You will be assessed and scrutinized from the moment you enter. It's not personal, it's not even a test, it's an assessment. You must understand, crisis for you and I is just history for them. No matter how serious or bleak things may be to us, they've seen it and lived through it before. They will not have the sense of urgency you and I do. You will be thoroughly probed."

"Not sure I like the sound of that." he replied.

"Now is not the time Mr. Cain." She was not amused.

"Sorry."

"They will ask you questions then answer your questions and will leave you with all you need to know, even if it is not the answers you're hoping for." With that she pushed open the door.

As he stepped in and saw eight people sitting at a table, he felt a sharp pain in his arm. 'Oh no, not again'. He knew someone had just injected Mallory again. He tried to reach her, but there was only silence. The oldest looking of the people in the room got up from the table and slowly walked toward him. He could tell from the cloudiness of her eyes that she was blind. McGonagall was stunned. She'd never seen Kalick stand before, much less walk. With each step she took she began to feel an energy emitting from him. She leaned into him and studied his face then she sniffed him.

"The so-called offset has arrived."

"Justice Cain, Kalick Penhold, the Oracle." introduced McGonagall.

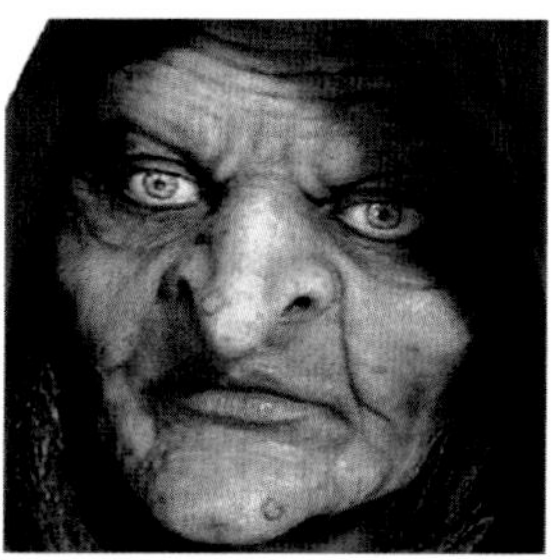

She sniffed again, "You have passion. Much of your power stems from your belief that you are fighting for the lives of others. However, your weakness lies in defending yourself. Why do you devalue your worth?"

"I have a job to do. I don't devalue my life. I just value the lives of all the people in my coven more than mine alone."

"You have no fear. This is a rare characteristic usually reserved for a much older warlock. You do realize fear is a necessary emotion to defeat Dark Magic? If you don't fear what the dark influence can do to you, what's to keep you from falling victim to it when forced to choose between what is right and what is easy?"

"A fundamental knowledge of right and wrong?"

"At your age, how do you know the difference?" stated a woman who looked to be the youngest of the group. She was beautiful. She looked him up and down, sizing him up.

"Perhaps now would be a good time for me to introduce you to the rest of the panel." McGonagall began with the younger woman. "Colina Crawford, she's a former Death Eater turned expert analyst for the panel. She knows their tactics and capabilities.

Elphias Doge, Hogwarts historian and columnist for the Daily Prophet.

Fenwick Grubber, former guard at both Azkaban and Nurmengard prisons. He's also an ex-auror.

Chapter 28 – The truth be told

Broadmire Voskoff, Durmstrang historian.

Bathilda Bagshot, the foremost magical historian of our time and author of 'A History of Magic'.

Andualum Mutombo, former Minister for Magic and expert on all Dark Lords throughout history. He is over eight hundred years old.

Finally, we have Jean-Michael St. Pierre, Beauxbatons historian.

The panel will now take questions in a quid pro quo format. You will state a subject and the panel will offer information. They, in turn, will pose a question of you. Keep your answers brief." Justice was offered a seat just in time before he fell. He was starting to feel the effects of whatever drug they had given Mallory.

"Place your wand on the table." they ordered. He did as instructed.

They examined it thoroughly. "Unicorn Ivory and Createaur hair, fourteen inches. I've not seen it's equal. Who crafted this instrument for you?" asked Mutombo.

"Krysta Marie Madison. It was her last. She referred to it as her Excalibur." he replied.

"Her work is legendary. She attended Beauxbatons you know?" Jean-Michael stated.

"She's an extraordinary witch." added Broadmire.

"Mr. Cain, why are you here?" He didn't respond. His eyes fluttered a bit. "Mr. Cain?" Elphias repeated.

McGonagall nudged him. "I'm sorry, what was the question?" Elphias asked it again.

Chapter 28 – The truth be told

"Are we keeping you from something Mr. Cain?" asked Colina.

"No Ma'am. I came to assist Harry Potter in defeating the evil that is headed his way."

"How did you know of this evil?" asked Colina.

"Marcus Reece, he's a telepath. I get feelings, I sense darkness. I'd been having the feelings and went to him, and he confirmed an evil presence was planning an attack on our coven."

"And did it prove true?" asked Fenwick, "As he had predicted?"

"Yes and no. The coven was attacked, but it was carried out by a group of foot soldiers and muggles."

"Muggles?" questioned the Oracle quietly.

"So, he was wrong?" questioned Bathilda.

"No, the presence was there, just not until the end. It was almost as if…" He began to fade.

"He wasn't there for you." The oracle finished his thought. He shook he head and snapped to attention.

"I have a picture of the presence." He reached into his pocket and pulled out a drawing Demetria had done based on his description. He laid it on the table, held his hand over the picture and it lifted into a three-dimensional photo. The figure was shrouded in a cloak with a long skeletal hand, glowing white eyes and upper and lower fangs glistening.

"Where did you get this?" Mutombo asked.

"My coven also has a portal practitioner. Her name is Demetria Sanders."

"There is no mistaking this image. Have you met this person yourself?" asked Mutombo.

"No, this was an image from a nightmare I had after the attack, but I'm sure it was at my coven the night of the attack."

"This evil has a name. The name is Alucard." Mutombo confirmed.

"You seem very distracted, shall we stop?" asked Fenwick.

"No, please, I need information."

"You may ask your questions." stated Kalick.

"Alucard?"

"The most notorious of all Dark Lords. He was the first Dark Lord to come into power by defeating the sitting Dark Lord in battle. He's so dangerous because of his indiscriminate killing of anyone who opposes him, man, woman, child, muggle or wizard. He began as a man but is no longer. He fell gravely ill as a child and on his death bed made a pact with the Reaper himself. His task is to collect souls to repay Death for mending him and making him the most powerful wizard of the age." explained Mutombo.

"But Death has a sense of humor. He made him powerful but made him age a rate that should kill him just before reaching his quota and fulfilling his debt." stated Bathilda.

"Alucard is a genius, a truly gifted wizard. He used his time on earth studying and learning ways to reach his goal and at the same time ensure he would not die even if Death did not honor their deal." explained Colina.

"Death is cunning and cannot be trusted. For those who

Chapter 28 – The truth be told

enter into an agreement with him, there is no way out." said Fenwick.

"Weaknesses?" Justice asked.

"He doesn't have any." Colina snapped.

"He is said to have an allergy to the touch of silver, but its effects are not fatal." said Jean-Michael.

"His chosen form will appear strong, but his age remains true." added Broadmire.

"The time to exploit any weakness has passed. He feasts on the pure blood of Ministry officials. He will be strong and virile." rebutted Colina.

"Tattenger?" Justice queried.

"She was well versed in all kinds of magic. She is said to have created a special skill, specifically for one last battle with Alucard, however, a battered body and advanced age kept her from ever having the chance to use it." stated Mutombo.

"When she died, all hope of dethroning him died with her." Colina told them.

"No, there is another." announced the Oracle.

"It's true. She has a blood descendant in Azkaban. I ushered her in myself." said Fenwick.

"Azkaban?" Justice suggested.

"Impenetrable. They've tripled the number of Dementors. The entire facility was relocated beyond the traveling distance of any Death Eater. You have to apparate to reach it and even then, there are only a handful of Ministry officials who can make the distance." explained Fenwick.

"A radial perimeter has been set in the sea. The water within the perimeter is cursed and Inferi patrol it, sinking unsuspecting ships that dare penetrate the boundary." said Elphias. "Only Ministry inspected, and approved ships get in."

"Inferi, Hippocampus and Kelpies in the water, Dementors patrolling the skies and corridors. Unless you're a prisoner, you can't even get there." said Voskoff.

"Strengths?"

"His, or yours?" asked the Oracle.

"His?" Justice replied.

"He's a shape shifter, but not a normal one. With most shifters, if one form is injured, the next form will still suffer the damage." said Voskoff.

"But not him. If the first form is injured, he shifts to a healthy form and the original then heals itself while not in use." said Mutombo.

"Keeping him in one form will be a key. He can shift to anything." whispered Bathilda.

"You've never lost a fight, have you Mr. Cain?" asked Kalick.

"I've been lucky."

"This is not favorable for you. If you've not known that moment of defeat, you may fight too long, rather than retreat to fight another day." reasoned Elphias.

"From what I understand, if I don't win the first time I face him there won't be another day for me, or any of us. Isn't that right, Ms. Crawford?"

"Do you think you're ready to face him?" asked Voskoff.

"Not yet, but if the time is now, I won't shy away from the challenge. Look, I don't have to win I just have to not lose. If I can keep him from shifting and keep him from getting whatever it is that he thinks will keep him alive, Death will do the rest, right?"

"How do you plan to do that?" asked Colina.

"With help."

"From whom?" asked Jean-Michael.

Chapter 28 – The truth be told

"Harry Potter. From day one I've always felt that Harry is the target, not me. I can keep the others safe if he fights. He can keep the others safe while I fight. Together I think we can wear him down."

"And if he doesn't fight?" asked Fenwick.

Justice was about to respond when Kalick said, "Enough! It is time we make our assessment. Give us a moment."

Justice was confused. McGonagall stepped over to him and gestured for him to go with her. "What's going on?"

"Come with me. The Panel will confer and let you know if they support your decision."

"Support my decision? Hold on," He stepped around her. "Excuse me. With all due respect to the Panel, I'm not asking permission to face him. He's coming, soon and I am going to fight. It's why I'm here."

"Justice, please!" shouted McGonagall.

"Mr. Cain, the Panel is going to assess the information from the interview. You ***will*** follow our recommendation. Alucard is unlike any force you've ever encountered. If you aggravate him and lose the wrath, he'll unleash on the rest of the magical community will be swift and severe. We must decide what the best course is for everyone, not just you or Harry Potter." responded Colina.

"I'm not going to let Harry face this threat alone." Justice plainly stated.

Kalick took notice, "You may not have a choice. Harry Potter may ***be*** the threat. He's been compromised."

Justice was shocked. "I've got to go. He's with them. If he's turned..." He paused, "Wait, you think...Harry is Alucard?"

"No, he's not, nor are you. He's not turned yet Mr. Cain. I have not foreseen it. Give us a moment please."

He stepped out of the room with McGonagall. "I warned you Mr. Cain, not to antagonize these people."

"I was just…"

"Silence!" she snapped.

After just a few moments the door opened and Broadmire asked them to come back in. As they approached the door he clarified, "Not you Minerva, just the boy." She was appalled but obliged.

Justice entered the room. Mutombo stood and spoke to him. "Mr. Cain. Your heart is in the right place. Your loyalty to your coven is inspiring. There is also no doubting your courage. However, the risk to the magical community out ways the commitment you have made to your people. We have decided to seek Alucard out and send a negotiating team to speak with him. We hold a trump card, so to speak."

"We believe he has returned. He's building an army and plotting an attack at some point, but we think for you to seek him out and confront him would force his hand and cause him to launch an assault on innocent men, women and children that would devastate our structure." explained Elphias.

"You see Mr. Cain we've experienced this threat before. We know what weapons Alucard possesses, and we honestly don't believe you have the command of the skills needed to defeat him." said Bathilda.

"You're either very brave or very stupid to have considered facing him. He's a monster, a very skilled monster. It will take an army of specialized magical mercenaries to even keep him at bay. Alone, with Potter, it makes no difference. He'll go through you like a knife through warm butter." Added Colina.

"Mr. Cain, we commend you for considering this task on our behalf, but it is a suicide mission. He's killed everyone

Chapter 28 – The truth be told

who's ever crossed path with him. How do you think he's survived for nearly a thousand years?" stated Voskoff.

"History has shown us that the first loss of a previously undefeated wizard, at the hands of a sitting Dark Lord, is usually fatal." contributed Jean-Michael.

"Sorry kid, maybe if you had more experience. Unfortunately, the only person who might be able to teach you anything truly useful to use against this particular Dark Lord, happens to be in the one place you can't access. Azkaban." said Fenwick.

"So that's it then?" Justice asked. Kalick stood up and walked toward him. Just before she reached him, he jerked forward and cried out. She stopped in her tracks. The others pulled their wands. Suddenly he did it again. 'Mallory?' He thought to himself.

"Justice?"

"Are you alright?"

"I'm being whipped, but I don't understand what's happening. It doesn't hurt. What did they do to me?"

"Not them, me. I…"

"Mr. Cain, you're bleeding." Mutombo pointed out. Blood was staining the back of his shirt. Jean-Michael waved his wand and Justice's shirt split down the back revealing large, raised welts with blood dripping from them.

"Explain this!" demanded Colina.

"I've seen those patterns before. That's the work of a trained Azkaban enforcer named Malikai Westerfield. They call him 'The Messenger', because once he's done with you, you've gotten the message."

"Westerfield? Why does that name sound so familiar?" He jerked again and they watched as another welt arose. "Mallory, you have to sell it. I transferred an ability to you to keep you from feeling any pain as a precaution."

"You're feeling it instead, aren't you?" She bit her own lip hard enough to make it bleed. She screamed out with every lash.

"Mr. Cain." said Kalick and she touched his shoulder. Images flashed through her mind and her hair stood on end. She released him and staggered back. "GET OUT!!!" The others stood and began toward the door. "Not you Mr. Cain!"

As the others filed out, McGonagall looked for Justice. "What, where's the boy?"

"Something's happening to him. Something dark." said Elphias.

"Well, is he alright?" she asked in a frantic tone. "Did he hurt anyone?"

"I'm linked to a female professor who was abducted. She's being tortured. I'm trying to find out where she's being held." he explained to Kalick.

"You did this?" she mumbled. "You've been touched."

"Yes Ma'am."

"And the marks? You transferred ability to her to keep her safe?" She paused.

"Yes, I didn't want to leave her unprotected."

"She's a friend, this professor? Perhaps, more than a friend?"

"Yes, I mean, no." 'Mallory, what do you see?'

"I don't know. Wait, he's coming for me. My blindfold came off. He's coming."

"Look around, quickly. Try to spot anything that will help me find you."

Malikai approached her and inspected her skin. There wasn't a mark on her. He screamed out in anger. He dragged

Chapter 28 – The truth be told

her back to the center of the room where he re-secured her blindfold, then he stood her up and hung her restraints over a suspended hook.

"Mallory? Are you still there? What's happening?"

"It's dark. Now I'm suspended, shackled to a hook."

He thought a moment. "Charista, can you hear me?"

"Justice?" she replied quietly. "What's wrong? It's two o'clock in the morning."

"Sorry, I need you. Can you see Mallory through me?" She concentrated. Her eyes began to glow yellow.

"Did you say Justice? What's wrong?" Hermione asked. Her sneezing had given way to dry skin and a swollen throat.

"Shhh!" snapped Charista. "I need to focus."

"Can you see where she is?" he asked. She was still blindfolded, but she did all she could to look straight down. "There's not much light. I can tell there's water on the floor. Wait, I can almost make out a pattern on the floor."

"Wake Demetria." he instructed Charista.

Hermione woke Demetria and grabbed a quill with her left hand. She tried to grab parchment with her right, but her fingers were growing increasingly numb. Demetria was still groggy from being awakened from a deep sleep. She sat at a desk and took the quill in her hand.

"You are pathetic." Jade said to Hermione as she grabbed the parchment and placed it in front of Demetria.

"Touch her hand, she'll do the rest." Justice instructed.

"Who are you?" the Oracle asked softly amazed by his abilities. She reached out and touched his shoulder.

Demetria drew the information being relayed to her. It appeared to be an etched 'S'. Her hand moved back and forth at remarkable speed then abruptly stopped. The drawing lay on the table. They all took a good long look.

"Come on people, anyone recognize it?" Justice asked.

"It can't be." stated Hermione softly. "It looks like…The Chamber of Secrets."

"The Chamber, at Hogwarts, that you told me about?" Charista asked.

"It can't be. I was there when it was destroyed." Hermione stated.

"Unless it was rebuilt." reasoned Jade.

"It's the only lead we've got. Where is it?"

"There was an entrance through a portrait on the third floor." She paused, "And the basilisk used to travel in and out of the castle using the pipes."

"The pipes, that's it, the night you were attacked in the prefect's bathroom. I followed Crouch through the drain to a huge cavern that let out into the Forbidden Forest." He turned to Kalick. "I'm sorry Ma'am, I've got to go."

Chapter 28 – The truth be told

"You're not ready to face him." she replied.

"Good thing he doesn't know that. Besides, if I'm not, she certainly isn't, bound and without her wand."

"What are you going to do if there are others with Malikai?"

"With all due respect Ma'am, I don't have time to discuss this right now, I have a friend in danger and I'm going to go do whatever I have to. However, if you must know, my plan is to use old school rules. When you're being bullied on the playground, you find the biggest, toughest kid and punch him in the mouth." He ran to the door.

"Mr. Cain," she pulled a necklace from her shirt. It had an hourglass hanging from it.

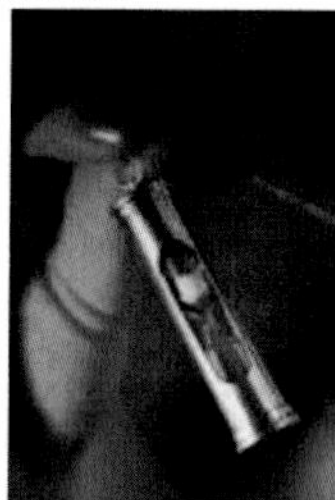

She tossed it to him. "This is your timeframe. When the sand runs out, he'll show himself."

He looked at it then at her. "Thanks." He turned to McGonagall. "They're here, on the grounds in the Chamber of Secrets." he told McGonagall. Before she could respond he apparated to the prefect's bathroom.

The panel members went back into the room along with McGonagall and saw Kalick standing there holding Justice's wand.

"He forgot it."

"And you let him go?" She paused, "Without it?" McGonagall questioned.

"Watch your tone, Minerva. Where did he come from?"

Kalick asked her.

"He came from America, he's just a student."

"He is far more than just a student. He is the Ranger." The others gasped collectively.

Chapter 29 – Temper, temper

"What do you want us to do?" Charista asked.

"I'm going back to bed. We've got two matches to win tomorrow, and we play the early one." said Jade.

"What about Justice?" Stormy asked.

"He'll be fine. This is what he does. He loves this stuff." Jade told them.

"He can't face Alucard alone." whispered Hermione as her eyes narrowed from the swelling in her throat.

"I'll go." said Charista.

"No, the team needs you rested." said Hermione, "I'll go."

"Oh my God! You'd be about as useful as a wet tissue. I'll go, it's the only way I'm gonna get any rest." Jade told them.

Charista touched her, "Here, now you can talk to him." Jade apparated without another word.

Justice entered the girl's bathroom, shouting, "Hello, is anyone in here?" He heard a voice say, 'I am'. It was Moaning Myrtle.

"Is anyone with you?"

"Yes." said a voice.

"Cover up, I'm coming in." He entered to find a fifth year Ravenclaw prefect scrambling to cover with a towel.

"You're not supposed to..."

"Sorry," he said then he turned to smoke and shot

through the bathwater and into the drainpipes.

'Ten more lashes and there's still not a mark on her'. Malikai thought to himself as he stood behind her inspecting his work.

"What're you goin' on about?" asked Malfoy.

Justice erupted up through the flowing stream that ran through the Chamber. It looked quite different than the last time he'd seen it. He sniffed the air and could sense that familiar hint of ash that he remembered from his coven. He heard a scream and bolted in the sound's direction. He stopped and sniffed again and knew Mallory was just behind a heavily bolted door to his left. It was then he realized he didn't have his wand. She screamed again as Malikai prepared to crack his bullwhip once more, this time with the whip glowing red hot at its tip.

"I wager this'll leave a mark." Malikai groaned.

"*Bombarda!*" Justice shouted. The door exploded knocking both Malikai and Draco down. Justice entered the room invisible and freed Mallory from the suspended hook she'd been tethered to. "I'm here." Justice whispered to her, but before he could remove her blindfold Malfoy cast a curse that sailed by him. Justice cast a shield around her and materialized.

Chapter 29 – Temper, temper

Draco took one look and vaporized. Justice raised his hand toward him, but before he could cast a spell Malikai had lashed out with the whip and sliced open his shirt. Justice finished ripping it off what was left of his shirt and looked down at his chest to see if he'd been cut.

Malikai swung the whip again and it wrapped around Justice's waist. "Alright, let's dance." Justice covered his mouth with his hand and when he removed it flames shot out and traveled up the whip causing it to erupt into a shower of sparks. Malikai dropped the whip and rolled clear of it. He turned his attention to Mallory. Justice glanced at her then tilted his head. A tattered wall hanging flew to his outstretched hand. He held it like a matador's muleta between her and Malikai. He shook it a few times then let it drop and she was gone. It appeared they were alone. Malikai smiled and slowly withdrew Mallory's wand. "That's not fair." Justice told him.

Malikai pointed it, but Justice vanished before he could cast a curse. Malikai glanced around cautiously. "Reveal yourself!"

A fixture fell from the wall and Malikai cast, "***Reducto!***" The item exploded and when the flames died down Malikai felt a tap on his shoulder. He spun and cast a curse that Justice ducked while executing a spinning foot sweep knocking Malikai off his feet. He dropped the wand and Justice caught it. Malikai thrust his hand upward and grabbed Justice by the throat. Justice grabbed the thumb on that hand and pealed it back into a thumb lock. Malikai winced in pain. "Where is Alucard?" he asked.

Malikai forced a smile. Justice applied more pressure. Malikai gasped. "He's not here and you won't find him."

"What form is he in?" Before Malikai could answer another hooded figure entered the room wand drawn. It cast a curse.

"***Aladusuch!***" Justice countered and the stream of green light from the figure's wand seemed to be absorbed into Mallory's wand. "***Confringo!***"

The figure dove to avoid the full brunt of the blast. Justice placed her wand to Malikai's forehead, "Tell me where he is!"

"He's…" Before he could finish there was another explosion. The other figure in the room was blasted against a wall. Jade entered the room wand drawn. She turned her wand to Malikai.

"JADE, NO!!!"

She cast a curse at Malikai hitting him in the arm. Justice pulled back from him. The distraction was just enough for Malikai to retrieve a knife from his pocket and stab Justice in his side. "NO!" she screamed. The disillusionment charm he'd placed on Mallory stopped, she became visible, and she removed the blindfold in time to see Justice transform into the wolverine. He opened his mouth wide and clamped down on Malikai's neck. He shook him twice and they heard a loud snap. He released his limp body and ran from the room leaving a trail of blood.

"Justice!" Mallory cried. Jade helped her up and led her out. The blood trail led them to him. He was back in human form, passed out on the bank of the stream. Firenze, the centaur came to their aid. As he lifted Justice up, he came to for a moment and spoke.

"We have to secure the Chamber."

"The Centaurs will stand guard. No one will enter or leave." Firenze assured him as he passed out again. A dozen centaurs appeared.

Firenze carried him and Mallory to the edge of the forest. The Headmistress, Professor Hunt and Professor Flitwick met them there. Jade lagged to not be seen. She was riddled with guilt. She took the car and went back to Beauxbatons. Mallory was examined by Madam Pomfrey and was found to be uninjured, just exhausted. When they asked Mallory, what had happened she couldn't remember. Madam Pomfrey gave her something to help her sleep, but before she could take it, she had to spit the pill out that Jade had given her that was already partially dissolved in her mouth.

Anthony Wright
Chapter 30 – Who am I?

The new dawn galvanized the Hogwarts team. Their play was inspired. Beauxbatons adjusted its game two loss. Jade's lack of sleep made her a step slow, and Rochelle Maynard noticed. She kept constant pressure on the Keep. She scored three goals, but luckily Charista was equally brilliant. Her third goal gave Hogwarts a **62 to 48** lead. Harry's feel for the speed of the Beauxbatons team was coming back to him. He'd spied the Snitch twice, but just as quickly lost sight of it. Time was running out. The Snitch was the last hope. The Beauxbatons Seeker spied the Snitch first and dove toward it. At just inches away Reggie cut across her path and prolonged the match momentarily.

Disaster nearly struck when Demetria fired a shot that was blocked away, but she recovered the Quaffle and shot again. It too was deflected moving Beauxbatons to just a ten-point deficit. Rochelle and Charista bumped and jostled the entire length of the pitch and when Cormac tried to knock her off course with a Bludger it misfired and nearly hit Jade. It caused Jade to get out of position for a split second and Rochelle took advantage tying the score at **62**.

Cam replaced Cormac for the final push and regulation time ended in a tie, so the rules of the tournament called for a shootout. Each team chose three players to take shots at the opposing Keep. Hogwarts chose Charista, Blaise and Stormy. Beauxbatons went first. Jade blocked the first two attempts with ease, but Rochelle's shot skipped off her fingertips and scored.

Blaise's shot hit the ring and bounded away. Stormy's shot was poked away at the last second. Charista was the last hope to force more time. She glared at her opponent and darted in feinting left and shooting right. The Quaffle got by the defender to once again draw the contest even. Double overtime.

Madame Maxime settled the crowd and announced, to the delight of the Minister of Magic, that the tournament rules now required the match to be settled with a 2-minute sudden death battle for the Snitch. The Snitch would be released and only the two Seekers would be on the field. The one who grabbed it would win the game for his/her team. If neither player was to catch it before the timer ran out the match would be declared a draw. Harry took his place opposite the Beauxbatons Seeker. It was his moment, his turn to be the Harry of old. The other players settled onto the ground and dismounted their brooms. They gazed up at the two players soaring high above the pitch. The Snitch was released, and it was as if the entire stadium held its collective breath. Harry flew like a man possessed. The Snitch ducked and dodged, bobbed and weaved and evaded the two competitors for ninety-five seconds before the Beauxbatons Seeker touched the Snitch's wings and knocked it off course. It fluttered and spun until it was secured in the palm of a hand. Harry held the Snitch aloft and the crowd erupted. They politely cheered excellent play despite the outcome not being in their team's favor. Both teams were now at three wins and two losses, and each had one match left against Durmstrang. While it was certainly possible both could lose to Durmstrang leaving the three of them tied for top honors, the likelihood was that they would both win and face a fourth and final epic battle. Only time would tell.

Justice opened his eyes and saw Neville standing with McGonagall and Madam Pomfrey. He glanced to his right and saw Mallory sleeping.

"You're awake? How do you feel?" Neville asked.

"I'm alright except for feeling like someone's standing on my stomach."

"You got stabbed and the knife went all the way through."

"I know, I was there." Justice said playfully. "By the way, where were ***you***?"

"I could hear Ms. Featherstone, but I didn't know where you were." he replied in a panic.

"I'm kidding."

"Well, well Mr. Cain. I'm thinking we should just move your house bed in here. It would save some time." said Madam Pomfrey sarcastically.

"I thought I was your favorite patient." he replied. She smirked and walked away.

"How do you feel Mr. Cain?" McGonagall asked.

"I'll be fine. How's she?"

"She's fine, thanks to you. Poppy just gave her something to help her rest. Justice, you risked your life for her?"

"She a good teacher and good teachers are hard to find, and she hasn't graded my last assignment yet."

"Do you take anything seriously?"

"I just did my job."

"I've heard you say that over and over, but it never really sank in until this moment. You really do feel you're here to protect us and apparently, you do have the skills to do it."

"Yes Ma'am, I do."

"What can we do to assist you?" she asked.

"Headmistress, there's someone here to see you." said Justin Fletchley.

"I'll let you know." Justice replied.

"Who is it?" she asked.

Chapter 30 – Who am I?

"I don't know Ma'am."

"Well, where are they?"

"This note says they're waiting in your office." That struck her as odd. She went there and as she entered the room she noticed a hooded figure sitting in the chair in front of her desk. She drew her wand and approached quietly and cautiously.

"You can put that away. I didn't come for a fight." stated the old woman. McGonagall knew she recognized the voice, but felt she had to be mistaken.

"Kalick?"

"I'm here about the Ranger." McGonagall was shocked. The Oracle had never been known to venture out of the confines of the Room of Requirement. "I need to return his property. He is still alive?"

"He's injured but recovering. He's in the hospital."

"Then he accomplished his task?"

"Yes, the young professor is safe."

"Extraordinary. Minerva, do you know what he is?"

"What do you mean?"

"Let me speak with him then I'll explain." She sent for Justice.

"You tell the Headmistress he has a serious wound. The blade may have been coated with something because it's not healing. He should not be moving around." barked Madam Pomfrey.

Justin turned to leave. "Wait," said Justice. "If she needs me, I'll go."

"Don't say I didn't warn you." snapped Madam Pomfrey.

"You have the cutest little wrinkle on your forehead when you're mad." he replied. She walked away in a huff.

Justin helped him up. He arrived shortly thereafter.

"Leave us." Kalick requested, concealed in her cloak. She did and Kalick withdrew his wand. "You left this behind, but then you didn't need it, did you? You can do magic without a wand."

"It still would have come in handy."

"Where did you acquire the skill?"

"It was a gift from Harry."

"I must say, I didn't expect you to be in one piece after facing Malikai."

"You're not the first to tell me that."

"Is he dead?"

"Yes."

"Impressive. You are quite a surprise."

"He wasn't there, Alucard."

"I know."

"How, because I'm not dead?"

"Because I'm an Oracle." She paused. She removed her cloak and she had taken on the form of much younger, beautiful woman with green eyes. "I thought this form might make you more comfortable. How far back do you remember?"

"I don't remember my parents, if that's what you are asking."

"You're special, more special than you know. Have you ever wondered why you can do what you can do? Yes, you've studied Elf magic and Goblin magic, but you knew instantly how to do whatever you learned."

"You're saying I already knew it? Because if I'm an elf or a goblin there's someone I owe an apology."

"You've been given these gifts for a reason."

"Yes, I know, to be able to kill Dark Lords."

"Well, yes and no. You feel it's because you're meant to fight for those who can't. You feel you are destined to face Alucard." She paused, "Perhaps you are. Perhaps you aren't. What concerns me is that you seem to feel that if you don't face him, or if you face him and lose, that you failed to fulfill your purpose. However, have you ever considered that you fulfill your purpose everyday with the lives you touch along the way? You fulfill your purpose everyday no one in your coven dies. You saved a life yesterday. That one saved life is worth more to that person than any hundred you'd save in your next battle. You think you still have something to prove, but to your friends you prove your worth every day. You've made their lives richer by knowing you now. They aren't going to think any less of you if you don't fight, or if you lose. You've already won. Having friends and people who love you is your victory."

"You don't think I can beat him. You've foreseen my fate?"

"No, oddly enough I can't see your destiny."

"Who am I?"

"Only you can answer that Mr. Cain. Your path is a work in progress, it's scripted, but it's in pencil. You still have the ability to change it."

"You're an Oracle, you see the future. What is it about me that make that different?"

"I am an Oracle. Do you know what that really is? Do you know what my capabilities are? I see many futures. None are set. I can make predictions, and many will come true, but usually that is the case of the weak minded. They hear their future and get drawn into thinking its set-in stone. When harm comes for them, they don't get out of the way because they think that's the way it is supposed to end for them. They don't realize they can change it. Things occur every day that alter the visions I have."

"I'm not sure I follow. I mean, no disrespect, but what's the point of being able to see that future if it can still be changed?"

"Do you play chess?" she asked. He nodded.

She lifted her wand and a chess board appeared. "You know strategy." The pieces began to move, one side then the other. "You look at the board and you see several moves in advance. It's easy when playing someone just as skilled as you, but in your case those types of opponents would be few and far between. Often, you'll predict what should be the next move of your opponent and they do something completely different. Your opponent has options. Each option vastly affects the pattern of the game. My visions are like that. I see every possible scenario."

"So, you've seen how this going to play out with him since you know his skill level."

Chapter 30 – Who am I?

"I know what his skill level was when he was at his peak. I have no idea what he's capable of now and even if I did, he is not the wild card in this contest. I have no idea of what your capabilities are since you don't know yourself. Heart cannot be measured. You have friends. Some can help you; some can hinder you. With Death Eaters it's easy. Friendship and love are not part of the equation."

"How well do you know him?"

"Pretty well."

"Of what you know about him at his peak and what you know of me right now, can I beat him?"

"That's not clear. Like you, he continues to evolve. You two are remarkably similar, but you don't know all that you can do. He, on the other hand, is fully aware of his abilities. He's been honing his skills for nearly a thousand years."

"Does he have a weakness?"

"Only his supreme confidence. He knows resistance is coming, but I know he doesn't know your potential. What he possesses that gives him an edge on any opponent is that there is no point at which he will concede. In any competition, the edge goes to the side that does not have a limit to what they are willing to do to win. He is willing to sacrifice everyone and everything around him to achieve his goal and stay alive. Can you say the same?"

"You know I'm willing to die for what I believe is right."

"Yes, I do, the question is how many of those around you are you willing to lose to defeat him? There's no shame in feeling for others, but there's no place for it in war."

"I'm here to fight. It's ***all*** I'm here for."

"You can say, with all honesty, that you'll let him kill your new friends and members of your coven to protect the remainder of the wizard community?"

"I won't allow them to die."

"Bold statement. What do you think will happen to them if you lose?"

"That's not an option."

"This is exactly what I expected you to say, he'll expect it too and it's what gives him the edge, right now." She paused, "Tell me about her." She slipped on a shirt and asked quietly, "Is it cold in here?"

"Who? Professor Featherstone?"

"The one who holds the key to your heart."

"I can't afford to stay close to anyone."

"It's a little late for that, don't you think?" She paused. "Do you find it odd that the first name you spoke was that of your professor?" Again, she paused. "Have you been seeing them both when you are with the professor?"

"How did you know that?"

"Oracle. Don't worry. It's a good sign for you. You'd be seeing the other one too if she wasn't an Elf."

"Wow. I guess you are able to see everything."

"Not everything. You do a pretty good job of shielding your thoughts of the ones you love, but there are many who love you. Your professor has an aura that allows her to appear as you want to see her and pretty much all you see when you look at any of them is the muggle born." Her voice tailed off. "Back to the real issue here, you can feel him, and he can feel you, but for now, he can't see who you are. You're both subconsciously able to block the others attempts to access one another's thoughts, but he may soon solve that riddle."

He changed the subject. "In any of the battle scenarios you've seen between he and I, have I won any of them?"

"I think you already know what the outcome will be. You said it yourself, you came here for one purpose. You haven't planned for anything beyond the battle."

"Meaning I won't survive it."

"How it ends is irrelevant to your future, it's your present that is the concern. You will know loss if you choose to go through with this."

"If ***I*** choose? I'm not the one forcing the issue."

"He said the same thing. His being there when your coven was destroyed was not mere coincidence. He was looking for the offset."

"Hold up, back up a moment. He who?"

"Alucard." she replied. Justice jumped to his feet.

"You saw him?"

"Mr. Cain, I don't see anyone."

"I'm sorry, I didn't…"

"It's alright Mr. Cain. Alucard can't see things the way I can. He does, however, have an ability to send and receive information in the form of written text. I have a journal. When he wants to communicate with me, he enters it in the journal in braille."

"Why would he want to communicate with you?" he asked, but feared he already knew the answer.

"He's my twin brother."

Justice closed his eyes and screamed. The walls of the castle shook. "You sit here across from me, a blood relation of

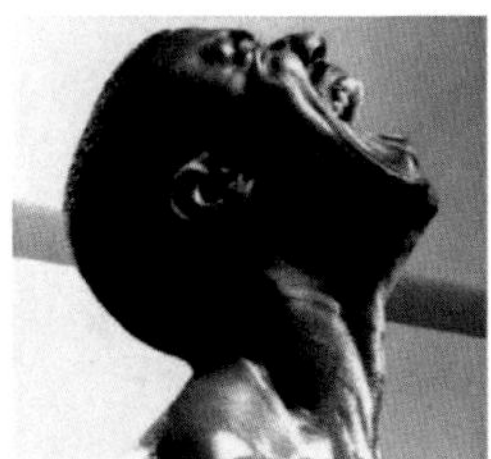

the Dark Lord I'm sworn to kill. What was all this? Are you gathering information for him?"

"He and I share a mother and father and a cellular bond, but our connection stops there. If he dies by your hand so be it. When I touched you, I saw some things more clearly than I ever did when I had my sight. I know why you rush to face him, why you feel you must. I too was once driven like you to kill him. He and I are twins, magical twins. We began as a single cell and were split into two babies. Our magic was in our DNA and when we split, we each got half the magical ability. I can do things he can't, and he could do things I couldn't. Heaven help us all if our magical ability was combined in one person.

He hated me for that, blamed me for not being as strong as he felt he was meant to be. As children, we were half as strong as others our age and had half the immunity to illness. He was born with his darkness and that rage and bitterness made him stronger than me. I was bedridden when he became school aged. I had no friends. I never went out. Very few people even knew I existed and even fewer know what I've just told you. The sicker I became the stronger he became. Ultimately, he was able to go to school, but I was too sickly. His power increased every day.

One day, however, I woke up and out of the blue I was feeling better. I was able to get out of bed and move around. It was the day that put all of this in motion. In the back of my mind I wondered how my recovery was affecting him. It didn't take long to find out. He came home in a fouler mood than usual. He was sick and angry. He came in yelling at me, and my mother stopped him. He started in on her instead. He wouldn't stop yelling at her. He made her cry. When my father came home and heard of what happened he confronted him. They began to fight. Alucard lost control. He was only twelve, but already had more magical ability than any of the seventh-year students at Durmstrang and many of the staff. My brother cast a curse that destroyed half our house. The rubble collapsed on top of our mother. My father screamed and cast a curse back and it hit Alucard full force. I thought Alucard was dead, but somehow, he remained clinging to life. My father was overcome with grief. He blasted away the debris and found her. In his rage, he wanted to kill us all. He set the house on fire with us both trapped upstairs. That's when it happened." Her voice tailed off. Justice didn't push. "Sometimes I can still feel the flames. That's when I lost my sight. I was dead and then…"

"You died?" he interrupted.

"Clinically, yes. Then he showed himself."

"He?"

"The Reaper. He came to me first. I made my deal. I wasn't ready to die. I make no apologies about it, but he wouldn't return my vision. That injury to me was what was keeping my brother alive. I made my peace with it, he offered me an out, eternal life without my vision, in exchange for keeping Alucard alive, or he would return my vision only to allow me to watch him take my family's souls. Alucard was my brother, we fought all the time, but I loved him and despite my parents being dead because of him, they were gone, and I didn't want to be alone. My choice was selfish and subsequently the wrong one, but that is my burden to bear. Death went to him next. We found Alucard in his bed. I heard his soul leaving his body. The Reaper offered him his deal and our lives changed in that instant. We'd both been touched."

"But I thought Mutombo said..."

"He was wrong. He knows the same story as everyone else, but I was there. We're both walking dead waiting for our time to run out. We have to be killed because we won't ever die."

"So, if I try to kill him are you going to try to stop me?"

"God no. I've tried to kill him myself. I'm tired Mr. Cain. There's nothing here for me anymore, but I've been touched. I can't die until I've fulfilled the terms of my deal. I thought when I tried to kill him it would break my deal, but I was never strong enough to even injure him. No one is."

"What about when he fought Fiona Tattenger? She tried to kill him. Why didn't that count?"

"Because I honored my deal then. He didn't get hurt. She hadn't been in power very long when he decided to overthrow her. He told me of his plan, and I had to help him, we're bound. If he dies, I die, but working together no one could ever defeat us because as he got weaker, I got stronger. I waited in the wings until she was vulnerable then I struck. I could finally read her mind. Then I used my ability and turned her minions against her. With only her brother and sister on her side she was no match for him. The others went into hiding. He was in charge, and I had to accept that I'd made the wrong choices in choosing to live the night of the fire, then in choosing not to let him die and keeping the power for myself. I sought out the only person I could talk to back then, Morticia Westerfield. Her husband, Craven, introduced me to Salazar Slytherin and he allowed me to stay in the

Chapter 30 – Who am I?

Chamber he'd built deep beneath the Hogwarts castle. The properties of the Chamber don't allow other witches or wizards to locate you. That's why you didn't know he had his minions hidden there. I ventured out from time to time and eventually found the Room of Requirement. I grew more depressed as the years went by and as the end of his term approached, I devised a plan."

"What do you mean, the end of his term?"

"Dark Lords reign for 100 years then they're replaced. Fiona had only been in the position for twelve years when Alucard replaced her. Since I couldn't kill him, I went to her to offer her a deal. She'd been working on a new magical technique to use against him."

"New magic?"

"Yes, but she hadn't quite gotten it to work the way she'd envisioned. Naturally, she didn't trust me, with good reason. So, I offered her the unbreakable vow. She wanted her family protected for a minimum of five generations. She knew I was immortal so it wasn't unreasonable, especially if we could get rid of him. We planned to hand down her knowledge from generation to generation and I assured her that hundreds of years down the bloodline one of her family members would be strong enough to seek the reckoning for what had happened."

"Me?"

"You're the offset Mr. Cain. Every hundred years since the dawn of time a Dark Lord takes his place in our community and during his reign an offset is born. The offset's purpose is to rise up and provide balance. There is always one offset for one Dark Lord. When Alucard displaced Fiona a second offset was produced creating a whole separate bloodline with the traits to defeat a Dark Lord. When

Alucard's first term ended, he shifted so the offset couldn't find him to fight him. They instead passed on the skills to their children and so on and so on. When Alucard decided to rise again, and retake his rightful place the result was two fully functional Dark Lord's, Alucard and Voldemort occupying the same time period and two offsets, Harry Potter and…"

"And me?" He paused, "Wait, if an offset is born when the Dark Lord takes his place among the Death Eaters, are you saying he's been planning this for the last seventeen years?"

"You have the skills to fight, but the Tattenger-Westerfield that is being held in Azkaban, Nicole, may hold the magical weapon you'll need to win."

"I just have to go to this impenetrable fortress, get it from her without her killing me then figure out how to use whatever it is."

"The clock is ticking Mr. Cain. He won't wait much longer." She took her shirt back off and pulled her hair back. "Damn hot flashes."

'Tell me about it'. He thought to himself. "Tell me something, Isn't the flying range of a Death Eater normally about a hundred miles? Because there have been an awful lot of escapes."

"That was a problem before they moved the prison. Now it's 250 miles out. That's even pushing the limit for Apparation. If someone was to escape now you can be sure they had Ministry help." She paused. "You're wound is bleeding again." She brought to his attention. "You need to rest now, but you don't have much time to heal. He won't wait much longer."

"Well, thank you. I think I have a clearer idea of how to do what I have to. My concern now is you."

"You're very clever. You're worried that if you are able to hurt him that it will make me stronger, and you have no guarantee that I won't use my strength against you to help him."

"If he and I fight and I hurt him you can be sure, with what's at stake, there won't be anything left of him for you to help. No, my concern is that if I succeed, you'll die with him."

"If that happens, I'll welcome the rest. As far as the other scenario, I can assure you I have no desire to be a Dark Lady, I never have. I give you my word, for what it's worth. After all these years, I do realize that I won't fight against him, but I promise I won't interfere in your quest. Fair enough?"

"You're an amazing woman. Goodbye Oracle."

"Goodbye Mr. Cain and good luck." She turned away to hide from him that tears began to drip from her eyes. She knew something about him that even he didn't. Just before Justice reached the door to leave, she asked him to send in McGonagall. She entered the room and took her seat at her desk. "This is going to get messy Minerva."

"How so?"

"He is indeed the Ranger, but he hides a darkness he, himself, is not aware of. You must brace the Order; a fight is coming. I've seen the battle between the Ranger and Alucard and I have yet to see a scenario in which Mr. Cain survives the encounter. In fact, I have not seen much of his past. It's being blocked."

"Blocked? Who could do that to you?"

"Not sure. At first, I thought perhaps it was Alucard, but now I fear it's someone else. Someone close to him. It frightens me Minerva."

"What if he doesn't fight? We can hide him, send him away."

"He will fight. To turn and run is not in his nature. He's convinced he must be the one and I now agree. When I touched him, I saw many things, many disturbing things that have placed him on this path, including someone close to him who has been poisoning him. That person will betray him."

"Who is it? We can take them into custody."

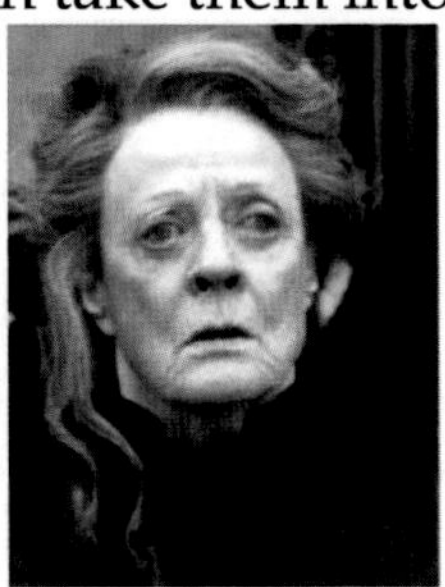

"Alucard thought of that, so I can't see who it is. Come, we need to gather the Panel and the Order members. Unless something unforeseen occurs, we could be facing the extinction of our species."

"You've seen Alucard defeat him then turn his rage on the rest of us?"

"I fear I may have envisioned something worse. Your Mr. Cain has the ability to absorb the magical powers of his opponents. Combined with the powers he already possesses and the underlying darkness that resides in him, if he wins, he could conceivably be even more of a problem than Alucard." She took McGonagall's hand and together they left.

Justice slowly made his way to Professor Hunt's office. He knocked on the door and she replied to come in. When he

Chapter 30 – Who am I?

entered the office, she immediately noticed he was hurt. "What are you doing here? You're supposed to be in the hospital."

"I need your help."

"Oh my," she ran to her window and looked out.

"What are you doing?"

"Looking for the flying pigs."

"I'm serious."

She looked at him and the smile left her face, "Okay, I'm listening."

"I have a theory, but it's gonna be hard for you to accept."

"If it's yours I know it's been thought out. Let's hear it."

Beauxbatons vs. Durmstrang

Rochelle Maynard was on a quest to not only have Beauxbatons win the tournament as the host school, but to claim most valuable player award honors as well. Her teammates looked for her at every possible opportunity. She took every shot the team got. She scored six times in the first fifteen minutes of play. The score was **78 to 8** before

Durmstrang scored their first goal. If looks could kill Viktor Krum would have been on his way to Azkaban. He normally wore a scowl, but this one had intent behind it. Rochelle fired off their first twenty shots, scoring eleven goals before the Seekers located the Snitch for the first time. **124 to 28** was the score when Beauxbatons added insult to injury by catching the Snitch to end the match. Durmstrang was officially eliminated from a chance at the championship and with Harry back Hogwarts was poised to force a playoff. Charista congratulated Rochelle on a well-played game. Rochelle was gracious on the outside but seething on the inside that her teammate didn't allow her to score a few more times to put the M.V.P. race out of Charista's reach. Charista got some soup to take to Hermione who seemed to be getting worse instead of better. She hadn't left the room since the previous day. Jade stayed out on the pitch and Reggie fired shots at her to help her practice. Harry looked on from the stands and saw Rita Skeeter stumbling behind Pius and some of the other Ministry officials trying to get an exclusive interview. Pius was constantly surrounded by guards as the threat of abductions was still very real. He congratulated Rochelle and when he glanced up into the stands he seemed to be looking directly at Harry. Harry's scar immediately began to throb.

Hermione had lost her voice completely. She tried but couldn't communicate with Justice. Charista walked in. "Oh, you poor dear. You look awful." She put down the soup and hugged her. "I feel so bad for you. Is there anything I can do to make you feel more comfortable?"

Hermione shook her head. She reached for a piece of parchment and scribbled a note. It was barely legible as she still had little use of her hands. Charista stared at it and when she deciphered the words she responded. "Yes, Beauxbatons won, and she played well." Hermione tried to scribble another note. Charista looked closely at it but couldn't make it out. Hermione began to cry. Even that looked painful, but remarkably she wasn't in pain, however, was losing use of her extremities. "That's it! We have to get you into the hospital." Hermione shook her head no. "Why not?" Hermione didn't answer. "At least let me tell Justice." Again, she emphatically shook her head, no. "Fine, then I'm not leaving you."

Hermione slammed her fist down on the end table and mouthed the word no. Charista began to feed her soup. Hermione used both hands to hold the quill and wrote something down. She pushed the paper to Charista and pointed at her with swollen fingers. Charista read the note. It had three letters on it:

M.V.P.

Charista hugged her.

THE ELDERS

"I need to call a meeting. I need them to hear me."

"That can wait. We need to get you back to the…"

"Now! I have new information and I need information as well. Things are getting sideways, and I have to right the ship before it's too late." Justice explained as he continually shook his hands to try to bring feeling back into them. Dani noticed.

"*Alright*. They wanted to speak to you anyway. I just don't know about this plan. You know this affects me too."

"You'll just have to trust me. Have you seen Marcus?"

"No." Her tone conveyed the fact that she already knew he was missing.

THE PANEL

The Room of Requirement was filled with Questers, Order members and the Panel members. McGonagall settled everyone down as Kalick moved to the head of the room.

"What's going on Kalick?" asked Mutombo.

"Did you speak with the young man?" asked Bathilda.

"Is he the one?" asked Colina.

"Yes, Mr. Cain is the Ranger. We have a problem." The people in the room gasped collectively. "He's going to challenge Alucard. If he loses Alucard will rain fire down on the magical community until no pureblood witch or wizard is left alive, but him and the blood sacrifice. The rest will breed themselves out of existence. Real magic will cease to exist for generations."

"How do you know he is ***the*** Ranger?" asked Jean-Michael.

"I touched him and the power I felt in him I have only ever felt in one other person, Alucard. I watched him transfer protection onto another witch so that he felt the pain inflicted on her. It's the same spell I used to protect the Tattenger bloodline when Alucard took power. There aren't many who can do it. He's seventeen. The things he knows can't be known by a seventh-year student."

"What are you saying?" McGonagall asked.

Chapter 30 – Who am I?

"I don't know yet. He's suppressing much of his past."

"Surely you've seen the battle scenarios between Alucard and the boy. What did you see?" asked Elphias.

"The visions are distorted."

"How so?" asked Bathilda.

"I see them face off then the vision is dark," she paused, "Then I see the boy fall."

McGonagall covered her mouth in horror. "Could the vision be wrong?" she asked, but she knew the answer.

"So, the next question is what to do about Alucard?" asked Voskoff.

"He'll be impossible to stop." mumbled one of the Questers.

"Our intelligence indicates he has been looking for our members. He wants the Hallows. We believe he has one already. If he gets his hands on the other two…" said another.

"All hope is lost." added Bathilda.

"I didn't say Alucard kills the boy." Kalick clarified. "Mr. Cain is facing the perfect storm. Alucard is his end game. True or not he believes facing him is his destiny. His very nature has made him many friends, but unlike Harry Potter, those friendships make him weaker, not stronger. He ***will*** try to save them all and will risk everything for one. But each person he uses his magic to save lessons his effectiveness and drains him of his life force. He knows this but doesn't care. He puts no value on his own life because…"

"Because he's an Alpha." McGonagall blurted.

"He's ***the*** Alpha, but that's not the reason. He has a deal with the Reaper." Again, there was a collective gasp throughout the room.

"Are you sure?" asked Mutombo.

"It's unmistakable. He will die once his fight with

Alucard is over. Our only hope is that he gets Alucard before Alucard gets him."

"Even if he wins, he loses." whispered Voskoff.

"This can't be." cried McGonagall, "Is there no way to save him?"

"His path is set. I just wish that was all." stated Kalick.

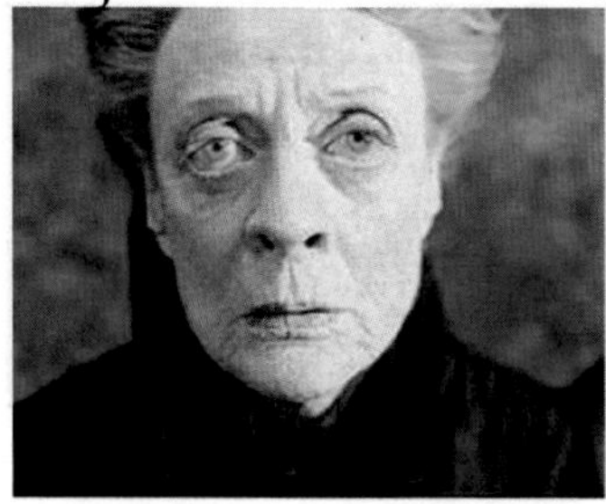

"There's more?" asked Jean-Michael.

"Tell them what you know Bathilda." she commanded.

"If what Kalick says is true, and we all know it is, there is yet another obstacle for Mr. Cain. Harry Potter."

"Harry Potter?" McGonagall questioned.

"Mr. Cain is an offset. Harry Potter is an offset. Throughout history there have only been two other times that we have had two living offsets in the same century. Cadmus Peverell and Nicholi Emilianenko. Cadmus used the Death Stick and killed the Dark Lord of his era. It was Nicholi who then cut his throat. The others were Albus Dumbledore and Gillert Grindelwald."

"But they were Death Eaters." reminded Colina.

"Yes, but neither was a reigning Dark Lord when they dueled for the Death Stick. They were offsets born to provide balance against the sitting Dark Lord of the time."

"Two offsets are one too many." said Voskoff.

"One will be turned by the promise of power, and they will face off before this story concludes it final act."

Chapter 30 - Who am I?

The Elders gathered in Professor Hunt's office. "Alright Justice, you've requested an audience and here we are." stated one of the members.

"I've asked you all here because our coven is once again in jeopardy. We've been displaced from our home. We're in a foreign land facing a very real threat. I have a job to do, but I can only do it effectively if I have all the information to keep the playing field level." He had their attention. "You know I've never asked before, but if anyone here knows who my parents were, I'd like to know." They all began looking back and forth to one another, but no one spoke. "Okay, fine. Has anyone seen Marcus?" Again, they began to mumble amongst themselves, but no one answered the question. "Okay, since it's got to be painfully obvious to each of you that we're falling apart, I say the time to act is now. Alucard is real and he's coming. I need to assemble the Alphas and we need to go find him and put an end to this. This guy is the most dangerous foe we're ever gonna face. I'll do all of the heavy lifting, but…"

"No." stated one of the Elders before Justice could finish.

"Excuse me?"

"We cannot risk it. We cannot authorize…"

"You cannot authorize?"

"We cannot authorize you to seek out an opponent for war. Your responsibility as ***our*** Alpha protector is to stay with ***us*** and make sure ***we*** do not come under threat here."

"Me seek him out. I'm just trying to be proactive here. It's not like we train for possibilities and hope that they never happen. This is coming. It could be today, it could be a month from now, but we are going to have to face it. I just think, with this particular individual it would be better to strike on our terms, rather than his."

"It's too soon." the Elder stated.

"What does that mean?" he asked. They whispered amongst themselves. "You know I can hear you right? You knew? All this time?"

"Justice…" Dani began.

"You knew and you were just using me?" Dani walked over to him and tried to reach out and place her hands on his shoulders, but he took a step back away from her.

"Justice, we weren't using you. We honestly believe you can defeat him."

"I trusted you. How many were there before me that you believed could defeat him? All this time you tried to make me believe I was protecting the kids and all the while I was your personal bodyguard? You didn't care if I survived, I was just being offered up to give you time to run."

"You don't understand. Our deal will end if we survive to the New Year. He gave his word."

"Do you hear yourselves? ***Death*** gave you his word he'd let you live if you survived until the New Year. Tell me something, what was the price?"

"What do you mean?"

"It's me, Justice. You know I've studied this stuff. I know the terms of a deal with Death. What did you have to give in exchange?" They didn't answer. They tried to act as if they didn't know what he was talking about. "Don't make me beat

Chapter 30 – Who am I?

it out of you." he said in a much different, no-nonsense tone.

"It doesn't matter. We're all dead. We're just awaiting our date. That's what we all have in common. That's what our coven is. Everyone in our coven has been touched by death, but you." Dani told him.

Another Elder began to speak. "A prophecy told us of the birth of a warlock with the bloodline dating back a thousand years. A warlock who possessed the skills to defeat history's worst Dark Lord. A Dark Lord whose one soul was worth a million to Death. Death wants that soul, and he is never going to honor any deal that causes him to lose it."

"You're an Alpha Justice. You have sworn responsibilities to your coven." barked one of the Elders. "Look at you, you can barely stand."

"And you didn't have any responsibility to tell me the truth so I could decide for myself if it was what I wanted?" He paused. "No, I don't think our contract is valid anymore?"

"He killed your parents." shouted one of the Elders stopping Justice in his tracks.

"What did you say?"

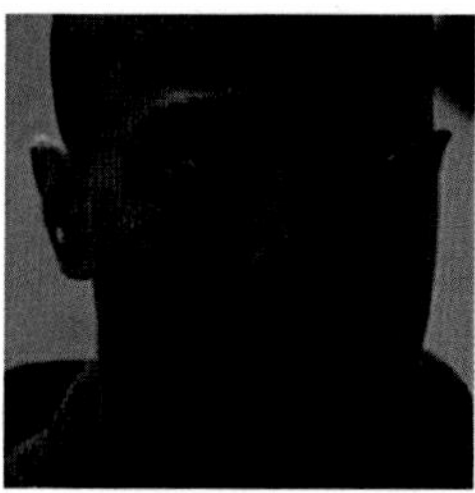

"Alucard killed your parents. He knew of the prophecy and tracked them down trying to destroy the bloodline and eliminate the threat against him. He didn't know you were alive. Your parents gave you up for adoption the night you were born to protect you." They all took a step back when lights in the room blew out. A gust of wind shot through the room and Justice's hands caught on fire.

Professor Hunt shouted. "Justice! I suggest you calm down and consider the consequences of your next move. You know the penalty for deserting your coven."

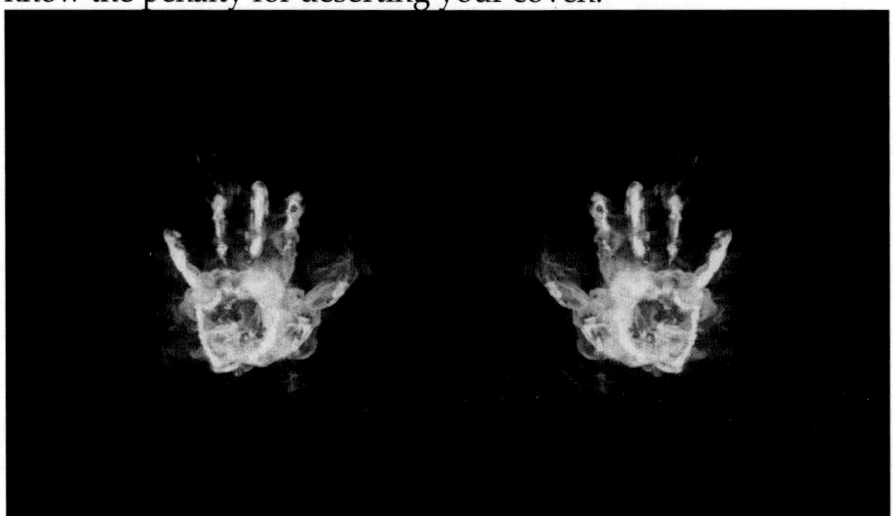

"And what's the penalty for the coven deserting me?" He just glared at her. The flames went out and the lights came back up. "It doesn't matter because it's not my coven anymore." He turned and walked out.

"Justice!!!" she called to him. She noticed him repeatedly flexing his fingers but dismissed it thinking it was the fire.

"Let him go. He'll realize he has no choice."

"Given what he now knows, I'm not so sure." Dani replied. She didn't notice him collapse in the hallway.

. "Is she ready?" someone asked.

"Who, Jade?" Dani replied.

"Yes."

"No, of course not." She paused, but I may know someone who is."

Chapter 31 – One-way ticket

THE FINAL MATCH

Hermione wanted desperately to attend the final match, but she could barely keep her eyes open. She'd lost the use of her hands and couldn't speak. She was deteriorating and finally had to be taken to the hospital. The hospital staff at Beauxbatons couldn't figure out the problem. They wanted to ship her to St. Mungo's, but she didn't want to leave without the rest of the team. Charista was supposed to be with the team getting ready to take the field, but she wouldn't leave. Wood came to the hospital to talk with her. He couldn't believe Hermione's condition, but he was there to try to win the tournament and knew he needed Charista. "I'll have Seamus or Hagrid come sit with her." he offered.

"No. Let Emmerick start in my place."

Hermione cried and shook her head no. She pushed Charista away. The three of them were at a standstill until Harry walked in. He appeared uneasy as he made eye contact with Charista. "How are you Hermione?" he asked as he sat down beside her and held her hand.

Charista was about to answer for her when she spoke for herself. "It's good to see you Harry." Charista was shocked. Hermione's body language changed completely. She adjusted her position and sat up. The swelling in her hands began to dissipate. She was confused by the fact that she didn't feel badly physically.

"Don't try to move, just rest. I was really worried about you." She began feeling better immediately, but also felt bad they were all fussing over her.

"All of you go, I'm feeling better, see? Play well and win for Hogwarts."

"Are you sure? I could stay with you." Charista offered.

"No. This is why we came. I really am feeling much better. Go, win. I'll be fine. I can use the time to prepare my report for the Triathlon. Represent us well."

"We will." Harry replied. "I'll come back as soon as we're done." He leaned in and kissed her on the cheek.

Justice grabbed his chest as he pulled the door open to Professor Flitwick's classroom.

"Don't have Seamus or Hagrid miss the match. I'll be fine." She attempted to stand up to show them she was able to care for herself, but she still wasn't that stable. Harry stood on one side and Charista stepped to the other.

"Are you sure about this?" Charista asked her. She nodded. "Liar." Charista said to her quietly as she leaned in to hug her one last time. She slipped off her glove and touched Harry's hand. As she pulled away her eyes were glowing yellow as she turned to Harry who had his back to her.

"What is it?" Hermione asked her.

Her eyes returned to their normal shade. "Nothing. We've got to go. You're sure you'll be okay?"

"I'm fine, go." She forced a smile.

Charista walked out the doors that led to the atrium. She glanced back one last time and Hermione mustered a smile and a wave. Charista seemed especially fidgety. The others assumed it was nervous energy about the match, despite never having seen her nervous before. She, however, knew the apprehension she felt was from an energy coming from Harry. It wasn't for Hermione. She also felt that Hermione's condition didn't appear to be a simple virus. This was a magical curse. An exceptionally powerful curse. When did it happen? Who did it? Charista wondered.

"CHARISTA!" Wood shouted.

"WHAT?"

"I need you here. The starting lineup is Charista, Blaise and Emmerick, Freddy and Cormac. Jade, of course, and Harry. The rest of you be ready, I'll likely use everyone in this one. We lose we go home. Constant pressure, let's go!"

The Quaffle went up and Harry bolted for the Snitch. Just seconds in he had his hand extended and was within inches of ending the match. Viktor was screaming at the top of his lungs. Harry could feel the Snitch's wings on his fingertips when he was hit hard on his blindside by both Durmstrang Beaters. Cormac was involved in the crash as well and came up injured. Cam was inserted and play continued. Rochelle had thirty-one goals in her six games. Charista had scored twenty-one through her five. Durmstrang struck first. Hagrid screamed for a violation as Jade was knocked out of position by one of the Durmstrang Chasers. Krum argued his player was just going for the Quaffle. Jade was furious and blocked the next ten attempts. Meanwhile, Charista didn't force any shots. She played within the plan of the offense, and she was amazing. She scored four times in a 2-minute span. Krum called time out to settle his team. When play resumed Blaise secured the Quaffle and flew up the right side of the pitch. He passed to Emmerick who took a shot that missed wide to the right, but Charista caught the errant shot and scored.

Gabrielle went to visit Hermione. She'd once again begun to fade, but so far still had her voice. She asked Gabrielle to help her to get to the match. Hermione tried to stand on her own and nearly fell. When Gabrielle touched her shoulder to stabilize her Hermione winced in frustration. When Gabrielle pulled her hand back, she saw a bruise where she had touched her.

"Oh my God!" Gabrielle couldn't believe she was in such a fragile state. "Are you sure you can make it?"

Hermione nodded and begged her. She helped her get dressed as carefully as she could, and they left. They arrived just in time to see Charista continue her brilliant play. They had to stand on the ground level since Hermione didn't have the stamina to climb the stairs. She was equally angry that she wasn't in any pain yet was crippled. Charista scored again giving Hogwarts a **158 to 26** lead. They were dominating in every aspect. It was Charista's eighth goal. Durmstrang decided to deploy a new tactic. "YOU PLAY PHYSICAL! I WANT BLOOD, I WANT BROKE BONES! THEY DON'T LEAVE ON FEET; THEY LEAVE ON STRETCHER! START WITH THAT ONE!" Krum pointed to Charista.

"Alright, let's settle down. We have a good lead, but they can still win if they catch the Snitch. Charista, you're the hot hand, do you think you've got two more in ya?" Wood asked.

Chapter 31 – One-way ticket

"I want this. I'll do whatever it takes."

"They're gonna try to rough you up when the match starts again. Be careful." stated Seamus.

"I anticipated that. We're gonna switch it up a bit. They can't hit what they can't catch. Speed team, you're in. Stormy, you and Demetria go in for Blaise and Emmerick. Reggie, you're in for Freddy. Charista, you score. Jade, you block everything and Harry, if you can't catch the Snitch make sure they don't."

"Got it." Harry replied.

"If we can score a couple more goals, we won't need to catch the Snitch." reminded Freddy.

Krum was shocked when he saw the Hogwarts lineup, but had already used his last time out. The Quaffle was about to be tossed when both Harry and Charista noticed Hermione near the bleachers beside Gabrielle. She looked awful. There were bags beneath her eyes. She had visible bruising on her skin, and she'd lost weight.

The Snitch was released. The Quaffle went up and the new insertion of speed was apparent immediately. Demetria grabbed the Quaffle and dove low avoiding the Bludger. She passed to Charista, to Stormy back to Charista, goal!!! **168 to 26**. Durmstrang attacked, and their Beaters fired the Bludger at Jade, but she simply slid just out of its path and blocked their shot. **170 to 26.** Charista got the Quaffle and raced down the right side. She passed to Stormy, but the Quaffle slipped out her hand and was caught easily by the Keeper. **170 to 28.** However, he threw a lazy pass toward his Chaser and Charista intercepted it and scored. **180 to 28**. She'd tied the record. There was still plenty of time left for her to score more, but she was content. She encouraged Harry to find and catch the Snitch to end the match. It would be much more satisfying to play Rochelle head-to-head for high scorer honors. Harry searched the sky. The Snitch darted by, and he set off after it, but simultaneously his scar began to throb. Jade's head began to pound. Demetria felt the pain of a severe migraine and Charista heard a high-pitched ringing in her ears. There was a hidden message in it. Krum noticed immediately and shouted to his players. They scored twice in fifteen seconds and changed the complexion of the match. **180 to 48**. Jade could barely stay on her broom. Charista fought through it. She took a pass from Stormy and attacked the Keep.

"Snap out of it, Jade, we need you." Reggie told her. Suddenly, just as quickly as they had all felt their pains, they went away. Jade accelerated at the last moment and avoided being crashed into by a Durmstrang Chaser. Charista fired a shot that was batted away, but Demetria collected it and passed to Stormy who scored. **190 to 50**. Harry refocused and flew off toward the Snitch. Reggie and Cam got between the Quaffle and the Durmstrang Chaser. When he lost sight of it Charista swooped in and scored, breaking the scoring record and giving Hogwarts a **200 to 50** lead. Harry bore down on the Snitch. The Durmstrang Seeker was right beside him. The Quaffle was up for grabs. Demetria grabbed it. The Beaters converged on her. She tried to pass it to Stormy, but it hit the ring and ricocheted to the Keeper. The official scorer mistakenly called it a block making the score **200 to 52.** Harry was inches away. He lunged and toppled off his broom taking the Durmstrang Seeker and a Chaser with him. The crowd was on its feet trying to sort out what happened.

Harry sat up and looked at the other Seeker. Harry's hands were clasped together. He opened them and there was nothing in them. The Durmstrang Seeker opened his hand and there was the Snitch, wings fluttering.

"DURMSTRANG WINS! BEAUXBATONS IS THE TOURNAMENT CHAMPION!!!"

Harry couldn't believe it. Charista led the players over to shake their opponent's hands. They all told her, despite the loss, she was clearly the Most Valuable Player. She didn't have time to enjoy the accolade because as she glanced into the crowd, she saw Hermione collapse. She heard Gabrielle scream, and, in an instant, she was there beside them.

"I'm taking her home right now!" Before anyone could say okay, or please don't go, she grabbed Hermione and disapparated. Jade had recovered enough to gather Cam, Freddy, Reggie, Stormy and D and direct them to the car.

Harry, surprisingly said, "I'll get her things and meet you all back at the castle." Jade was shocked he didn't want to come with them.

Charista communicated to Justice they were on their way. He told her to go straight to the hospital wing. He'd be there waiting when they arrived. He went to the Owlrey and dispatched several letters and packages. He looked at the little Arctic Tern Neville had gotten him. "Don't worry little guy, you'll get your turn." One parcel was addressed to Krysta Marie Madison.

BAD TO WORSE

"Oh my God." Was his reaction when he saw her condition.

Madam Pomfrey went to work on her immediately.

McGonagall and others gathered around offering to do anything to help. Justice stepped over to Bill Weasley and whispered something in his ear. Bill looked at him with a confused expression. Professor Hunt approached.

"You will tell Ron?" Justice asked Bill.

"Of course? Are you alright?" Bill noticed him bleeding.

"What is it?" Professor Hunt asked as Madam Pomfrey approached them.

"I don't know. I honestly don't know. I've never seen anything like it. She's alive, but I think she may lose her right arm. Her condition is so advanced." She paused, "She may be dying." She had a tear in her eye. She was genuinely saddened by the fact that she didn't think she could save her.

Justice closed his eyes and appeared to be in deep thought. His eyes could be seen moving back and forth rapidly beneath the lids. Suddenly they opened. He reached for a rag on an end table. He lifted his shirt where his stab wound was, and he tore away the bandages. He wiped at the wound until the blood stains were gone, all signs of the wound was gone as well. "Charista," Justice began. She was crying uncontrollably and holding Dobby.

"I'm so sorry Justice. I should have protected her."

"This isn't your fault."

"He was there, Alucard. He was there, or close. He's broadcasting a message to Death Eaters that he's looking for the Hallows."

"Don't worry about him right now. Can you please bring Ron here immediately? He should be here for her, just in case."

"Of course."

"Is that alright Headmistress?" he asked out of respect.

"Go." she approved.

Justice stepped to Charista and took her hand. "Sorry to have to ask this of you at a time like this, but..."

"Don't mention it. You know I'd do anything for you and Hermione." He nodded. Once she left the room, she opened her hand and realized he had passed her his wand and a note. She opened the note and read it to herself.

Back in the room, Dobby looked away. He disapparated just as Jade and the others came running into the hospital. Mallory walked up to Justice and hugged him. "Thank you." she whispered.

"My pleasure. I need you. We never finished my lesson."

"Any time." she replied.

"How about now?" As he held her, she felt a sensation much like a tiny electric shock. She could see electrical charges in his eyes. He let her go and she felt slightly lightheaded.

"What was that?" Mallory asked as she shook her head.

Professor Hunt walked up to Justice. "Don't even think about it."

"You know, you really need to back up off me. You can't tell me what to do anymore remember? Your privileges have been revoked."

"What are you two fussing about?" McGonagall asked.

"Hermione is like a Goddaughter to me, but you are forbidden to interfere."

"Can…Can you help her?" McGonagall asked.

"I think so." he replied.

"No!" snapped Dani. "He's on suspension from being an Alpha. If he tries to heal her, he loses his strength level. He must save his abilities to protect the coven. Even Hermione…"

"Don't speak her name!" Justice snapped at her causing her to recoil in fright.

She continued. "She would tell you not to break your contract. One life is not worth the sacrifice of your ability to protect hundreds from your own coven."

He didn't look convinced. "I don't have a coven anymore; I was kicked out." Jade and the others looked at one another confused.

Professor Hunt turned to McGonagall, "Surely you agree."

McGonagall looked at Hermione then back at Dani. "Justice, if you can save her, save her."

"Is this true?" Neville asked. "About the coven?"

"What difference does it make? If I let her die what good are my powers anyway? I don't know if I can save her, but I have to try." He turned to Hermione.

Chapter 31 - One-way ticket

Then McGonagall remembered what the Oracle had said about him helping others. "Wait! Poppy, is there nothing else you can do? No potion…" Madame Pomfrey shook her head.

"What about St. Mungo's?" Professor Flitwick asked.

"I'm afraid it's too late." she replied.

"Neville, what about the Westerfield potion? Perhaps it could slow down the symptoms." Bill asked.

"It's worth a shot." Neville rushed by his Gram to the potions room and brought back the solution. Charista and Ron arrived. Justice stepped over and whispered something to Seamus and Dean. Together they left the room immediately. Justice began to walk toward Hermione and Professor Hunt grabbed his shoulder. He spun and cast a curse that blasted her across the room. Mr. Crisp grabbed him around the arms.

"Big mistake young man. One that I've been hoping you'd make since the start of the semester."

"Mr. Crisp!" McGonagall called.

Crisp leaned in and whispered to Justice. "I can't wait until I am alone with her to extract the whereabouts of that cloak she has." Justice began to struggle causing Crisp's sleeve to ride up his arm revealing his Dark Mark. He was a Death Eater. Justice spun and grabbed Crisp by the throat. He slammed his palm to Crisp's forehead and a light appeared to emit from his hand. Marcus entered the room quietly.

"Extracting information was a surprisingly good idea. '***Extract!***'"

Crisp fell to the floor limp. Flitwick cast, "***Incarserous!***" and bound him. Neville and Dean reentered the room. Jade reached for her wand and Charista's eyes were yellow.

"No Jade!" Justice commanded. Finally, she listened to him and stood down.

McGonagall approached Justice. "Give it to her Neville."

Justice begged. They administered the potion and within moments her breathing seemed to stabilize.

"Mr. Cain, you've been witnessed assaulting two members of our faculty. The first indiscretion warranted a suspension. The second is a crime that requires immediate imprisonment in Azkaban prison."

"No!" shouted Jade. Marcus hid in a corner.

"It's okay. It was worth it." he told her.

"I'm sorry Mr. Cain." said the Headmistress.

"I left you no choice." he replied. The Oracle listened in from beneath her hood in the back of the room. Filch, Bill and Seamus escorted Justice from the room.

"I can't believe this! You let this happen." Jade accused McGonagall. "And you!" She turned to Professor Hunt.

"Jade, that's enough. You need to calm down. What good is it going to be for you both to be sent to Azkaban?" Charista asked as she placed her hand on Jade's shoulder.

"Take your hand off of me." Jade demanded.

"Or what?" Charista stepped nose to nose with her.

"Yeah, cat fight." said Freddy. Cam smacked him in the head.

"This is getting out of control." stated McGonagall.

"Did I hear you mention you've lost control?" asked a familiar voice. It was Dolores Umbridge.

"What are ***you*** doing here?" McGonagall asked.

"I'm here on behalf of the Ministry. As the Ambassador for Magical Education, I have been asked to personally oversee the proceedings of the Triathlon."

"How did you get onto the grounds?"

"It wasn't long ago, Minerva, that I was the Headmistress here. Not everyone has forgotten that." She glanced over at Hermione. "What's wrong with the mudblood girl?"

"We don't know, but don't bother pretend as if you care."

"Don't worry, I won't." she said with a smile.

Mallory walked by her and said, "All of my students, come with me." She wanted to gather the group together. Professor Hunt called to Charista. Marcus slipped away.

Dani gathered herself and approached Charista. "The Elders of my coven have authorized me to extend an offer to you to join our coven as an Alpha."

Jade rolled her eyes and walked out. "After what you did to Justice, you dare ask me that and right now? Besides, Jade is next in line if you're looking for a fill in until Justice comes back, and he ***is*** coming back." She walked by her and followed the others out of the room.

They all gathered in Mallory's classroom. "Alright, who here has any idea what's going on?" she asked.

"He's lost it. It's all my fault." said Demetria, sounding guilty and remorseful.

"What are you talking about? This has nothing to do with you, drama queen." retorted Jade.

"I should have touched him before they took him." said Charista.

"I think you've touched enough of our group." said Jade. "You shouldn't have let them take him."

"What was I supposed to do, grab him and disapparate? Then we'd both be on the run."

"Think about it Jade, Justice ***went*** with them. If he wanted to get away, he could have. You know that." reminded Cam.

"Yeah, stop being such a Hag." said Freddy then he cowered behind Cam.

"Stop it, all of you. He's our friend." stated Mallory.

"So that was friendship when you had your arms wrapped around him in the hospital?" said Jade sarcastically.

Mallory ignored her jealous ranting. "He'd never leave one of us in trouble. We need to figure out how to help him." said Stormy.

"I like her." whispered Neville to Dean.

Chapter 31 – One-way ticket

"Get in line." Dean whispered back.

"We need Marcus." Jade said.

"We need Hermione. She'd know what to do." said Ron.

"He touched you before he left the room. What did he take?" Jade questioned Mallory.

"I don't know. We'd been working on a few things, but we didn't get to complete the project."

"What was it?"

"It was between the two of them." snapped Charista.

Jade took offense and stood up. "I have had about all I'm gonna take from you! I don't care if you are an Alpha in my coven now, I don't have to…" Mallory cast a protective barrier between them.

"Is that what this is about? I didn't accept. If they need an Alpha to fill in for Justice, it should be you."

"Jade, cut it out. You're always looking for a fight. We all know Justice. He's got a plan. He's always got a plan, right?" Cam asked.

Harry followed Gabrielle to Hermione's room to collect her things. He found her beaded bag with the undetectable extension charm on it. He began packing her things when he came across her journal. He looked around and made sure no one was watching. He knew he shouldn't, but he opened it and began to read some of the last passages. His eyes grew narrow, and he abruptly slammed it shut.

One of the ministry escorts that had come with Umbridge was waiting for Justice at the front entrance. Flitwick released Justice's binds; Bill shook Justice's hand. Seamus hugged him. "Sorry about everything guys. Look after things for me. Take care of Hermione." He stepped to Filch with his arms open. "Come on. Give me some love. You know you want to." Filch just sneered at him.

"Alright, alright, that's enough. Let's go." said the official. The two of them disapparated to Ministry headquarters. Justice was taken to the lower level holding area, placed in a room with three men and searched.

"Where's your wand?"

"I have no need of one. ***Imperious!***" He cast. "***Sleep!***" he commanded. The three men guarding him collapsed to the ground. He gathered them together. "***Obliviate!***" He searched them and confiscated their wands. He pressed them together then tilted his head back and swallowed them. He gulped a couple of times and stepped through the door reaching back and touching the door handle which fused it shut. He had two wands drawn on him immediately. He put his hands up. "They said one of you three is going to transport me to the facility."

"Eager to get to Azkaban, are you?" One of the guards grabbed him by the collar. "We'll change that." He was yanked away toward another room within the bowels of the Ministry. Two of the guards stopped at the door as the last led him inside where there was a large fireplace. "Listen up, cause here's the instructions and I'm only gonna say em once. Take a breath, but not too deep or your lungs'll explode."

"Is it a long trip, here to Azkaban?"

"The longest ***you'll*** ever take. In fact, it's too long for anyone to make it all the way without a stop. You try and you'll die. Only a few of us know the way. If you survive it maybe I'll introduce you to a Dementor, they're just dyin' to kiss young ones like you."

Justice stopped in his tracks and stared at the fire. "We're not going by Floo are we? I've only done that once before and had a bad experience."

He squeezed Justice's arm tight now that they were alone. "Rumor has it you had a part in the death of a friend of mine, Malikai. Does that name ring a bell?" Justice glanced up at him appearing frightened. "You scared boy? You should be. Lots of people die on the trip over. No one's even gonna miss you. Now come on, let's get on with it. Keep your mouth shut. We just get in and I say Kitaro and we're there before you know it."

"Kitaro, I thought we were going to Azkaban?"

"We are. It's the secret halfway point. I told you know one can make it to Azkaban in one jump." He pushed a button that doused the flames.

"I see. Thanks."

"Thanks? For what?"

"***Langlock! Incarserous!***" The man fell, bound, onto the ground. Justice stood him up, shoved him into the fireplace and said, "***Oblivion.***" The guard disappeared. He then stepped into the fireplace and said, "***Kitaro.***" What Justice didn't know was that Kitaro was booby trapped. The moment he arrived on the island he was under siege. He nearly got trampled by a stampeding heard of Erumpent. Erumpent are large grey

African animals weighing nearly a ton. They have a thick hide that repels most charms and curses, a large sharp horn upon its nose and a long rope-like tail.

He turned invisible and made his way to a tree line for cover. He materialized and could hear the crackling of the other fireplace, the one that would take him to Azkaban. As he pushed the dense foliage aside, he took notice of the type of flower that was growing. They were remarkably familiar.

He took some. Soon he came to a clearing. He could see the fireplace but was sure he was being watched. Something was waiting for him to step into the open. He took a breath and ran about three steps into the clearing, and they came swooping down toward him, Griffins.

Unlike Hippogriff's, like Buckbeak, with the head and forelegs of an eagle and the body and hind legs of a horse, Griffins had the head and forelegs of the eagle and the hind legs of a lion with fully functional claws. They eat raw meat. In this case Justice knew he was raw meat. He disappeared and evaded them continuing to the fireplace. He was just a few feet away when he found the entrance suddenly blocked by a huge Chimaera. "What is this, some kind of mutant circus?" The Chimaera had a lion's head, a goat's body and a dragon's tail.

Chapter 31 – One-way ticket

It was vicious and bloodthirsty. It was much smaller than the Griffin, but the Griffins wanted no part of it. It lunged at him, and he dove to avoid it. He cast a protective sphere around himself, but while inside it he couldn't get into the Floo. He was reduced to being a hamster in a ball for the Chimaera to play with. He was flipped and banged and rolled side to side to the point of getting dizzy when he had what was initially thought to be a stroke of good luck. The Chimaera stopped batting him about and backed away. His vision cleared slowly, and he watched the animal's odd behavior for a moment. Then he realized there was something causing it to back away. He turned slowly and saw it approaching. It was a Nundu. A Nundu is a gigantic leopard that moves silently despite its size and whose breath could cause disease virulent enough to eliminate entire villages.

"Great!" He knew what it was but had never seen one in person. It bounded over his protective sphere and subdued the Chimaera in one bite then turned its attention to Justice. He knew he couldn't even make a break for it with it this close. He'd be infected in minutes. The huge animal slammed its clawed paw down on his protection several times before it looked up and scanned the sky. It heard something approaching. Justice looked up, and in the distance, he saw Buckbeak swooping down toward him. There was someone on his back.

'Harry?' he thought initially, but when it got close enough, he could see it was Dobby. Dobby dove off the creature and cast a spell that stunned the animal for a second. He was a good hundred feet from the beast. It charged toward him. Justice removed his protection, cast one around Dobby and shouted "*Alarte Ascendare!*" The huge animal was shot high into the air. Justice ran to Dobby. "I don't know how you knew where to find me or even why you'd come, but thank you."

"My daughter cares for you very much."

"I feel the same for her." He looked up, "I wouldn't be here when the Nundu comes down, if I were you." Dobby looked up.

"Good idea, sir. By the way, he wasn't there."

"Who?"

"The evil one, sir. I went to Beauxbatons and there was no sign of him. No trace at all."

"Thanks Dobby."

"Good luck sir." Then he snapped his fingers and disappeared.

Justice ran to the fireplace and said, "Azkaban!"

Chapter 32 – The Dark Lord's heir?

Harry arrived back at Hogwarts carrying the Most Valuable Player trophy to give to Charista. The mood was solemn. There was no fanfare. Neville filled him in on everything that had taken place. He went to see Hermione and found Ron sitting at her bedside. "How are you, Ron?"

"I'm alright, better than her."

"Has there been any change?"

"Not really." Ron tried but couldn't hold his tongue. "Where were you?"

"What d'you mean?"

"What took you so long to get here? Your best friend is lying there fighting to stay alive and you stayed behind!"

"I had to get her things." Harry's tone was eerily calm and distant. "I'm not gonna have this conversation with you, not right now."

"Fine, we can have it during the Triwizard tryouts."

"You've decided to compete, against me?"

"Don't act so surprised. The tryouts are open to anyone over seventeen."

"You can do what you want. I won't try to stop you. I do have one question though, when did you decide to enter?"

"Just now." He got up and left the room.

Harry sat down beside her and took her hand. She

opened her eyes and said his name.

"I'm here Hermione."

"Where am I?"

"You're in the hospital wing at Hogwarts." She tried to sit up. "Take your time."

"How long have I been here?"

"Since yesterday. You collapsed at the tournament, and we brought you here straight away. Do you remember anything?"

She thought to herself then said, "I remember my chest hurting then my head. Is anyone else sick?"

"No, I don't think so."

"Why is this happening to me?"

"I don't know." 'It shouldn't be you'. he whispered to himself.

"What do you mean?"

"Nothing."

Madam Pomfrey ran to the bed surprised she was awake, much less talking. "Praise Merlin, this is a very good sign." She turned to Harry. "It was looking pretty bad for a while there, but perhaps you were just the medicine she needed. Just don't overdo it." she told him, "She needs rest."

"Okay. I won't stay long."

"Her recovery is remarkable. I don't understand. She was literally at Death's doorstep." Poppy noticed, "Come with me." She walked him outside and told him to wait. She returned to Hermione's bedside and checked her vitals. Everything had dropped across the board. "Mr. Potter." she called. He came back and Hermione showed immediate improvement.

"You stay with her until I can figure out a way to stabilize her condition. Can you do that?"

Chapter 32 – The Dark Lord's heir

"Sure, I'd do anything for Hermione."

Draco sat in a room as Alucard sat before a roaring fire. "My Lord…" Malfoy began, but Alucard simply raised his hand without speaking. There was a knock at the door. The door opened and a hooded Death Eater stepped in.

"He's here my Lord."

"Show him in." Marcus entered the room. "What news do you have for me?"

"He's on his way to Azkaban."

Draco was stunned. "And the girl?"

"Hard to say. She's alive but hasn't made much progress. She's incapable of performing magic in her condition and the longer the poison is in her system, the more permanent the effects."

"Shouldn't we attack now, while he's gone?" Draco asked.

"You're afraid of our young friend, are you?" asked Alucard.

"No, I just don't see why we're waiting."

"You don't need to see. You just need to do as you're told." He paused.

"You're right to be afraid. I've studied Justice for years, seen him in action. He lives for this. The irony is that his fate is to die in this battle." Marcus stated.

"Who are you?" Draco asked.

"He's someone I trust. Unlike your, Voldemort, a true Dark Lord knows how to use people. You want to kill him, fine, you may get that honor, but why kill one, when you can kill two with one stone?" Alucard asked. "Marcus, enlighten Mr. Malfoy."

"Harry gets his strength from the girl's love and friendship. Her condition will require her to stay close to him causing his strength to increase while also creating additional tension between him and Justice."

"You're turning them against each other."

"If Justice is at full strength, he kills Harry, leaving him alone to fight us, advantage, us. However, Harry's increased power through the girl levels the playing field and should leave the victor mortally wounded and no match for you, Draco." Draco was unaware that the girl Marcus was speaking of was not Charista, the intended target, but was in fact, Hermione. "The one wrinkle I didn't see coming was Justice leaving the coven. I never thought he'd turn his back on them, especially not after he confirmed you were here. If he's not in the coven, perhaps he won't even fight you. What would be the point. But, If the move is permanent, Professor Hunt will have to follow the law of the Alpha code and strip him of his powers. That will leave him as helpless as a muggle. We wouldn't even have to kill him. Harry, however, would be both strong and confident and a worthy adversary. You'd have to kill him yourself, father."

'Father?' Draco was dumbfounded.

"Everything is coming together. You're sure about the cloak?"

"Yes father, I was with him when he put it in his vault at Gringotts. I would have taken it from him then, but he wasn't alone."

"Let me guess, Weaselby was with him. As inept as he is at magic, he'd probably have cast a curse that knocked both him and Harry out for you." said Draco sarcastically.

"It's fine. Soon, Harry will bring me the cloak himself. It's the wand we must find. Peeves failed me. It's too bad really. I thought he might have been of use, but alas he too must die, once and for all."

"Father, he knows." Marcus hesitated and swallowed hard. "He knows about the pills." Alucard's eyes grew narrow.

Mallory insisted Jade and Charista were to end their feud. They were both going to be needed, working together, to fend off Alucard's evil. Alucard was a shape shifter but couldn't simply turn himself into Harry to enter Gringotts because his evil aura was so strong the goblin alarms at the bank would be triggered the moment he set foot in the door. He could, perhaps, have pulled it off as a mere Death Eater, but not as a Dark Lord. No, Alucard's arrogance was leading him to believe Harry himself, would bring the cloak to him in exchange for the life of someone close to him.

"You're really his son?" Draco asked Marcus.

"Yep. Marcus Reece." he introduced himself.

"What's that like? Being the son of a sitting Dark Lord?"

"I barely know him. I was raised by foster parents. They died in a car crash. For the longest time I had nightmares that I caused it. I still don't know for sure."

"Your dad, he doesn't have any weaknesses, does he?"

"He's not a fan of silver, but other than that, none that I know of, why?"

Draco pretended he didn't hear the question and changed the subject. "What about this Justice character? What's his story?"

"Ah, Justice, the warrior. He's not afraid of anything, which makes him so dangerous. That and the fact that he loves it, you know, the fight. He doesn't know how to lose."

"You sound like you're in love with the guy."

"I'm going to love being the one to kill him, once and for all."

"Sorry to ruin your plans, but he's not gonna make it back from Azkaban. I left him a little surprise along the way. I made the deal that sent a Nundu to Kitaro Island myself. Besides, if he somehow makes it to Azkaban, he's got the Dementors to deal with and the Floo network that goes from the ministry to the island only goes one way. ***If*** he makes it back to Kitaro from Azkaban, he'll be stuck there. We've seen the last of him, it's just Potter and the mudblood."

"I wouldn't go celebrating just yet. If you're right and he doesn't return, we'll have a distinct advantage, but there are still several more Alphas that are sworn to protect the coven, so unless father's plan is to avoid them all together, there's still gonna be a fight ahead of us."

"I've taken care of that too. We'll have plenty of numbers to overwhelm them when the time comes."

"Really? Interesting that I haven't seen that in any of my visions."

"Is that your gift? The ability to foresee things?"

"If gift is what you want to call it. It's only about a month's window for the really strong events, minutes for the minor stuff."

"Still, it comes in handy, right?"

"Sure, I get to see everyone close to me die a full month before it happens. I'm not like an Oracle; I can only foresee events that involve me. Events that I'll be there to see unfold."

"Tell me something, why is he waiting?"

"There's a prophecy that the Hallows will all be in one location on a certain day. It just happens to be the same day that he'll pay off an obligation that in turn will make him the most powerful wizard ever."

"He isn't already?"

"If he was, do you think he'd be expending so much energy looking for the Hallows to ensure his invincibility? He's the most powerful Dark Lord, but for every Dark Lord there is an offset. An equally powerful witch or wizard sent to fight for the other side."

"Justice?"

"Or Harry. The prophecy wasn't clear. Just because Harry fought Lord Voldemort doesn't mean he was Voldemort's offset. That's why he wants to turn one of them against the other."

"Whatever."

"He's not gonna turn Justice. We just have to hope the mudblood survives long enough to help Harry hurt him. How much poison was in that necklace, by the way?"

"We're routing for Potter to win a fight?"

"Trust me, we'd rather face Harry than Justice. With Harry, we know what we've got. Justice is unpredictable. Best of all, because of the mudblood girl's feelings for Justice, Harry, given the chance, will kill him."

'I know that feeling'. Draco thought to himself, still unaware that the necklace had gone to the wrong target.

"Justice would never just kill Harry, he has too much respect for him being an Alpha."

"Harry's an Alpha too?"

"Yeah, he just doesn't acknowledge it." If it plays out and Harry wins, everybody can get what they want."

"Yeah," Draco replied. "So, do you share his powers?"

"No, I can do some things, but I'm nothing like him. It's strange, there are certain things I can't do, can't even learn. It's like every spell was written on a piece of paper then torn down

down the middle and I only got half. I'm good at what I can do though."

"But if he loses, your father, you're next in line, right?"

"I'm no dark wizard. I'm his blood, so when he called, I came. This is his moment and I want to be there to see it."

"You said Justice won't survive the battle."

"I said I don't see Justice beyond the battle."

"What do you see?"

"Draco." called Alucard. "I have an assignment for you. It's your turn to earn your keep. I want you to use your contacts at Hogwarts and find the wand. Aberforth wouldn't have taken it far. Search his room, search his tomb. Rip his body open if you must. Bring me that wand."

"Yes, my Lord."

"Take Marcus with you. He can oversee things. As a student, he'll be able to move around freely."

Marcus looked surprised. "Um, father, I left the school, where am I supposed to tell them I've been?"

"You were abducted, of course, but you escaped. You'll be a hero."

They both turned to leave. Then Alucard spoke again. "Draco."

He stopped in his tracks. "Yes, my Lord."

"Don't let me down."

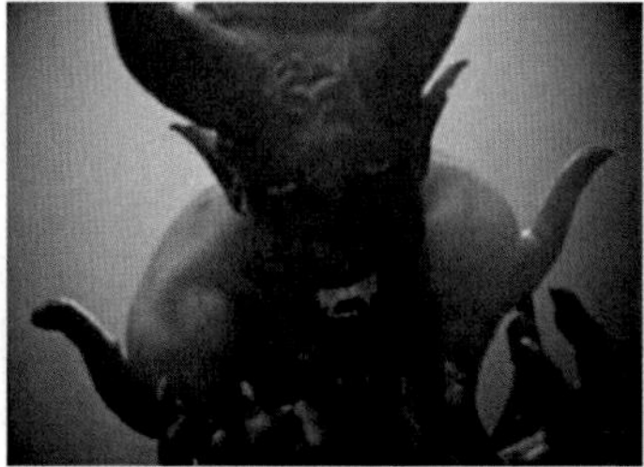

"No, my Lord, I won't."

Chapter 32 – The Dark Lord's heir?

Hermione made a miraculous recovery. She was sitting up and talking albeit with a raspy voice and aside from still not having use of her right hand and only partial use of her left, she felt well enough to leave the hospital wing. Her first order of business was to see the Headmistress. McGonagall was shocked to see her walking, but pleased she appeared to be on the mend. She was still battling with Poppy's accusation that Harry was somehow connected to her illness. He was the source of her recovery, but by association, was the cause of her deterioration. She noticed the difference in Harry and had it been Ron, perhaps, but Harry could never do that to Hermione in her opinion. She pleaded with the Headmistress to allow her to take part in the Triathlon. McGonagall was hesitant but knew how important it was to her to have a complete academic resume. She also knew how much Umbridge would hate it. "Agreed, provided you continue to improve."

Harry stayed close as she put the finishing touches on her project. She had to reconsider her finale, however, as her plan had been to play a piano duet with Mike Ambrose, but without the use of her hands that would be impossible. Ron was extremely uncomfortable with the idea that Harry was sticking so close to Hermione, but if it was keeping her healthy, he'd live with it. Besides, he was being kept busy by Charista training for the Triwizard tryouts.

Mallory confronted Professor Hunt. "We need to talk."

The timing caught her off guard. "About what?"

"About Justice, about what's going on. I don't buy it."

"It is what it is. Justice is a big boy. He's been moving away from the coven for a long time now. It was just a matter of time."

"You're not fooling me. Justice ***is*** your coven. He'd never just leave, especially not right now. He trusted you."

"Then he wasn't very smart, was he?"

"This doesn't make sense."

"Just prepare your students for what's coming. They rely on you and by the way, we have an opening for an Alpha."

"How dare you. I came to see you out of professional courtesy. Guess that was just wishful thinking. This isn't over." Mallory stormed out.

The door had barely closed behind her when Professor Hunt heard a voice. "She's a clever girl. She's onto something." Professor Hunt grabbed her wand and pointed it in the direction of the voice. "You can put that away. I'm not here to hurt you. Your Mr. Cain is quite the enigma. So young, so talented, yet burdened with the responsibility of protecting an entire coven. It hardly seems fair."

"Who are you?"

"No one of consequence. I'm simply curious why he's in this position."

Chapter 32 – The Dark Lord's heir?

"What position?"

"I don't know him as well as you do, but while he strikes me as loyal enough to fight for your coven out of the sheer goodness of his heart, he seems as if he's being pushed."

"What's your point?"

"He's been touched."

"I don't know what you're talking about."

"Of course, you do. You've been touched too. You should know we can recognize one another."

"Why are you here?"

"He's destined to die within a month. Spending it fighting a powerful Dark Lord to protect a school full of orphans seems a bit wasteful and irresponsible."

"If you know him at all, you know he's not going to be forced into anything."

"Including being forced out of his coven." Kalick pulled her hood onto her head.

"I don't know who you are, but I'd stay out of it if I were you."

"Well, you're not." she snapped.

"Hey!" shouted Dani, taking exception to the tone. "Whatever his plans are they're his plans."

"So, he ***does*** have a plan."

"You'd have to ask him."

"Perhaps I will."

"It was a figure of speech. You stay away from my student."

"Or what?"

"You need to leave this office now!"

The hooded figure pulled its hood back. "Is he, perhaps, more than just your student?"

"How dare you!" Dani cast a curse at her, not knowing

if it was Alucard himself. It rebounded and Dani was knocked to the floor. Kalick stepped over to her. "If you love him, and I sense that you do, stop him before he dies in a way unbefitting the way he lived his life. Alucard is a killer. He'll take everything from Justice, before he takes his life. Many will suffer in the name of him trying to honor his commitment to Death. The choice is yours." She vanished from the room.

Professor Hunt sat down in her chair and tears began to well up in her eyes. 'No, the choice isn't mine. I sure hope you know what you're doing'. There was a knock at the office door. "Who is it?"

"It's Hanover. May we speak for a moment?"

"Just a moment please." She wiped away the tears from her cheeks. She reached into her desk and pulled out a vial that Justice had given her. She drank down the liquid contained in the vial and more tears rolled down her cheeks.

Chapter 33 – Nicole Westerfield

Hermione told Harry she wanted to bathe before the Triathlon began. She asked Stormy if she'd mind relieving Harry of his duty for a short while. They agreed and Harry said he'd meet her back at the common room in an hour. Harry headed outside and down to the Quidditch pitch to get in some flying practice before it got too late.

Unlike the actual tournament itself, the tryouts had preset tasks. There would be a display of magical skills and once each participant performed each of ten escalating complex spells, they would be graded on completion, accuracy and speed. They would then duel to eliminate one another until there were only two. Harry was exempt from having to compete in those prelims. The three contestants would then compete head-to-head in a swimming event, a foot race and a flying competition.

Charista, Fred, George and Neville had taken Ron under their wing and were helping him train. Harry looked as if he'd been slapped in the face seeing Charista helping Ron, of all people, to compete against him. He walked by them without speaking. As he emerged from the dressing room Wood called to him. "Harry, I need to speak with you a moment."

"Can it wait Oliver? I need to practice."

"No Potter, it can't! In my office, now!"

Harry followed him into his office and when Wood turned to face him Harry had his wand in his hand.

"Look Potter, I don't know what's going on with you, but something's not right. You need help."

"What I need is you off my back. Sorry Oliver. ***Stupefy!***" Harry bound him and sealed him in a trunk. Wood was right. Something wasn't right with Harry. However, even Harry, himself, didn't know what it was.

Hermione was already feeling sluggish. She began to disrobe and when she removed her shirt, she was frightened at what she saw. "Oh my God!" Stormy stated. The necklace Harry had given her was but an imprint in her skin. It had literally melted into her flesh.

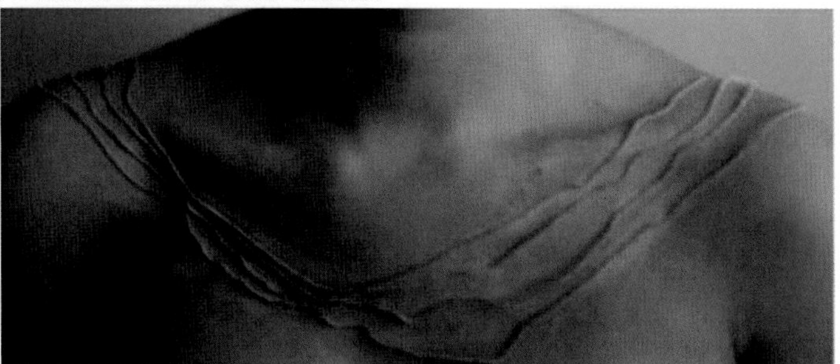

She collapsed to the ground, once again feeling weak. She couldn't stop crying.

"I hate this. I'm stronger than this. What's going on?"

AZKABAN

Justice had arrived at the prison at the tail end of high tide and a storm. He was sitting in a small room being processed by a guard. He grabbed his chest.

"What's your problem?"

"Nothing, I'm fine. Can you tell me what time it is?"

Chapter 33 – Nicole Westerfield

"Time for you to keep your mouth shut." The man continued with his paperwork. "Alright, we're done here. You're in luck, you get your choice of cells. Just this morning we got a mandate from the Ministry to move all the prisoners to Nurmengard. Guess they're finally gonna refurbish this place. Bout time too, with all the breakouts." He paused, "Odd though that they would've still sent ***you*** here and unescorted."

"I won't be the only one here, will I?"

"Ha! You're scared. Well, you should be." He paused and looked at Justice who looked as if he might cry. "Don't fret, you won't be alone. The three of us guards are more than enough to keep an eye on the likes of you. There is one that didn't get shipped out."

Justice paused and scanned the sky, "Who's that?"

"Name's Westerfield. You don't want any part of that. That one reeks o' crazy. She's a real threat, but don't fret, she's all the way up on fourteen. You'll likely be down on one or two. Attacked a teacher, pshhh, light weight. Let's go."

They stood up and headed from the office toward the huge triangular building. Justice paused and again asked, "What time is it?"

The guard sighed and looked at his watch then replied, "What do you care, you got a date?"

"I'm expecting something." At that moment, the tiny Arctic Tern, that he released from the Hogwarts Owlrey, swooped down and dropped his wand to him. He caught it and spun casting a spell. "***Petrificus Totalus!***" A stream of blue light shot from its tip hitting the guard. "Thank you, Neville." He entered the building firing curses, freezing the guards in their tracks. He watched as the ice crept along the walls indicating the Dementors were drawing nearer. He began to ascend the stairs. He reached up to his throat, tilted his head back and stuck his fingers in. He pulled out several small items. "*Engorgio!*" The items grew and revealed that they were explosives he'd gotten from Seamus. He began placing them as he climbed the stairs. The first ten floors were generally reserved for the lessor infractions. The upper floors were for the murderers and Dark wizards. He encountered his first resistance on the eleventh level. The halls were patrolled by Red Caps.

The little dwarf like creatures were easily blasted aside. Then he encountered a Quintaped on level twelve. The five-legged fur covered beast snarled and snapped at Justice who was undeterred.

He further confused the beast when he ran directly at it and when he got within a few feet of it he summersaulted over it causing it to bend backward until it fell over onto its back. He was surprised when he entered the hall of the thirteenth level and found it empty. He stopped, closed his eyes and inhaled. There was a Lethifold hiding somewhere.

Chapter 33 – Nicole Westerfield

They were extremely rare and extremely dangerous. He was sure it was there despite being confused at how the creature, native to tropical climates, was able to survive in the balmy, salty sea air. With its uncanny resemblance to a standard black cloak, it was nearly impossible to see in the dark corridor. He knew they could be fended off by a patronus charm, but chose instead to cast, "***Lumos Solem!***" The intense light emitted from his wand caused the creature to give away its position on the ceiling near the end of the hallway. "***Petrificus Totalus! Descendo!***"

He froze the creature then forced it to drop from its perch and he ran toward it, leapt and glided over the top of it. Finally, he'd arrived on the fourteenth floor. Again, the floor appeared vacant. He sniffed the air but detected nothing. However, when he took his first step toward the holding cells, he heard the ice crackle beneath his feet. He knew the Dementors were inside. He hurried up the hall inspecting every room. He found her. He set one of the explosives to open the door. "Stand back!" he instructed. The door burst open and the instant he stepped in a curse was cast at him from seemingly out of thin air. It hit him squarely in the chest and knocked him against the wall.

"GET OUT!!!"

"Okay, I deserved that. My name is…" He began as he looked around the room trying to find the source of the verbal command. Another curse flew at him that he deflected. He turned invisible and reappeared standing right beside her. With a flick of his wand, she was pinned against the wall. "Stop it! I'm not here to hurt you. I think we can help each other."

He paused, "How did you do that?" He looked at her face.

It was old and her clothes were ripped and dirty. For a moment, he thought she was the wrong person. He'd expected a much younger woman, but the guard had told him she was the only prisoner there. It had to be her.

"I don't want your help! I don't need your help!"

"You want out of here, don't you? I read your file. I now you're innocent."

"We can't get out. There is nowhere to go."

"Leave that to me."

"Who are you?"

"I'm the guy who's been chosen to fight Alucard."

"***Alucard***? What do you know about him?"

"Not enough, that's why I'm here. I was told your relative, Fiona Tattenger, was working on a weapon to use against him."

"You just saw it. It's called Focus Energy Targeting, but it's obviously not ready. I hit you with a direct hit and you barely flinched."

"Don't fault yourself for that, I have a unique ability. It's a long story. The hit was actually rather good for not using a wand, but right now we need to get out of here."

"I told you, we can't get out. There are Dementors out there. We can't get by them. I've tried." She paused then screamed as two large Dementors entered the room.

"*EXPECTO PATRONUM*!" Justice shouted and a silver wolverine burst from the tip of his wand. The Dementors retreated. "Let's go." It's what he needed his wand for.

She withdrew into the corner. "You cast a patronus."

"Yeah."

"Death Eaters can't do that."

"I know, now let's go. Besides, who said I was a Death

Chapter 33 – Nicole Westerfield

Eater?"

"Are you going to kill me?"

"Only if you don't get over here!" he demanded.

"I can't. I…"

"I don't have time for this." He grabbed her, put her on his back and ran into the hall. The Dementors were everywhere. He recalled the wolverine to him. *Diverse, Aladusuch!*" The animal split into two wolverines and each headed in a different direction forcing the Dementors away. "We have to go right now!" He threw one of Seamus' devices down the hall. "***Expulso!***" A huge explosion severely damaged the structure. He ran down the hall. She was heavier than he expected. They got to level ten, and all the magical creatures were blocking the exit. "***Agua Eructo!***" he shouted without breaking stride. A flood of water shot from the wand and washed them all down the stairwell.

"What did you say your name was?" she asked.

"Justice." he shouted.

"We're being followed."

Suddenly explosions began to ring out in succession from the floors above them. They continued to run until they made it out of the building. The building imploded on itself destroying the floors above level four. Justice fell and Nicole landed on top of him. The tide was in, and the water violently crashed against the rocks around the base of the island.

Nicole stood up slowly and offered him a hand up. She gazed up at the clouds. "My cell didn't have a window. I haven't seen the sky in five years." He watched as she seemed to grow younger before his eyes.

"There'll be more of it once we get to where we're going."

"I'm not going with you."

"What are you talking about? You can't make it back alone. We're out. Two more stops and you can go home to your family."

"I'm the last of my family. For years, all that kept me alive was my hatred of Alucard. Rage kept me strong. When my mother taught me Focus Energy; I could barely knock over a book through another object. I'm better now, but all my strength is gone. He'd kill me before I could even try it."

"We can do it together." He paused and thought, 'Would she then become the new Dark Lord?'

"No, you can do it. I can tell you what you need to know then you can develop it."

"There's no time." He took her hands. "You're okay with me knowing the technique?" he asked.

"Yes." she replied, confused by the question.

He squeezed her hands, and she felt a surge of current go through her. In the transfer, she gave him the details of the story he was to tell everyone once he got back. It was his alibi. He released her hands.

"That's it?"

He had what he needed. With the next crash of the tide dozens of Inferi crawled onto the shore. Justice tilted his head back like a Pez dispenser and up popped one of the wands he'd taken from the Ministry guards. He handed it to her. She examined it then pointed at the unconscious guard. With a flick, the body was hurled into the rubble.

"You are extraordinary. You know, if I were younger, or you were older…" She looked into his eyes, tilted her head, "It wouldn't have made the slightest bit of difference, would it? You're bound to someone, aren't you?" She paused. "Whoever she is, she's a very lucky girl." Justice reached out and held her hand. "Don't leave any part of him moving."

"I'll see what I can do. Are you sure you won't come

with me."

"My destiny is different from yours. You go and don't underestimate him."

"I won't." He turned then look back one last time. She smiled and cast a spell toward the sky and the storm cleared and the tide seceded. "If you change your mind, the midway point is an island called Kitaro."

"Kitaro, got it. You'd better hurry." she told him. "I'm not the witch I once was. I don't know how long this spell will last." The fresh air had restored her youth and beauty and he was momentarily lost in her stare. He took a breath and disapparated.

Anthony Wright
Chapter 34 – A moment like this

Stormy put Hermione's arm around her and helped her down the hall to the common room. Hermione's voice was failing her, and she couldn't speak the entry words clearly enough for the portrait to open.

"Flamingo Cardigan." Stormy stated and the portrait swung open. They made it to one of the sofas before Hermione collapsed. Her voice was gone. She looked pale and thin. Everything looked painful. She reached for her wand and tried to conjure a flame in the fireplace, but nothing happened. She figured perhaps it was because she couldn't speak. She tried a different spell that didn't require her to speak. It didn't work either.

Harry entered the room. She gestured to him and tried to show him that she was unable to perform magic. He sat in a chair across from her.

"Harry." she whispered, struggling to get his name out. "The necklace, where did you get it?" She swallowed hard. Her throat was dry and raw. Everything hurt for the first time.

"I'm sorry? What was that?" he mocked as he removed his robe and sat down on her bed.

She pulled her shirt open to show him the imprinted pattern in her skin. "Where did you get the necklace?" she asked. Her voice was returning little by little, her strength was as well. "Why Harry?" She was able to sit up.

Chapter 34 – A moment like this

"You're bound to him? Bound? Really?" he lashed out.

"What are you talking about?"

"You finally found someone you can trust?" he read from a page he'd torn out of her journal.

"You've been reading my diary?" The look on her face was pure heartbreak. "How could you? What have I done?" Her voice was growing stronger. She took the page from him.

"You don't even know him. He doesn't love you the way I do. No one does!"

"Harry, what's wrong? Talk to me. Why are you acting like this?"

"I don't need you. I don't need anybody. ***I'm*** the chosen one. You want him, you can have him. Let him save you." He got up and stormed out.

"Harry!" she called to him then suddenly she felt weak in the knees. Her legs were going numb. She found herself wishing Justice was around.

Ron walked into the common room. "Hermione, there you are. The triathlon's about to start and..." He stopped talking when he saw her curled into a ball crying. He ran to her. "Hermione? Are you alright? Hermione?"

KITARO

Justice literally appeared out of thin air fifteen feet above the ground and fell hard to the earth. At first, he was disoriented and not sure he was on Kitaro since it was snowing and when he'd left to go to Azkaban the temperature was nearly triple digits. The fall knocked the wind out of him, but he still had to react to the fleeing heard of Erumphant. He rolled out of the way of the first wave then caught his breath in time to stand and act as a matador for the last pair. He held up his wand and flicked it in a downward motion. A red muleta dropped down and he stood his ground.

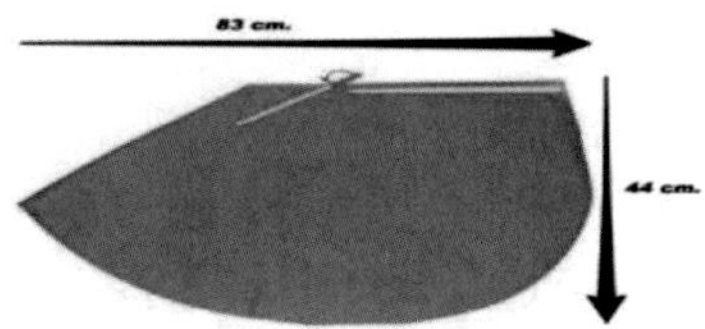

The two huge beasts charged straight for him and when they got within a single stride of him, he swept the muleta over the both of them and they disappeared.

He was on Kitaro alright. He remembered what he'd learned in the coven about the island. He thought it was just a myth, but the magical properties of the island were quite evident. The island was the only place on earth said to support every known climate and environment, side by side, simultaneously. He began to walk due east and sure enough, within moments he walked out of the snow and into a desert like climate. It was unbelievable. He stood on hot sand yet reached out his hand and felt snow in his palm. It was as if he had stepped through a doorway that didn't actually exist. He let out a sigh and caught his breath. 'Now where would they be?' He asked himself. He turned and started to walk until he came to a tropical climate then found a tall tree. He tilted his head back and looked straight up. There it was. 'That figures'.

Chapter 34 – A moment like this

It was an Occomy nest. The Occomy is typically found in the Far East and India It's a two-legged, winged creature with a serpentine body.

They can reach fifteen feet in length. They are aggressive by nature, especially in defense of their eggs, whose shells are made of the purest, softest silver. Justice figured there were eggs in the nest, and he had a plan for them. He was going to apparate but was exhausted, so he had to climb instead. He started up and transfigured into the wolverine by his third step. With his added strength and razor-sharp claws, he had no trouble scurrying up the tree, but quickly found additional motivation when he looked down and saw the Nundu climbing beneath him. He hurried and reached the nest, transfigured back and found a huge clutch of the eggs. He

placed three into his pocket. The Nundu was almost upon him when he leapt down, grabbing the animal around the neck causing it to fall with him. "***Arresto Momentum!***" They both stopped in midair, a mere foot before the ground then they fell. The moment he hit the ground he transfigured. His wolverine self was about one tenth the size of the leopard, but he stood his ground. The Nundu roared and all the other animal species on the island took notice. It displayed its teeth, saliva dripping and snarled at the little wolverine. Justice's fur stood on end, his back hunched.

They stared into one another's eyes as they inched ever closer until they were nearly touching.

FADING

Protections were down at the school due to the visitors arriving. Ron got Hermione to the hospital wing. Madam Pomfrey was frantic. She'd never seen this kind of magic.

When she inspected the marks from the necklace, they were almost undetectable. Hermione was born to non-magical parents, but Madam Pomfrey knew her to be a talented and powerful witch. To have lost her magical ability was shocking. She couldn't speak and the atrophy in her right arm was severe. Arrangements were being made to send her to St. Mungo's immediately. Her condition was deteriorating rapidly. Headmistress McGonagall altered the rules a bit to allow Hermione to compete. Instead of the participants reading their own essays, Demetria, who had already won the other groups honors, would read them. They were all very thorough and informative. There was a short intermission as they tabulated the scores. McGonagall sent Charista to check on Hermione in hopes that she might be feeling up to making it to the final round but knew she had originally intended to play the piano. McGonagall was very aware of her hands' condition. They were both unaware of her relapse. Charista went to Hermione's bedside and was stunned to see her so sick. Hermione struggled to sit up. Charista propped her up with pillows. She gestured for water and Charista got it for her. She took a few sips to loosen her throat and whispered the words.

"Have you seen Harry?" she asked.

"No." She paused. "Hermione, I hate to pry, but do you remember what happened before you started feeling sick?" She tried to remember. "I ask because I feel this is a curse that was put on you ***and*** I feel that with the way Harry's personality has changed that…"

"I know." she whispered. "I just don't want to believe it. There must have been poison in the necklace like with Katie Bell last year, but that was Malfoy, a Death Eater trying to impress a Dark Lord."

"I know. The question is where did he get it?" Just then Stormy walked in.

"You're ahead. Your essay scored the highest. Ravenclaw got eliminated. Jade is second then Justin. He's gonna go first in the presentation round. The displays are being brought in one by one to be judged then they'll start the talent portion. It gives you a little more time. How do you feel?"

Before she could answer Harry walked in. "How is she?" he asked Charista.

"So, you care now?"

"What's that supposed to mean?"

"Where did that necklace come from? Why are you doing this?"

"Doing what?" Charista's eyes began to glow yellow. "She has a protector, she'll be fine. Oh, that's right, he's in Azkaban prison. He's not coming back. I can make you feel better. I can protect you." She began to cry. She turned away from him. "Hermione, I love you. I'd never hurt you. If he loved you, he wouldn't have gotten himself thrown out. He'd be here with you. So, where is he?" No sooner had the words left his lips Lilacs and Orchids began popping up all over the room. Her pain subsided. She figured it was her proximity to Harry.

"Hermione." Charista said, "Look." She could barely open her eyes, but she did and for the first time in days she smiled. Charista made a move toward Harry with an ungloved hand and he apparated.

"Let him go." she whispered, "He needs some time."

"Mike," Justice called to him. Mike Ambrose was supposed to be Hermione's partner in the talent portion of the competition.

"Justice? When did you get…?"

"Shhh!" Justice gestured for him to come over. "Mike, I

Chapter 34 – A moment like this

need a favor."

"Sure, what is it?" He looked down at Justice's shirt. It was ripped open. "Is that ***blood***?"

"I need to borrow you for a little while."

"Okay."

Justice reached out and touched Mike on the face. Mike vanished and Justice transfigured into Mike's exact replica. "***Sleep!***" Justice commanded and Mike passed out. He caught Mike's invisible body and dragged him into an unoccupied room. "Thanks buddy. Sleep tight." Justice rushed to the hospital wing. Stormy came out just as he arrived.

"Oh, hi Mike."

"Hello." He entered the hospital wing and saw Charista sitting beside Hermione. The moment he stepped into the room all the flowers opened. Charista noticed. Madam Pomfrey was shuffling back and forth removing the flowers. She was talking to herself, fussing and was further infuriated when each time she removed a bunch of flowers another appeared in its place.

"Madam Pomfrey, I believe you're needed at the judges table." he told her.

"I can't leave now. I have an extremely ill patient."

"Charista and I will look after her."

She sighed but agreed to go. "You call me if anything changes in her condition, you understand? I'll be right back."

"Yes Ma'am. She looks much better to me, must be the flowers. Nice touch." he said. She smirked and hurried off.

"How did you get here?" Charista asked as she hugged him.

"I just came up the hall." He walked over to the bed.

"Do you know how big a chance you're taking coming back here?"

"How did you know?"

"Just because you don't look like you, doesn't mean your scent changed."

"Wow, I'll have to remember that." he replied with a smile. "And how's our patient today?" he asked as he sat down beside her.

"Not so good." she whispered. Charista told him about Harry and the necklace. He felt so guilty at having been the one who put it on her. He noticed the bruising and discoloration of her right arm.

"Alright, Charista would you be so kind as to take Jean's project to the judging station. We'll be down in a minute."

"Of course." she smiled. She was excited. She hugged

him tightly. He moaned. The smile disappeared from her face when she looked down at his shirt and she asked, "Is that blood?"

"I got scratched by a cat." Hermione's breathing became increasingly labored. "This has gone on long enough. Jean, can you hear me?" he asked. She nodded her acknowledgement.

Chapter 34 – A moment like this

"I'm gonna hold your hands, okay? I need you to close your eyes and listen to the song and sing along when you think you can." She looked confused. He looked at the hospital room door and it locked itself. Music began to play in her head. "Once my voice starts don't open your eyes until my voice stops and don't let go of my hand. Can you do that?"

"What are you going to do?"

He took her hands, and she immediately felt a current run through her body. "Justice, don't. It'll weaken you to help me, remember?" She opened her eyes and looked at him. His eyes were all white and he appeared to be in a trance. She closed her eyes quickly. He began to sing.

" If you say my eyes are beautiful, It's because they're looking at you
And if you could only see yourself, You'd feel the same way too
You could say that I am a dreamer, Who's had a dream come true
If you say my eyes are beautiful, It's because they're looking at you"

Color began to return to her cheeks. Her breathing stabilized and she sat up on her own.

" If you wonder why I'm smiling, It's because I'm happy with you
And the warm sensations touch my heart, And fill me through and through
I could hold you close forever, And never let you go
If you say my eyes are beautiful
It's because I just love you so"

His voice began to weaken. With his help, she stood up. He pulled her to him, and they began to spin slowly. He felt her grip tightening. The lights in the room began to flicker.

" Now my heart is an open door
Won't you come inside for more?
You give love so sweetly now
Take my love take me completely now"

Their fingertips slipped apart as she spun and danced. He sat on the bed and watched her strength return as his faded. She began to sing loud and strong.

" If you say my eyes are beautiful
It's because they're looking at you
And my eyes are just the windows
For my feelings to come through"

They sang back and forth to one another. His voice was soft compared to hers. The ceiling disappeared and was replaced by an enchanted sky full of stars. Justice hadn't done it. He sang and she answered.

" And by far you are more beautiful
Than anything I've ever known." he sang.
"If you say my eyes are beautiful"
" If you say my eyes are beautiful." she responded.

Together they sang, the stronger she sang the softer his voice became.

" If you say, my eyes my eyes are beautiful
It's because, it's because, they're looking at you."

The music stopped and she opened her eyes. She was standing in front of a mirror. Her hair was styled. She was wearing a beautiful white satin gown and heels. Her makeup was flawless, and she felt strong and healthy. She couldn't stop smiling. She turned to thank him and heard him sneeze. The smile left her face and she rushed to his side as he slumped down onto the pillow.

"What did you do?" she asked.

"I'm alright. How do ***you*** feel?"

Chapter 34 – A moment like this

"Spectacular, but I never wanted this. I didn't want you to have to suffer my illness."

"That's why I didn't ask. I'll be right behind you. You can still make it to the judging…" He sneezed. "I can fix your hand, but not until after the competition. You'll need to lie down afterwards. It's not a fun process." He sneezed again. "I placed a cast on it." It looked like a white lace glove. "When I held your hand, I felt the bones shifting, they were deteriorating. I reversed it, but it will take quite a while for them to heal on their own."

"You're amazing."

"Don't let it get out." Madam Pomfrey walked back in and nearly fell over.

"Miss Granger? What are…How did…?"

"I know, right?" She spun. "I don't want to leave you." she said to Mike.

"What's wrong with you Mr. Ambrose?"

"Just an upset stomach Ma'am." He sneezed. "Go." he told Hermione. "Go get your trophy."

"You're going to the triathlon?" Madam Pomfrey asked as she checked her out. "Your vitals are strong." Hermione nodded. "You better hurry. Justin just got done with his juggling routine. I'll get you some bicarbonate, Mr. Ambrose."

"How'd he…" Justice began but sneezed before he could get the question out.

"He dropped the items three times and each time he did, so too did his animated figure. Miss Malone is about to sing."

Hermione paused with a look of panic on her face. "Justice? I mean Justin really dropped what he was juggling?" She caught herself. She turned from him to her and back. "What am I going to do? I was going to play the piano but can't with my arm."

"Jean, this is your time. This moment is only going to happen once. You're a senior. This is it. Seize it." He could see in her eyes she was unsure. He stood up slowly. "Let's go."

"What about your stomach?" Madam Pomfrey asked.

"I'm feeling better, and I have a feeling we're not gonna want to miss this." They walked toward the door, and he felt his left arm beginning to tingle.

Madam Pomfrey thought to herself a moment, 'What did he call her?'

Mallory burst into the hospital. "Hermione?" she said as she saw her not just standing but dressed. "You look beautiful."

"Thank you. So do you." she replied.

"How do you feel?" she asked as she looked all around the room.

"I'm better, thank you."

"Hello Miss Featherstone." Justice said.

"Hello Mr. Ambrose." she replied as she continued to look around. Before long, her eyes were fixated on Mike.

"Is anything wrong?" he asked.

"I just had a strong feeling." She looked more closely at him. "I thought I felt…"

"You have amazing instincts." he said.

"Justice?" Her eyes grew large.

"Shhh!" He glanced around for Madam Pomfrey. "This

Chapter 34 – A moment like this

is your doing." he whispered gesturing to his appearance.

"I was never this good at it." she walked around him.

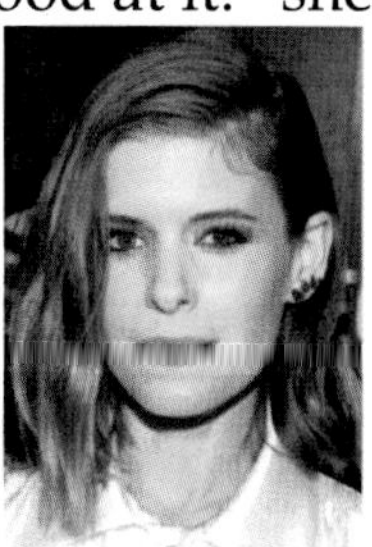

"We'd better get going. I'm gonna need to speak with you later. We need to discuss Harry."

"Okay. I'll gather the others."

"First, could you do something for me?" He leaned in and whispered something in her ear, interlocked his fingers then pulled out his phone and quickly found a picture. Mallory nodded, smiled, hugged him and walked off. Where she'd hugged him it left a bruise.

As they walked into the judging chambers Jade was standing on stage. The music began and she performed a rousing rendition of 'All I want for Christmas'. Her project theme was winter in New York City. Her display was of Central Park with a huge Christmas tree and little figurines ice skating around it. She was wearing a skimpy, formfitting red satin Mrs. Santa Clause outfit with black gloves and matching boots.

The women in the crowd were stunned while the men in crowd were cheering and whistling. She finished to a thunderous round of applause. Hermione was nervous. McGonagall walked to the podium. She was speechless. "Well, that was quite a performance. Thank you, Miss Malone. So, I guess..."

Justice walked up to the podium beside her. "Hermione is ready Ma'am." he whispered.

She looked at him then back to see Hermione standing in the wings. She couldn't believe her eyes, especially after what Madam Pomfrey had told her of Hermione's condition. Jade couldn't believe what she'd just heard. "Ladies and Gentlemen, our third participant is ready to perform." She could barely contain her excitement. She was so pleased Hermione was feeling better. Meanwhile, Hermione was nervous. She kept rubbing her throat and shaking her good hand as she paced back and forth.

"Jus...Mike, I still don't know what I'm going to do out there."

"Sing. You have an amazing voice. This was meant to be. You can win this thing. Just walk out there and give it your all."

"What if my voice fades again?"

"It won't, trust me." He kept trying to flex his fingers to bring feeling back to his left hand. He reached down and grabbed his arm. It began to throb, and he sneezed again.

"I don't know if I can do this alone right now."

Mallory got his attention from the opposite side of the

stage. She smiled and gave him a thumb's up sign.

He looked at Hermione and said, "You don't have to. I have an idea." He whispered in her ear then walked around to the other side of the stage. He saw Professor Hunt standing in the wings. "Hello professor."

"Hello Michael."

"You look lovely."

"Why thank you Michael." She responded, but immediately questioned how the comment made her feel. She walked away.

The curtain on the stage opened and Hermione walked out to a spirited round of applause. "Good evening." The crowd gave her a standing ovation. " My display is of Hogwarts. I've spent more time here over the last seven years than I have at my home. Right now, it is my home. I love it. I love it here with all my friends, old and new, so my display represents Hogwarts, old and new." Her display lit up and it was an exact miniature replica of the castle. A tiny carriage made its way through the main gate and a tiny person got out. The front door to the castle opened and a young woman walked out to greet the visitor. The detail was incredible. Everyone could tell it was Justice and Hermione. "For me, Hogwarts has been a series of memorable moments strung together, one after the other. Moments like this one, being here today." The lights dimmed and a black piano with keys on one side and a saw tooth pattern on the other was illuminated. She walked over and sat down. "I was going to play a duet with Mike Ambrose for you, but I've got an injured hand." Suddenly a second piano, it was white and a mirror image of the first, slid into position and the jagged patterns interlocked forming a heart.

Mike was seated at the second piano dressed in a tux. He had a cast on his left arm.

"Shall we?" he asked. The crowd applauded. Together they began to play, Hermione with her left hand and he with his right. She began to sing softly.

" What if I told you it was all meant to be?
Would you believe me, would you agree?
It's almost that feeling we met before
So tell that you don't think I'm crazy
When I tell you love has come here and now
A moment like this. Some people wait a lifetime
For a moment like this, some people wait forever
For that one special kiss, Oh I can't believe it happening to me
Some people wait a lifetime for moment, like this."

Chapter 34 – A moment like this

The two figurines in the display bowed to one another then began to dance. Justice used his mind to tell her, 'Come on, this is your time. Your voice can take it, go for it'. She looked into his eyes and began to sing stronger.

" Everything changes, but beauty remains
Something so tender, I can't explain
Well I may be dreaming, but till I awake
Can't we make this dream last forever? And I'll cherish all the love we share
A moment like this. Some people wait a lifetime"

The crowd joined in and sang background. Tears poured from McGonagall's eyes. She was so proud. Hermione sang stronger, straight to Mike, and the crowd reacted.

"For a moment like this, some people wait forever
For that one special kiss, Oh I can't believe it happening to me
Some people wait a lifetime for moment, like this."
" Could this be the greatest love of all?
I want to know that you will catch me when I fall, So let me tell you this
Some people wait a lifetime, for a moment like this,
Some people wait a lifetime, For a moment like this, some people wait forever

(all of Gryffindor house sang the chorus)
For that one special kiss, Oh, oh, like this
Oh, oh, oh, Oh I can't believe it happening to me
Some people wait a lifetime for a moment like this, Oh, oh like this."

Fireworks launched and lit the sky above the tiny display. The crowd exploded in applause led by the Minister of Magic. They gave her a standing ovation. They applauded for five minutes straight. The entire school was aware of how sick she'd been and was astonished by how she'd recovered.

Even Jade was seen applauding albeit not as enthusiastically as some others. McGonagall took the stage and proudly announced, "I think it's clear. Ladies and Gentlemen, we have a winner."

Chapter 35 – Justice's return

Malfoy arrived in Hogsmeade under cover of a cloak. Marcus was right behind him. "What are you doing here? Your father gave you a job to do and it's not following me around."

"I can't go back to Hogwarts."

"Do you know what your father will do to you, to us, if you disobey him?"

"Do you have any idea what Justice will do to me if I show up at Hogwarts without an explanation? The last time he saw me he was asking me to help the professor. Then she gets kidnapped. He's not stupid, quite the contrary."

"You're his friend, what's he gonna do?"

"He'll kill me. It's what he does."

"Are you trying to tell me you're more afraid of Justice than of your father, a Dark Lord?"

Marcus paused and thought, then answered, "Yes."

Draco found that interesting. "Alright, look. You can come with me, but you have to do something first."

"What's that?"

"You have to make the unbreakable vow."

"With you?"

"If you do, you'll have to make sure nothing happens to me. You'll have to protect me from ***whoever*** wins the war. When this comes to a head one of those two will be left standing and that's when I'll make my move."

"Your move?"

"I have a plan, but I need more than your word if I'm gonna put my neck on the line."

Marcus thought about it. He didn't see Justice in any visions after the battle. Did that mean Justice would die in the battle? If Alucard wins, would he be spared? If Justice defeats Alucard, who kills him? Either way, he couldn't go to

Hogwarts, he needed an ally. "Okay."

Malfoy extended his arm. He wasn't sure Marcus was going to go through with it, but figured the sooner he started, the sooner he'd find out for sure. Marcus reached out and took it. Draco placed the tip of his wand to their linked hands and spoke, "Will you, Marcus Reece, watch my back and pledge your loyalty to me, Draco Malfoy and do ***my*** bidding without hesitation and without question?"

"I will." A thin flame wound its way around their arm and bound them.

"Remember, from now on, if I die, you die." He paused. "Now come on and see what real power looks like." Draco led him to the Hog's Head. It was boarded up. It appeared no one had been inside since Harry and Neville had rescued Aberforth. Draco checked to make sure they weren't being watched then blasted away the boards blocking the entrance. He walked in with Marcus closely behind him. Once they closed the door behind themselves, Draco looked around and noticed a few bar stools knocked over and lots of dust and cobwebs. He waved his wand, and the debris began to swirl around and fly back into place. Once the place was tidy Draco pulled back his sleeve, closed his eyes and pressed his fingers to his Dark Mark. Within moments Death Eaters began to materialize from black vapor. They had been hiding nearby. There were ten in all excluding Draco. They'd come from all over, Germany, Australia, Sweden, South Africa, Ireland, China, Japan, Mexico, Italy and America. They were all wearing masks.

"Welcome my brothers and sisters. Thank you all for coming."

"Why have you brought us here?" asked the Italian.

"I have a proposition for you."

Chapter 35 – Justice's return

"What's that?"

"Each of you are the sitting Dark Wizards and Witches in charge of your area. Do you enjoy running your areas as you see fit?" The tension in the room was thick and Marcus was formulating visions of things potentially turning bad quickly. They seemed to nod in agreement. "Well, your freedom to run your own areas is about to go away. There is a true Dark Lord, the strongest I've ever seen, and he's about to unleash his army. If he takes power, he'll kill you all then take control of your people."

"Let him try." spouted the German.

"Who is this bloke?" asked the Australian.

"You've all heard of Alucard?" Collectively they gasped. "He's planning on using his army to take over the Ministry here, he's already taken or turned half the senior staff then he's going to move from territory to territory eliminating each of you until he's running everything."

"How do you know all this?" asked the Swedish Death Eater, who they now all knew was a woman.

"I'm his apprentice."

The German wizard drew his wand, "Then this is a trick. No one who knows of Alucard would ever believe you would dare cross him. Alucard has been around forever. Even as old as he is, he's still more dangerous than all of us combined."

Marcus placed his wand to the man's temple. "Lower your wand and hear him out." The Death Eater reluctantly did as he was told. "That's better, we're all friends here."

"A threat has come to Hogwarts in the form of an American. There's a prophecy my father told me about before he died. It stated that he's the Dark Lord's offset. From what I've seen there's a good chance that if these two square off the winner will be left so weak from the battle that we'll be able to take him. Once he's out of the way we'll be free to claim our own territories again, and with no one standing in our way, all of us together can restore the wizard community to its former glory. We can finally get rid of the Muggles and Mudbloods. We can capture the blood traitors and lock them away. The pureblood witches and wizards can run everything the way my descendant Salazar Slytherin intended."

"Nice thought, but where you gonna put them?" asked the Chinese Death Eater.

"Who?"

"The Mudbloods and Muggles? There are too many to kill."

"We'll lock them up in Azkaban. Let the Dementors have their way with them."

"Haven't you heard? Azkaban was destroyed. Everyone was moved to Nurmengard." said the American.

"Destroyed, how?" Draco barked. "That can't be! That ruins everything! The American offset was there. If it's destroyed, he might be dead."

"Justice?" Marcus said calmly. "He's not dead. *He* destroyed it." Malfoy looked at him trying to process what he was saying.

"Justice? You don't mean Justice Cain?" asked the American. Marcus nodded. "Well, well, must be my lucky day. Count me in."

"You haven't heard the plan." replied Draco.

"Doesn't matter. Your boy here is right, he's not dead." He reached up and removed his mask. It was Aldrich, Jade's foster brother. "I owe him." His face was burned on one side. He ripped open his shirt and revealed the knife wound in his shoulder. Marcus was stunned.

'How can this be? He wasn't a wizard, and he was killed

in the explosion at the coven, or was he?' Images began to flash in his mind of that night at the coven. As he hid, crouched down at the end of the corridor, he recalled Justice's blasting curse slamming Aldrich against the wall and knocking him out. The memory flashed ahead to when the fire was set in the hall by the hooded figure. There was a second explosion, but his recall now told him that Aldrich's body was yanked down the corridor out of sight before the explosion. Someone pulled him away and Marcus now knew who it was. Seconds after Aldrich was moved a hooded figure appeared beyond the flames. It had to be Alucard. Marcus then turned and ran through the door at the end of the corridor and was followed shortly by Jade and Justice. Jade was hysterical. The reason she'd gone back was to save her sister and instead she ended up watching her sister die.

Even Justice had no way of knowing that when she began running the wrong way down the hall, it had been deliberate. She was trying to get to Aldrich. She really was in love with him and was distraught over the possibility he too had been killed. She was harboring a secret from all of them, while Marcus was harboring one of his own. The Dark Lord ***had*** placed him under the Imperious Curse, but it was still him who cast the spell from behind Justice that killed Inara. It was Marcus who had been given the poison vitamins. He gave them to Jade and told her what they could do. She decided to give them to Justice as revenge for him Killing Aldrich and Justice did whatever she asked of him because he felt guilty that Inara had died while under his protection. It was then that he vowed never to let a protection he'd cast fail again.

If Jade found out it was him, not Justice that caused Inara's death, she'd kill him. If Justice found out that Jade held him responsible and was setting him up for a betrayal, he would kill her. The question was would Justice listen to him at all or simply feel he was just trying to stave off his own punishment. The answer was he couldn't take that chance.

Aldrich went on to tell the others about Justice and the significant threat he presented. Draco was wise enough to know, from Marcus' reactions, that he didn't want the others to know that he was there in the coven the night of the attack. Likewise, Marcus had been aware that Draco too had been there that night. Marcus was on edge, however, waiting to hear if Aldrich was going to explain how he became a Dark Lord. When it began to appear that the explanation was not going to come voluntarily, Marcus asked out right.

"So, are all of you pureblood wizards?"

"Aye." acknowledged the Irishman. "Surely, you know you can't be a Dark Lord if you're not." Aldrich didn't answer.

"So how exactly did you become a Dark Lord?" Marcus asked. He wanted to see if he was going to catch him in a lie.

"Me? I may be the first of my kind. I was a civilian. No magical blood at all. Then I had my run in with that Justice jerk. I hated him from the moment we met. I would have killed him, but I got distracted. I got knocked out and when I came to, I was on fire. Fifteen more seconds and I'd have been a goner, but Death wasn't ready for me. Instead of death, I was sent to hell. I made a deal with a hooded devil in exchange for my life. I vowed that if I ever crossed paths with Justice, I'd kill him. The deal was accepted, and I was given the tools of Dark Magic. My human blood was transfused with pure magical blood, and I was reborn. I started hunting all the civilian supporters, the right to choose bastards, the live and let live pansies. Then I caught your message in the Daily Prophet about recruiting."

"You must be pretty good to have deciphered the code."

Chapter 35 – Justice's return

stated Draco.

"Let me get this straight, your human blood was replaced, with pure wizard's blood? How did that happen exactly and how did you get a copy of The Daily Prophet?"

"Aldrich pulled aside his collar and showed two puncture wounds on his neck. "I got the paper off a girl. I don't know where she got it."

"You were bitten?" asked the Mexican Death Eater.

"Ironic, isn't it? I've become one of the things I hated the most in the world, but now I have the powers to kill them."

"So, what is the plan?" asked the Japanese Death Eater.

"The Dark Lord is planning an attack during the Triwizard Tournament at Durmstrang. He plans to kill the most notable Dark Lord slayer we know, Harry Potter." Marcus explained.

"What about this Justice character?"

"Let me finish! Justice Cain is a warrior. He's powerful, but he thinks of protecting his friends first. The way to defeat him is to get him fighting then let him see his friends being killed. He'll give up to save them, then we can kill him, if the Dark Lord hasn't already."

"What about Potter?" asked the South African.

"Potter only thinks of himself. He's not powerful at all. He's lucky and his friends protect him. Especially a mudblood named Granger. Separate him from them and he'll be easy to defeat, and I already took care of that."

"The biggest threat with Potter is his friend Charista." added Marcus.

"Exactly. Potter's fallen for her, so I used that against him. I went to him with a cursed necklace for him to give to her. As soon as she put it on its poison would start to seep into her skin. Not so fast that she'd notice, but fast enough that by the time she did figure it out its effects would be irreversible. Without her all he's got is Weasley and that's almost like having another person working for us as daft as he is." Draco laughed. It was then that Marcus knew Draco thought the necklace had been given to Charista. His expression went blank, and he tried to get Draco's attention. "While the Dark Lord attacks at Durmstrang, we'll attack Hogwarts. The Slytherins will get us in and attack from the inside while we attack from the outside."

"Um, Draco, may I speak with you for a moment?" asked Marcus.

"Not now." he replied.

"It's important."

"What part of NOT NOW, do you not understand?"

"Perhaps you need to teach your little friend here his proper place." Aldrich suggested.

Draco raised his hand and Marcus cowered. "Sorry my Lord."

"That's better. Now, if you've got something to say, spit it out."

"I just had a suggestion sir. I thought if Alucard is planning his attack and we know where and when. It's when he'll be the most prepared. We don't know if anyone including Justice knows about it yet, but surely if he does, he'll have the entire castle prepared. We know he's out of Azkaban and you were pretty sure that wasn't possible. He's formidable, Alucard is lethal. We may be better served to let the events play out."

"He's right. These blokes are already on edge. They're both gearin' up. They'll be like tryin' to catch a Chupacabra with your bare hands before the tournament starts."

"Precisely, what if…we let them battle and allow

Chapter 35 – Justice's return

Alucard to relax after killing Justice, let his guard down?" reasoned the Swedish Death Eater.

The Mexican Death Eater turned his wand into a knife and said, "Then we can slit his throat."

"Careful, all of you. It won't be long before he puts a taboo curse on his name." reminded the South African.

"Are you scared?" asked Draco.

"My people know Alucard very well. We know what he's capable of."

"And I know what Justice can do. I agree with the others. We're with you, but we don't have the element of surprise before the battle. If we wait, perhaps the Dark Lord will be wounded, even mortally, and we can waltz in and take the castle without resistance." said Aldrich.

"Once the Dark Lord is gone, who will take his place, you?" asked the Swede.

"I don't care about being a Dark Lord. I'm just tired of being told what to do." said Draco.

"He made you his second in command, why do you want to kill him so badly?" asked the Irishman.

"My mother is dead. He killed my father. You just come when I call. I'll know when the time is right. I'll be there to see who gains the advantage."

Justice staggered off stage and found Neville. "Wow Mike, if I didn't know better, I'd have believed the two of you were a couple. I didn't know you two were that close." Neville noticed Mike wince in pain. "What's wrong?"

"Come with me." He sneezed then led Neville to a quiet corner and asked him to hit him.

"What?"

"I need your help. Punch me in the stomach as hard as

you can."

"Mike, I…" Justice braced himself then smacked Neville in the forehead. Neville punched him in the stomach and Justice lurched forward and out of his mouth popped the necklace that had poisoned Hermione. He transfigured back into his own image to Neville's surprise.

"Justice, you're back? How did you? When…what is that?"

"I'll explain later. Take this, but don't touch it with your bare hands. I can't let the others see me yet."

"Okay, but what do you want me to do with it?"

"It's cursed. It contains some sort of poison. See if you can extract it for me. Don't tell anyone else, can you do that?"

"Sure."

"Thanks. Tell only the Headmistress that I'm at the gate."

"Okay." Justice vanished. As Neville ran down the corridor toward the potions room, he saw the real Mike Ambrose stumbling groggily down the hall.

"Within moments the Headmistress, Ms. Featherstone, Charista and Professor Flitwick were headed to the main gate. Hagrid was doing his best to delay Umbridge and her guards. Mallory and Charista sensed his presence as they approached. McGonagall waved her wand and the gate opened. They looked in every direction then he appeared from the tree line.

Chapter 35 – Justice's return

"Hello Headmistress."

"Mr. Cain, what are you doing here?"

"I wasn't sure where else to go."

"Why aren't you in Azkaban?" asked Umbridge as she pulled her wand.

'Thanks Neville, the Headmistress only'. "You haven't heard?"

"Heard what?"

"There was an explosion at the prison just as I was being processed. The guards ran inside and told me wait by the Floo station. I did, but the explosions continued. Finally, a guard ran out and ran into the Floo, so I followed. He was injured. Just before we left the island, I thought I saw what looked like curses being cast back and forth. We left together."

"And what happened to the guard?"

"When we arrived where the floo let out, he looked to be in pretty bad shape. He told me how to get back and I was going to get help. I tried to convince him to stay put, but he stumbled out of the Floo and was trampled by a huge beast. I made my way to the other Floo portal, but it wouldn't work to return me to the Ministry. So, I concentrated and apparated and ended up floating in the water near the coast. I washed ashore and after resting I came here as quickly as I could."

"Oh, you dear boy, you're lucky to be alive. I've heard that's part of the security measures that make Azkaban so effective. Most people can't apparate the distance back to the mainland."

"This is all very touching, but the fact of the matter is, without an official notification, you are an escaped convicted criminal." Umbridge pointed her wand.

"Dolores! Considering what he's been through to get back here, we should at least check with the staff involved to see if they still want to enforce the charges or consider this a lesson learned." She paused. "Prior to the incident, Mr. Cain was an honor student. He has no history that would suggest this would ever occur again."

"All we have is his story. There is no..." as she spoke an owl glided down over them and dropped a copy of the Daily Prophet into her hands. The headline read:

"EXPOLOSIONS ROCK AZKABAN"

She went on to read, "Investigators are hard at work to determine the cause of the explosions, but early indicators are that they may have been the result of an escape attempt by one of the inmates. It is undetermined how many people may have perished in the collapse of the ten uppermost floors, but at least four bodies have been recovered thus far. Three were guards on duty and one is yet to be identified. Among the unaccounted for are the inmate known as Nicole Tattenger-Westerfield. She appears to have gotten a hold of a wand and set off numerous explosions before reaching the outer perimeter where she likely succumbed to the Inferi and Dementors. The search continues. There is some confusion among the members of the Ministry regarding the population of prisoners normally housed at the prison. No one is claiming responsibility for a transfer order made for today's date that sent the captives from Azkaban to Nurmengard just hours before the incident. Westerfield is thought to have living relatives who may have had something to do with the deception, although authorities are yet to establish a motive for the actions." She paused and looked at all of them. "Well, I'm sure I'll be needed at the Ministry to help sort out this mess. Be sure to tell the winner congratulations."

"She has a name! It's Hermione Granger!"

"Indeed." She turned to Justice. "Don't leave the grounds. The Ministry will be in touch regarding your sentencing." With that she disapparated.

Chapter 36 – A changing of the guard

"Well, welcome back Mr. Cain."

"Thank you, Headmistress."

"I don't expect any more incidents involving you."

"No Ma'am." She turned and walked away. The others ran to him and hugged him. "How is everyone?"

"Confused." answered Mallory.

"Nervous about the tryouts." added Charista.

"They need some reassurance about what's going on with you and your coven." Mallory told him.

"Are you alright?" Charista asked him, sensing his weakened state.

"Yeah, long story. I need to see Cam and I need to know what's going on with Harry. Can we get everyone together?"

"I'll arrange it." said Charista. "We definitely need to talk about Harry. Something's not right. He's been avoiding me. I tried to touch him, but he pulled away. He's hiding something. It's almost as if he's afraid of me."

"Interesting."

"I'm glad you're back." she said with a smile then ran off.

'Me too'. he replied.

Cam, Freddy and Stormy came bounding down to the front gate. Cam ran up and hugged Justice. "We heard you were back. How are you?"

Chapter 36 – A changing of the guard

"What was it like, Azkaban? Was it as bad as they say?" Freddy asked.

"I'm okay and yes, it was as bad as they say. We've got a lot of work to do, and time is getting short. Charista's getting everyone together."

"By everyone, you mean…"

"No, not Professor Hunt, just us. Come here." Cam walked over and Justice touched his hand.

"Got it. We'll meet in the library in an hour." Some of the others followed Cam back toward the castle.

"I'm glad you're back. You still have time to train." Stormy pointed out.

"Train? For what?" Justice asked her.

"You're going to enter the tryouts, aren't you?"

"No way. There's another threat we need to look for. I don't have time for the tournament. I need to find it. I slipped, I lost focus and Jean almost died. I can't let that happen again."

"What happened to Hermione wasn't your fault. You saved her, just like you saved me." Stormy reminded him.

"She was poisoned." Freddy added.

"That's what caused the sickness?"

"Yeah, and whoever did it is gonna pay." said Cam.

"It had to be someone who was working for Alucard right?" Stormy asked.

"Probably, but there's something about the way it was done. Using a necklace with a slow dispensing poison, it just doesn't seem like his style."

Mallory thought about it, "Yeah, why not just kill her?"

"Exactly. I need to keep my eyes open." Justice replied.

"What did you have in mind?"

"I'll tell you with the others." He looked up and saw

Hermione running toward him.

"Justice."

"Jean." She hugged him then noticed everyone looking.

"You got everything straightened out?"

"Yeah, for now."

She looked from him to Mallory. "I'll go get things going." Mallory told him and headed off.

He reached out and hugged her again. "How are you feeling?"

"Fine, how about you? Can you still do magic?"

"Yeah. Neville gave me a hand. I think we got it all. The thing is something's been bugging me since I got back."

"What is it?"

"You're a gifted witch, that's not in question. I'm convinced you're gonna play a key role in this war before all is said and done, but you're muggle born?"

"So?"

"So, no offence, but why would they go after you like that? What ability do you have that the most notorious Dark Lord ever, would be so afraid of?"

"I don't know. You mentioned before that Harry draws his strength from our relationship…"

"Yeah, but why have ***him*** be the one to give you the necklace? You're the smartest one here. They had to expect you'd figure out it was causing your illness and could ultimately turn you against him making him vulnerable. He may not be the sharpest tool in the shed, but he wouldn't do something that would weaken his own magic."

"Maybe they were trying to kill two birds with one stone. He weakens me, but he can heal me, so he gains my loyalty out of necessity. Our reconnection gives him confidence until they attack then they turn me against him

Chapter 36 – A changing of the guard

making him weak in battle."

"Perhaps, but that's a lot of moving parts."

"They also knew you'd try to heal me which would weaken you and you played right into their hands."

"See how you are?"

"What?"

"I thought I was on to something, and you just explained it all away."

"Well, with that out of the way you can finally relax for a bit." Hermione suggested.

"Oh, I'm not done. We still need to take care of that hand. We're gonna need you at full strength. I have something new I need to teach you."

"Oh really?" She smiled. "Still, it is odd though."

"What?"

"That Alucard would poison a necklace the same way Draco did last year with Katie Bell."

"You've done it again." Justice paused, "Draco, that's it."

"What have I done?"

"Draco. He's with Alucard."

"That's highly likely."

"When we went after Neville, Draco and his father were there along with some of their underlings. There was no sign of Alucard. I don't think he'd ever been there. I think the Malfoys were running the show and Barty Crouch was there healing. Draco gave your friend a necklace a year ago and likely did it again this time. The thing is, given the way he feels about you, I'm not convinced you were his target."

"Then Harry…"

"No. I don't think that either. When exactly did he give it to you?"

She thought for a moment, "He was in the hospital wing

at Beauxbatons after the attack. Wood said he thought Harry attacked him, but Ron said it was a hooded figure who attacked Wood then isolated ***him*** from Harry and attacked Harry as well."

"If that's accurate, what or whoever attacked Harry could have placed a spell on him and is using it to control him. It could have given him the necklace and told him the target."

"Then it could have been intended for any of us."

"Not exactly. Being a woman's necklace, it would have been intended for a woman. Being embedded with poison it would have been intended for someone powerful."

"Someone Draco considered a threat."

"He knows you're a threat magically, but he's in love with you according to the Genealogy book. He wouldn't risk you dying from the poison, so I think we can rule you out."

"Jade wasn't there, and he doesn't even know Stormy."

"Flipping the coin, we've both sensed it." He reasoned.

"I know. Harry's affection for Charista. You know, now that you've mentioned it, that day in the hospital wing I thought I heard him mention her name, but when she didn't appear, I dismissed it. He may have just been too weak for her to pick it up given his condition at the time."

"Or she chose not to respond knowing how you feel about him. She really is your friend first."

"How I ***felt***."

"Hold on a minute." He stepped to her and took her right hand. He raised it to his lips and kissed it. "I've given up on steering you in his direction, but don't forget, he's likely being controlled by the Imperious Curse."

"That may be, but…" She gazed into his eyes.

"But, enough about Harry." he began. He lifted her hand to his lips once again. She tilted her head back and closed her eyes. He blew hard onto her thumb. 'CRACK'!!! The bones could be heard loud and clear. With a quick wince, she passed out from the shock and he caught her. "Now let's fix that

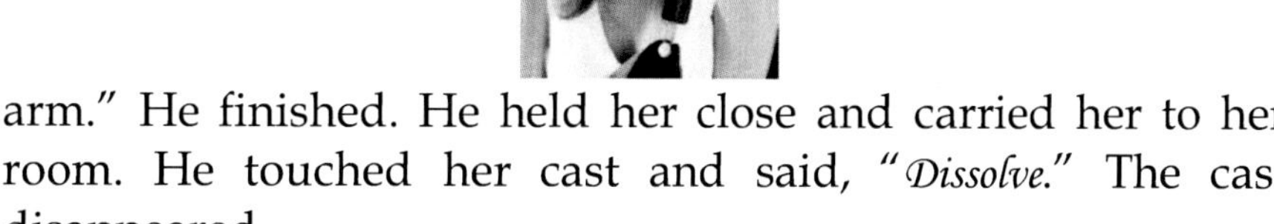

arm." He finished. He held her close and carried her to her room. He touched her cast and said, "*Dissolve.*" The cast disappeared.

Justice arrived at the library. The gang was practically all there. Demetria was noticeably absent. There was heart felt greetings on both sides. "Hey everybody. It's good to see you all. Neville, Ron, Reggie, Stormy, Cam, Freddy, Jade, Mallory and Charista, I've missed all of you."

"We've missed you too."

"Thank you all for coming. I asked you all here because I have something to share with you that could come in handy."

"What is it? Some new kind of magic?" Ron joked.

"Yes, actually. I learned it from Westerfield's relative. She was the reason I went to Azkaban."

"The reason you went. You mean, you staged that attack? You ***wanted*** to go?" asked Mallory.

"I knew you had a plan; you always do." stated Cam.

"Don't give me too much credit. It didn't go quite the way I planned, but I made it and may have found something to help us in our battle."

"Should we wait for Hermione?" encouraged Neville.

"No, she's resting. I'll show her later. Now I haven't had a chance to work on it much yet. Nicole…"

"Nicole?" asked Charista and Jade simultaneously.

"Nicole Tattenger-Westerfield. We only spoke briefly, but she told me the one thing that seemed to give Alucard trouble was magic he'd never seen before. Fiona began working on something she called Focus Energy Targeting."

"How does it work?" Ron asked.

"Well, what's the one thing we've all been taught that all magic needs to be effective?" he asked as he set two books upright on the end of the table, one in front of the other.

"Eye contact and line of sight." answered Hermione. She had just entered the library. Charista was the first to reach her and hug her. One by one they all greeted her and welcomed her back.

"As usual, you're dead on. How are you feeling?"

"Very well, thanks. Don't let me interrupt."

"Yes, please continue." Jade requested.

"Alucard isn't afraid of anything he can understand or see coming. But, with Focus Energy Targeting you can cast a spell at objects that are blocked by other things."

"Can you show us?" asked Stormy.

"I can try. Demetria really should see this. She's really good at picking up things like this." He glanced around. Hermione walked over to him.

"Thank you." she said as she wiggled the fingers on her healed hand.

"You're quite welcome." He smiled and looked deeply into her eyes. "Guys, can all of you gather around for a moment? Get in close. Just form a circle." Charista stood on one side of him, Hermione on the other. "Could you all hold hands? I'd like to give a silent thank you for this reunion." He lowered his head, stood silent then moved his hand to Charista's bare forearm and said, "*Aladusuch!*" Collectively they felt a surge of electricity then he let them go. They looked back and forth at one another then Mallory spoke.

"That was nice, thank you."

He nodded then turned to the others, "Let's continue. You have to focus on the target's mass. In this case, you know what's back there. Try to picture it and when you're ready…" He looked at the books, pointed his wand and said, "*Focus.*" The second book fell over.

"That was awesome." shouted Freddy. "Did you see that? Do it again." he requested enthusiastically. They set it up again. Justice turned his back and concentrated. Nothing happened at first.

"Freddy can make things fall over, using just his ugly face." Jade commented.

"Hey!" replied Freddy.

"*Aladusuch, Focus!*" he said, and the book fell over. "Alright, line up. Let's see what you can do." First up was Neville. "Just point and focus on the second object.

Neville tried his best but knocked over the front book. Stormy did the same. Mallory got the rear book to wiggle a bit before the front book fell. Jade stepped up and blasted both books off the table.

"Take no prisoners, leave no witnesses." she said then turned her back and walked off. Ron went next. He cast his spell and blasted a hole in the front book.

"It's okay. This is our first time. It's a difficult concept." They set them up again and Charista took her turn.

"*Focus!*" She knocked over the second book.

"Well done." Justice acknowledged.

"Naturally." said Jade in a jealous tone. Justice set the book up again as the others congratulated Charista.

Hermione stepped up and pointed her wand. "***Focus!***" The second book fell over.

"Whatever! What good is knocking over books gonna do?" snapped Jade.

"You're right. Set it up again." Justice commanded. They did. He focused, "***Focus!!!***" The second book exploded. "That's the goal."

"Whoa!" said Ron.

"Awesome!" said Cam.

Hermione and Charista inspected the front book and saw a burn stain on the back cover. Further inspection revealed more pages inside were smoking. "It's a work in progress. I'll figure it out." he explained.

"Of course, you will." stated Charista.

"How did you pick it up so fast?" Stormy asked her.

"I worked for the Westerfield's for years. They all whispered of it and dabbled with it, but no one ever figured it out. This is the first time I ever got it to work and that's from seeing Justice do it and from the magic he passed to us."

"That's what that was?" Ron asked.

"That's why she was the target." Hermione mentioned.

"Target? Me?"

"We've deduced that you may have been the intended target of the poison necklace, not Jean."

"Why me?"

"Because you're the most powerful of all of us." Justice clarified.

"I'm not more powerful than you."

"At best, my magic may be more diverse, but that's only because you don't do the silly illusions that I do."

Chapter 36 – A changing of the guard

"Oh brother, are we done with the mutual admiration society stuff?" asked Jade sarcastically.

"What is your problem?" snapped Justice.

She was shocked he spoke to her like that in front of the others. "You know, I thought I was glad to hear you were back. I thought I was glad to know that despite turning your back on your coven, that you still intended to fight for us, but now I see we're probably better off on our own. The Elders were right."

"The Elders? What are you talking about?"

"They didn't think you were coming back from Azkaban. They had to make decisions to ensure the safety of the coven."

"Justice, I was going to tell you about it. It was only temporary and now they'll reverse their decision." said Cam.

"What decision?"

"The Alpha's needed an Alpha One."

"No." Hermione shook her head.

"And with my spot open…" Jade began then looked over to Cam.

Both Justice and Freddy looked at Cam. "I was gonna tell you, I swear."

"What the hell were you waiting for? How could you?" Freddy asked angrily as he approached Cam.

"Guys, stop it. It's alright. They didn't know I was coming back. They did what they had to do. Good for them. I don't blame you Cam, they got a good man."

"And me?" Jade asked.

"You're still not ready. You don't think like a leader. You're too impulsive."

"You're just jealous of my power. You always have been."

"Really Jade? I'm jealous? Jade, I love you. You know that. You have unlimited potential. This was always gonna be the plan, you and I working together. We get you reinstated and in time you would take over. You know it won't be long."

"Don't say that."

"Jade, you better than anyone know your time is coming, but not now."

"I told you I was sorry! I told you it was over!"

"Jade, this has nothing to do with that."

She grabbed her head. He reached out and touched her shoulder. "Are you alright?" he asked as he cast a protection charm over the others. He'd seen her like this before. She spun, wand pointed, and he caught her wrist in midair. "Jade!" he shouted to get her attention. She clearly looked confused and startled. "Jade, it's me. We're okay."

She looked into his eyes and began to cry. He pulled her to him, "***sleep***", he muttered. He lifted her into his arms and carried her toward the door. Charista watched with her eyes glowing yellow. Cam stopped him at the door.

"I'll take her. You know; that Alpha thing."

"Yeah, I know." He handed her to him. "Cam, be careful. Look after her, but this stinks of an inside set up. This wasn't coincidental. Someone's manipulating us apart. Smart."

"I'll bet its Professor Hunt. She's been acting totally weird. She hasn't even acknowledged what happened with you." Cam told him.

"That would be my doing. She must have felt compromised. I gave her a way out. She'd never turn against us."

"Well, Marcus is still missing and now so is Demetria."

"What do you mean?"

"I specifically told her to meet us here when I saw her

after the Triathlon. She just disobeyed a directive from an Alpha."

"So, she knew you were, ***are***, an Alpha?"

"Yeah, I told her. Everyone else knew, but you and Freddy. You were gone and I didn't know how to tell Freddy."

"It's alright," He patted Cam on the head, "Take her to her room so she can rest. We'll talk more later." Suddenly Justice shuttered. He had a thought, and it wasn't happy.

"So, what do you think's going on?" Ron asked.

"I'm working on it. Did anyone see Harry at the Triathlon?"

"No. Last I saw him he was headed toward Hagrid's"

"Hermione, if…"

"What did you call me?" she asked. He paused a moment.

"Jean, if Harry doesn't know for sure you're not still under the effects of the poison, you may be better served, at least in the short term, to let him think you're still ill. Just until we find out for sure if you were indeed the target."

"I don't know if I can pull it off. I guess I can try."

"It's just a thought." He turned to Ron. "Okay, how are you coming along with your training for the tryouts?"

"Alright, I guess. Everyone's been helping with my transfiguration. That first leg has me a little concerned. I mean, I'm an okay swimmer, but there are all kinds of things in that lake. I barely survived three years ago."

"I'm sure you'll do fine. Just remember, you can't transfigure until you hit the water."

Ron thought about it, "What am I saying? Now that you're back it doesn't really matter. It's gonna be as it should be, you against Harry." Justice just shook his head no.

"I can't believe you're not gonna try out." said Mallory. "No offence Ron."

Ron shook his head, "None taken, I agree. He should be in there."

"No, Ron's our guy. I have something else I need to do during the try outs."

"What's that?" Stormy asked.

"I need to go to Diagon Alley."

"Justice? You're not serious. You just got back here from Azkaban. The Headmistress isn't going to allow you to go on a field trip." Mallory reminded him.

"You heard what that ogre Umbridge said, you're not to leave the grounds until they're done investigating what happened at Azkaban." added Charista.

"That's why it's better to ask for forgiveness, rather than permission."

"I can't hear this." Mallory told them.

"I'll go." said Charista.

"Thanks, but no. Now that I'm not an Alpha I don't have to abide by their rules." He checked his watch. "The mail

Chapter 36 – A changing of the guard

should be here any minute, right?"

"Yeah, why?" Neville asked.

"You're gonna receive a package. Keep it hidden until I ask you for it, okay?"

"Sure, what is it?"

"A bargaining chip. Everyone be on your guard. I don't know where Demetria is, but if anyone sees her, I need to know about it right away. We may have a mole. It's none of you. I'm pretty sure it's one of ours. Just be careful who you tell what."

"So, what are we looking for in Diagon Alley?" Hermione asked.

"Oh no. I'll do everything in my power to help keep you safe, but I'm certainly not gonna put the Valedictorian in harm's way and risk you being suspended, expelled, arrested or killed. In fact, with less than twenty-four hours to the try outs and a week to the Triwizard Tournament, it may be best for all of us to stay away from all of you." He realized, in that moment, that he was keeping them safe and putting them in danger at the same time. He had to take a stand for their own good. It wasn't going to get any easier, not with this enemy.

"That's silly. There's safety in numbers. We stick together and we can keep each other safe." Hermione pointed out.

"Hermione listen to me." his voice changed. "Everyone gather around!" he commanded. "This isn't a game anymore. I feel something has shifted. I'm feeling it in the castle. I came back for one reason, to fight. Thanks to some great intelligence from several of you, we know where and when the fight's going to take place. I was born for this, you weren't. You all have long lives to live, bright futures, families to go home to after the school year and families to start, as well as careers that are going to make all our lives better. I intend to make sure that happens. I can keep you all safe, but not if I'm babysitting. I've done what I can for all of you, now I have to fulfill ***my*** destiny. I'm a killer, it's what I do. It's all I know."

"So, stop."

"I can't. I don't want to. For me killing is like eating chips. You can't stop after just one."

"Don't joke about this." she pleaded.

"I'm not joking. It's who I am." He turned to face Hermione, "It's ***all*** I am."

"And he's back." stated Jade who had just walked back into the room. "That's the guy we're all used to."

"No, it's not." Hermione ignored her and kept talking to him. "You're much more than that."

"Two members of the coven are missing. Professor Hunt's memory was wiped of me. Neville and Stormy were kidnapped, you were attacked and poisoned. All of that was because of me because I'm here. I promised I wouldn't let you get hurt; I broke that promise. I never break promises. Enough is enough."

"I know someone else who used to think everything bad that happened was somehow his fault and he could solve it all by himself. If we had listened to him, he'd have been killed. We didn't listen then and we're not listening now."

"YES! YOU ARE GONNA LISTEN AND LISTEN WELL, because I'm only gonna say this one more time. If you all want to live, stay out of my way. I'm gonna have my hands full enough with him." He turned to leave.

"That's it then? Are you done?" Hermione asked.

"Why? Are you gonna cry about it?"

She slapped him. "I'm done crying. You're trying to act like we all just met you. It's too late. We know who you are, who you really are, so save the act."

"You have no idea who, or what I am."

"You want to walk away; I can't stop you. I'm asking you not to walk away from us, from me. Not tonight. You said it yourself. We've all suffered many losses and the one constant in our safety is you. All of us here owe you something. So, if you want to leave right now you go ahead, but when we needed you, you were always there. When you need us, we'll be there for you. And don't you dare forget your promise to me." She turned and walked away.

"You can't make us stay away." Charista told him.

"Actually, I can." he rebutted. He turned and stepped outside. The moment the door closed he banged his head on the wall.

"That's not going to help you, giving yourself a concussion."

Without even looking up, he recognized the voice. "Oracle." With a wave of her wand invisible barriers sealed them off from view. He could see out but couldn't be seen.

"So, it's begun."

"What's that?"

"The chess match." She paused. "You're very clever, trying to push her away. Think she'll listen?"

The others began to walk out of the library. She began to sniff the air as if she was waiting for a specific scent. Justice knew he and Kalick were hidden, but when he noticed Kalick paying particularly close attention to each person who walked out of the library he blackened the walls of the barrier out of habit. 'She was blind, right?' he thought to himself. There was no way she could see them, yet she stared in their direction as if she was taking inventory. Could she be trusted? With what he knew about her he couldn't be sure. He looked into the eyes of her younger face, and they were no longer cloudy, they instead were beautiful and green and stared right back at him. "Was it you?"

"Was what me?"

Justice lifted his hand and Kalick was pressed against the wall and immobilized. "Why are you here, now?"

"Killing me isn't going to help your cause."

"Understand something, these people are important to me. Your brother wants a fight, I'll give him all he can handle, but he will have to kill me if he touches any of them."

Chapter 36 – A changing of the guard

"You mean your friends? You can't even say it. Do they know the real you? What you're really capable of?"

"They're gonna find out."

"You can't protect them all. I have foreseen it."

"I'll ask one more time! Why are you here?"

"My brother is paranoid. Like you, he senses dissention in the ranks. Unlike you, however, he will kill anyone he thinks isn't following his orders."

Hermione, meanwhile, was straightening things up in the library. "So, who was that show for?" Charista asked.

"You saw through it too? How did you know?"

"The Wrackspurts. Between the two of you they were practically dancing a ballet."

"I saw his plan when he touched me. He's planning to go after Harry's cloak. He's going to try to break into Gringott's."

"Are you sure?"

"I saw it."

"Hermione, you know what I think of Justice. You know I've always maintained that I trust him."

"Of course."

"Justice is one of the smartest wizards I've ever met." She paused. "He could easily have looked up all the information we all have about Alucard."

"Go on."

"What if…what if he's going after the Hallows for himself? Is that even a possibility?"

"No, what are you saying?"

"Hermione. You utilize logic better than anyone. Just for a second, consider the possibility. We've been convinced a fight is coming, yet we've never seen this enemy. We're told he's a shape shifter, so we wouldn't recognize him if we did see him. He wants the Hallows. You say you've seen that Justice is going after the cloak. People have been disappearing and we know he can come and go as he pleases."

"So can you." she countered.

"You were attacked by something and there he was. Ms. Featherstone gets kidnapped and he's able to communicate with her then he finds her where no one else could. Professor Hunt argues with him, Crisp confronts him, and he wipes both their memories. He moves like both a Death Eater and a member of the Order. Who else have you ever known who could do all that?"

"He healed me."

"How did he know how?"

"This is nonsense. He cares for us, all of us."

"I know he cares for you. But wasn't Harry doing the same thing? You were sick, he came around, you felt better, and you began to trust in him. Justice heals you by extracting a poison from you that Madame Pomfrey couldn't even identify. He gave you a reason to trust him. He's given all of us reasons to trust him. I'm just saying, what if that was his plan? To gain our trust then attack us. He knows our weaknesses. What if…he's Alucard?"

"I can't believe that. I won't. I thought you were his friend?"

Chapter 36 – A changing of the guard

"I am. I really am. I don't believe it either. I just had to see your reaction."

An owl found its way to Neville and dropped a package into his hands, just as Justice had told him would happen. It was post marked from America. Neville read the return address label. It was from Krysta Marie Madison, the wand maker.

"I apologize for handling you that way."

"I understand. It's very difficult for you to put your trust in me. He's my brother after all. Your chances are improving.

The fact that you returned from Azkaban shows your resourcefulness. Alucard is going to have his hands full. Just remember, you're not Potter. Your strength is not derived from your friends. They are your weakness. When the time comes, you'll have to let them be exposed to focus on your task. You cannot allow them to be a distraction, he'll exploit that. You may have to let some of them die to achieve your goal."

"So, you keep telling me."

"Are you prepared to do that?"

"I told you that's not an option."

"We'll see. As far as the chess match goes, remember, it

will start with the loss of pawns, but soon there will be back row casualties. You may even have to sacrifice your queen to achieve the opportunity to attack the king." As if on cue, the barrier cleared and Charista stepped out of the library. She immediately looked in their direction, despite not being able to see them. The barrier dissolved and Kalick was gone. Justice vanished as Hermione exited the library. Charista looked at the spot where Justice had been standing and could smell that he'd been there.

Justice was standing at a window in the Hufflepuff common room when Justin walked up to tell him he was being summoned to the Headmistress's office. "Thanks." He headed to see her and passed Professor Hunt in the hall. She smiled pleasantly and found herself staring at him as she walked by. She stopped, "I'm sorry, you look so familiar to me, but I can't place where I've seen you before."

"I'm in your Muggle Studies class."

"Really, I don't recall seeing you recently. I'm so sorry."

"It's okay, I've been away." The Headmistress could be seen approaching from up the hall. He felt his eyes welling up. "Professor, perhaps I can come see you after my meeting to get the assignments I've missed. Will you be in your office?"

"Yes, that will be lovely."

"Okay, bye."

"Bye, bye." She walked off just as McGonagall arrived.

"You two must have made up?"

Chapter 36 – A changing of the guard

"She's a very forgiving woman."

McGonagall looked from him to her as she disappeared around a corner. "Shall we?"

"Yes Ma'am." They went to her office and sat on either side of her desk.

"Mr. Cain. I called you here because I heard you still haven't submitted your intension to try out for the tournament."

"No Ma'am."

"If it's a matter of not having had time to fill out the paperwork, I can tell you, there are some advantages to being the Headmistress. I can pull some strings." She grinned.

"No Ma'am, that's not it. With all that's gone on I just feel that Harry is a better representative for Hogwarts."

"I was born during the day, Mr. Cain, but not yesterday. As an Alpha, isn't it your responsibility to protect him? These may just be tryouts, but they are every bit as potentially hazardous as the actual tournament will be, I assure you. And where better to protect him than right beside him on the course."

"That may be true, but one, it's not allowed by the coven and two, I'm not an Alpha anymore."

"Whatever do you mean?"

"I've been stripped of my status and replaced by Jade."

"I see. Well, if that's the case I guess ***she'll*** have to withdraw. Justice, if I remember correctly, you were dismissed from your coven and two, you may or may not have the title of Alpha anymore according to some. You're an alpha to me, but you are the offset. You are the best chance for the survival of the students here at Hogwarts and I will do whatever I have to, to ensure their safety."

"I attacked a teacher."

"Professor Hunt appears to have gotten over it and Crisp

wasn't injured, he doesn't recall the incident, and frankly, I like him better this way."

"Yes Ma'am."

"If you Ma'am me one more time."

"Yes Headmistress."

"So, I'll notify the committee you'll be participating."

"If you're sure you want me."

"Of course."

"Then count me in. I'll go start the prelims."

"You're a previous champion. You're exempt from having to qualify. You just need to be there at the starting bell of the first event."

"I'll be there."

"Justice; don't let me down. I expect you to give Potter a real run for his money."

"Oh, I intend to."

Justice went to see Professor Hunt. She was seated at her desk when he walked in. "Hello again." she said.

Chapter 37 – Two Champions

"Hello Professor." He looked at her. "You changed clothes?"

"Yes, I guess I wanted to feel pretty today."

"You look beautiful every day."

She blushed. He immediately felt the sadness in his heart of her not recognizing him. 'Poor Neville and Hermione'. For him it was just a few days. For Hermione, it was months without her parents and for Neville, years. Was it easier that they hadn't seen their parents since it happened? To be standing so close to someone you cared that deeply for and have them not recognize you at all. He certainly couldn't imagine feeling any worse. The hardest part was that he'd have to let it continue a little longer. He had Neville's potion, but couldn't be sure it would work even if he figured out how to give it to her.

"Mr. Cain are you alright?" she asked. Her body language revealed her to suddenly be apprehensive, nervous in his presence.

"I'm fine and you? How do you feel?"

"I feel very well thanks. As well as I can remember." In watching her he certainly didn't recognize any ill effects.

"Mr. Cain," she said as she glanced up at him to notice his eyes glued to her every move. "May I say something and not have you take it the wrong way?"

"Of course."

"This is highly irregular." She paused, "I'm very confused about you."

"How so?"

"I find myself thinking about you constantly since I passed you in the hall. I read your file and it says you've been in my class since the start of the school year, yet I don't seem to have a recollection of you."

He smiled. "Professor Hunt." He stood and could see her recoil.

"Please, let me finish. This is difficult enough for me." He sat back down realizing the internal difficulty she was experiencing with the situation's circumstances. "You're a very handsome young man and your file paints you as quite extraordinary. Straight "A's" in every class you have with your female professors. Your only blemish is with Mr. Crisp. I have you as a straight A student and then I came to an entry that shows we had a physical altercation that I don't remember."

"I can explain."

"What do you think of me, Mr. Cain?"

He sat back in his chair. "You're beautiful, more beautiful even than I remember. I'm so glad to see you looking so well. You're exceptionally intelligent and caring and I love you. I love you more than you'll ever know."

She stopped him. "Mr. Cain!"

"Justice. Please, you've always called me Justice."

"Mr. Cain," she paused and looked very troubled. "Are you attracted to me?"

Chapter 37 – Two Champions

He started to laugh. "Dani..." he began, and she raised her eyebrows.

"Professor Hunt." She cut across him, "Because I feel an attraction to you, a closeness that's confusing me to a point of being uncomfortable. I've heard of students becoming enamored with their teachers, but..."

"**Professor Hunt**, relax. It's not like that. There's a reason you feel the way you do..."

"Is that why we fought? Did something occur between us that I've suppressed from my memory? Did Crisp find out about us why you attacked him as well? You went to Azkaban over it. If it's true, I should have been sent there too. I barely remember you, but the way I feel, even right now, it couldn't have been one sided..."

"Alright stop! It's not what you think. We didn't do anything inappropriate. I can explain."

THE ARGUMENT

"So, what are you saying? He is a recognized Triwizard Champion. He is no longer restricted by the antiquated rules of his coven. The rules are clear on this point. What is unprecedented is having two current champions at one school."

Pius and Umbridge conferred. "Pius, this candidate's championship is not recognized in this country."

"Dolores, the wizard community is one community

worldwide. We must embrace our brothers and sisters."

"It's not fair. I earned the right to compete. I was better than everyone so far in the prelims." Jade interjected.

"It is the will of your Elders, not our rules that are keeping you out." reminded McGonagall. "Be careful what you wish for."

"So, Headmistress, you are granted this exemption. This also changes the rules of the event a bit." Pius told her.

"How so?"

"This has become a challenge match between two champions. The tryouts are over."

"No! He won't agree to that. He won't compete."

"***He*** has no choice."

"***You*** have no choice, Dolores. He thrives on the competition. You want to see him perform at his best? Allow the other qualifiers to compete as well. You will have two finalists. Let the prelims determine the other two."

"Fine, but only seniors will be allowed to compete, and the flying portion of the course will take place in a labyrinth that I will set up." Dolores flaunted.

"Fine. Just remember, these are tryouts, not the actual tournament."

"You just have the contestants there on time."

Chapter 37 – Two Champions

Jade turned and stormed out passing McGonagall who was wearing a sheepish smile. The students were gathered in the Great Hall and McGonagall made the announcement about the tryouts.

"Ladies and gentlemen. Ladies and gentlemen. Your attention please. The preliminaries are nearly complete. The two finalists from each house will be chosen and the names will be posted on the board near the door. The rules have been altered slightly but did not affect the selections already chosen by the committee, with one exception. Jade Malone was promoted by her coven to Alpha status. The bylaws of their coven restrict the participation of their Alpha's from such competitions. Her name will be withdrawn from the list of candidates. All the finalists will be seniors. And lastly, we have two automatic qualifiers, not just one."

The students began to stir. Hermione was in attendance but sat quietly by herself as Harry looked on. She would occasionally sneeze, and she kept silent to promote the charade. Justice stood with Mallory against a wall.

"Harry is an automatic finalist as the winner of the last tournament. The second automatic finalist also won a version of the Triwizard competition."

"No way. He's an Alpha!" Harry shouted.

"He was recently demoted from Alpha status making him eligible to compete and he has agreed to do so. Justice Cain is the second finalist."

Harry was incensed. He stomped out and Justice pursued him to the outer courtyard. "Harry."

"Leave me alone, Justice."

"Harry, hold up a moment, I need to talk to you." Finally, he ran up and tapped Harry on the shoulder. Harry spun around. His eyes were red. Justice could swear he saw fangs in his mouth which confused him momentarily. Harry punched Justice and knocked him down. Harry jumped atop him, wand drawn and pressed it to Justice's throat. Justice placed his hands-on Harry's chest to create some space between them. "Harry, it's me, Justice. I'm not here to fight you. I came to explain that none of this was my idea. I mean, you know from Quidditch, that I love competition. If it was up to me, my final four would be, you, me, Charista and Jade competing, representing the four houses. That'd be a hell of a test, right?"

Harry's eyes returned to normal. Justice tugged at his shirt a bit and was able to see the bite marks on his throat explaining what was going on with him. "Harry, I can help you. Have you lost the ability to do magic without your wand?" Harry didn't answer, but Justice felt Harry's grip begin to loosen. He started to get up and suddenly he was blasted backward. Charista's eyes were still yellow. As Justice looked around more, he could see half the school was standing in the courtyard looking on. Professor Greenway grabbed Charista. As a reflex Charista turned and cast a curse that sent the professor flying toward a wall. She braced for impact, but never hit it as Justice silently cast, '***Aladusuch***' and stopped her in midair. He sprang to his feet and rushed to Charista. He threw his arms around her and cast a shield just in time to deflect a curse from Harry.

"***Expelliarmus!***" cast McGonagall and Harry's wand flew to her.

"Charista, it's me, Justice. We're okay." She turned toward his voice, her eyes still glowing yellow. "We're okay." He repeated and her eyes returned to normal. He removed the shield charm. McGonagall immediately called for all of them to report to her office. Pius went to join them.

Chapter 37 – Two Champions

As Justice released Charista she said, "I'm in trouble, aren't I?"

"It may not be as bad as we think. Let's let it play out. And thank you, by the way."

"You're welcome." She smiled. She turned to walk off, and Justice opened his hand. In it was the key to Harry's vault that he normally kept around his neck.

The three of them sat in McGonagall's office. She and Pius were in a heated debate. '*Muffliato*' kept them from being overheard. They walked over to the three of them. "Explain yourselves!"

"It was my fault." Justice spoke up. "I went to Harry and was a little overzealous in the way I tried to get his attention. As I grabbed for him, I tripped and pulled him down on top of me. Naturally, given our history, Charista thought we were fighting and was just trying to separate us."

"And the professor?"

Justice spoke again before Charista could respond. "Again, I startled her. She was trying to protect me, and I deflected the spell she'd cast, and it rebounded onto the professor. We all know how accurate she is with her spells."

"So that's the story you're all sticking too?"

"I cast the spell at the professor. I knew what I was doing."

"I see."

"Very admirable of you to confess Ms. McDonald, but I'm equally impressed with Mr. Cain attempting to dissuade the blame to himself." said Pius.

"Be that as it may, you must be punished. You are a member of the staff. You should know better. You are remanded to your house for one week." Her face showed remorse as the words left her lips. "Had it not been witnessed by the entire student body…"

"It's okay Headmistress. I deserve it and more. Thank you for being so even handed in your punishment. I'm lucky to not be banished. Please tell Professor Greenway, I am terribly sorry."

"A week will cause her to miss the tournament." Justice pointed out.

"I'm sorry Mr. Cain. I have no choice."

"What about us?" Harry asked. Before McGonagall could respond Pius interjected.

"Do you intend to wage a charge against Mr. Potter?" he asked Justice.

"No sir, I fell."

"So, you said. Well, with no charges to be filed I see no reason to impose a punishment at this time."

McGonagall's mouth fell open. She turned to them, "50 points from Ravenclaw and 10 points each from Hufflepuff and Gryffindor for your ***fall***. Don't let it happen again. Your first event is at 7:30 am tomorrow. The duels will begin at dawn. I don't want to see either of you until then."

"Yes Ma'am." The three of them left the room. Justice could still hear Pius and McGonagall talking.

"Pius, how could you? What message does this send?"

"Minerva, with the genuine animosity that exists between them this could be even better than the actual tournament. You said it yourself. It's unprecedented for there to be two legitimate champions competing against one another at the same school."

"It'll be a great show if they don't kill each other first."

Harry walked away from them. "Charista, he's been bitten, that's why he's been acting so strange."

"Can you heal him the way you did Hermione?"

Chapter 37 – Two Champions

"It's a different type of problem. I'm not sure. I better talk to Neville and Cam. I'm sorry about the house restriction. I really do wish you and Jade were competing with Harry and me. That would be so fun."

She smiled halfheartedly. The length of the punishment would make it impossible for her to go with the winner to Durmstrang. "I've let you down."

"You could never let me down. Is there anything I can do for you?"

"You've already done it." She hugged him and walked away.

Justice began down the hall and was flagged down by Professor Flitwick. "Hello Professor."

"Hello, yes. I have your package." he whispered. He handed Justice a gold silk bag. "I'm sure you'll find it to your exact specifications. Be careful with these."

"I will. I'm sure they're perfect. Thank you again."

"Good luck Mr. Cain. Use them well."

"I intend to." He hurried off to the Hufflepuff dorm. He changed his outfit and waited for the rest of the Hufflepuffs to go to the Great Hall. Now that he was going to be participating in the events he'd have to sneak out of the school, get to Diagon Alley in London, get into Gringotts, one of the most secure locations known to wizard kind, into Harry's vault, then out and back undetected before the start of the tryouts. It was going to be tight if not impossible. At least the bank was always open. Wizards could need access to their possessions at any time. The staff would be minimal, and he had the key. He had one last thing to do. He needed to make copies of Harry's glasses and wand. Bill had told him that was part of Gringotts security system. All wizards and witches, known or not, were required to present their wand for identification and their key. He placed the key he had in the palm of his hand and closed his fist around it. He placed his other hand over a cup of cold water. Within seconds the water began to boil. He poured it into the fist with the key without spilling a drop. He wrapped his other hand around his clinched fist then opened it until the palms were flat against one another. When he separated his hands, there were two identical keys. The chain the key usually hung from was already broken. He headed toward Harry. 'Here we go again.' He was going to bump him and upon impact he was going to slip the key into Harry's pocket. He started across the room as the board was unveiled showing the names of the other participants. There were two from each house. Justice was just a few steps from Harry when Hermione bumped him. Not hard enough to draw attention to them, but hard enough for her to lift the key from him.

"If it's not around his neck, he'll know something's up. I'll take it from here." she said, and she headed toward Harry before he could stop her.

"Jean, wait..."

Justice gritted his teeth then noticed she was approaching him without a cast on. "***Steleus!***" The spell made her sneeze repeatedly, but the effects would be temporary. She tapped Harry on the shoulder. "***Ferula!***" Justice cast and as Harry turned to her a cast formed on her healed hand.

She cleared her throat a few times then struggled to speak softly. "Harry, can we go for a walk?"

Chapter 37 – Two Champions

He looked her in the eyes then looked around until he saw Ron talking to Neville and Blaise and he saw Justice at the beverage table. "Sure." They left the room together as a crowd gathered around the board. The names on the list were:

Gryffindor – Ron Weasley & Blaise Zabini
Hufflepuff – Stormy Knight & Reggie Fields
Ravenclaw – Oz Gotschall & Alfredo Tejada
Slytherin – Robyn Banks & Emmerick Tepis

Justice followed Harry and Hermione at a safe distance. Hermione began to speak more loudly and clearly as they walked. Her gait also improved as it had around him when she had been sick. He followed them to the Black Lake, and she reached out and held his hand.

"Harry, I know we haven't spent much time together recently and I regret that. I miss you. I miss us. I feel so much better when I'm around you."

"It's good to hear you say that."

"I still love you, Harry. Nothing's going to change that."

'Alright, Jean, that's enough'. Justice said to himself.

"Look Hermione, I know I shouldn't have read your diary, but…"

"It's in the past. I've forgotten about it. You should too. Here and now is all that matters. And right now, I want to go swimming."

'What'? Justice said to himself.

"What?" asked Harry. "Are you crazy? It's freezing in that water. I'll be in it soon enough."

"Come on, join me." She removed her top and trousers and placed her socks in her trainers then walked out to the end of the dock.

'Hermione Jean Granger, don't you do it!' Justice said to himself. She extended her hand to Harry.

"No! No, absolutely not." he insisted. She walked over to him and placed her arms around his neck, then removed his glasses. "Come on Hermione, you know I can't see without them." He reached for them.

"Just a quick dip, please." She kissed him on the cheek.

He sighed, "You're mental you know that?" He removed his shirt and immediately felt the key was missing. "My key?"

"It's right here." she told him and reached down at his feet. He squinted to try to see, but the darkness combined with his horrible vision left him helpless. She held up his key then took hold of him, "I'll put it here with your wand and glasses." He continued to disrobe and together they jumped in. Justice turned invisible and rushed over while the sound of her laughter and their splashing concealed his steps.

"***Geminio,***" He made copies of the wand and glasses. He left the real glasses and the copied wand. He needed the original since the goblins would certainly recognize a copy as fake. He cast a hot air charm with Harry's wand then touched it to the copy. "***Aladusuch!***" He cast a spell on the wand so that if Harry tried to use the wand to dry them off it would work well enough to fool him temporarily.

"Oh my God, Harry. You were right, it's freezing in here." She hurried out and he joined her. Justice stood at the tree line of the Forbidden Forest and watched as Harry did in fact dry them off with the wand. As they got dressed, they heard a sound approaching.

"Blimey 'Arry, what're you doin' ere? And who's that with ya? Ermione? You two ought to know better than to pull a stunt like this the night before the tournament. Now git!" Hagrid scolded them.

They hurried to the castle. Justice followed to make sure Harry didn't get too close. He followed them into the common room. It was late, so they were alone. "Well, goodnight." she said.

"Hermione, wait. Outside, tonight…"

'Here we go'. Justice braced himself.

"I thought."

"Harry, it was nice to spend time together, but it's late and like you said, you have to compete in the morning."

"Wait a minute. You came on to me like that then suddenly you just turn it off again?"

"Harry." He advanced on her, and Justice cast a barrier between them, but Harry stopped when he heard a voice from up the stairs.

"It's a little late, don't ya think?" Ron said.

"Stay out of this Ron."

"I don't think so."

Harry pulled out his wand. "Stop it!" shouted Hermione. "I am so sick of this. We're always fighting. I hate it."

"Go ahead, curse me? You'll be thrown out of the tournament."

"It's Justice's fault."

"Stop blaming everyone else. There's a Dark Lord organizing an army to fight us. You're the only person here who's defeated one. We could all use your help. Instead, you're just trying to beat Justice at something, anything. I'm so tired of both of you right now. I just want it to be over."

"Then what? Say we fight and win, whatever that means. Then what? Do you plan to leave with him? Or were you thinking the two of you would stay here, together? He told you before, he's here to fight. Once that's done, he'll either be dead or he'll leave. You have no future with him. It's me that loves you Hermione, me. Why can't you see that?"

"I can't do this. I can't think around you, any of you."

Chapter 37 - Two Champions

She walked by them and into the girl's sleeping quarters.

"Well done mate." said Ron as he turned and went back to his bed. Harry sat down on the couch and Justice grabbed a piece of parchment and left the room.

Justice got to the front steps and sat down. He hated her torment. He placed his hands on his head and thought. He wrote a note and folded it into a paper butterfly and set it free.

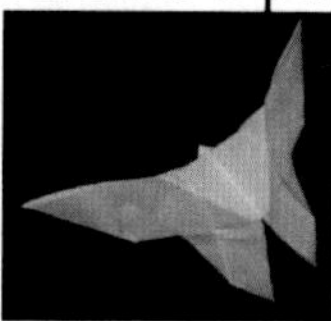

He made his way to the forest and out the hole in the fence. He stopped there and sniffed around. He rubbed his hands together quickly then blew into them. A glittery substance flew and settled onto the ground. "***Reveal your secrets!***" The glitter formed patterns of footprints leaving the grounds. He could tell Demetria had been through it recently and there was another scent as well. He returned to the car and went back into the Forbidden Forest. It was just after midnight, and he anticipated two hours each way. He just couldn't leave without knowing Hogwarts was secure. He knew time was short, but he drove to the opening to the Chamber of Secrets. The car stopped, the doors and trunk popped open. He got out and the doors closed. He closed the trunk. He was immediately surrounded by four centaurs.

"Nice work guys. I just need to take a quick look around." They stepped aside and he walked in.

Anthony Wright
Chapter 38 – I love you, goodbye

Draco and Marcus sat on opposite sides of a table in the Hogs Head. "They're here." Marcus said.

"Who's here?" Draco asked as he pulled his wand. He went to the door and looked out. Two Death Eaters were standing outside with something between them. Draco let them in.

"We brought you the Goblin, Griphook."

"Griphook, you work at Gringotts?" Draco asked. Griphook nodded. "We need to get into a vault there."

"I can't help you."

"Oh, you can, and you will." He pulled a knife and placed it to the goblins throat.

"Killing me won't get you into Gringotts."

"Not getting me into a vault at Gringotts ***will***, however, get ***you*** killed. That I can assure you."

"If I get you through the doors, then what?"

"Then you'll lead me to the vault, open it and I'll get what I need."

"We can't get in without a key. That's part of Gringotts security."

"Are the vaults never accessed for maintenance?" asked Marcus.

"Only when they are unoccupied, or the witch or wizard who owns the vault is confirmed dead."

"Who makes the keys?" Draco asked.

Chapter 38 – I love you, goodbye

"What do you mean?"

"My family has held a vault for many years. My father told me, when he opened his vault, a key was made for him. Who made the key?"

"There is a goblin named Shambolt. He makes the keys when the vaults are assigned."

"Can he make a duplicate?" Marcus asked.

"I don't know."

"For your sake, you'd better hope he can."

"If we get him to make a key to Potter's vault you can get us inside?" asked Marcus.

"***Potter's*** vault? You're searching for the Cloak of Invisibility."

Draco stabbed the little goblin in his left hand. The goblin grabbed his wrist and writhed in pain. "What do you know of the cloak?"

"I was the one who let him in the day he left it."

"Can you get it?"

"I saw where he put it, but no." Griphook moaned. Draco twisted the knife. The goblin cried out. "Perhaps if I had the key I could go in alone and find what you seek."

"No deal. We go in with you."

"It can't be done. Perhaps if Potter, himself was to be persuaded to join me."

"We don't have time for that."

"What about polyjuice potion?" asked one of the Death Eaters."

"It wouldn't work beyond the lobby. It could get you through the door, but not into the catacombs."

"Transfiguration?" asked Marcus.

"Perhaps, but it would take an immensely powerful wizard to pull it off."

"Alright! Marcus, take Creese and Brighton and the goblin and go to the key maker. Get a key and get to the vault. Send him in to get our package. If he's not in and out in twenty minutes, kill everyone in the building." Draco commanded.

"What are you going to do?" Marcus asked Draco.

"I think it's a good night to collect another bargaining chip."

Marcus paused and closed his eyes. He saw Griphook walking down the front stairs of Gringotts toward him with a package under his arm.

"What's with you?" Draco barked.

"Nothing, I'm ready. This should be a walk in the park."

HERMIONE

The tiny butterfly fluttered its way up the walls of Hogwarts tower until it found Hermione sitting in an open Window. Her face was stained with tears. It came to rest upon her shoulder and to her amazement, as it unfolded it began to speak to her in Justice's voice.

Chapter 38 – I love you, goodbye

"Hello Jean, it's me, Justice.
You may want to go somewhere secluded to listen to this.

She glanced around and everyone else was fast asleep. She went down to the common room and sat by the fire.

"I recently told you I was done pushing you toward Harry, but I've given a great deal of thought to you and I and the way I feel for you. When I was an Alpha a relationship with you was forbidden. Now I see it's simply not fair to you, to us. I have no claim on you. I was prepared to give up being an Alpha if it meant I could be with you, but Alpha or not, I now know our paths are running parallel with no intersecting point. I don't know if I can defeat this foe, but thanks to you I have no fear of facing it. You've given me strength and purpose and I know what I must do and it's best if I leave now to focus on that task. Thank you for all you've done. I wish you only the best."

The parchment refolded itself into a mouth, kissed her on the cheek then began to sing.

"Wish I could be the one
The one who could give you love
The kind of a love you really need

Wish I could say to you
That I'll always stay with you
But Jean that's just not me

You need someone willing to give their heart and soul to you
Promise you forever, Jean that's something I can't do
Oh I would say that I'll be all you need
But that would be a lie

I know I'd only hurt you,
I know I'd only make you cry
I'm not the one you needed,

I love you, goodbye

I hope someday you can
find some way to understand
I'm only doin this for you

I don't really want to go
But deep in my heart I know
This is the kindest thing to do

You'll find someone who'll be the one that I could never be
Who'll give you something better than the love you'll find with me
Oh I could say that I'll be all you need
But that would be a crime

I know I'd only hurt you, I know I'd only make you cry
I'm not the one you needed, I love you, goodbye
Leaving someone, when you love someone
Is the hardest thing to do
When you love someone as much as I love you

Oh I don't want to leave you, Mione it tears me up inside
But I'll never be the one you needed, I love you, goodbye

Jean it's just never gonna work out, I love you, goodbye

Hermione sat sobbing aloud. "Keep it down, we're trying to sleep here!" barked one of the portraits in the room.

"Nice voice." said another one.

"Get a grip girl." spouted another. With a wave of her wand all the pictures in the room went black.

Justice looked around thoroughly through the debris. There was no sign that Alucard had ever been there, but there was plenty of evidence of Draco. He entered the room where Mallory had been held and he closed his eyes. He could recall the image of her bound in the center of the room. He pictured

Chapter 38 – I love you, goodbye

Malikai and then Draco. He remembered him standing against a wall and touching it with his bare hand. He walked over to that spot and sniffed the wall. He hurried out of the cave.

He told Firenze to keep a keen eye out. He sensed Draco was close. He reached for the door handle of the car and stopped in his tracks, "What are you guys doing out of bed?" Cam and Jade stepped out from their concealments. "Guys, please keep your eyes and ears open today. I'm gettin a feeling." He noticed the trunk was open and closed it. "You really need to fix this." he told Cam.

"You should be in bed. You're competing in a few hours." Cam reminded him.

"I've got an errand to run first."

"Now?" Jade asked.

"What's McGonagall going to say when you're not here for the tournament?"

"I plan to be back in time."

"We're Alpha's, we can't let you leave." Cam told him.

"You can try to stop me."

"Where are you going?" Jade asked.

"I really can't say. Besides, the less you know, the less you'll be forced to tell. It's a win, win. Can you please just keep an eye out? Something doesn't feel quite right. Check the perimeter. Someone's been through the gate. And don't confront Harry."

"You can't tell us what to do. You're not an Alpha anymore."

"I know. I wasn't commanding, just suggesting." He turned to walk away.

"Ice."

He stopped, "Yeah?"

"Need some back up?" she asked.

"No thanks. Like you said, you're Alpha's now. Your place is here keeping the coven safe." He walked over and got into the car. Cam leaned into the passenger side window.

"Be careful."

"You know me."

"That's what I mean." He smiled.

Justice drove off. He checked the time and if all went well, he'd be cutting it very close. He kept thinking of Hermione and the look on her face. The thoughts filled him to the point that he began to smell vanilla cookies. He finally arrived in London at nearly 3 am He parked the car a couple blocks away from The Leaky Cauldron. He put on the glasses and a hooded cloak and closed his eyes. "Alright Mal, let's see if the lessons paid off." He transfigured into the exact image of Harry Potter, all the way down to the scar. He pulled his cloak over his head and exited the car.

Marcus, Griphook and the two Death Eaters had been going over the plan one last time at the mouth of the pathway that led to Knockturn Alley. "You have twenty minutes to get in, get the item and get out. Try anything funny and everyone in the building dies, understand?"

"Vault 687 is several levels down. It'll take that long to get to it after convincing Shambolt to make a new key. I'll be out within an hour. It's the best I can do."

"Just hurry. We haven't got all night."

Griphook entered the building and headed to the rail car platform that transported the customers to their vault. There was a tiny door at the end of the platform with a light shining through it. Griphook pushed the door open.

"Griphook." said a deep, sullen, raspy voice.

"Shambolt."

Chapter 38 – I love you, goodbye

"What can I do for you?"

"I need to get into a vault."

"Which one?"

"687."

"687 is occupied."

"I'm aware of that."

"Do you have the key?"

"If I did, I wouldn't be here."

"Leave your authorization, I'll make a duplicate. You can pick it up tomorrow."

"I need access now!" He pulled out a dagger.

Shambolt turned to him slowly.

Justice entered the bank with little fanfare. He made his way down the pathway beyond the dozens of goblins sitting on their high stools. They barely seemed to notice him. He reached the podium at the end of the path and removed his hood.

"Ah, Mr. Potter. It's good to see you."

"Good day to you as well. I need to access my vault."

"Is everything alright?"

"Oh yes, fine, brilliant. I'm just planning a sudden trip and need to gather a few things I've placed here for safe keeping."

"Very well. Your key please."

He placed it on the counter. "And your wand?" He placed it beside the key. The little goblin thoroughly inspected the wand then satisfied, he returned it to Justice. "I'll have someone take you to your vault right away." He scampered off. Justice felt the eyes upon him. He had to remember it was Harry they were looking at, not him. The goblin returned. "Mr. Potter. This is Arbagast. He will show you to your vault now."

"Follow me please." said the goblin in a tiny voice. He was escorted through a door that led down a dark, dank corridor that emptied into a rail system.

"Watch your step." The tiny elf requested. The two of them climbed in. The car sped off descending deeper and deeper into the bowels of the building. There were few lights, but each time they passed one they saw the bank's guards gathering. Something was up. They were suspicious.

'How did they figure it out so quickly?'

Arbagast didn't seem to know what was going on, so Justice figured if he could just get into the vault before they came for him, he'd at least have a fighting chance. He needed that cloak. He couldn't stop thinking of Hermione's face. The rail car began to slow down and when it came to a stop, they were shocked to see the vault door was ajar.

"Wait here." Justice instructed the little goblin. He could hear voices coming from within the vault.

"You won't get away with this Griphook. Need I remind you the penalty for a goblin robbing the bank is death?"

"Shut up Shambolt!" he barked. "It's got to be here."

Chapter 38 – I love you, goodbye

"Just tell me what you're searching for. Perhaps I can help you find it."

"Yes Griphook, do tell us what you're looking for." Justice said.

"Griphook's mouth fell open. He was holding the dagger to Shambolt's throat. "Stay back!"

"Griphook, put the knife down."

"I need your cloak, where is it?"

"Tell me why you need it?"

"It's none of your concern."

"I beg to differ."

"If I don't give it to them many will die."

"Who's them?"

"Death Eaters."

"They're here?"

"They're waiting for me and I'm late."

"How many are there?" The goblin sneered at him but didn't respond. "They're coming, we haven't got much time."

"Exit the vault with your hands up!" shouted one of the guards. Arbagast had alerted the guards that the vault was open when they arrived.

"Last chance! I can get you out of here, alive, but I can't let you have the cloak, and I won't help you if you keep that knife to his throat."

"They're goblins, not wizards. Your magic won't have any effect on them. Now where is the cloak? Tell me or I'll slit his throat." He barely got the words out when a curse flew from the tiny opening in the door. Justice sensed it and ducked out the way. The blast didn't hit Griphook but came close enough that he flinched, and the dagger stabbed Shambolt. It was a goblin made blade, so what appeared, at first glance to be a superficial wound, was fatal. Justice waved his hand and the vault door shut. He knew they couldn't stay inside long, but it would buy him some time. Shambolt collapsed to the ground, mortally wounded. Justice could tell Griphook was genuinely frightened for what he'd done to his old friend. He never intended to hurt him. He pointed the dagger at Justice to keep him at bay.

"Griphook, listen to me. They're gonna get in here. What's done is done, but you don't have to make it worse by attacking me."

"I'm not afraid of you, wizard. In your world, the great Harry Potter may be powerful, but wizard magic is no match for goblin magic."

They began hearing explosions at the door getting louder and louder. "They're almost in. What's it gonna be?"

"Shut up! I need to think!"

"I don't have time for you to think." He raised his hand. "***Obliviate!***" Nothing appeared to happen and Griphook grinned. "***Aladusuch!***" he commanded. Griphook stopped grinning and had a blank stare on his face. "***Sleep!***" Justice called out and Griphook fell to the floor. Justice blew in his palm and glittery dust settled on the objects in the room. Some settled in a shape with seemingly nothing beneath it. "There you are." Justice grabbed the cloak. It was wrapped around the Genealogy book. He pushed the book down into his waistband just as the door was blasted open. He pointed his wand, but never cast a curse as Hermione stepped into the doorway.

Chapter 38 – I love you, goodbye

"Hurry, more are coming."

"How did you? What are you doing here?"

"No time, let's go."

The two Death Eaters with Marcus were growing impatient. "It's been too long, something's wrong." one said.

"I'm going in." said the other. They exited the building they were hiding in and approached the bank's front door.

"Hang on guys." Marcus stood by the door but didn't follow. He closed his eyes and again could picture Griphook bringing him the cloak. He still felt everything was going to be okay. When he opened his eyes, he saw the two Death Eaters entering the bank. The goblins in the lobby were scampering back and forth as they were waking up from the effects of the sleeping gas bomb Hermione had set off when she arrived. She'd broken in and gotten it from Fred and George's shop before she followed Justice into the bank.

"Jean? How did you get here?"

"I stowed away in the trunk of the car."

"You were in the trunk all that time?" She nodded. He shook his head and couldn't help but smile. He noticed she was still wearing her cast. "Here, put this on." Justice handed her the cloak.

"I have one." she said pulling it up from her waist where it had been tied. "The resemblance is uncanny." she said as she inspected his 'Harry' face. "It's eerie actually."

"This is Harry's, cover up." he commanded and with a snap of his fingers he tried to turn invisible himself, but it didn't work where they were. The vaults were immune to the properties of wizard magic, but inside the hollow underground mountain that was the location of the mine's rail system, magic could only work in the form of curses from a wand. That's why, for most customers, wands were collected and kept in the lobby. Only the prestigious customers were allowed to keep them.

Justice could hear the voices and footsteps approaching. Hermione told him to get under the cloak with her. He reminded her they'd be exposed.

"I'll be fine. I'm glad to see you, but I wish you wouldn't have come." He pulled the cloak closed around her. "Don't take this off, no matter what, until you're back at Hogwarts. Okay?"

"I won't let you get hurt and I won't let you get caught." She turned and disappeared.

THE SEMIFINALS

The sun crested over the eastern horizon. There was a buzz of excitement throughout the school. The ministry officials began arriving and the Great Hall was decorated befitting the event. The matchups were set for the first round. The tryouts would pit house against house, but also friend against friend. It was each man for himself.

"Good morning ladies and gentlemen. Welcome to the semifinals. Scores have been tabulated and the seeding's are as follows. The eight seed is from Ravenclaw, Oz Gotschall. He will face the one seed from Gryffindor, Ronald Weasley. The seven seed is from Slytherin, Robyn Banks. She will face the two seed from Hufflepuff, Stormy Knight. The six seed is from

Hufflepuff, Reggie Fields and he will face the three seed from Ravenclaw, Alfredo Tejada. And in the final match of the first round the five seed from Gryffindor, Blaise Zabini will face the four seed from Slytherin, Emmerick Tepis. You two gentlemen, please take your place on the starting platform?" McGonagall requested.

The two men saluted one another. "As explained, this is a single elimination tournament. The winner will advance, the loser will retire. Good luck to both of you. Begin!" Pius instructed.

A curse flew by Justice's head. "***Defodio!***" His blast chipped off pieces of the rocky wall near the opening the guards were coming from. That gave him an idea. He touched his wand and said, '***Aladusuch, Temporus!***' For the rest of the time he was in the bank all of the spells he cast with his wand would be treated as Goblin magic. He pointed his wand. "***Aladusuch!!!***" A huge wave of water surged from each opening behind the guards for six levels. The waves washed about thirty guards and goblins from their tunnels and sent them free falling into the dark abyss below. He pointed his wand downward. "***Arresto Momentum! Aladusuch!***" He didn't want them dead, just out of his way. As he glanced downward toward them, he heard a sound coming from the level he was on then he was hit by a curse cast from the very top level. It knocked the glasses off his face, and he transfigured back to his normal appearance.

"*Fumos!*" He cast and gray smoke obstructed the view from above as the sound got louder and louder. He stumbled forward dazed and was dangerously close to the rails. The curses continued to fly blindly toward him as he shook his head to clear his thoughts. They got closer and closer and just before one struck the exact spot where he was standing, a rail car came whizzing by and he was snatched onto it.

"What the…"

"Are you alright?" Hermione asked as she pulled the cloak from over her head. "You shaved." She noticed. The curses couldn't keep up with the rail car, but the men casting them turned their focus on the tracks before them. Justice began returning curses. He covered her with the cloak where she'd be protected from curses and aimed his wand.

"*Come forth!*" He flicked his wand and down dropped the muleta and from it flew a mighty Griffin. He cast "*Baubillious,*" upward and a beam of white light shot out. The Griffin understood. It flew up and attacked the men on the top level. The rail car stopped at the lobby platform. The two of them got off and Hermione helped support him. They headed to the door, but just before they opened it Justice heard something.

"Stay behind me. I'll clear a path. You get to the door and go outside."

"I can help you. My magic will work now."

"No Jean, I have a bad feeling. Let me handle this, please. I couldn't stand to see you hurt."

"I won't get hurt, I'm ready to fight."

"I know, and I feel sorry for whoever you release your anger on. But trust me on this one, please."

She noticed he was trembling. "Okay, I'll go." She looked behind him and the Griffin was flying toward them. "Justice." She paused. "Um, Justice." She pointed as it got closer and closer. Finally, It was upon them. "Justice!"

Chapter 38 – I love you, goodbye

He pointed his wand and it exploded into a million pieces of confetti and was collected by the wand. Justice calmly entered the lobby. He'd cast a protection shield charm and it effectively deflected all the curses being sent his way. He finally released it once he saw the front door open and close. He cast a cascading jinx.

"***Stupify!***" All the goblins casting spells at him fell over. He kept his wand poised because he still felt a presence. He heard a whisper and his eyes locked on the marble column that hid the source. Justice pointed his wand and the column exploded knocking Creese to the floor with shards of marble stuck in his body. The second Death Eater stayed hidden, and Hermione pulled the cloak off. She'd never gone outside.

"Was that Focus Energy?" She cast a spell at a goblin behind Justice before it was able to throw its dagger. "See, I saved you again. We need to talk about that butterfly. Now aren't you glad…"

"LOOK OUT!!!" he screamed as the Death Eater charged out and stabbed her through with a sword. The blade entered her back and pierced through her stomach. Justice saw the blade poking through her body. Brighton stayed hidden behind her as he ripped the blade out.

The match was graceful. Technically flawless. Back and forth it went until finally it was announced, "Winner, Emmerick Tepis."

Match two saw Freddy's over aggressive style work against him as Reggie advanced easily. He shook Freddy's hand and took his place with Emmerick. Stormy and Robyn were very evenly matched from a 'skills' standpoint. They both wanted to win, and it was the slightest tactical error that ended the tournament for Robyn. As expected, fueled by loud cheering by his brother's Fred and George, who had just made it for the start of the match, Ron stuck to the game plan his trainers had laid out for him and he dispatched Oz rather quickly.

"The round two matchups will be as follows, Ronald Weasley will face Reggie Fields and Emmerick Tepis will meet Stormy Knight. The two winners will both advance to the finals but will face off in a head-to-head duel with the loser receiving a fifteen second penalty at the start of the second task. The two matches will take place simultaneously."

The building began to shake. "*Liquefy!*" A beam of blue light whizzed by Hermione's hair, even moving a few strands. Brighton began to swell then exploded like an overfilled water balloon. Hermione stood in shock. She turned to face Justice. Something wasn't right.

She lifted her shirt and looked at her stomach. There was no wound. She touched her stomach and back, there was no scar. It was as if it never happened. "How is this possible?" She looked up at Justice and saw a red stain growing larger just above his waist. He fell to his knees. She stood in shock.

Chapter 38 – I love you, goodbye

She ran over to him and caught him before he collapsed to the ground. She placed her hands on the wound, "I am so sorry. This is my fault. You told me to keep the cloak on. You told me to go outside. You told me not to come. You said goodbye and now I've gotten you..." She needed to stop the bleeding. She needed her wand but didn't want to release the pressure on the injury. She closed her eyes and decided to try a nonverbal spell. "***Vulnera Sanentur!***" Nothing happened. Her face showed her state of concern. He placed his hand on top of hers and blinked slowly. She tried again. "***Vulnera Sanentur!***" The blood stopped flowing out but didn't return to the body as intended. His goatee sprouted back onto his face indicating that parts of his body were healing more rapidly than others.

"Thank you."

"For what? I didn't heal you."

"No one could." He turned his head and coughed into his hand and saw blood. "That's new." He paused. "That was a goblin made sword. You did amazing to close the wound. You saved my life." He struggled to get up. "We've got to get out of here before anyone else shows up."

"Okay." He began to stagger forward, then paused, "Wait a moment, there's likely at least one more Death Eater out there. Griphook said they were waiting for him to bring out the cloak. These two were likely scouts that came in to see what was keeping him."

"So, let me go out under the cloak to see if I can find him. I owe you that."

"You don't owe me anything. No, I think I have a better idea, but I need you to please listen to me this time." He looked at his watch. "The duels will be starting in a few minutes. I need you to take the car and get back to the school. If you're caught out of bed, you'll be suspended, and we can't afford that right now."

"What about you?"

"I'll get there, trust me."

"Surely you're not planning to still compete. You're too weak."

"I have to. They want a show. Wait sixty seconds then walk straight to the car, get in and go. The return coordinates are already programmed in. Don't stop, don't look back. And no matter what you see, do not, intervene. Can you do that?" He paused, "For me?" She hugged him and looked into his eyes. He leaned down and kissed her. "I love you, Jean. Goodbye." He folded the cloak, placed it in a bag, turned and walked to the door. As the door opened, he transfigured into Griphook.

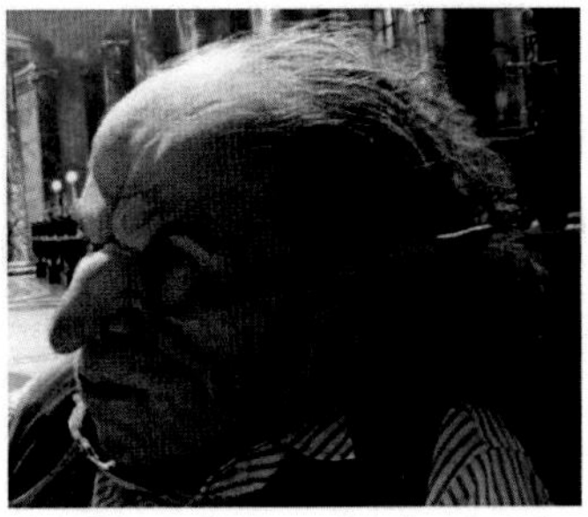

'I love you too'. she whispered and he heard her.

He began down the stairs with the cloak beneath his arm just as Marcus had seen. Marcus stepped out of the building and rushed up to him. Justice grew furious when he saw him.

"You got it. What took so long? Where are Creese and Brighton?"

"They're dead. They came in firing curses and the guards killed them. We need to go. The ministry will be here any moment."

"You're right. Give me the cloak."

"Perhaps it would be better if I held on to it until we get back."

Chapter 38 – I love you, goodbye

Hermione slipped out the front door and rushed to the car. She got in and the car took off immediately.

"Give me the cloak now, Griphook!" Marcus pulled his wand. Justice felt the same energy surge he had felt at the school. Marcus glanced down and noticed a blood stain growing beneath the goblin's shirt. Justice grabbed him around the throat and began to squeeze. As she ascended, she saw Marcus being choked. Then she saw him roll over on top of the goblin. Justice was too weak to subdue him. She tried to open the door, but it was locked. The windows didn't roll down either. She cast a spell at the window, but it couldn't penetrate through. She was helpless. She screamed out.

Marcus then began choking the goblin. The goblin's arms went limp and fell to his side. Marcus grabbed his knife, held it high above his head and said, "Now you die goblin. I'm taking the cloak to Draco." He thrust downward and Justice transfigured back to himself.

"***Aladusuch!***"

The knife blade hit is skin and shattered into dust. Justice reached up and grabbed Marcus' throat with one hand and slammed him to the ground. He climbed atop him.

"Justice?" Marcus said with a frightened look on his face. "I-I don't understand."

"Good idea." He placed his hand on Marcus' forehead. A silver light emitted from his palm and Marcus shook violently. "***Extract!***" he commanded and within moments Marcus was being stripped of his magical ability as well as his memories. Justice looked down at him. He could feel himself squeezing the life out of the boy. Just a few more seconds was all it would take for him to extinguish Marcus' life.

"I'm sorry Justice." Was the last thing Marcus said before his body went limp.

"Charista, I hate to ask, but I need a ride." Charista appeared.

"It would be my pleasure." She then noticed his condition,

"Oh my goodness."

"I've been worse." he replied.

She took his hand. "Where are we heading?"

"Hogwarts. I've got a tournament to complete in." He paused, "But I need to make one quick stop first." Together they disappeared.

The four participants bowed, and the matches began. Emmerick was the first to score a point, followed by Ron. Ron then took a two to zero lead as Stormy defended well to keep Emmerick from increasing his lead. Ron momentarily became overconfident and soon found himself even, two to two. Emmerick was clearly the most technically proficient, but Stormy used a balanced attack and constant pressure to avoid the upset and come from behind to win. Reggie had turned the tide and Ron, retreating in defense, fell backward and on his way down scored the winning point.

Pius enthusiastically announced the final would be Gryffindor versus Hufflepuff. Ron Weasley would be up against Stormy Knight. Neville was torn. He didn't want either to lose. He was, however, comforted by the fact that regardless of the outcome they would both be advancing.

Charista and Justice arrived in the chess room. She got him laid out on a table. "Don't move!" She disappeared and seconds later reappeared with Dobby.

Dobby looked him over. "Hello Dobby." Justice struggled to say to him.

"You can't even consider competing. You're hurt too badly. It would be insane." she stated.

He ripped open his shirt open so Dobby could access the wound. Charista stared intently and softly bit her lip. Justice noticed Dobby looking at her.

"You were stabbed with a Goblin-made blade. Justice Cain is very lucky indeed. You, Sir, should be dead."

"That's what they keep tellin' me." Dobby did what he could. "Thank you. I need to get cleaned up."

"I could help you in the shower…to the shower." she correcte4d herself. "I can walk you there."

"DOBBY will take Justice Cain to the showers." Dobby said sternly.

"You've both done enough. I can get myself to the shower. Charista, please go now. I shouldn't have called you. We can't let you get caught out of your room. We're gonna need you later, please."

Dobby nodded to her. "You can't compete, I mean it." She leaned down and kissed Justice on the lips. She smiled then vanished. Dobby glared at her. He then turned to Justice.

"Tabby is right, Sir; with rest you can recover. If Justice Cain doesn't let himself heal; he may not survive."

"Justice Cain doesn't have a choice. Thanks for coming."

"Justice Cain is a very extraordinary wizard."

"I'm just a guy with extraordinary friends and one of them is out there and he's in trouble. He's the one we all need to place our faith in. He needs my help." He reached into his waistband and grabbed the Genealogy book. "Dobby, can you destroy this book?" Before he got an answer, he absorbed the most recent information in it. "Oh my God."

"Yes sir. Dobby can destroy it. But why sir?"

"It's very dangerous to Harry Potter."

Hermione entered the room. "Justice." She ran to him and hugged him. "How are you? I saw you and Marcus…I tried to stop. I tried to come back…"

"I'm okay. It's okay. How are you?"

"Me? I'm fine thanks to you. You saved my life ***again***." She paused, "You did it when you touched us all in the library." He smirked and handed her the cloak.

"I know what happened with Harry. He attacked Wood and hid him in the Quidditch pitch somewhere. I have to find him." He scribbled a note and asked her to give it to Seamus.

"You're hurt. I'll go. I'll find him."

"No. I've got this. When I found Marcus, I was able to find out that he was helping Draco. I also think Draco is here or will be. They were plotting against Alucard. It's gonna be dangerous out there today. Please stay inside. I need you safe. I need to get to Harry. I know what I have to do. Where are the tryouts?"

Chapter 39 – The finals

"The final match is just about to start between Ron and Stormy. Someone said Harry is already on his way to the starting point."

"Okay, it's time." He blew as hard on his thumb as he could, but nothing happened. She grabbed his hand and blew. He cried out in agony. She burst into tears at the thought of him being in that much pain. He collapsed to the ground. "Thank you." he said to her then struggled to his feet. "Jean, please don't leave the castle." He leaned in and placed his forehead to hers. "And whatever you do, do not come to the final task."

"I found out what being bound to someone means." she whispered to him.

"We can talk about it when I get back."

She nodded. He walked out. Dobby took her hand. "Justice Cain will be alright Miss. Dobby is sure of it." Together they disapparated.

He put on fresh clothes then sprinted down to the Quidditch pitch. He ran right by Rita Skeeter. "Mr. Cain! Mr. Cain, we didn't think you were going to make it."

"Funny how that's always a thing."

"A quick word for my rabid readers?"

"No time, catch up to me later, gotta go change." He yanked his shirt off then suddenly caught a whiff of something odd. He slid to a stop. In the distance, he could hear Ms. Featherstone announcing the participants. She introduced Stormy first, as she had lost the duel to Ron and would be starting with a fifteen second disadvantage. Ron was announced to a rousing round of cheers from the Gryffindors. She announced Harry and the decibel level was off the charts. As the returning school champion, he was the odds-on favorite.

Justice turned and rushed up to Rita. He leaned in close

to her and sniffed. She blushed and grinned showing the red lipstick stuck to her teeth. "***Mr. Cain.***" He showed no interest as he continued to sniff the air. Then he stopped.

"Draco. He's here."

"What was that? Did you say Draco? As in Malfoy?"

"Excuse me." Justice began to follow the scent, but ran into McGonagall, Pius and Professor Hunt.

"Mr. Cain, why aren't you dressed for the final?" McGonagall asked.

"Hello again Justice. Welcome back." Professor Hunt said fondly. Justice smiled and nodded.

"They've already announced the other contestants. The event starts in less than a minute." added Pius.

"I'll be there." He continued to follow his nose into the supply room.

Rita and her quick quotes quill were hot on his heels and when he stopped and turned toward her, she was staring at him. "Oh my."

She snapped back to the task at hand and even she had to admit she began to smell something awful. She just figured it was old gym socks. Justice tracked it into a storage area and to a large chest that was covered with broomsticks and Quidditch pads. He could hear his name being announced. He shoved the items off the chest and found it padlocked. He pulled his wand as Rita came into the room. "*Cistem Aperio!*" The chest burst open and bound, down inside, was Oliver. Justice climbed down inside and pulled him out. His breathing was labored, and he looked dehydrated. "Ms. Skeeter, come here please." She was shocked at the discovery. She rushed over and was again startled by the sound of the cannon signifying the start of the event. Harry and Ron dove in side by side. The moment Harry hit the water he transformed into a dolphin and dove toward the lake floor to find a Gryffindor shield with the Gryffindor symbol on it as the first task. Ron transformed halfway into a shark, but then transformed back causing him to lose valuable time. He tried again, and completed the transformation then began his search.

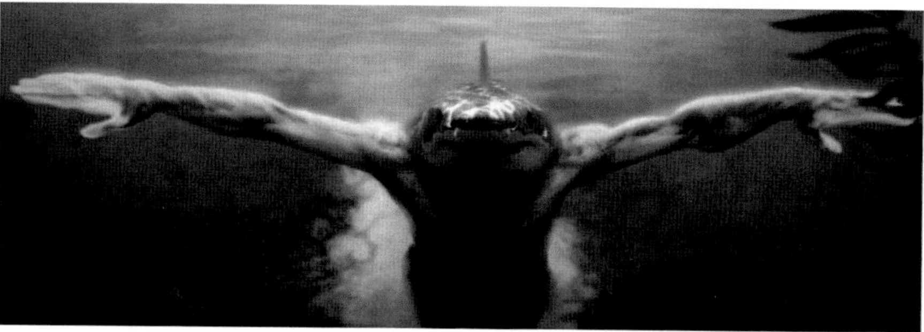

Justice grabbed the flower from the hat she was wearing and squeezed it in his hand. He held it over Oliver's mouth and drops of water began to fall onto his tongue. He gasped and Justice clapped his hands together and they made a thunderous sound then he rubbed them back and forth quickly. Once they began to glow, he placed one on Wood's forehead and one on his chest. Wood began to shake.

"What are you doing?" Rita asked. He had removed the incident from Wood's memory.

Jade and Cam ran into the room. They knew the sound

and what it meant. They moved Rita aside and Cam said, "I've got this, go!"

"You win this thing for all of us." Jade told him.

"Draco is here, on the grounds. Find him! I've got to go to Harry." Freddy stood in the doorway. Justice grabbed his shirt, "Freddy, find Jean."

"Who?"

"Hermione. Find her and don't let her out of your sight."

Without a word, Freddy ran off toward the castle. Justice heard the second cannon blast as he exited the dressing room signifying Stormy's start. She hit the water and transformed into a sea lion and darted through the water on her quest. Justice ran through the stadium and the students erupted. He streaked through the exit and down to the docks in a full sprint. He dove from about twenty feet away from the water and as he hit the water he transformed into a swordfish. It was perfect execution. At one point, he was fish underwater and human above.

"Amazing!" Pius said.

Chapter 39 – The finals

Justice swam by Stormy and searched for Harry. Harry had a huge lead. For most it would have been insurmountable, but Justice wasn't most.

AN UNINVITED GUEST

Hermione paced back and forth. She was so worried about Justice. She was riddled with guilt about what had happened. She wanted to be at the stadium to show support for all the participants. She had close ties to all of them, even Stormy, but Justice had been severely injured because she went against what he asked of her. She was determined to listen this time. She placed her Bearded Dragon, Camille, on her shoulder and went to the Great Hall. It was vacant in the castle with everyone at the competition. She was very tense. She didn't know how Justice was doing with his injury. How would it affect him?

Charista was pacing back and forth in her room as well. She too was worried about Justice. Dobby had come to her after leaving Hermione. As her father, he was concerned that she was emotionally vulnerable. He sensed her fondness for Justice and wanted to remind her that she was an elf. She looked human, but she wasn't, and he wanted to protect her.

Hermione began to flex the fingers on her healed, but casted hand. She sat down at a piano and began to play with one hand. She couldn't take it. Her arm was starting to itch beneath the cast anyway. She touched it with her wand, and it disappeared to the surprise of Draco who had in fact slipped onto the grounds and was watching her through a window, waiting to make his move. He was just about to enter the room when she began to play. The music filled the castle and Charista could hear it. She was drawn to it. She figured everyone was supposed to be at the tournament, so she took a chance and went to investigate. She entered the room quietly and concealed herself in a corner. Before long Nearly Headless Nick, Moaning Myrtle and even Peeves had found a place in the room and settled in to listen.

Harry had found the shield and accelerated through the murky depths. Ron was still struggling to find his shield. Stormy was drawing nearer to the concealed Hufflepuff item. Justice was gaining ground quickly, but knew he had to find the shield, or he wouldn't be allowed to continue and would lose Harry. He cut through the water like a warm blade through butter and spied the object. He speared it with his sword and soon found himself in Harry's wake. He momentarily lost focus as even underwater, he was able to hear and feel the music. He began to transform back into Harry. His hair grew straight, then he refocused and propelled himself forward. They were barely a third of the way through the first event and it was already a two-horse race.

Hermione rubbed her throat; it was feeling much better. She closed her eyes and began to speak to herself. 'Justice, I don't know if you can still hear me, but I wrote this for you. It's from the notes in my journal. I hope you like it'. She cleared her throat. Draco crept forward but hesitated when she began to sing.

"Sweet love, sweet love
Trapped in your love
I've opened up, unsure I can trust
My heart and I were buried in dust
Free me, free us
You're all I need when I'm holding you tight
If you walk away I will suffer tonight

Chapter 39 - The finals

I found a man I can trust
And boy, I believe in us

I am terrified to love for the first time
Can you see that I'm bound in chains?
I've finally found my way

I am bound to you, I am bound to you

Stormy found her shield and tried to make up some ground but was so far behind that when she saw Ron losing his focus and partially transforming back into his human form, she knew she had to help. Harry and Justice needed to surface for air and when they did more obstacles of the task became apparent. Kelpies and Kappas were visible on the surface and were blocking the path to the shoreline.

They were still half a mile out and with merpeople and grindylows below and these formidable water demons on the surface, this task suddenly had become very treacherous. Justice was distracted by her words. He was able to hear her as if he was sitting in the room beside her.

So much, so young, I've faced on my own
Walls I built up became my home
I'm strong and I'm sure there's a fire in us
Sweet love, so pure

I catch my breath with just one beating heart
And I embrace myself, please don't tear this apart

I found a man I can trust
And boy, I believe in us
I am terrified to love for the first time
Can't you see that I'm bound in chains?
I've finally found my way
I am bound to you
I am bound to

Stormy and Ron surfaced with Ron coughing trying to clear the water he had swallowed. Stormy used her wand to cast "***Periculum!***" sending red sparks high into the sky to signal their location. The song inspired Justice and with a burst of speed he charged at the Kelpies. The horses whinnied and thrashed as Justice sailed through the air up and over the line of defenders then dove down and maneuvered through and around the merpeople who were poised with their tridents. Harry followed him and before long they found themselves approaching the shore.

Suddenly the moment's here
I embrace my fears
All that I have been carrying all these years
Do I risk it all? Come this far just to fall?
Fall

Oh, I can trust and boy, I believe in us
I am terrified to love for the first time
Can you see that I'm bound in chains?
And finally found my way
I am bound to you

I am, ooh I am
I'm bound to you.

Harry was spent and crawled to shore. Justice was revitalized by the song. He used a burst of speed to propel himself out of the water and onto the shore. Harry got to his feet quickly. They each had a set of their fresh clothes with cloaks and shoes waiting, and they both began to change.

"Harry, we need to talk." Justice looked into his eyes and could tell he didn't seem quite right. He was especially fidgety, and he began to sniff the air searching for something. He found it when he looked down and noticed Justice's wound bleeding. Through this section of the course, they were restricted from apparating. They had to run, on foot, to the third and final stage. "Harry?" Justice looked at him. Harry opened his mouth and flashed a huge pair of glistening fangs. Justice held his hands out in front of him.

"Take it easy Harry. I know about the bite. I don't want to hurt you because I know this isn't the real you." Harry slashed at him with long claws and Justice was scratched on his neck and arms. He didn't take the full impact but could tell Harry's strength was amplified in this state. Justice took off running on the path and Harry gave chase.

Camille became very restless and scratched Hermione on the neck and arms to get off her. She ran across the top of the piano to the window. 'What was that about?' Hermione asked herself then suddenly saw a flash in her mind of Justice running and Harry chasing him. Camille clawed at the window until Hermione got up and walked over. Charista was standing in a dark corner of the room wiping away tears. She was moved by the song and was just about to go talk to Hermione when she was grabbed from behind by Draco. He placed a rag over her mouth, and she passed out without a fight. Hermione didn't notice as he dragged her outside of the room. Hermione began to feel as if Camille was sensing something as well, she opened the window and Camille crawled out. She pointed her wand, "*Engorgio*!"

Ron and Stormy followed the crowd to the bleachers surrounding the third stage. The labyrinth filled the Quidditch pitch. From the top, it looked like a lush green maze, but it held many secrets for Harry and Justice. Justice had built a sizable lead and could likely have just continued to the third stage and never looked back, but he began to feel himself losing energy. He was tiring and began to hear strange sounds and suddenly the air became thick, and the sky grew dark. He ran through a clearing and just as he was about to reach the other side. He heard Harry call out from behind him. "Justice! Help!" Was it a trick? Was it a trap? Justice stopped and looked back to see Harry had fallen and was surrounded by giant spiders. They seemed to be everywhere. Justice ran back toward him.

He pulled his wand, "*Arania Exumai*!" A stream of light shot from his wand and blasted the spiders away. He ran to Harry and extended his hand. Harry took it and stood up revealing that he had a slightly twisted ankle. They stood back-to-back.

Chapter 39 – The finals

"Got any suggestions?" Harry asked. Justice thought about a way out. There were just so many of them, hundreds. They were everywhere.

"I'll try to draw them off. When I do, you run." Justice spun and landed on all fours in the form of the wolverine. He snarled and pawed at the ground then charged at the closest ones. He bit them and rolled over avoiding being bitten or stung, but there were still too many of them.

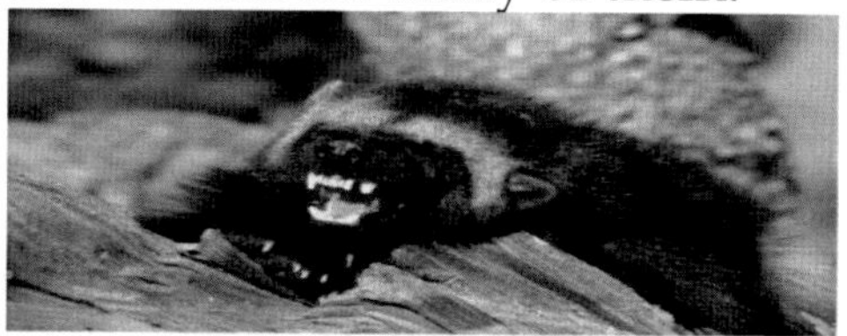

On his ankle, Harry wasn't going to make it out. He began casting "*Flipendo!*" which knocked them aside, but reinforcements continued to arrive. The situation was becoming dire when Justice transformed back into his normal form.

"We need some more help. Get close to me." He pointed his wand, flicked it and the muleta dropped down. "Get ready to run!" With a wave, a large Graphorn charged out. It immediately charged through the barrier of spiders,

trampling them. "GO!" Justice demanded and Harry followed them. As he reached the edge of the clearing safely, he glanced back and saw the wall of spiders shut behind him once again sealing Justice in. He hesitated before trying to conjure a firestorm. "No Harry, you'll set the whole forest on fire. I have a better idea. GO!"

Harry turned to run and some of the spiders tried to follow. They stopped in their tracks when they heard a thunderous sound approaching. Trees began to topple. Harry was just able to dive out of the way when the Graphorn came charging back. 'That's odd'. Justice thought. "It looks frightened. But what could have…" he began shouting to Harry then saw Camille the size of a school bus charging into the clearing.

She shot out a huge sticky tongue and began eating the spiders. They crawled all over her, but her hide was too tough for their stingers to penetrate. Justice pointed his wand and the Graphorn was absorbed back into it. They now seemed to ignore Harry completely and he decided to go for help. Finally, the largest spider of them all, Mosag, mate of Aragog, began to descend from the trees above. She was the reason for the darkness of the sky. Justice thrust his wand upward and cast, "***Fianto Duri, Protego Maxima***!!!" Some of the smaller spiders tried to run out and disintegrated on impact with the shield. Justice had also unknowingly sealed out Cam and Jade who had come to help.

Chapter 39 – The finals

Camille shook and flung the spiders off her. Some of them flew against the barrier and disintegrated. The rest gathered behind the large Acromatula, and she began to stalk them. Justice realized she was large enough to do damage to Camille, so he pointed his wand, "*Reducio!*" Camille shrunk down and ran to him. He cast, "*Erecto Duro, Aladusuch!*" A small stone cage appeared, and he placed her inside. The spiders were drawing nearer. He rubbed his hands together and produced a piece of parchment from thin air. He tossed it into the air causing the spider to jump back momentarily. They began to advance again, and the moment the parchment hit the ground, Justice extended his hand and said, "*Come forth!*" The three Zowls that Demetria had drawn for him literally popped up right off the page.

Three large wolf-like creatures stood poised facing the spiders. The first, Blaze, had fire burning on the tip of his tail. He flicked his tail, and the fire was flung toward them searing a patch of them instantly. The other two, Bolt and Blizzard shot streams of electricity and shards of ice, respectively. The spider's numbers were dwindling rapidly.

Once there was just a handful left the rest began to scurry away back up into the trees. Those that ventured too high were disintegrated. The others stayed put in the canopy.

The large Acromatula stood her ground and despite the three magical creatures all concentrating their special gifts upon her she refused to give ground. Justice recalled them to the page when she began to spit venom at them. "Okay, I've got something special for you." He dropped down the muleta and said, "***Come forth!***" The Nundu emerged from it and the huge spider began to retreat. The Nundu gave chase following it into the trees and pouncing on it. They both fell to the ground. The Nundu exhaled and toxic gas surrounded the spider. It began to feel the effects immediately and the Nundu wasted no time attacking. Once it had completely subdued the beast it turned its attention onto Justice. He spun and transformed into the wolverine and stood his ground. The Nundu snarled and growled in triumph, then lied down. Justice transformed back and pointed his wand. The Nundu was once again absorbed into it. "***Finite Incantatem!***" The barrier disappeared and Jade and Cam ran to his side.

"Are you alright?" Jade asked.

"I'm fine."

Cam noticed the blood dripping from his shirt and the scratches on his neck and arms. "You don't look alright."

"This was from earlier. Has Harry finished?"

"No, it's still a long way from here to the third stage." she replied.

"Then I've gotta go."

"Justice, I don't think this was a coincidence. As an Alpha, they put me in charge of security. You were right, as always, I'm not ready. There's an issue, but we're on it."

"What she's trying to say about this situation is they told us about all of the planned booby traps and this wasn't one of them."

"What's going on? Is everyone alright? Did you find

Demetria?"

"No, actually…" he hesitated.

"Who else is missing?" They could tell he was growing truly angry.

"She's fine, Freddy found her." Jade said, knowing Hermione was who he was most concerned about.

"We'll take care of it. You finish." Cam reasoned.

"I'm going to finish because there is something I have to deal with right now, after that the three of us are going to dance." He looked them both in the eyes then ran off. He could have taken the information from them if he wanted to, but he could feel himself growing weaker and he still needed to deal with Harry. When Harry emerged from the forest line limping, but first, the crowd cheered. Rita had only told Pius and McGonagall about Wood. McGonagall wanted to stop the tournament immediately, but Pius wouldn't hear of it. Harry made it to his broom and flew into the maze. Justice came running out of the forest and jumped straight onto his broom. McGonagall and Mallory both saw the blood and Mallory ran down, grabbed a broom and flew into the maze behind them. They ducked and dodged and avoided the Tentacula vines that were lashing out at them. The corners were sharp, and the high hedges made it almost impossible to tell when you were facing an actual dead end. The rules, however, stated that you would be severely punished if your feet touched the ground within the boundaries of the stage. Pius and McGonagall were curious why Dolores chose not to be present for the event since she was the one who had designed the labyrinth.

Justice could smell Harry. He knew he was drawing ever closer to him. He'd used ***Agua Eructo*** to wash away the blood from his wound to mask the scent, but the wound continued to bleed, and he continued to lose energy. He had the ability to heal quickly but had sustained so many injuries on top of having placed the protections on Hermione, Mallory, and Charista that it was taking longer and longer to recover.

"Excuse me Minister, this urgent message just arrived for you." said Professor Sprout.

The minister read the note then handed it to McGonagall. She looked heartbroken. "Surely you don't believe this, do you?"

"Minerva, I have no choice. An accusation has been made and it must be followed up." Dozens of ministry guards began to emerge at the entrances and exits.

Harry ran into a dead end. He pulled back on his broomstick and when he turned around there were five Dementors swooping down on him. Ice formations kept him from pulling his wand as one by one they took turns approaching him and sucking the life force from his body. Justice found him and cast a patronus that drove them away. Mallory saw what happened and noticed Harry was about to fall off his broom. She swept in low and caught him as he slumped over. His weight forced her to land to support him. The ground was crawling with Runespoor. They were striped orange and black three headed serpents.

Of the three heads only the one on the right was extremely venomous, but with so many, it was impossible to keep track of which was which. Justice released Blizzard, the ice Zowl. Runespoor were a favorite food of that species as they were immune to the venom. Justice slowly moved forward as the

Chapter 39 – The finals

Zowl cleared a path and Harry glanced up in time to see a Dementor coming up behind Justice. He cast his patronus and the stag charged out. Justice turned in time to see the Dementor driven away. He turned back to thank Harry and saw one of the vines lash out and cut Mallory on the neck. No blood appeared from her wound but did drip from Justice's neck.

"Oh no, Harry!"

Harry smelled the blood, and his claws and fangs sprang out. Pius cast "***Deletrius!***" and the hedges and magical creatures vanished, all but the Zowl. Harry lunged at Mallory, but Justice cast "***Everte Statum!***" and knocked Harry away from her. Harry scrambled to his feet and grabbed Mallory again. He used her as a shield between himself and Justice.

Pius tried to cast "***Expelliarmus***" at Justice, but the Zowl jumped in its path and blocked the spell. Everyone could see what was unfolding. Justice cast a transparent shield around the three of them. He wasn't strong enough to shade it. They could be seen, but no one could get in. Hermione ran up and McGonagall screamed to her, using ***Sonorus,*** not to touch the shield. Pius cast a Shield Penetrating spell at it, but Justice countered with an Unbreakable Charm and Pius' spell just bounced off. Justice pointed his wand and Blizzard turned toward them.

"Let her go Harry. This is between you and me." Harry didn't respond. It was as if he couldn't even hear him. "HEY!!!" Justice shouted and got his attention. Mallory grabbed Harry's wand and slipped out of his grasp. Blizzard ran and jumped and knocked them both back and knocking off Harry's glasses. Justice seized the opportunity to cast a barrier between them. She was safe with Blizzard outside of the barrier. Justice put away his wand. "Alright, I'm right here. You want me, come and get me." Harry's face began to contort then he charged and leapt at him.

Justice caught both his arms at the wrist and held him at bay. Harry's aggression gave Justice added strength. He stood him straight up then wrapped his leg around Harry's and tripped him. He forced Harry's arms to cross his body and used them to block Harry's mouth from trying to bite.

Justice looked into his eyes, "Harry I can help you."

Suddenly Harry had a burst of energy and flung Justice off him. He ran to attack and Justice rolled over, sweeping Harry's legs out from under him. Justice scrambled over and forced his arm beneath Harry's chin then locked him in a rear naked choke position. Harry clawed at his arms, but Justice gritted his teeth and tightened his grip. Harry was on the verge of passing out when Justice released him and pushed him aside. He choked and gagged, grabbing his throat.

Justice released the barrier and pointed his wand. "***Return!***" he commanded and the Zowl ran and jumped back into it.

"Justice Cain! You are under arrest!" stated Pius.

Harry sprang to his feet and ran at Justice. Hermione shouted, "Look out!" Justice spun and in one motion and plunged his wand into Harry's chest.

Everyone gasped. Harry fell back onto the ground and lied motionless. Madam Pomfrey rushed toward him. Justice placed his foot on Harry's chest. "***Tergeo, Aladusuch!***" Fluid squirted out of the exposed end of the wand to the onlooker's horror. He pulled the wand out and wiped it clean. Madam

Chapter 39 – The finals

Pomfrey placed her hand on Harry's throat then turned to Pius and McGonagall with a look of shock on her face. Hermione covered her mouth. Ron's mouth fell open in disbelief. Justice placed his wand lengthwise between his palms and whispered, '*Geminio*', then pressed his palms together until the entire wand disappeared. He pulled his hands apart and his wand erupted into a ball of flame. He whispered, '*Reducto!*' and the ball burst into particles and then went out.

Pius cast a body bind curse and wrapped Justice up. "Guards! Escort Mr. Cain to Nurmengard. You are charged with the murder of Harry James Potter and the abductions of both Dolores Umbridge and Charista McDonald."

"Charista?" he shouted. "What are you talking about?"

Hermione approached him holding Charista's gloves. "She's gone. We can't find her anywhere." Dobby stood silent with tears in his eyes.

"You were late to the first event this morning Mr. Cain. That was the last time Dolores was seen. Where were you?"

"He was with me, all night." Jade blurted without hesitation. The announcement drew some very strange reactions, including a high five from Freddy and Cam.

'You wish'. Hermione thought to herself.

"No, I wasn't. Thanks Jade, but I don't need you to lie for me. I have no alibi, but I wasn't with her."

"Take him away." said Pius. "Tell no one of this."

"Wait!" shouted Professor Hunt. "Justice Cain. As

Alpha Selection Committee Chairperson, it is my duty to administer judgment for this offense. You have brought disgrace on the American contingent for the last time. As set forth in the bylaws of our decree, you are hereby banished from our coven and as described in your oath, you must now suffer 'The Reconciliation'. Alphas, what say you?"

One by one the remaining Alphas stepped forward and shouted, "AYE!" Jade agreed reluctantly and Cam didn't speak.

"You are to be stripped of your magical ability. Present your wand." Justice tilted his head back and extracted a wand from his throat. He handed it to her. She held it aloft for all to see, pointed her wand and said, "*Reducto!*" The wand disintegrated. "Bow!" she commanded. He complied.

"NO! YOU CAN'T DO THIS!!!" Hermione shouted. Ron held her. Mallory went to comfort her.

"Here, you should have this." She handed Hermione Harry's wand.

The professor placed her hand on Justice's head, '*Aladusuch*', and light began to pass between them. The American Elders stood and looked on intently. The light stopped and he slumped to the ground. She took a step back. Hermione didn't want to look, but once she did, she couldn't turn away.

The guards grabbed hold of him. He looked around and found Hermione and he winked at her. "Justice!" she shouted. She ran to him and hugged him. She slipped the invisibility cloak beneath his cloak. Two by two the guards apparated. Hermione ran off toward the Owlrey.

Neville glanced down then reached into his pocket and when he pulled his hand out Justice's wand was in it with a note wrapped around it. He shoved it back in as he looked around to see if anyone else noticed. He pulled it out and it looked as if it was filled with some type of fluid. He unscrewed the top of the wand and smelled the contents. He recognized it. He immediately looked down at Harry.

"He's not dead." Neville shouted as he put the wand away. He ran down toward Harry as everyone looked on. Mallory bent down and looked at Harry's hands. The nails were normal and surprisingly well manicured. She opened his mouth and there were no fangs. Neville ran to Harry. "He's been petrified." Neville opened Harry's mouth and poured in some of the fluid from the wand. Within seconds Harry opened his eyes and sat up. Pius yanked open his shirt and there was no sign of a puncture wound.

"Madam Pomfrey?" Pius asked for her opinion.

She looked him over. "I'll have to take him back to the infirmary for a more comprehensive examination, but he appears to be fit as a fiddle."

"Perform your exam. As for the rest of you, Hogwarts is on immediate security lock down. Students, you will follow your prefects to your houses and be counted. I want everyone accounted for in thirty minutes, now move!"

McGonagall addressed the staff. "The staff will convene in the Great Hall in thirty-five minutes to be briefed."

"That's enough Minerva. The ministry has had its eyes on Mr. Cain for some time now. Ever since the Americans arrived these abductions have been occurring. It is documented that on several occasions he has been out of his room after hours and he has left the grounds without authorization. He has assaulted multiple students and staff. This is clear cut. I will not reverse my decision. He is to be held at Nurmengard until his tribunal and that's final. Address your staff. Let them know no one is to leave the grounds without Ministry approval."

"You're making a mistake. You know the prophecy. You know he's back and is planning a war. Sending that boy away leaves us vulnerable to attack."

"You're right. A mistake has been made, appointing you as Headmistress. However, that's one mistake I can fix right now. You're fired. You have one week to vacate your office. Hanover Crisp will take over as acting Headmaster." he said as he left the room.

Hermione and Ron sat at Harry's bedside during his examination. "Guys, I'm fine. I feel great actually."

"How did he do that? I saw with my own eyes, he stabbed you in the chest. His entire wand went into your body." Ron questioned.

"It must have been one of his illusions." Harry reasoned.

"But there was blood, your blood, squirting out onto the ground like a bloody fountain."

"There's something else. I think Justice wanted to be sent to Nurmengard." Hermione added.

"Are you barkin? Who would want to be sent to a wizard prison?" Ron asked. "Twice."

"He went to Azkaban on purpose." she retorted, "And

when Professor Hunt stripped him of his powers, she used his spell."

"So?" Harry replied.

"He once told me that he was the only adult human who could perform the spell and that if I ever heard anyone else use it, he'd either given them that power, or it would be ineffective. I think they may have planned that."

"With that guy, you never know. Nothing ever seems to surprise him." Harry conceded.

"So, what do we do? Even if he meant to go to Durmstrang, what good does it do if he's in the prison?" asked Ron.

"On the other hand, what if it ***was*** real? What if he has been stripped of his powers?" What was that about? Without his powers, he'd be a sitting duck in that prison. Either way, we have to get him out of there." stated Harry.

"Really?" Hermione asked.

"Of course. He's one of us." He paused. "Besides, if it was staged, I'm finally starting to realize that to defeat Alucard we'll need his abilities. You two better get going. As soon as I'm released, I'm going to go see McGonagall about Justice and the tournament."

"You're not still thinking about competing, are you?" she asked.

"No, but it may be a way to get to the school."

Ron and Hermione got up and started for the door. "I'll go talk to Professor Hunt." said Hermione. "Oh, by the way," she handed him his wand. "Try not to lose this again."

Ron opened the door and walked blindly into Hagrid's enormous girth. "Ron, what're you doin' ere? You're supposed to be in yer common room countin the students."

"I did." He pulled out a list with the head count. "I just

had to check on Harry."

Hagrid looked up. "Ermione, 'Arry."

"Hello Hagrid." they replied.

"Git to yer house and don't let anybody see, understood? Use yer cloak."

"I don't have it."

"What do you mean?"

"Long story."

Hagrid stepped aside to let him go by. "And the staff is gatherin, so you'd better get a move on." he told Hermione. "Hope yer up and about soon." he told Harry and continued to find Madam Pomfrey.

Hermione sat in the gathering and inched her way toward Professor Hunt. "Professor?"

"Hermione dear, call me Dani."

"Dani, the ceremony with Justice?"

"Yes. I know that was difficult for you to witness."

"I know it was staged." Dani looked at her. "The spell you used," she paused hoping the Professor would simply offer up an explanation, but none seemed to be forthcoming.

"What about it?"

"I know what it does." She paused. "And what it doesn't."

Professor Hunt turned to face her. "***Muffliato***." She leaned in close, "You really are the brightest witch I've ever met. How many other people know?"

"Just Harry and Ron."

"Did it look convincing enough?"

"Yes, for the students and staff here, but I figured it out..." She paused, "Why risk it, there, in front of everyone like that?"

Chapter 40 – Nurmengard

"It was his idea. He needed everyone to think it was real. He's not sure who can be trusted."

"So, what's his plan?"

"Plan? Its Justice. He makes it up as he goes."

"If it wasn't his powers, what did he transfer to you?"

"What do you mean?"

"The flow of the transfer went from him to you, not the other way around."

"You are extraordinary. You don't miss a thing."

"I missed Charista being taken."

"That wasn't your fault. Whoever took her came through the school's security and through all of us. They are very skilled and very motivated."

"So, what was it?"

"My memories of him. He'd wiped them from me just in case I was abducted. He wants to protect me. He wants to protect us all."

"Can he? Is he that powerful?"

"Justice is the most unique Warlock I've ever known. His potential is limitless. He draws power from his enemies. He draws power during battle, that's why he's never been beaten. He has weapons they don't, but during battle he can take from you what you do best and then use it against you. Can he defeat Alucard? I don't know. Alucard is unlike any previous Dark Lord. Then there's the prophecy."

"You've seen it?"

"Yes, it's a requirement of being a member of the Elder council. The members of our coven share a bond. Justice has been entrusted with keeping the sanctity of that bond. It's an enormous burden he chose to bear. He and he alone has the power to save us all."

"But every sacrifice he makes for us makes him weaker."

"You can't tell him that. Hermione dear, there are still a lot of things you don't know about him. Things that make the future you envision for the two of you impossible."

"What do you mean?"

"When we're done here meet me in my office. I'll explain."

NURMENGARD

Pius arrived at Durmstrang shortly after Justice. He walked into a dimly lit room where Justice sat surrounded by a dozen guards.

"Leave us." he commanded. The guards left the room. Justice sat, head down, bound with magical chains. "You are quite the enigma Mr. Cain. It is difficult to know where your true loyalties lie."

"I know the feeling."

"Did you have anything to do with any of the abductions that have occurred?"

"Aren't I supposed to have an attorney present?"

"Answer me, or I'll have to use other means."

'This ought to be good'.

"What did you say?"

"Nothing, look, I'm just as concerned about the people who are missing as you are. I didn't have anything to do with any of them being taken, but if you let me go, I'll find out who did."

Chapter 40 – Nurmengard

"I see." Pius withdrew his wand. "***Legilimens!***" Pius focused his attention but saw nothing. He tried again, "***Legilimens!!!***" He saw flashes of light and flickering, but there were no images. "***LEGILIMENS!!!***" he shouted. "This can't be right."

Justice looked up at him. "Your nose is bleeding." Pius pawed at it. Blood was flowing freely. "Perhaps it's because my powers were taken from me. Have you ever performed this spell on a muggle?"

"Silence!" Pius snapped. He was frustrated at not being able to extract any information. Justice, on the other hand, had read dozens of Pius' memories and was at least able to see that while Pius was aware Alucard was back, he at least, was not feeding him information. He really didn't know if Justice had been involved in the abductions but wasn't going to confront Alucard about it. His intension was to keep Justice confined until he needed him, then attempt to unleash him against Alucard. He simply didn't see Justice as as big a threat as Alucard. Pius was frustrated. He pointed his wand, "***CRUC..***"

The door flew open, "Are you alright Minister? I heard elevated voices." said a guard in a slow paced, low tone. His face was covered by a full helmet.

"How dare you disturb me during an interrogation!"

"My apologies," the guard bowed. Justice looked up.

"Where are the others?"

"Tending to other prisoners. With all transfers from Azkaban there's barely room left."

"Fine." He turned to Justice. "I'll deal with you later. Take him to his cell."

"Yes Minister." The guard cast a body bind curse and ropes extended to and around Justice. "Move!" commanded the guard. Without a word, they made it all the way to the very top level of the prison. The room wasn't even a cell. It was a storage closet that was being fitted with an enchanted door. A worker had a broom sweeping the floor on one side while a torch was welding the door's hinges. There was a tiny window, about 6 inches by 1 foot in the wall and a 1 foot by 4-inch slot in the door that they could slide food through. When the guard swung the door open, the broom was trapped behind it. "Hurry up! The cell is need, now!" said the guard.

"I'm almost done." said the worker.

"Does door work?"

"Yes, I just need to finish cleaning."

"He is prisoner, not guest, leave it. I finish, Go!" The worker walked out. The guard shoved Justice into a corner. He released the binds and walked to the door. "Door is enchanted. Once it is close, whatever touch door turn to stone. Don't touch door."

"Thanks Viktor." The guard turned to him and nodded. "How did you know I was coming?"

"Mionee send letter." He held it up. "You can see pitch from window. You will know when they arrive."

"Viktor, something bad is about to go down here. You have to get as many of the people as you can off the campus as quickly as you can."

"Why? What are you going to do?"

"It's not me. You're a historian. I know that from when I touched you on the island. A Dark Wizard is coming to perform a cleansing here."

"How you know this?"

"Because I'm here to stop it."

Harry was waiting on the stairs to McGonagall's office when she walked up. "Mr. Potter, what are you doing here?

Chapter 40 – Nurmengard

You should be in bed."

"Headmistress, Justice is innocent. We can't leave him in prison."

"Since when do you care about Mr. Cain? The two of you were trying to kill one another a few hours ago. One of you succeeded."

"He wasn't trying to kill me. He was trying to heal me. And yes, he succeeded."

"Mr. Potter, I'm glad to have you back, but I'm not sure there's anything I can do for you. I've been sacked. Mr. Crisp is going to be your new Headmaster."

"They can't do this."

"They can and they have. Besides, it's not as if I could send you to Nurmengard."

"No, but what about the tournament? It starts the day after tomorrow."

"The minister would never allow you to still compete. You didn't win the tryouts."

"But I didn't lose either and as the previous champion I have an automatic entry. The rules are absolute, the Goblet of Fire makes the selections, and they constitute a binding magical contract. Not even the Minister can overturn it."

"Go on."

"The selections are made tomorrow morning. If my name is put into the cup, the Goblet must select me and allow me to compete."

"We just have to figure out how to get your name put in."

"The two people who could get in and out aren't here." He paused, "What if ***you*** went?"

"The order to keep me out would have gone out the moment the Minister left Hogwarts and with Dobby out looking for Charista…"

"How's he handling this?"

"He was inconsolable."

"We have to get out of here."

"Pius placed a restriction on the grounds. No one can apparate in, out, or within the grounds. All communication is cut off. Not even owls can get out at this point."

"I'll think of something." He turned to leave.

"Potter."

"Yes Headmistress?"

"Good luck."

"Luck, that's it." He reached into his pocket and pulled out a vial of Felix Felicis. "Neville gave it to me before I left for the Inaugural Quidditch Tournament. Obviously, I never used it. He made it himself." He lifted it to his lips and drank.

"How do you feel?"

"Brilliant." he replied, "Professor, may I use the pensive?"

"Of course." She gestured him in its direction.

He retrieved the vial Aberforth had allowed them to take before he died. Harry poured the silvery liquid in and submersed his face.

Crisp came into the office. "What are you still doing here?" he asked McGonagall.

She headed him off, so he didn't see Harry. "This is still my office until I've removed all of my things." With an inconspicuous wave of her wand, the door to the closet that concealed the pensive, closed. Crisp began further into the office. "Mr. Crisp! You may have been named acting Headmaster, but these are my students. If any harm comes to them…" Harry pulled his head out the pensive and was just about to pull the door open to tell McGonagall what he'd seen

Chapter 40 – Nurmengard

when he heard raised voices.

"That sounds a lot like a threat."

"You better believe it's a threat." She paused, "As outgoing Headmistress I am entitled to one final decree. Harry Potter is to be allowed to compete in the Triwizard Tournament."

"That's out of the question!" Crisp snapped back. "He'd never…"

"***Imperio!***" Harry cast.

"Of course, Minerva, I will honor your wish, provided his name is drawn from the cup."

"And as is customary he will be allowed ten members for his entourage and two chaperones."

"Now that…"

"***Imperio!***" Harry cast.

"Is of course customary." The two of them left the room. Harry slipped out shortly after. He met with Ron, and they put together a list of the people he wanted to take with him to the tournament.

"Demetria, Marcus and Charista are missing. Jade and Cam are Alphas now and wouldn't be allowed to go." Ron pointed out.

"That's fine. We'll take Neville and Stormy, Blaise, Reggie, Freddy, Dean and Seamus."

"With me and Hermione that leaves one spot and two chaperones."

"I figured I'd ask Emmerick, and we'll need Ms.

Featherstone. Hermione seemed to feel Professor Hunt has some kind of direct link to Justice, so she might come in handy."

"That Emmerick is a creepy bloke. You sure you wouldn't rather have Robyn Banks?"

"Yes Ron, I know. She's cute, but I want creepy. We'll stick with Emmerick. You check with each of them first thing in the morning. Now we just have one detail left."

"Getting your name into that cup."

THE VISION

Hermione and Dani sat in her office and the door slowly opened. "Professor Trelawney?" Hermione questioned.

"Yes dear, it's me. Professor Hunt asked me here to share with you a vision that's been haunting me for weeks now. It's growing clearer and more intense with each passing day."

"What is it?"

"Come." She motioned for Hermione to sit at a table beside her. She placed a Crystal ball in the center of the table. The three of them joined hands. "Clear your mind. Prepare yourself my dear. The images are quite disturbing."

The crystal sphere on the table began to glow and suddenly it cast a beam of light toward the ceiling. It showed Justice grabbing a hooded figure by the throat. The figures face could not be seen. Then it showed the hooded figure's hands. The nails on the fingers were an inch long each and pointed. In one violent thrust it plunged the nails into Justice's torso, to Hermione's shock and moments later Justice released the figure and bowed his head down.

"NO!!!" Hermione screamed snatching her hands away

from the two teachers. Professor Trelawney was in a trance-like state and didn't even notice. The image disappeared the moment the connection was broken. "That image is wrong. Justice made me a promise."

"He made our coven a promise as well." Dani turned to Sybill and snapped her fingers. The Professor blinked several times and looked around.

"I'm sorry dear, were you saying something?"

"No. We're fine. Thank you."

"Oh, okay. Good day." She walked out.

"Hermione, there's something I need to tell you about Justice. He's even more unique than you know. He was born with a gift. The powers he possesses were inside him all along. He was born with a purpose."

"I know, he's an offset."

"He and Harry share many bonds. They are the same. They're both offsets, they're both burdened with the protection of their coven. They were created to stop the Dark Lord from winning the war and forever changing the wizard community."

"But Harry already defeated a Dark Lord, Voldemort."

"Voldemort was a test. There is only one true Dark Lord. Use your logical mind. Why do you think he's has lived through all other Dark Lords? Harry and Justice were born in the same year. There were ten others as well, all with a common fate, to fight the most powerful Warlock in our history. This event is unprecedented. This is the war to end all wars. This threat only fears one thing, age.

He is aging at a rate that will not kill him but will render him ineffective at a point in the near future. He cannot stop it; he cannot reverse it. However, he made a deal with the one person who can. If he wins, if he fulfills his commitment to that person, he will receive the gift of true immortality."

"I don't understand. He is immortal, how else could he have lived this long, and where are the others?"

"He's not immortal yet, he's enchanted. The others have been hunted down, one by one and killed. Only four are still alive and now that Justice got himself sent to Nurmengard all four will be in one place at the same time. It plays right into his hands, but I've learned to trust Justice's instincts. This entity is the Lord of Lords. He too is unique. When he kills, he absorbs the years of his victims, unfortunately for him, it just extends his life, it doesn't stop him from aging. He's figured out a way to maintain his strength by drinking the blood of pureblood wizards. But if he achieves his goal he will be rewarded with the gift of eternal youth. He will be strong; he will be young, and his reign will last forever."

"How can Justice defeat him? Do the others know they're offsets?"

"I doubt it, but it's possible. The others would have had handlers as well."

"Handlers?"

"Yes, I was assigned to Justice when he was born."

"So, you meeting him on the street and taking him in wasn't a coincidence?"

"He told you about that?"

"Sort of." She paused, "So if you were assigned to protect him why did you wait until he was older to take him in?"

"It was safer for him. He didn't know he had powers until

he was eight years old, so he wasn't targeted. You-know-who knew of some of the offsets right away and got rid of them immediately. I'm sure he always had an eye on Harry but didn't see him as as big a threat. Harry is different from the rest. He doesn't have the killer instinct the others do. He's always needed help to survive. Justice was the second born that year and is by far the strongest. As far as knowing he was an offset, he just found out not long ago, but I think he's always felt it, inside."

"Do you know who the others are?"

"No. Not for sure, for their safety. We have been keeping an eye on one that we suspect is the first born. Her skills are off the charts and once she and Justice were brought together and there was a definite chemistry."

"She?"

"Yes, she's a student at Beauxbatons Academy."

"Rochelle Maynard."

"How did you know?" Hermione rolled her eyes when her suspicions were confirmed.

"I met her. She mentioned she knew Justice and it just all fits now. I mean, I understand. She's quite lovely and seemed nice. She plays Quidditch."

"No, no, don't do that. You don't have to worry about her, trust me. I was out of line when we met, and I tried to steer you away from Harry. I did it for your own good. I know what these guys are facing, and I didn't want you to get hurt. I had no idea you would have the effect on Justice that you have."

"What do you mean?"

"Justice has a magnetism that's undeniable. Every woman he's met has fallen victim to it, trust me, I know. It's not his fault. But he's the sincerest young man you'll ever meet. He cares for everyone which is unfortunately his Achilles heel. He's been tempted by many ladies over his years with the coven, but he's never let them get too close."

"What about Jade?"

"What relationship those two ever had has always been exaggerated by Jade. He was always respectful and careful with her feelings, but she has her own agenda. He loves her and she's in love with the idea of them being together."

"And Rochelle?"

"You know, on the surface I'd have thought that if anyone would have had a chance, it may have been her due to what they share, but he was the perfect gentlemen as always. No, he was all business. I can't be sure she was spared though."

"When did they meet?"

"She stayed with us for a while and competed in the American version of the Triwizard Tournament. She gave him a run for his money."

"I see. She mentioned that she had heard of me."

"I'm sure her guardian told her about you. The information we were given was on Harry. His name doesn't get mentioned without yours, but I edited the information, I didn't let him read about it himself. I dare not let him get his hands on any of the written materials. The thing is, you've gotten in. He reacts to you differently than he's ever reacted with anyone before. It just concerns me that fate is not on your side, timing wise. Justice has an obligation that…"

"That should never have been his burden to bear." They both turned to see a person standing in a dark corner. They could tell from the voice that it was a woman. However, her face was covered by her cloak's hood. They both drew their wands. "Put your wands away. I'm no threat to you."

"You again? Who are you?" Dani asked as she stepped in front of Hermione.

"Now that's ironic. You stand in front of a powerful witch as if you care for her wellbeing, but you haven't told her why Justice is forced to face the Dark Lord on your coven's behalf." She removed her cloak and stepped to the window. She appeared deep in thought as she gazed out.

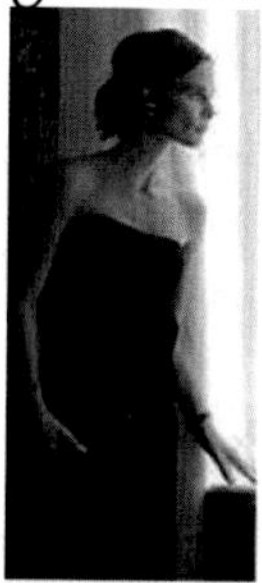

"How do you know about our coven?"

"You two know each other?" Hermione asked.

"Yes. I'm the Oracle. My name is Kalick. I've been listening to your story Professor. It filled in some gaps for me." She sniffed the air and turned toward Hermione. "I hadn't seen you as the one to capture the Ranger's heart. But now I know why. I'd been seeing the visions from the female perspective. I've seen the futures they hope for. The wicked blond, the elf and the ginger."

"Are you referring to Jade, Charista and me?" Hermione asked.

"Yes, yes and no. There is another with hair of flame."

"Do you mean Ms. Featherstone?" asked Dani.

"Mallory, descendant of Dumbledore. That's the one."

"She's interested in Justice too?" Hermione asked.

"You're getting sidetracked." reminded Dani.

"The young Mr. Cain is exceedingly difficult to read. May I?" She reached out for Hermione. As she stepped closer Hermione was able to see that she was blind. Hermione stepped forward but kept her wand at the ready. The Oracle placed her hands-on Hermione's face.

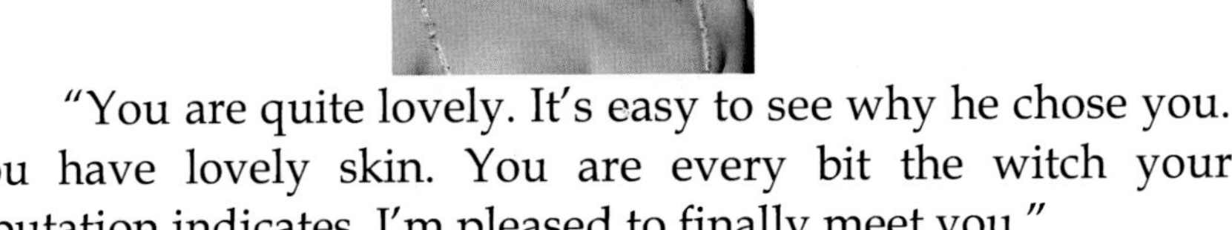

"You are quite lovely. It's easy to see why he chose you. You have lovely skin. You are every bit the witch your reputation indicates. I'm pleased to finally meet you."

"Thank you. Where did you come from?"

"That's not important right now. You have other questions for me?"

"Yes, if I may. As an Oracle, can you see what Justice will face?"

"The thing is destiny is a relative term. No future is set. I see what will happen on a specific course, but circumstances can still change. However, there are some futures that are set in motion that cannot be changed, isn't that right Professor?"

"Like what?" Hermione asked.

"Would you like to tell her, or shall I?" Kalick asked Dani.

"I don't know what you're referring to."

"Sure you do, just tell her the simple truth."

"What truth?" Hermione asked.

"Justice Cain..."

"Oracle, don't. Please!" Dani pleaded.

"What?" Hermione asked.

"Will not survive the fight."

"I've seen him fight. He's never lost. I understand You-know-who is strong, but Justice won't have to fight alone. We're all willing to help."

"It won't make a difference."

"Oracle!" Dani snapped.

"Why not?" Hermione questioned.

"His fight is not just against Alucard." They gasped and Kalick noticed. Everyone had been careful not to say his name for fear of a taboo curse, but as his sister, Kalick was immune. "While you're with me you're safe from the taboo curse. If he loses, Alucard will kill him. If he wins, he must honor his coven's commitment."

Hermione was stunned, "What commitment? What are you saying?"

"Many years ago, the American Elders made a deal with The Reaper. Alucard came to America in search of the offsets. Back then he was destroying everything and everyone at every stop. He left nothing standing. When the Reaper came to our coven it was clear someone was going to die. Death touched everyone there. Do you have any idea what it's like to not just know you're going to die, but to know when?"

Hermione listened to Dani's confession, but all the while her mind was trying to use the information to find some way to help Justice. "The coven did what it had to do to survive." Dani continued.

"And it was to sell out the unborn Ranger." added Kalick.

"So, what you're telling me is Death foresaw Alucard coming to your coven to kill everyone there to eliminate any threat against him. Death arrived and offered the coven a deal. In exchange for the lives of the Elders they were to give Justice to Death?" Hermione surmised.

"Yes."

Tears poured from Hermione's eyes.

"Hermione dear, you have to understand, the way Death goes about his business, when he visits you, he claims a soul. There typically is no negotiation. This was many, many years ago. The Elders you see here today were babies. Their coven protectors were offered a deal, one future soul for hundreds of saved lives. They had no way of knowing Justice would ever appear. Many of them who were spared that day went on to grow up and do miraculous things for our community. Many have died of old age which released them from their obligation. Their souls are at rest. But for those of us who came later, we too wanted to live. Death visits us regularly and shows us dates and times that our staff and students would have died were the agreement not in place. Thousands have been saved. By agreeing to the terms Death shrouded us from Alucard. He gave us the ability to remain hidden from our enemies, including Alucard. But the muggles got smarter and more determined as the years went by. They posed a constant threat. They periodically found our hiding places and we'd have to uproot everyone and move. Death would notify us when there was another witch or wizard born and we'd assign an Alpha protector to it. When the time was right, we'd leave the safety of the coven and go collect the new members. What we didn't know soon enough was that outside of the coven we were not protected by the agreement. Many lost their lives just outside the walls of our property.

The most frightening day of our lives was the day The Reaper showed up and let us know that Justice had been born. It's the day the clock started ticking for every member of the council. I was given the assignment and the rules changed so that the few Alphas we had left were always kept within the coven boundaries. We were forbidden to venture out. The mindset was the same. The needs of the many outweighed the needs of the few, or the one.

When I met Justice, I knew immediately he was special. He didn't have the fanfare that came later with baby Harry, but you could feel his power. The Death Eater's society had spies everywhere. That year, 1995, each month another offset was born. Justice in February, Harry in July. Rochelle in January. The Death Eaters leaked the locations of each one over the next several years. One by one potential Dark Lords set out to try to kill them and put themselves in position to take over as the one leader of all Dark Wizardry. Several Alphas and several offsets were killed, but a handful survived by escaping. Alucard was awakened after Harry was found, but was unable to be killed, by Voldemort."

"That's right," Kalick interjected, "He felt it deep within himself. The threat had come who was especially intended for him. The soul, so coveted by The Reaper, was also the bargaining chip Alucard needed to achieve his true immortality. He was so tired of collecting souls all those years only to have offsets maturing who would threaten his life before he could fulfill paying his debt to The Reaper. It became a race. He needed to regain his strength to kill the remaining offsets, while at the same time trying to find a way to ensure his eternal life should either of the other goals not be reached."

"Justice doesn't know about this, does he?"

"No. The Elders discussed it and felt it would be unfair to have him try to concentrate on fighting with this looming in the back of his mind." Dani replied.

"Please tell me I didn't just hear you use the word fair. What part of you knowing he's going to die, no matter if he wins or loses, yet still asking him to fight for you all, is fair?" asked Hermione.

"My sentiments exactly." added Kalick. "I like her."

"Hermione, you care for him, so your judgment is clouded. Justice believes, as we all do, the needs of the coven are more important than any one of us individually." Dani explained.

"That's easy for you to say when he'll be the one fighting."

"If he fights and wins, he'll save us all."

"But ***he'll*** die."

"He'll die either way."

"Yes, thanks to you and a group of people who never gave him a choice."

"He'd fight anyway, it's what he does, it's who he is."

Chapter 40 – Nurmengard

"It's who you manufactured him to be."

"If there was a way out of this, I'd gladly do it. I love him. I practically raised him. I was the one who took him from his real parents and put him with foster parents before Alucard found them and killed them. I didn't make this deal. This was done many years ago. Before Justice. Before me."

"But that's not why you believe in it. Tell her the rest." Kalick taunted.

"There's more?"

"Mr. Cain was given the burden of protecting the members of the council before he was born, but since then he's taken on much more." revealed Kalick. "She's correct, every member of the American coven has been touched by Death, because had the agreement not been accepted, Alucard would have wiped out the entire coven, every man, woman and child. But the noble Mr. Cain had a different plan. He found a young girl on the verge of death and before he could get her to the coven Death came for her." said Kalick.

"That's when he met Death face to face for the first time." said Dani.

"And Death knew he was the Ranger. It was ***his*** soul that Death coveted." said Kalick.

"So, Justice made his deal. Without knowing his fate was already sealed. He offered his life in exchange for hers. The Reaper could sense how unique Justice was. He'd always regretted agreeing to the deal with Alucard. He knew Alucard couldn't be trusted. He knew Alucard was searching for a way to cheat Death. Having a sense of sport, The Reaper countered Justice's offer. He agreed to let Justice live until Alucard's deal came due. His plan was to have Justice fight Alucard to the death with him claiming the loser for himself. If Justice agreed he'd allow every witch or wizard our coven found on Death's doorstep to heal and thrive. Justice, being who he is, wasn't afraid of dying so he accepted. Alucard's soul was the only soul Death wanted even more than Justice's. That's when Justice approached the Elders to allow us to actively seek out our brothers and sisters throughout the country. We took in as many as we could find.

Then, one day, they found us. Alucard found muggle minions and used them as spies. One of them turned out to be Jade's foster brother. He led Alucard to us."

"The sad part for Justice is that he believes he has a chance to defeat Alucard, not knowing that even if he does, it won't save ***him***."

It was so much to process. Hermione couldn't think, she felt so bad for Justice but was torn about what to do. She wanted so badly to tell him, have him run away beneath the invisibility cloak but knew in her heart he'd never do it. She rationalized the only chance any of them had was to defeat Alucard to keep him from killing everyone after the battle. She left the room and walked to the outer courtyard. She made sure no one was around then vaporized. You couldn't apparate within the grounds, but they hadn't anticipated anyone moving like a Death Eater. Once outside the restricted area she closed her eyes and concentrated. "Justice, can you hear me?" He was sitting on the floor, his legs folded, eyes closed. He was breathing in deeply and listening trying to pick up a sign that Charista was near when he heard her. His eyes fluttered a few times then he heard it again." Justice, can you hear me?"

"Jean? Is that you?"

"Oh Justice, how are you?"

"I'm okay, but I can hear in your voice that something is wrong. What is it?"

She fought to speak as clearly as she could. "I'm just worried about you. Everything has fallen apart. You're in prison. I want to come help you. I want to be there with you."

"No, you stay put. Stay inside, stick close to Ron and Cam. How's Harry?"

"He's fine, Justice this is just so unfair. You should be here with your friends, with the people who love you."

"Jean, hold your hand up."

"What?"

"Just put your hand in the air." She did. He held his up as well and she immediately felt as if he was standing before her touching his palm to hers. The sensation stopped for her because he moved his hand to his face and said he could smell Orchids and Lilies.

"Justice, listen to me. Can you get out?"

"Not sure, no one's come since your friend brought me to my cell. Thank you for that, by the way."

"You're welcome. Viktor is a good friend. I'm going to try to get a message to him to see if he can help get you out. You have to leave, just run away."

"Jean, you know I can't do that. It's my fault Charista is missing. I can't leave her out there. I've been trying to reach her but haven't gotten a reply. I tried you and Mallory too. I was just starting to think maybe I couldn't penetrate these walls."

"There's a protection on the castle. We can't apparate

within the grounds and no communication is going out or coming in. Justice, you do remember your promise?"

"Yes, I do."

"I just…" She felt tears coming on.

"Jean."

"Wait, there's something I need to tell you." She paused.

"Jean, before you say another word, I want you to know, I'm not a guy who needs to hear the words. I feel it. I feel it each time I breathe in. I hear it each time you say my name. I love you, Jean." She burst into tears. "I love you and it's that love that makes me unafraid. It's that love that has me

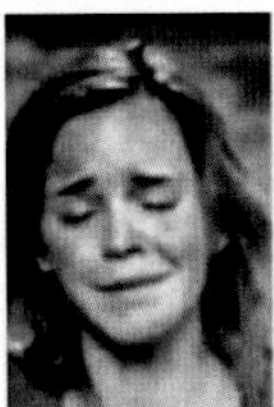

prepared to face whatever is coming. As long as I'm alive, you don't have to fear anything. As long as I'm alive, ***he'll*** always have to worry about me."

"Justice, I love you too." He closed his eyes, and the walls of the cell began to burn.

"Just hearing you say it, even once, makes my life complete. Hold out your hands." She did and he moved his hand in a circle and a bouquet of flowers appeared in front of her." She began to cry aloud.

"We're coming for you. We need you to help us get in if you can. We need to get Harry's name into the Goblet of Fire before midnight tonight. With everything in lockdown it's the only way any of us will be allowed out."

"Jean, I've been sitting here in this cell, and it's given me a chance to really think. I don't think any of you should come here. Not even Harry. Forget about the tournament. It'll be better for me if none of you are put in harm's way until the battle is over. It's almost here." He looked at the sand in the hourglass Kalick had given him, and it was almost out. "I can feel them getting closer."

"Justice, I'm not going to just sit here while you fight."

"I kinda figured you'd say that. I'll see if there's anything I can do to get Harry's name in the cup, but please consider what I said. Don't come here. There's no one here yet, but I can already feel the energy. It's unlike anything I've ever felt. I mean it, don't come here."

"I'll consider it."

"Damn it, Jean! I meant it!" Justice stood up and paced back and forth a couple times. "Jean, you said communications were blocked in and out of the school grounds, so how are we able to communicate?" He waited for an answer but got no response. "Jean? Where are you?" Still nothing. He reasoned she had to have gone outside the grounds to reach him. Now he had to hope she'd gone back why he wasn't getting through.

She was concentrating on something else, so she wasn't picking him up. She'd placed a rock atop a boulder and moved until a tree obstructed her line of sight. She concentrated on the rock. 'Focus'. She pointed her wand, "***Focus, Reducto!***" The tree appeared fine. She stepped around and the rock was gone. She smiled then saw the back side of the tree smoldering with a huge chunk blown out of it.

"Very impressive." said a voice from the darkness. She spun in the direction of the voice.

"Who's there?"

A faint scream was heard by Jade as she and Cam and a few others patrolled along the school's perimeter. Jade sprinted to the gate but saw nothing. She closed her eyes and

and when she opened them, they glowed white. She scanned the area and saw what appeared to be a spectral trail dissipating into the air. She inhaled and her eyes returned to normal. She smelled vanilla cookies. She glanced down and saw the bouquet of flowers. "Oh no."

Justice tried not to jump to conclusions. 'She's fine, right? She just went back inside. She's far too smart to let anyone get the jump on her'. He took a deep breath, closed his eyes and concentrated. '***Expecto Patronum***'! At Hogwarts, the Gryffindor students were asleep in their beds when a bright light began to emit to the point where it woke Neville up. He shielded his face and the light suddenly whisked away, shooting through the castle and out across the grounds. McGonagall looked on from her office window and a grin appeared on her face. The light reached the perimeter fence and burst through the protections sending a shower of sparks cascading down.

Moments later the tiny ball of light came to a stop at the foot of the bed of yet another student. This one was on the campus of Durmstrang. The student awoke to see the light manifest itself into the shape of a wolverine. It began to speak in Justice's voice. "Hello?"

Justice began to feel sleepy.

"Hello." The student replied. "***Justice***, is that you?"

Finally, he was able to connect with her. "Yeah, how are you?"

Chapter 40 – Nurmengard

"I'm shocked actually that you've contacted me this way. When you didn't come to the tournament with the Hogwarts team, I thought maybe you didn't want to see me."

"No, it wasn't that. It's complicated, but right now I have to ask a favor if you're up for it."

"Of course, anything. You know that."

"I was wondering if you could add Harry Potter's name to the Goblet of Fire?"

"I don't see why not, but how did you know I'm at Durmstrang for the Triwizard Tournament?"

"Because you're the most qualified at Beauxbatons, you're the most competitive woman I know, and you easily could have won the competition in America and…"

"And what?"

"I smelled your perfume the moment I set foot near the campus." He yawned and his eyes began to feel heavy.

She jumped up and looked all around. "Oh my God, you're here?" she asked in a panic. "You can't see me right now, can you?"

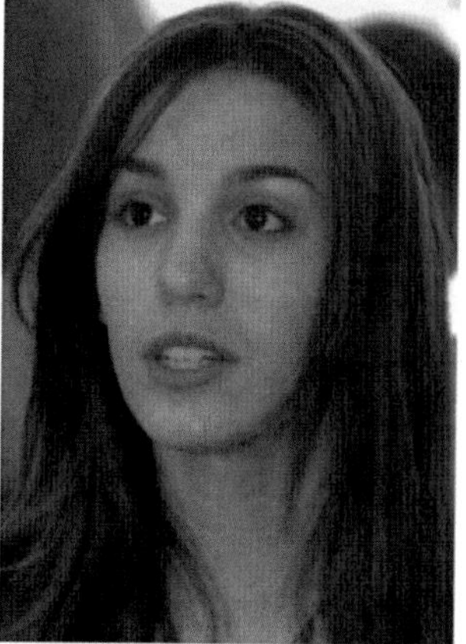

"No, no. I'm close, but I'm not here for the tournament." She calmed down. "The Goblet will only accept entries until midnight. That doesn't give you much time. I hate to have to ask this of you the first time we've spoken in several months."

"What are friends for?" She paused. "We are still friends, right?"

"Of course."

"Justice, I meant it when I apologized for my behavior last time."

"Rochelle, the past is the past. Forget about it."

"Thank you. I'll go right now."

"Thank you." He lied down and fell asleep.

Anthony Wright
Chapter 41 – Round one

As dawn approached Justice woke up and could see people arriving at the school. As he ran his tongue over his teeth, he could taste a metallic residue. He heard students and staff buzzing and saw the construction being finalized at the stadium for the start of the tournament. He felt very uneasy.

McGonagall removed the protections on the perimeter fences to allow mail to arrive and within moments hundreds of owls descended on the Great Hall. Neville's Gram worked feverishly to get breakfast ready for the staff and students in Dobby's absence. Jade and Cam told the Elders of her suspicions about what had taken place and Mallory, Ron and Harry tried to gather the group he intended to take with him to Durmstrang should the plan have worked.

They got their conformation when a copy of the Daily Prophet plopped down at the staff table and the headline read:

"CHAMPIONS CHOSEN FOR TRIWIZARD TOURNAMENT"

Durmstrang champion: Alexi Voscov
Beauxbatons champion: Rochelle Maynard
Hogwarts champion: Harry Potter
Aidan Morgan Academy champion: Justice Cain

McGonagall's mouth fell open, shocked. She placed the paper in front of Crisp and went to tell Harry to gather his things. She found him and the others and moments later Jade and Professor Hunt found the rest of the group.

"Has anyone seen Hermione?" Ron asked.

"Harry, Ron, I have something I need to tell you." said Jade. "I think Hermione's been taken.

"What?" Harry asked in disbelief.

"When? How?" Ron asked.

"I think she went outside the perimeter fence, and someone took her. I heard a commotion. It sounded like a muffled scream. When I got to the fence, I found the remnants of a spectral trail. Once the protections were removed, I went outside and found this." She handed Harry her Time Turner neckl00000ace. Everyone on Harry's list assembled. Without
Hermione, they were still one short. Ron and Harry wanted to leave as quickly as possible. They hurried toward the Slytherin house entrance and saw Robyn walking down the hall.

"Excuse me, Robyn, may we have a word?" Harry asked. She turned back toward them. They explained about the trip and the inherent danger. She accepted without hesitation.

Before they left McGonagall pulled Harry and Ron aside. "Boys, listen to me. We don't know for sure that Miss Granger's been taken. You have to be focused on what needs to be done, or we'll lose you both. You thought Voldemort was dangerous to deal with, multiply that by ten and you'll begin to approach what Alucard is capable of. He's been alive for nearly a thousand years. He's a killing machine and a master of disguise. You're all going to have to work together to keep each other alive. No ***one*** person can defeat him. Stay focused. If you find her and Charista, bring them home safely."

Chapter 41 – Round one

"We will."

Neville walked up to McGonagall and handed her a note. "Justice asked me to give this to you. He said you'd know what to do." He walked off. She opened the note and read it. She stepped over to Mr. Filch and whispered something to him.

"Right now?"

"Yes, Mr. Filch." He turned and grabbed Mrs. Norris then left the room. Harry and the others gathered. Professor Flitwick created a portkey for them. They all took hold and off they went.

Draco walked into a room lit by a fireplace. "Ah, my young apprentice has returned. Do you have something for me?"

"Yes and no, my Lord. I wasn't able to acquire the cloak. I'm sure you heard; something went wrong at Gringotts. I questioned some of the vendors who were working that night. They eventually told me they thought they saw Harry Potter enter the bank that night."

"What of Marcus?"

"He hasn't been seen since that night. I don't think he felt he could face you without having returned with the wand."

"Was I not clear in my instructions to you?"

"My Lord, he insisted. He's your son. He wanted to impress you." Alucard began to advance on him. "My Lord, we both know Justice Cain is too dumb to run away. He's going to come to us. He doesn't stand a chance against you, but I brought you some insurance just in case." He snapped his fingers and Crabbe and Goyle carried in a body wrapped in a covering. He walked over as they laid the body on a table.

"He'd do anything for you not to hurt her." He unwrapped her and there, lying unconscious, was Charista.

"I'll deal with you later." Alucard told him. He touched his wand to the table Charista was on and a magical cage assembled around her. "It's time for me to meet my adoring public."

DURMSTRANG

Harry and the others arrived at the school. Welcome! Welcome!" They were greeted by a tall robust man draped in a fur lined cloak and hat. "We've been expecting you. My name is Nicholi Putkin. I am Headmaster here. You are Harry Potter, no?"

"Yes sir, pleased to meet you."

"Likewise. Please, come in."

Chapter 41 – Round one

They were escorted in. The school was dark and drab in its appearance. The halls were lined with torches. The group visually inspected everything as they were shown to where they could freshen up.

"Guys, we need to find Justice, Hermione and Charista."

"Reggie, Blaise and I will look for a way to the prison." offered Freddy.

"We can go down to the stadium to check out the security." said Stormy.

"Do we have a plan, mate?" Ron asked.

"Still workin' on that. For now, just keep your eyes open. We don't know the layout of the castle, so if you're checking a room and someone finds you, just tell them you're lost."

"Stay together. You're safer in pairs or groups. No matter what, we all rendezvous back here in one hour." Mallory instructed. She, Harry and Professor Hunt got changed and went to check Harry in. The others explored the castle looking for anything out of the ordinary. They all split into pairs. Dean and Seamus, Robyn and Emmerick, Ron and Freddy, Neville and Stormy and Blaise and Reggie.

"This is ridiculous, we're supposed to be looking for signs of Death Eaters inside the perimeter, everything here would point to this being Death Eater training camp." Reggie pointed out.

Dean and Seamus were the first to see something that gave them pause. Three hooded forms were huddled together pointing at locations within the stadium. As they turned to walk away Seamus could swear he saw one of their faces clearly enough to identify him as Vincent Crabbe. They began to follow the group down the pathway that led beneath the stadium. They lost sight of them and agreed to turn back, but when they did, they found themselves surrounded.

THE EXODUS

Crisp found McGonagall and asked her why she'd requested all the students be assembled. "If you'll follow me, Mr. Crisp, I'll show you." She walked at a brisk clip, and he followed closely. She turned a corner and when he followed, he found himself nose to belly button with Hagrid. Hagrid grabbed him by the arm and lifted him up. "*Petrificus Totalus*!" McGonagall called and Crisp became as rigid as a board. "Take Mr. Crisp to the dungeon, please."

"It'd be my pleasure Ma'am." he replied.

"Mr. Filch, is everything ready?" she asked.

"Yes Ma'am. The carriages are arriving as we speak."

"Alright, let's move, quickly. Did you send the owls?"

"Aye, Headmistress."

SHALL WE BEGIN

"It's begun." Harry told Mallory and Dani. "We don't have much time. We've got to find Hermione. I know she's here."

"If she's here, we'll find her." Dani assured him. He got signed in and took his place with the other contestants. The Durmstrang Headmaster approached the podium.

"Ladies and Gentlemen. Welcome one and all. The proud sons of Durmstrang have worked extremely hard to prepare our school to host this incredible event…"

"And a fine job they've done, but I think I'll take it from here." said a voice from high up in the rafters. It appeared to be a student. All eyes turned toward the source. "Please, don't be alarmed. You have nothing to fear."

"Who are you?" Pius asked, "Show yourself!"

Chapter 41 - Round one

Alucard cast a meteolojinx. The sky darkened; the clouds burst into flames. Rochelle flew with incredible speed avoiding the flames cascading down like raindrops. Alexi wasn't so lucky. The flames ignited his broom and he spiraled to the ground and crashed. She saw a tiny opening and darted toward it. Simultaneously she, from her broom, and Mallory from the ground, cast '*Partis Temporus*!' A small hole remained open long enough for her to shoot through it.

Alucard cast a curse at Mallory that knocked her off her feet. She was shocked she didn't feel any pain. A welt arose on

Justice's chest as he sat in a trance on the floor of his cell trying with no success to reach Hermione or Charista. With the sky dark, Alucard said to himself, 'This used to be so much more fun'. He was confused as he looked over the crowd. The total number of people he could see was far less than he had anticipated, less than he needed to collect his number of souls. He summoned one of the Death Eaters. "Take some men and release the prisoners." His eyes turned white, and he looked to the sky. Suddenly dozens of abductees he'd bitten himself, or had bitten, began to appear.

Justice sat breathing in slowly and deeply, his eyes closed. On the floors below him Death Eaters were releasing the prisoners as instructed. They were just outside his door when the last grain of sand dropped in the hourglass. Seamus led the others through one of the tunnels that Peeves had told Justice about. Justice had confided the location in Seamus in the form of a note he'd given Hermione to give to him before the try outs. Neville, Blaise, Reggie, Ron, Freddy, and Dean were hiding outside when the Death Eaters entered the prison.

"Seamus, we can't let them get out. What can we do?"

"I've got an idea." he replied. They all scurried off around the perimeter of the building.

Two Death Eaters approached Mallory who had continued to lie still. The others didn't know she wasn't hurt. Emmerick cast a curse at them knocking them back. Alucard took notice. Mallory was a trophy he wanted. He cast a curse at Emmerick that Emmerick deflected.

He held his own momentarily, but Alucard was too strong. He cast a curse that disarmed Emmerick then he cast, "***Avada Kedavra!***" It all happened so fast. Mallory jumped up and fired curses, Harry, Dani and Stormy joined in. Alucard's vampire minions began snatching the students.

Ron and Reggie took some explosive charges Seamus had given them and while Dean, Blaise and Freddy fought off the former ministry officials, they made their way to the entrance of the prison building and planted them. Seamus had hoped to catch some of the prisoners exiting the building, but the explosives went off and sealed the doorway trapping everyone inside.

"What did you do?" Dean asked.

"How is Justice supposed to get out now?" asked Blaise.

Justice's eyes opened as the door to his cell swung open.

Chapter 41 - Round one

Two men came in. They were unafraid since no prisoners had wands, but Justice was unlike other prisoners. "*Protego Duri! Flagrante!*" he called. The two men's clothes burst into flames as they screamed and staggered around. Justice knocked the Death Eater's wand out of his hand and slid it in place to keep the door from locking. Justice kicked the man closest to him in the chest and it knocked both backward into the door. They both turned to stone and fell over. Justice stepped to the door, but with the two stone bodies lying against it he couldn't get out. "Great!" It turned out better for him since he could hear other Death Eaters and prisoners approaching. He clapped his hands together and when he pulled them apart, he was holding his ear buds. A Death Eater stuck his arm into the room and cast curses blindly. Justice looked back, "*Waddiwasi!*" The wand propping the door open was launched away and the door slammed against the Death Eaters arm causing it to turn to stone and he fell to the ground. Suddenly another explosion rocked the building disabling the protections on the prison. He turned up the music, looked around and spied the broom against the wall. He cast a flying spell on it and threw it through the window slit. Justice vaporized and dove out of the window slit. He fell freely until he caught up to and grabbed the broom. Neville and the others saw him materialize and pull up on the broom and they cheered. The commotion gave away their position and curses began flying their direction. Justice flew upward and stopped. He whipped his head from side to side targeting each of the sources of the curses. With a cascading jinx, he launched a fiery offensive that scorched all the targets.

Blaise and Freddy cast "***Inflatus,***" at the singed targets and they swelled until they lifted off the ground and floated away.Justice swooped down and asked, "Where is everyone? We can't let Harry get taken."

"They should be at the stadium."

"Find a place to hide, I'll deal with Alucard."

"We didn't agree to come here to hide." said Neville as he handed him a package.

"There's a bunch of the Death Eaters in the halls of the castle searching for more people. We can surprise them if we go through the secret passage back to the school." Dean explained.

"Yeah, that note Hermione gave me tellin me about the hidden tunnel came in handy. We're with ya." added Seamus. "What I don't understand is how you knew we were even comin here?"

"I just figured, from what I've been told, you wouldn't want to miss an opportunity to blow some stuff up." Seamus smiled and nodded. Justice created a Port Key for them and told them to find and help Harry. He'd take care of the men in the school. He vaporized and shot through the tunnel.

Alucard retrieved his cloak, grabbed Robyn and forced the others to drop their wands. He and his team rounded up Harry and the others. He cast "***Depulso,***" and sent them away. "Take the souls, now!" he commanded and with each person bitten a small ball of light could be seen floating through the air to a necklace that hung around his neck. "This was too easy." he told Draco. "Finish up here and bring the quarry to the coven. Leave no one alive. We need them all."

Justice entered the school undetected and began an assault on the Death Eaters who were searching the halls for more students. After subduing twelve men he vaporized and flew into the stadium. He could hear a voice and knew it was Alucard. Was he too late? He flew in that direction but stopped when he found Emmerick's body.

"I'm going to convince Mr. Potter to give me his cloak then I'll just need the wand." Alucard waved his hand, and the clouds began launching huge fire balls that exploded when they hit the buildings. Alucard vaporized. The team arrived in the center of the stadium. Justice cast a counter meteolojinx and the fire turned to water dousing the flames. He flew back down to be with the others as Ron stood up to cheer and was hit by a curse.

Reggie and Neville screamed. "Ron!" Freddy, Blaise and Dean watched as Justice rematerialized and fell to the ground.

"Wait a minute." Dean questioned, "The curse hit him," he pointed to Ron, "But he took the hit." he pointed to Justice.

"Yeah, he does that." Freddy told him.

Ron was stunned. He felt his chest and realized he wasn't hurt. Justice looked around and saw the vampires attacking the students. He pointed his wand to the sky, "***LUMOS SOLEM, MAXIMA!***" The sky became filled with sunlight and the vampires burst into flames. "You need em all, do you? Let's see how you like this. ***Accio broomstick!***" He flew hard back to the prison. "***Bombarda Maxima!***" He fired at the base of the building, and it collapsed upon itself.

Draco, shouted for them to forget about the others and head back to their lair. Crabbe and Goyle pointed their wands at the guys as they tried to calm Ron from his excitement. "*Depulso,*" and they all disappeared. Krum and the staff were able to surround the remaining Death Eaters. Justice noticed the last of the souls trailing off into the horizon. He accelerated and when he got close enough, he leapt off the broom, vaporized and followed them. Ministry guards and Order members arrived to help.

Chapter 42 – Alucard vs. Justice

Justice arrived at an elaborate estate and within seconds of materializing he could smell Charista. He saw the others being escorted into a building. They were in Wiltshire, England at the former site of Malfoy Manor. The building had been rebuilt and was vast and well-guarded. Justice needed to

get inside quickly. He knew once Alucard found out he didn't collect all the souls from the prison he'd likely take the lives of his friends immediately. He found a perch in a tree where he could locate the guards. He pointed his wand as if looking through a scope. He was just about to cast a curse when his eyes shifted. "So, are you gonna help, or are you just here to watch?"

"Just waiting for my cue." Jade replied.

"How did you find me?"

"I felt you."

"Felt me? What are you talking about? You know this is why we've always had a problem with you being an Alpha. You should be with the others."

"They're safe. The place you rebuilt in Little Hangleton is perfect. No one would think to look there beneath the rubble. When did you have time to do all that?"

"On my way back from Gringotts. I just felt that once this thing began, Hogwarts would be next on the list." He didn't want to tell her that he had extracted the plan from Marcus. There was no reason she should hold any animosity against him, Justice had already taken care of him. "That's not the point."

"We can talk about this later, are we gonna do this or what?" She turned and pulled her wand.

"Easy tiger, this isn't one of your kick the door open and

start shootin' assaults. This requires stealth, skill, a plan."

"Fine, we'll do it your way. The boring way'.

He pointed his wand as if it was a rifle. "Range me."

She looked through a pair of omnioculars, "Ten o'clock, 150 yards." He zeroed in and moved his finger as if pulling a trigger. The Death Eater fell over.

"Goodnight."

"Twelve o'clock, 210 yards."

"Goodbye."

One by one they eliminated fourteen guards. "You're really gonna do this?"

"Of course, what do you mean? This is what we've trained for."

"No one's trained for this." She paused. "You know I've always had complete confidence in your abilities. Your bravery is unquestioned, but this is the Lord of all Lords. This is a legend and you're alone. Are you sure you're ready?"

"Don't have a choice, now do I?"

"You always have a choice."

"You know I don't, and you know why, but you do. I won't think any less of you if you want to sit this one out."

"Don't make me hurt you."

"I just need to get to Harry."

"Then let's go." He grabbed her arm and vaporized. They materialized just inside the perimeter fence. She squinted then shut her eyes. She began to feel pain in her head. Suddenly she heard a voice in her head. 'Kill the Elf.' She shook her head trying to clear it, then heard it again. 'Come to me, NOW! KILL THE ELF!'

"Jade? Are you okay?"

She looked at him. "Yeah, yeah, of course." Dogs charged at them. Justice raised his wand, but Jade forced it down. "I've got this." She pointed her wand, "***Freeze.***" They stopped, some in midair. "You realize this is likely a trap?"

"Oh, I know it's a trap. I have to go in. They're inside and I'm their only hope. I just need to free Harry."

They snuck inside. She tapped him on the shoulder and silently indicated that she was going to go one way while he went a different way. He shook his head no, but she crawled off before he could stop her. He had to scramble away because someone was coming. He recognized the voice, it was Draco.

"Stick close to me, we're gonna have to move fast. He's gonna lose it when he finds out how short he is."

Justice waited for them to pass by him then crept up behind them and slammed Crabbe and Goyle's heads together knocking them out. Draco didn't even notice. He just kept talking. Justice dragged them into a closet and gagged them. He followed Draco to the sitting room where Alucard sat covered by his cloak. Justice still hadn't seen his face. He was about to go in when he caught Charista's scent again. He followed it and found a room being guarded by two men. He didn't need to kill them he just needed them away from the door. He cast a Pus Squirting Hex at one of them and yellow goo squirted from his nose onto the other man.

"Yuk!" he shouted. Then Justice cast a Stinging Jinx at the other. "Ouch, great, I'm allergic." Justice cast a Trip Jinx on them, and they took off, stumbling down the hall. He entered the room and saw Charista in the center of the room in the cage. Her eyes began to glow.

He approached her cautiously. She lied down and curled up into a ball. He called to her, but she didn't respond. He touched the cage and received an electrical shock. She looked at him, something didn't seem quite right. He tried to speak to her, but the barrier on the cage restricted any sounds. As he inspected the cage she recoiled. He noticed her body language and began to shake his head no. She lunged at him and received the same shock he had. She grabbed her head as if she had a severe headache. Something was broadcasting to her inside the cage that he couldn't hear. She was being tortured with high pitched frequencies. He needed to get her out, but suddenly he stopped and looked around. He felt a presence in the form of energy. He could tell it wasn't Alucard. "***Reveal your secrets!***" he commanded, and the room illuminated, and he could see the others, Mallory, Dani, Ron. They were all blindfolded and hanging by chains binding their wrists. He raised his hand and was about to break the chains securing them when he heard voices approaching from outside. "***Finite Incantatem!***" The lights dimmed and he ran and hid. A hooded man entered the room.

"Incompetents!!! I should kill you all!" He glanced around the room. He lifted his hand, and the others became visible and their blindfolds disappeared.

"Wake up!" They all began to stir.

"So, you're Alucard." Harry stated.

"This is one of many forms I've taken over the years. Do you like it?"

Chapter 42 – Alucard vs. Justice

"It's just as disgusting as the rest of your personality."

"Oh, that makes me sad. I've worked so hard on this personality. Oh well, it's a work in progress. I, on the other hand, am thrilled to meet the famous Harry Potter. It's quite an honor for me knowing that I will be the one to do what Voldemort couldn't. You see, I've heard of your exploits. About how brave you are. I'm not sure you've heard of me. Perhaps I can show you what I'm famous for." He advanced on Harry and grabbed his face.

"I'm your huckleberry." Alucard paused and looked around the room to nothing but blank stares. 'No one? Really? You people have got to watch more movies'. Justice thought.

Alucard stopped in his tracks and released Harry. "So, we have company." Justice cast a protection barrier around the others. "Let me guess, the fabled Ranger, is it? I was so hoping to meet you but had heard you weren't going to be able to make it to our little party. I was told you ran into a little Ministry trouble."

Justice released the barrier and concentrated on each of the others until the links on the chains they were suspended by, fractured. With the slightest yank, they'd be free. Now he needed a diversion to get them out. He was set to cast a spell when Dobby appeared. Harry had seen Charista and the moment he did it registered in the Genealogy book. Dobby hadn't destroyed it yet. Dobby was furious. He raised his hands and cast a spell at Alucard. It was deflected by Draco. Justice blasted Draco against a wall then ran toward Dobby. "*Aladusuch*!" He dove at him, but Alucard's curse found its mark. Justice rolled over and had Dobby in his arms. When he looked down at him, he realized he was too late. He carried Dobby and laid him down behind a barrier.

Draco grabbed Harry and crawled out of the room.

Justice stood up. His body was engulfed in flames. He balled up his fists and gritted his teeth. Then he let out a growl and a blast of flame shot in every direction. Every Death Eater in the room was consumed, all but Alucard. None of the group was harmed.

"Very Impressive. Was that anger?" Alucard asked. "It's been so long since I've let anyone live long enough to display emotion, I can't be sure."

"No, I'm not angry." Justice replied.

Alucard paused, "No matter, as much as I'd love to stay and play, duty calls. I do, however, have a game you may find to your liking in my stead." He snapped his fingers and Charista's cage opened as he disappeared. Justice went to follow him but was blasted against the wall by Charista.

"Charista! What the bloody hell are you doin? That's Justice. He's your friend." Ron told her. She turned to him and blasted him back as well. His chains broke easily. Ron was shocked the blast didn't hurt. Justice moaned. She looked down and saw Dobby's body lying on the ground. They all realized they were free with just a slight tug.

"Ron, get everyone out of here. Get to Harry." He handed them a package that contained a new Krysta Marie Madison's wand for each of them. "Charista, we don't have to do this. It won't end well." She stood up and her eyes began to glow yellow. "Oh boy." She fired spell after spell at him and they all bounced off his protection shield. He wouldn't fire back. He knew she was under the influence of the Imperious Curse. He was going to try to stun her, but when he rolled out into the open, he saw Jade standing behind Charista with a dagger.

"NO!!! he screamed, but it was too late. Jade plunged the knife in. Justice rushed to her side and caught her as she fell.

"You're welcome." said Jade in a sarcastic tone. Without

looking at her he cast a spell that began to squeeze her throat. He slammed Jade against a wall, her feet dangling several inches above the floor.

"*Cauterize! Aladusuch!*" he said and placed two figures inside Charista's wound. She screamed out in agony, but quieted as he pulled them out slowly and the blood flow stopped, but she was hurt badly. Elves were vastly different than people. He removed his cloak and placed it under her head. She appeared stable. He leaned down and kissed her and slipped her gloves on. Her eyes opened and his flickered and his grip loosened on Jade's throat.

"Do you see? Do you see what she's costing us? Why? Why didn't you ever love me? It's all I ever wanted."

"And you didn't care who from. I tried Jade. I tried to show you there was something else, something more. You're better than this. You knew she was under the influence of a curse, but you didn't think. You never think, you just do, and I don't have time for that anymore. What's at stake here is about our kind, it's about more than you, than us. It always has been. That's what you never got, that's what kept us apart. She grabbed her head. That's why I never supported you being an Alpha. I love you Jade, but you crossed a line this time." His wand dropped into his hand and a steel point appeared from its tip. He spun and threw it and it stabbed her in the temple. She fell back onto the ground, her eyes still open. He walked over and yanked the wand and the metal tip stayed lodged in her skull."ALUCARD!!!" he screamed, and Charista covered her ears. When she released them, she shook her head and realized she was free of the curse. Her eyes returned to normal. She saw Justice, then Dobby.

"Justice, I'm sorry." Charista whispered.

"Shhh!!! I'm the one who's sorry. Dobby was…"

"You did all you could. I may have been cursed, but I could still see that." she sobbed uncontrollably as she looked down at her father. Justice touched her hair and she hugged him. "I know we still have work to do. I'm going to pull it together, but I have to ask. We both know what I am beneath this exterior, but if things were different..." She pulled her hair back.

"In a heartbeat." he replied without hesitation. He helped her out of her filthy shirt and used his handkerchief to wipe her face. "Anyone would be lucky to have someone so special, so gifted to care for and to care for them. My heart belongs to someone special, but you will forever have my friendship." He hugged her. "You've done more and given more than we should ever have had to ask of you. What I need from you now is to take Dobby and go."

"But you're hurt, you're weak. You need my help." She removed her glove and touched his face. "Tell me the truth. In your condition, can you beat him?"

Chapter 42 – Alucard vs. Justice

"I've never lost." He smiled. "Why don't you sit this one out? I'll take it from here." He moved her hand to Dobby. "***Depulso!***" They disappeared.

"You have been a continuous disappointment to me." Alucard told Draco when he found him searching for the cloak. "But, for some reason, I still believe in you. I just think you need a little push in the right direction." Alucard's eyes glowed white and his fangs glistening in the flickering light of the torches. Draco cowered as Alucard crouched over him and bit him repeatedly.

Ron and the others crept along a corridor trying to find a way out, but they didn't know their way around the school. They went through a door that let out into a dining room. They headed for an exit door. They got about halfway across the room when the lights went on and Alucard stepped into view. He was still shifting back to his human form as a dozen Death Eaters entered and surrounded everyone.

"I'm losing my patience. I need the cloak and the wand, now!" he told Harry.

"The cloak is in a vault where you'll never get to it, and I don't know where the wand is."

"Then I guess you are of no use to me." Alucard took a step toward him and was hit with a curse that knocked him across the room.

"Stay away from my friends." Justice told him. "***Eructo Barrier!***" said Justice and a half wall formed around them, shielding them from the Death Eaters. He was recovering quickly, but it was all he had the strength to do at that moment. Dani and Mallory fired spells at the Death Eaters to keep them at a distance and told the others to stay down. Justice was strong but continued to feel a step slow. He just felt sluggish and now wasn't the time.

Alucard's wand sprayed fire toward the barrier as he scrambled to his feet. Justice dove behind the barrier. Ron looked over to Justice.

"We don't need a barrier. Their curses don't hurt, watch." He stood up and cast a curse.

"No Ron!" shouted Harry. A deflected curse hit him squarely in the chest. Ron fell back.

"See, it didn't hurt at all." he said as he rolled over and saw Justice, lying beside him, clutching his chest. "What's wrong with ***him***?" he asked Stormy. She smacked him in the forehead. "Oh."

"Not all of you are protected and for those of you who are, I'm not sure for how much longer. I'm prepared to face him, but I can't have one of you take a hit and cause me to lose focus. Either go, or stay here, but stay down. Don't fight unless you have to." The hits were taking their toll on him.

"I'm ready," Harry told him.

"No Harry, this isn't what I had envisioned. With Je…Hermione still missing, it's best if you go and keep the others safe. I'll try to wear him down so if he does get by me, you'll have an easier time of it. If this goes sideways neither of us might make it out."

"I'll stay with him." Mallory told him. "The rest of you go."

Chapter 42 – Alucard vs. Justice

"I don't have time to argue. I'm gonna to try to draw him off, that's when you can make your move." He turned to go, and Dani stopped him.

"Justice, there's something I have to tell you."

"No, there isn't."

"You don't know all the facts." She grabbed him. "The Elders…" She paused, "You don't have to do this. It won't make a difference."

He placed his fingers to her lips. "It will to me. I know about the deal. I've always known."

"Wait! You what?" She stared at him with a puzzled look on her face. "Then why would you still risk your life for us when we lied to you like that?"

"It's what I'm here for. This is my path, I chose it. It's okay." He hugged her.

"What is she saying?" Freddy asked.

A Death Eater ran around the barrier and cast a spell at her. Justice deflected it and cast his own causing the Death Eater to disintegrate. "Alucard, you and I need to finish our dance. What do you say you let these people go? Your clock is ticking and even if you kill us all you're still well short of your goal." He handed Harry his cloak. "Long story."

"You have no idea what my goals are. As for your deal, I'll pass, but we can finish that dance now. In fact, I have a perfect dance partner for you since you apparently didn't find our little elf friend to your liking."

Justice peered around the corner and saw Alucard holding Demetria by the hair. He scrambled back and took a deep breath. "Are you okay, D?"

"Why wouldn't she be? Oh, you thought I'd hurt her because she was disloyal. Because she betrayed me, her own father?"

"What did he say?" Freddy asked.

"Get ready to go, take them one at a time once I distract him." He tilted his head back and pulled out the Azkaban guard's wand.

Justice snuck a peak and Alucard could see the confusion on his face. "You didn't know?" Alucard grinned, "Oh this is even better than I could have hoped. You didn't know I sent her to your coven to spy on you for me?"

Justice became so angry the walls and ceiling began to crack. "Justice, there's no way man." Freddy told him. He motioned for Harry to start to lead the others out.

"Enough stalling, here's how this is going to go. You're

going to show yourself, I'm going to kill your friends, then kill you, but first you're going to give me the cloak. You have three seconds before I start by killing her."

"Or, how about this, you let her go and I'll let your son go." Justice stood up and removed his own cloak, He held it up then let it drop and when it did Marcus was standing before him. Alucard's expression went blank.

"Marcus, my son. What has he done to you? Are you hurt?"

"I'm fine."

"Are you sure?"

"Yes father."

"Do you have the wand?"

"No father, I..."

"***AVADA KEDAVRA!!!***" Alucard cast and killed Marcus on the spot. His soul floated up to Alucard's chest and settled in a small amulet that hung from his neck. "So much for your plan." Justice saw where the souls were being collected.

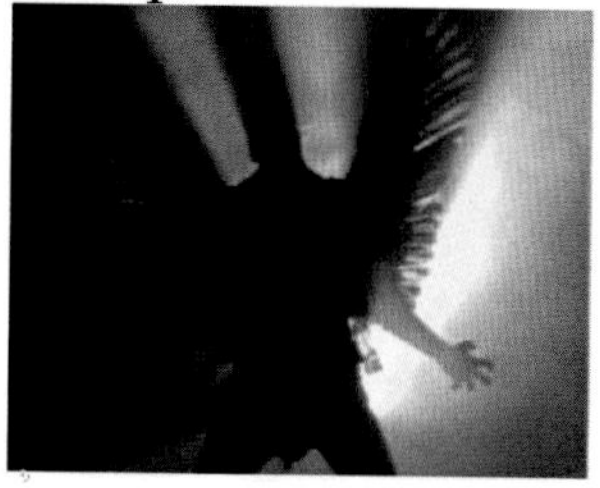

He rolled out into the open and cast a spell at Alucard. Alucard retuned a spell that Justice deflected. Crabbe and Goyle had come to. Goyle ran toward him and began firing spells from behind him. He was dueling them at the same time with his two wands and gaining strength quickly. Finally, he cast a Finger-removing jinx at Goyle and when Goyle brought his hand downward to cast another spell his wand flew across the room, as he had no fingers on his hand to grip it with.

Goyle screamed, held his fingerless hand to his face then screamed again. He ran toward the wand but Mallory cast, "***Lacarnum Inflamarae,***" sending a ball of flame across the room. It hit the wand and it burst into flames. Goyle saw the wand burning and screamed then he looked at his fingerless hand again, and screamed again.

"Wait!" Justice shouted. He knew Alucard was ruthless but hadn't figured he'd kill his own son.

"For what? You don't have anything left that I need."

"I thought you wanted the Elder Wand.

"You don't have the wand."

Justice tilted his head back and pulled out the package Neville had given him from his throat. He unrolled the wrapping and held up the wand. Alucard stepped to him.

"Let her go." He snapped his fingers and a flame lit in the palm of his other hand. Alucard cast her aside.

Robyn tried to hold back a scream. Harry had gotten each of them by the Death Eaters. Dani and Mallory were the only ones left. Draco sniffed the air and followed the scent. It led him straight to them. He blocked their exit and exposed his fangs then roared at them. Harry cast a curse at him but missed and Draco hit Harry with the back of his fist, knocking him out. He searched him and found the cloak. Reggie cast, "***Expulso,***" causing an explosion between them and Draco. Blaise and Dean tried to grab Harry, but more Death Eaters had come and forced them back into the Dining room.

Alucard shape shifted into a lion and he and several Death Eaters charged at Justice. "***Come Forth!***" he commanded and the three Zowls leapt from the wand and immediately began fighting the Death Eaters. "***Beast-mode!***" Justice spun and turned into the wolverine, but he was three times his normal size. He charged at Alucard and the two of them clawed and bit and rolled over and over. Justice maneuvered into position to grab Alucard by the throat, but he wasn't strong enough to finish him. Alucard slashed him across the chest then ran over to Demetria, knocked her down and placed his mouth over her throat.

Justice returned to his normal form. Alucard placed his claws to her chest and snarled. Draco told Justice to call off the Zowls or Alucard would kill her.

"***Return!***" he commanded and the three of them did as they were told.

CAPTIVE???

Hermione and Kalick simultaneously opened their eyes. Hermione had been knocked out with chloroform. That's why Justice couldn't reach her and why he felt so sluggish. She stumbled out of the bed and realized she was in the Gryffindor girl's sleeping quarters. She was alone. She tried to apparate, but the restrictions had been restored on the castle. She went to the door and could hear voices. She retrieved Bellatrix Lestrange's wand from her beaded bag and crept up the stairs until she could see into the Common room. Pansy Parkinson was telling Sally-Anne Perks and Millicent Bulstrode that she was hungry.

"Go to the Dining Hall and see if you can find anything edible."

"Come with us. She'll be out for hours." stated Millicent. "The rest of the army will be here before she wakes up."

"No, Draco told me to make sure she doesn't leave the house until he gets here. I'm gonna stay, I might even go up there and cut all her hair off. I hate her. Little Miss Perfect." The others laughed.

"We'll be right back." They left and Pansy sat back down on the sofa. Hermione waited a bit to make sure the other two girls were far enough away then cast "***Muffliato!***" She pointed her wand and cast a Toenail Growth Hex. Pansy's toenails grew right through her trainers and into the floor. Then she cast "***Taranalegra,***" which forced Pansy's legs to dance uncontrollably. With her long toenails anchored to the floor this was very painful. Pansy screamed, but no one outside the room could hear her. Myrtle and Peeves came in and took great delight in what they were seeing. Hermione remembered her laughing when Ron's curse at Draco rebounded on him in their first year and she cast "***Slugulus Eructo;***" the same slug vomiting curse Ron had suffered. She tossed Pansy a wastebasket as she left the room. A troll patrolling the halls spotted her and began to yell. "***Silencio!***" she cast, but the damage was done. The other girls ran back toward the Common room. Hermione looked around for an escape route.

She headed straight for a stained-glass window. The troll closed the distance in just a few strides and prepared to swing its club. As she ran, she cast, "*Periculum*," behind her. Red sparks flew from the tip of her wand, blinding the behemoth and it tumbled over her and right through the window. Hermione vaporized and the two girls followed. She cast spells at them but was inaccurate while vaporized. She needed to re-materialize. She did so at the opening in the fence and the moment the two girls appeared they were surrounded and bound by Firenze and the other Centaurs.

"Thank you." she said.

"We've got them, friend of Harry Potter, go." he told her.

She ran through and concentrated. She tried to reach Justice, but he was busy being beaten. He had to surrender to them and Alucard was going to kill him but couldn't find the wand. Although he was being whipped, Justice could feel his strength returning the more awake Hermione became.

Hermione stopped and closed her eyes and Charista appeared. They hugged immediately and Charista told her where Justice was. She told Charista what Millicent had said about the army coming. "I'll be ready for them."

"Be careful. I'll return as soon as I can. I just feel I have to go help him."

"Go. I'll be fine." She transformed into the unicorn and ran into the grounds stopping to converse with Firenze.

Hermione apparated to Malfoy Manor. She snuck into the house passing the still frozen dogs on the way. Justice silently cast a spell that broke his chains. Draco called to Alucard, "My Lord!" He ran over to him and handed him the cloak.

"The true Cloak of Invisibility." Alucard said aloud.

Justice looked around the room and targeted the Death Eaters.

"And now for the wand." He approached Justice, grabbed his head and yanked it back. He reached into Justice's mouth and pulled out the wand. Hermione entered the room through one door. Kalick entered through another and pointed her wand at Justice. Hermione shouted for Justice and when he heard her name, he felt a surge of power. She told him to look out, he turned invisible. There was an explosion that blasted away a huge section of the roof.

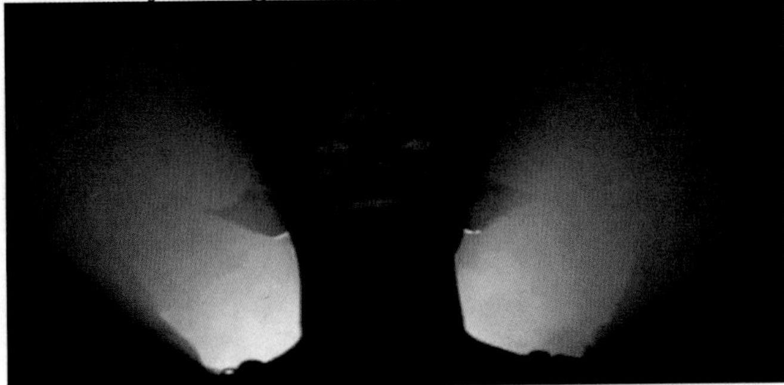

The Reaper had arrived to collect at least one of his prized possessions. Justice reappeared and cast a cascading jinx, "*Oblivion! Aladusuch!*" The Death Eaters burst into confetti.

"STAND BACK! I NOW POSSESS ALL THREE OF THE HALLOWS! I FEAR NOTHING! I AM INVINCIBLE!!!

Alucard grabbed Justice and pressed the wand to his temple. Draco looked up at Hermione, "It can't be." In Alucard's presence Hermione's wound began to drip blood. He tilted his head back and inhaled. His nostrils flared; his eyes rolled back.

Chapter 42 – Alucard vs. Justice

"The blood sacrifice has arrived." he said. Kalick stepped closer. With Alucard distracted, Justice turned invisible and slipped out of his grip. Alucard started toward her and suddenly a second Hermione stepped out from behind the first one. There were two, both identical. This time Justice even remembered to duplicate the Vanilla perfume. Kalick stopped and took a step back. The Reaper hovered over them, seemingly intrigued by the developments. Harry came to and Draco grabbed him and forced him to watch. Alucard pointed his new wand and told them not to move. Justice cast a protective shield over the others and stood side by side with the real Hermione. Alucard approached and sniffed them one by one. He still couldn't tell which was the real Hermione but did realize the blood he smelled wasn't coming from either of them. He grabbed one of them by her face and tilted her head from one side to the other. "Kalick, come." he called to her.

She approached them and he guided her hands to one of their faces. She touched the face and felt the eyes, the nose, the mouth then she moved to the second one and repeated the inspection. The Reaper pointed its staff and Kalick's vision was restored momentarily.

Justice cast, "***Imperio!***"

"That's her." she said. He threw the other one to the side. It was the real Hermione. He grabbed the face of the one that still stood before him, tilted it to the side and expose her neck.

"Now would be a good time." she said.

"What did you say?" Alucard asked. He pulled her closer.

'Jean! Justice said to her using his mind.

'I can't do it, I'll hurt you'. she replied.

'DO IT, NOW!' Justice reached up to the Elder Wand in Alucard's hand.

"Show yourself, now, or she dies." Alucard shouted, "Who are we kidding, she dies either way. ***AVADA KEDAVRA!***" Nothing happened.

Justice snapped the wand in two. "It would have worked if the wand was real. Thank you, Krysta Marie Madison." Alucard positioned her between and the others.

The real Hermione stood up from across the room, pointed her wand, "***FOCUS! ALADUSUCH!***" A curse shot from her wand straight at Justice and Alucard. It went through Justice and blasted Alucard back against the wall. Alucard was shocked and disoriented. As he tried to get to his feet the Resurrection Stone fell from his pocket. He couldn't believe he had gotten hit with a curse through another person.

"I did it?" Hermione questioned.

"You did!" Ron shouted.

Justice ran to Alucard. He was still in Hermione's image. Alucard grabbed him by the throat. "NO!" Hermione screamed. She noticed blood staining the back of Justice's shirt. He had gotten hurt from her attempt. He transformed back into himself and grabbed Alucard by the throat as well. He snatched the amulet from around Alucard's neck without him noticing. He punched Alucard in the stomach and grabbed his throat again lifting him off the ground and slamming him against the wall. Alucard's face turned skeletal, his fingernails grew to inch long, razor sharp daggers. He opened his mouth exposing his fangs. He thrust his fingernails into Justice's torso and Justice moaned.

"NO!!! YOU PROMISED!!!" Hermione shouted at him.

He looked over at her then slumped to the ground. Mallory, Dani, Ron, Harry and the others could see the life fading from his eyes.

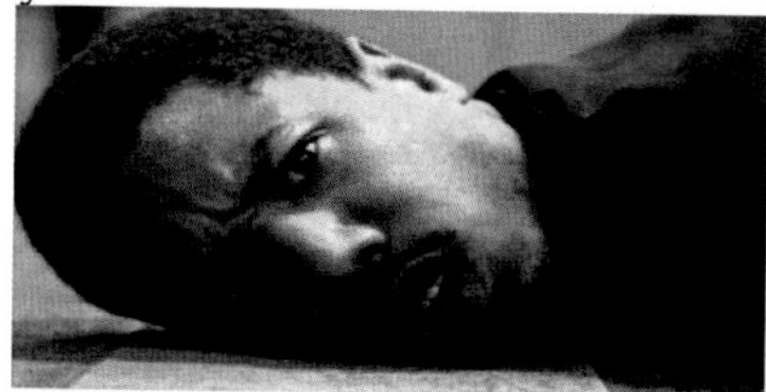

"Don't be ashamed, your fate was set long before this. I was just the vessel to escort you to the other side." Alucard picked him up and thrust his fingers in deeper until they poked out of Justice's back. "How does it feel to lose?"

Justice's head slumped forward. Draco pulled back his sleeve and pressed his finger to his Dark Mark. "*Morsmordre*!" He was calling for backup since Alucard had won the battle.

Justice's friends were inconsolable. Everyone was crying. Then Neville said, "Wait." they all looked up and Justice began to move. He grabbed Alucard's arms and held them in place.

"I don't know how it feels. I've never lost. And now I am angry. *IMPERVIOUS! ALADUSUCH! INCENDIO!*" He burst into flames.

He pulled Alucard tightly to him. Alucard ignited. "***INCENDIO MAXIMA!***" The flames burned so hot the others ran for cover. They didn't realize Justice had placed a protection on them that kept them from harm. It was just the Death Eaters who were spontaneously combusting. Justice reached into his pockets and when he pulled his hands out, in between each of his fingers, was a razor sharp, goblin made, solid silver dagger.

He plunged the daggers deep into Alucard's chest. Alucard drew in a labored breath. His chest began to burn from the sliver. He tried to pull the daggers out but couldn't get a grip. When he did, his fingers were singed. 'Thank you, Professor Flitwick'.

He looked up at Justice and screamed. "YOU!!!"

Justice pulled out the silver Occomy eggs and shoved them into Alucard's mouth then he slammed his palm into Alucard's chin. Draco took the Resurrection Stone, grabbed Harry and Hermione then vaporized and disappeared. Justice slammed Alucard with a head butt that knocked out two of his fangs. Alucard's eyes grew large when he glanced down and realized he'd also been impaled by the sword of Gryffindor, which Demetria was holding. She was, in fact, a worthy Gryffindor in need and the sword came to her. He tried to transfigure. If he was successful, he could heal himself in another form, but Rochelle burst in and cast a Homorphus Charm that changed him right back. Kalick fell to the ground and took in a deep breath. Justice looked over to her. "Thank you for setting me free." she said to him. Then her robes caught fire and she simply closed her eyes.

Chapter 42 – Alucard vs. Justice

Justice grabbed Alucard by the elbows and yanked upward breaking both of his arms. He grabbed Alucard by the back of the head and kneed him in the stomach, then pulled his head down and kneed him in the chin. He lifted his leg and placed his foot on Alucard's chest then kicked him away forcing Alucard's fingers out of his body. Justice staggered over to Demetria. He caressed her face and nodded. He stumbled over to Alucard, knelt behind him and placed his arm beneath his chin. He locked it in place with his other arm. He had Alucard in a sleeper hold and he applied pressure until Alucard passed out. Then, with a quick jerk, he snapped his neck and pushed his lifeless body aside. It was over. The Reaper nodded to him and collected Alucard's soul then disappeared. The others ran over to him and just as Reggie was as close as arms distance away, Justice collapsed.

Reggie caught him and laid him down. "YOU DID IT!" He paused. "I can't believe you did it, you defeated Alucard."

"Where are Harry and Jean?" he asked.

"Draco took them." said Demetria.

"Where's Jade?" Blaise asked. Justice didn't respond. He struggled to get up.

"Justice, you can't help anyone in this condition. We have to get you to a hospital." Dani told him.

"You know that would be a waste of time for me." He noticed her arm bleeding. "Your arm," he paused, "It was you. You're the blood sacrifice?"

"What's he talkin' about?" Seamus asked.

"Not anymore." she said to him, fighting to hold back tears.

"He's dying." They all looked up at the person who said it.

"Who are you?" Dean asked as he pulled his wand.

"My name is Rochelle Maynard. I'm a friend of Justice's."

"What are you doing here?" Stormy asked her.

"It's my turn. Like Justice, I'm an offset. I was one of twelve, but now I'm one of only three who are still alive, soon to be two from the looks of him. I can help him if you let me. I can ease his suffering."

"How?" Dani asked.

She began taking her clothes off.

Chapter 42 – Alucard vs. Justice

"Um, what are you doing?" Reggie asked.

"Changing into something I can fight in. The twelve of us were always meant to help one another, but people and circumstances have always worked against us. Separating us as children, they thought they were protecting us, but they were just making us weaker, more vulnerable. The twelve of us were meant to fight Alucard together, but as we grew, we all came to know, through planned encounters, that Justice was the best of us. So, the prophecy shifted. It was unprecedented. At some point in his life, Justice was in contact with all the other offsets. Alexi was the last. Our offset assignments changed and each of us was assigned other potential Dark Lords to defeat. Nine of us failed and Justice unknowingly took on the burden of each of the assignments, one by one. With Alucard, he's now killed eight potential leaders of the Death Eaters. I killed one. But that wasn't my assignment. Harry was shifted to Voldemort, Justice was assigned to Alucard, Alexi was assigned to Kalick, and I am assigned to the last threat of this century, Draco Malfoy."

They all gasped. "I just need to find him. He's recruited an army and they planned to strike three days from now, but when Draco thought Alucard might defeat Justice, he summoned them now and they're gathering in force."

"So how do we find them?" Mallory asked.

"With as many as there are supposed to be it shouldn't be too hard, the problem is time. We don't have any. We don't want to have to follow a trail of bodies to track them down. We need to know their first target so we can stop them there."

"So where do we start?" asked Freddy.

"With him. The prophecy states that he'll know where I need to go."

"Do whatever you can for him. We need him." Demetria told her.

She finished pulling her hair back into a ponytail then knelt over him and kissed him.

"Yeah, that should wake him up." Ron stated.

She said an incantation over him then placed his wand

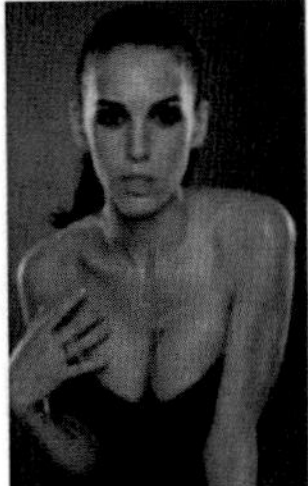

between his teeth. She inhaled deeply and blew into his thumb. He screamed out in agony.

"STOP IT, YOU'RE KILLING HIM!!!" shouted Stormy.

He began to breathe very shallow then suddenly stopped all together. Everyone was sobbing when just as suddenly he arched his back and inhaled then began to cough. "Thanks for comin' back. Are you alright?" he mustered.

"Thanks to you." He held her hand and they both closed their eyes.

"Hermione, can you hear me?" she asked.

"Yes. Who is this?"

"It's Rochelle, where are you?"

"Hogwarts." She paused. "They're coming."

"Hermione?" Rochelle paused, "Hermione?"

"We've got to go." Justice said.

"I gave you all I could spare to keep you alive long enough to make the trip to a hospital. I don't know that they'll be able to save you. You certainly aren't in any condition to help me. You were amazing, as always. You did what none of the rest of us could have. Don't try to steal my thunder."

"Thank you." Neville said to her.

"Thank you for being such good friends to him." She turned to leave.

"I'll go with you; you can use a hand and I can show you the way. Demetria offered. "Besides, I owe him. He's the only family I've got left. What Alucard said about me spying on

Justice..."

"It's okay. We all knew that was a lie. He was controlling you, Marcus and Jade. He knew, trust me." She motioned to Justice. Justice strained to say no to try to stop them.

HOGWARTS

Hermione was in a daze. She saw what happened when she tried to use the Focus Energy Targeting, she may have killed Justice. She was being dragged around like a rag doll and was too shaken to fight it. Harry had gotten a shroud placed around his head so he couldn't speak or tell what was happening until they arrived. Draco used the chloroform once again, and put her to sleep. Then he awaited the arrival of his guests.

Rochelle took Demetria's hand. "That was very brave of you, choosing Justice over your own father."

"Justice has always been more of a father to me than Alucard ever was. I love him."

"We all do, no matter how hard we try not to." She paused. "When we get there, you show me the way in then you go. Justice built a safe house in Little Hangleton for the students and staff. You'll be safe there."

"I can fight. I'm strong and I'm not afraid."

"I can tell, but this isn't the time or the place. You're the daughter of the most powerful Dark wizard ever. What magic you do possess came from him. Let the Hogwarts professors help you develop it for good and you could end up as Minister of Magic."

"I can't think beyond right now, I just want Justice to survive and heal."

"That may be a request beyond us. Offsets have a difficult enough task guiding their future, Justice has much more at stake than the rest of us. The way to honor him is to not undue his great work by allowing another Dark Lord to simply step in and take the place of the one he put down. As you said, I too owe him. He saved my life too. I fell in love with him the moment we met and to try to impress him I did some foolish, reckless things. One of them nearly cost me my life. I was crushed during a challenge in the American version of the Triwizard Tournament. He was well ahead and was rightfully going to win easily, but he turned back when I was injured. He dug me out and performed the same technique on me that I did on him back there. I should have died. He then offered to let me win since the risk I had taken showed him how badly I desired the trophy. I talked him out of it and withdrew from the competition. I left the country to attend

Beauxbatons. I never forgot what he did, and I never stopped loving him. But my time with him taught me what we were here for, and I refocused and was able to complete a task. I've been aspiring to live up to what I thought would make him proud ever since."

"That's funny, that's the same thing that's always driven me to be the head of my class, trying to impress him. I had something similar happen to me that I've never spoken of to anyone before. I looked up to Jade, our Keeper."

"The pretty blond?"

"Yes. I thought of her as a big sister. She would constantly sneak out of our coven to go back to see her foster family. One night I followed her. I tried to stay back far enough for her not to notice, but all it did was get me lost. I was still young and hadn't been at the coven very long so I couldn't find my way back. I was stranded for hours. I was walking down an alley that I thought was the one our coven was hidden on, and three men stopped me. I knew I wasn't supposed to use magic outside of the coven, I wasn't supposed to be outside at all. I tried to run, but they were so fast and so strong. They grabbed me and shoved me back and forth. I pulled out my wand, but one of them snatched it out of my hand and broke it. They knew I was a witch. He stabbed me in the neck with it and they left me to die. Justice found me moments later. He pulled it out, healed me and covered me. He turned invisible and found the men. They were going to tell about me. I didn't see what he did, but I heard the screams. He came back covered in blood and took me home. The next morning, I woke up and there was a box on my bed. I opened it and there was a brand-new Krysta Marie Madison wand in it. He never told anyone, and we never spoke of it again."

A CHANCE FOR REDEMTION

Justice reached out and Neville and Blaise helped him up. He leaned into Neville. "Bring Jade to me."

"Where is she?"

"She's in the next room. Be careful with her."

Ron, Dean and Seamus carried her into the room and laid her body on a table. "Who did this to her?" Ron asked.

"I did." Justice replied. He walked over to her and pulled the metal tip from her temple. "When I first met Jade, she'd been beaten so badly she had bleeding on her brain. Our doctors did everything they could, but there was always a possibility that the injury could rupture, and she could bleed out. One of the times she snuck out of the coven she was attacked. She was gone for three weeks. When we finally found her, I could tell something was different about her. It turns out they had performed an operation on her and placed something in her brain that they used to control her. They tried to use her to lead them to us, but her love for us caused her constant conflict." He unscrewed the tip of the metal piece that had been lodged in her head and inside was a cylindrical computer chip. "This was why she was always so aggressive and conflicted." He snapped it in half. "They activated the tracker several times and it was always preceded by severe headaches, because she'd subconsciously suppress the signal. It's how she found her way here. That's why whenever she complained of headaches, I would always ask her if it was like before."

"That's been in her head all this time?" Dean asked. Justice nodded.

He touched his wand to her wound. "***Aladusuch!***" The wound sealed. He caressed her face and spoke softly to her,

Chapter 43 – Draco the Dark Lord

"Get up lazy bones." Slowly her eyes opened. She looked up at him. "Welcome back. How do you feel?"

"Better than I have in a long time." she whispered.

"Good, cause I'm gonna need you."

"You're hurt." She noticed. "What happened?"

"It's just a scratch. Seeing you like this makes me feel better." He stepped aside. The others stepped over to her and hugged her and welcomed her back.

She sat up and rotated her head. "What happened?"

"Long story. We'll tell it later. We need to get to Hogwarts."

"Who's the target?"

"Draco Malfoy, but he's got an army with him."

"We can take em. What's the plan?"

"Still working on it, but we don't have much time. Are you able to travel?"

"There's only one way to find out, but I could ask you the same thing."

"I'm feeling a little better."

"You don't look it."

"I'll be fine. This isn't over. Let's saddle up everyone. I need some suggestions." he asked.

"We need to get into the castle grounds then lock it down so that no matter what happens to us inside they can never leave." said Mallory.

"We also have to keep more Death Eaters from getting in behind us to catch us in a crossfire." said Freddy.

"They'll attack from both the ground and the air, so we could use some aerial support." Dani pointed out.

"Got it." he said. "Follow my lead. We'll rendezvous at the point in the forest where we first arrived at the school."

Jade took Justice by the arm. "Thank you, for everything. Thank you for still having faith in me after everything that's happened. I will redeem myself."

"This is your favorite part. You've always been good in a fight. Besides, you've helped me just as much as I've ever helped you."

"Liar." She smiled.

"There are going to be a lot of them everywhere you look. Aim true and be careful." He created a port key. "Anyone not ready for this go to the safe house. I'll completely understand. There's no shame in choosing to live to fight another day. To die today is not the destiny of everyone here. If I have my way, it won't be the fate of ***anyone*** here." he said and staggered.

"Are you sure you're up to this. You still look a little…" Blaise noticed.

"It's not me. It's Jean. They must have drugged her." he explained.

"We're with ya." said Seamus.

"Yeah!" the others echoed. "Whatever you need."

"Until the end." Mallory added.

"Alright, grab hold." They all touched the port key. Justice touched the pile of hands last and again placed a protective charm on them. They disappeared.

THE BATTLE

They arrived and saw the sky littered with Death Eaters

Griffin

chasing Rochelle and Demetria. Rochelle was zipping back and forth fighting them off. Demetria was not as skilled a flyer but was holding her own. She flew low and cast curses back behind her knocking the Death Eaters to the ground. Justice looked around and found a Death Eater on a Firebolt. "Wait here!" he told the others. "Freddy." he called. Freddy braced himself.

Justice ran toward him and turned invisible just as he got close. Freddy dipped down then propelled his invisible body into the air just as the Death Eater passed over their heads. It was as if the Death Eater had hit a solid wall. He fell to the ground where Dean and Reggie pummeled him. The broom seemingly landed itself. Justice materialized. He pointed at the broom, "***Geminio!***" The broom duplicated a dozen times. They each mounted one and prepared to take to the air. "Give them a hand, would you?" Justice asked of the group. Stormy, Reggie, Ron, Blaise, Robyn and Mallory took off. They attacked the pursuing Death Eaters like fighter jets, each with a wingman.

Curses showered down at them. Justice, Dean and Dani deflected them. There were three Death Eaters bearing down on them and simultaneously they slumped over and spiraled into the ground. Cam, Charista and McGonagall flew down and greeted them. Cam hugged Justice then Jade hugged Cam to his surprise. "Just go with it." Justice told him. He looked over to Charista, "Glad you could join us." he smiled.

"I wouldn't miss it for the world." she replied.

"Status?" he asked.

"There are at least a hundred coming from Hogsmeade,

they'll be here in a matter of minutes." Cam told him.

"There's nowhere to hide here." McGonagall pointed out. "We'll have to make a stand."

Justice looked around, "That's not entirely true."

"I'll take a group in on the ground. We have to find Harry and Jean." Jade offered and Cam turned to go with her.

"Guys, hang on a minute." He tuned in to Rochelle so she could hear him. "Lead them toward the castle, quickly. Keep them close to the castle if you can. Don't go to the lake or the forest." Neville, Dean and Seamus flew off and the Death Eaters followed.

"Justice, don't even think about it. It's too big even if you weren't hurt." Dani told him.

"He's not planning what I think he's planning is he?" Charista asked.

I think I'm getting my second wind. He pointed his wand into the air, "***Griffin, Come Forth!***" Another mighty Griffin flew out of the tip of the wand and landed before him. He ripped a piece of the cloak of one of the fallen Death Eaters. He held it up to the Griffin then made it transform into vapor. The Griffin inhaled the scent then flew off. Justice faced the grounds, closed his eyes and said, "***Vanish!***" The entire school disappeared. "Let's go." He led the others to the opening in the fence. They stepped through and he told Cam to seal it off.

Cam repaired the fence. "Charista, Dani, Headmistress, can you please target the brooms. We need them on the ground."

The three of them began casting spells at the Death Eaters who were chasing the group. They began dropping from the sky. Justice, with everyone inside, pointed his wand. "***Fianto Duri, Repello Inimicum, Maxima! Aladusuch!***" He placed a dome over the grounds. He, himself, was outside the barrier.

Chapter 43 – Draco the Dark Lord

Chimera

Once the dome was in place the castle reappeared but was not yet visible through the barrier. "I'll be back." He vaporized and flew to meet the approaching army. He landed on the ground and since he vaporized like a Death Eater the army landed. The leaders of the Germans, the South Africans, the Irish, the Japanese and the Italians approached.

"Greetings." Justice said.

"Who are you?" asked the South African.

"Draco sent me. The fights begun. It's just over the hill. How many strong are you?"

"Each of us brought about seventy members, as agreed." said the German.

"Over four hundred." Justice calculated.

"With the five hundred waiting in the castle dungeons we should slice through those Ministry idiots in no time." said the Irishman.

"So, what is plan?" asked the Japanese Death Eater.

"The Ministry and the Order have a line of defense that stretches about a quarter mile. You should form a line. Space yourselves about every ten feet, you'll overwhelm them."

"Alright, let's get in there. I can't wait to slaughter those traitors." said the German.

"Ditto." Justice said to them.

"You heard the man, spread out in ten-foot gaps. Fly down their throats!" he told them. They flared out and took off.

"You're accent, it's American, no?" asked the Italian.

"Are you with Aldrich's group?" asked the Irishman. Justice's expression went blank.

"Yeah, Aldrich's group." He tuned in to Charista and Rochelle. 'There are about five hundred more of them in the castle dungeon. I'm on my way back, how are you doing?"

"We're just about done with these." Rochelle replied. "I was just thinking this is way too easy."

"That was about seventy-five against fifteen of us. There's a big difference between five each and thirty plus." Charista reminded them.

"Yeah, well that's only if I can get rid of the four hundred, I have with me. We need Harry and Jean. Jean, can you hear me." He didn't get an answer.

"Where are they?" Crabbe asked Draco.

"Who cares? We've got the filthy mudblood, the American will come to us. Have the others stay hidden until he arrives."

"The staff and students aren't here. We've checked the entire school, they had to have known we were coming." said Goyle, still favoring his fingerless hand.

"Did they Pansy? Did they know we were coming?" A shirtless Draco had her hanging from a beam.

"I told you, there was no one here when we brought her the first time. If someone told it wasn't me. Please, Draco, let me go."

"You want down?" he asked her, "Fine." He showed his fangs and leapt onto her biting her throat. Crabbe and Goyle turned away as Draco jumped down from her and wiped her blood from his face.

"What about the Phoenix's fighting outside?" Crabbe asked.

"Is any of them Justice?"

"Not that we can tell."

"Blaise?"

Chapter 43 – Draco the Dark Lord

"Yeah, he's out there."

"Get him and kill him, bring me his head. Get her out of here. It's time for the ritual to begin. Bring him to me."

"He's lost it." Crabbe whispered.

"Yeah? You tell him." Goyle replied.

The Death Eaters flew in a line with ten foot spacing. Justice led them and increased his speed as he got close to the school's perimeter.

"It's supposed to be here." said the German leader. All they saw was vacant land before them.

"No, no. It's farther over the hill toward the water." Justice told them. They sped up to keep pace. He disappeared just short of the barrier and flew in a loop. Hundreds of them flew blindly into the protection and disintegrated. He was positioned behind the rest that pulled up in time. "*Aladusuch!*" Their brooms vanished. They hit the ground and began casting curses up at him. He pointed his wand, "*Come Forth!*" The Zowls, the Graphorns, the Nundu and a Chimera charged out. Justice cast, "*Fianto Duri, Repello Inimicum, Maxima! Aladusuch!*" The Death Eaters were sealed in. They took off running away. Justice opened a pathway into the school grounds. And as soon as he stepped in, he was met by Firenze.

"We will take it from here. You go, fight the darkness. Good luck, Mr. Cain. They will not get through us."

"Thank you."

Hermione slowly awakened. She had been asleep about an hour and was still disoriented. She walked into the common room. There was no one there. Everything was neat and tidy with a warm fire burning in the fireplace. She made her way up to the boy's dormitory, but all the beds were empty. She ventured into the hall. Everything was intact and in proper order. Something wasn't right. It was quiet in the castle, too quiet. She began to hear sounds in the dining room. She pulled the doors open and fire raced up the walls. She was sucked into the room. Ropes lashed out and bound her wrists. She was being pulled toward the center of the room through a crowd of Inferi. They clawed and pulled at her as she was dragged toward the center of the gathering.

The crowd parted and she could see Harry tied to a table. He cried out when he saw her. His chest was bare and in the center of it he bore the Dark Mark. A hooded figure crouched over him and as it turned to face her, she could see it clutching a long dagger in its hand and its eyes were glowing red. It grinned at her bearing dozens of pointed teeth. It reached toward her, and she felt the fingers wrap around her throat and squeeze. She tried to scream, but no noise would come out. She found herself face to face with the creature and could smell its putrid odor. It flicked a forked tongue out at her then appeared to smell her. Her heart ached.

"Kiss me!" It hissed.

"What?" She could see the creature holding the Resurrection Stone in its hand.

"Kiss me and I'll let him go." Harry squirmed. "NOW!" It demanded. "Or I'll kill him."

She looked at Harry then back at the creature. Tears were streaming down her face. She closed her eyes tightly and leaned forward with a look of disgust. Just before the two made contact the creature pulled back its hood. It was Draco Malfoy.

"Malfoy?" she recoiled.

He removed his cloak and raised the knife high into the air. He began to chant an incantation then screamed and

Chapter 43 – Draco the Dark Lord

plunged the dagger deep into Harry's chest. Blood squirted onto his chest. He began to jump around and rub the blood in and in doing so clawed himself repeatedly.

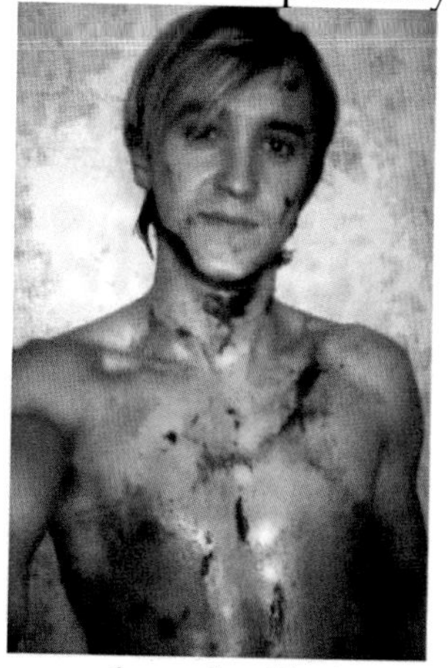

Finally, he screamed and all the windows in the room blew out. She clutched her chest and began to lose consciousness. The windows blowing out was Charista, Jade and Demetria storming the castle. Malfoy fired curses at them. Crabbe and Goyle ran back into the Great Hall being chased by Mallory, Blaise and Stormy.

Draco laughed hysterically as he waved his wand and lit the ceiling on fire. The others raced in. McGonagall pointed her wand and put out the fire. Draco grabbed Hermione. "Drop the wands, all of you, or I'll kill her!"

Justice vaporized and entered the castle. He could smell Draco the moment he entered the building. He raced through the halls and made his way to the Great Hall.

"Pssst!" He looked around then heard it again. "Pssst!" He noticed Nearly Headless Nick motioning for him to follow.

"There's another way into the Hall. I can show you, but we need to do something about the ones in the dungeon."

"I need to know she's alright."

"Follow me." They went upstairs to a broom closet. There was a vent opening concealed by a painting. "This vent let's out in the Great Hall above the staff table." Justice nodded to him then vaporized into the vent. When he reached the opening, he could see Harry on the table with the dagger stuck in his torso. He saw the others bound and being watched by Crabbe and Goyle. He saw Pansy Parkinson staring blankly with fangs showing. He saw Jade standing in front of Aldrich who had his hand around her throat, and he saw Draco holding Hermione by the hair. He heard a sound behind him and without looking back a flame lit beneath Peeves.

"I'm here to help." he pleaded. Myrtle and Nick were there too. Justice was skeptical, but Nick nodded to him.

"Take this to the dungeon. When Draco gives the signal for the Death Eaters to come up, you open this vial, understand?" He handed Peeves the amulet. "You all have friends in there."

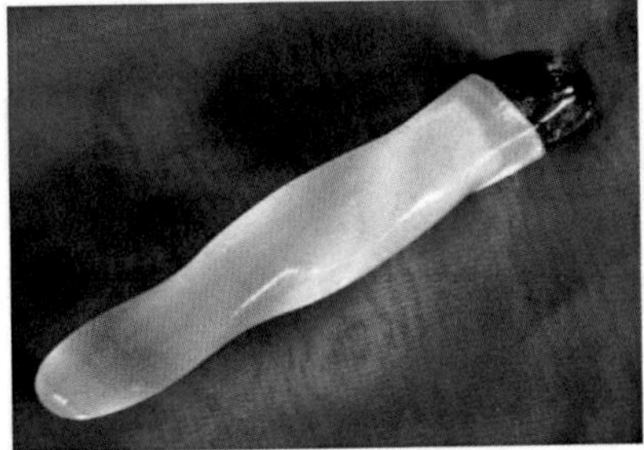

"Jean, can you hear me?" he asked.

'Justice? Yes, I can hear you. I'm so glad you…' she answered telepathically.

"Brace yourself, things are about to happen quickly." He tuned into Rochelle. "Are you done playin' around?"

'It took you long enough'.

Chapter 43 – Draco the Dark Lord

'Charista, get ready.'

'Ready when you are'.

He used '*Sonorus*' and his voice was heard throughout the Great Hall. "Y'all gone make me lose my mind." Draco and the others looked around.

Cam said, "Up in here."

Then Freddy echoed, "Up in here."

"Y'all gone make me act a fool."

Cam and Freddy again echoed, "Up in here."

Draco shouted, "SHOW YOURSELF!" He pulled Hermione near and placed the knife to her neck. "I'll do it!" He poked the blade in just enough to pierce the skin. When he pulled the knife back there was no blood. Draco didn't understand. Blood did, however, drip from Justice's neck. He cast a switching spell just as Draco raised the dagger again. Hermione was now in the vent and Draco plunged the dagger into Justice's side.

"*Aladusuch*!" He cast and all the chains broke, the Alphas were free. "Now Jean!"

"*Focus*! *Aladusuch*!" Draco was blasted back against the wall.

Both Rochelle and Charista fired Arrow shooting spells at him pinning him against a wall. Hermione climbed down out of the vent and approached him and as she got to his impaled body, he was still lashing out with his teeth trying to bite her. The sword of Gryffindor appeared in her hand. He vaporized to try to escape, but Hermione shouted, "*Aladusuch*!" and captured the smoke in a ball of energy.

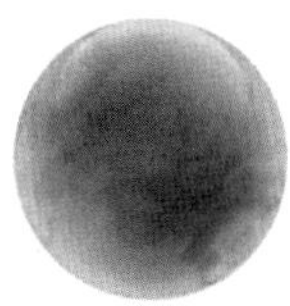

Justice stretched out his hand and with a downward motion made the energy ball slam to the ground and explode leaving Draco lying there back in his human form. "Thanks, Charista." He had used the elf magic he had taken from her when they fought at Malfoy Manor.

Rochelle fired arrows that once again secured him.

Justice turned to Aldrich. "You should really take your hands off her. It didn't work out too well for you last time." Blood streamed down his leg from his stab wound and he fell to one knee.

"Look at you. You can barely keep your eyes open. She's comin' with me. She belongs to me, always has, always will."

"You don't control her anymore. She can make up her own mind."

"You have no idea of the bond she and I share. You really need to hear her say it. Tell him, tell him who you love, who you've always loved."

"You disgust me. All the things you and your friends did to me. All the times you beat me and Inara. I should have killed you years ago."

"Watch your mouth. He's the one that killed Inara." Ron, Neville and Seamus stepped closer to him with their wands poised. He pulled her close to him to use as a shield.

"Back up! Back away! Jade, tell them to back away!" He turned to her and whispered. "I'd never hurt you; I love you."

"*Focus! Aladusuch!*" Justice cast and Aldrich flew across the room. Jade turned and ran to him. Her wand transformed into a 10-inch serrated knife. "Jade, don't get too close." he warned. Aldrich grabbed her and stabbed her with his dagger. She staggered back and pulled the blade out. They were both shocked to see she wasn't injured. Justice collapsed to the floor.

Draco yanked his arm free of the arrows and touched his finger to his Dark Mark to call the other Death Eaters from the dungeons. The doors swung open, and Peeves was right there with the amulet. He unscrewed the top and the souls were released. The souls joined their undead bodies, and they overwhelmed the Death Eaters. Professor Paramore floated over to Peeves and thanked him for releasing the souls, "Who do we have to thank for our liberation?"

Peeves thought about it for moment, but even he knew there had to be honor amongst spirits, so he told the truth, "His name is Justice Cain."

Paramore nodded then joined the attack on the Death Eaters. The screams were deafening.

Draco screamed and Rochelle cast "***Lumos Solem, Maxima!***" The sunlight shown through and Draco, Aldrich and Pansy burst into flames.

Simultaneously, Hermione and Jade lifted their blades and swung. Both Aldrich and Draco's bodies dropped to the floor. Pansy slumped to the ground. Crabbe and Goyle dropped their wands and put their hands up. Firenze galloped into the castle with Dolores Umbridge draped over his back. "She was found wandering in the forest dazed and mumbling. Her memory had been wiped. She has no idea who she is."

Hermione ran to Justice. She was crying. There was so much blood. Rochelle ran over as well. "Do something! Blow on his finger like you did before." Demetria begged of her.

Rochelle knew he was beyond any magic she could do for him. Hagrid rounded up the magical creatures between the barriers and the barriers magically closed in on one another disintegrating everything still trapped between them. The Zowls disappeared.

Mallory and Ron walked over to Harry. Mallory was able to detect a slight pulse.

Ron braced him and pulled the dagger out of his chest. Just then Albus, the Phoenix, flew into the room and landed beside him. It cried into the wounds.

They placed Justice on a table beside Harry. Hermione blew into his thumb repeatedly, but nothing seemed to help. He caressed her face. "It's okay. It was always meant to be this way."

"Why did you change places with me. If you hadn't, you'd be okay."

"No. I wouldn't. This was my deal and I'm ready to go. You're safe. That's what matters. I wish I had a little more time. There are a couple things I had left to do."

"Don't leave me, not now."

"I'll always be with you. I just have to rest." His eyes began to flicker. He motioned to Rochelle. She stepped over. "Take care of them. You and Harry are the only ones left. Help each other. It's not going to last forever with no Dark Lord. Stay sharp." he asked for Charista. She stepped close to the head of the table. "You were amazing." He tugged at her glove. She removed it and touched his hand. When he let her go, his nose began to bleed a little. "Thank you, all of you. This was the best few months of my life and if I had it to do over again, I wouldn't hesitate. Thank you, Headmistress, for allowing us to come here and for being so kind to us. Mallory, what can I say, you've been an inspiration. D, straight A's. Guys, Stormy, Robin, it was great playing Quidditch with you all. Jade, I love you. Now you're ready to be an Alpha. Dani, you practically raised me. I love you. Without you I'd still be roaming the streets performing card tricks for change. He coughed several times. "I can't see Harry, where is he?" Harry was right beside him. His vision was fading.

Dani took his hand and placed it on Harry's shoulder. A surge of energy passed from him to Harry. His hand slipped off and hung beside the table. "Tell him he really is as great as advertised and I want a rematch with him, Charista and Jade.

Thank professor Flitwick, Bill Weasley and especially Neville. They were the true heroes in this battle. He reached blindly for Hermione's hand.

Jean, you're the best person I've ever met." He couldn't keep his eyes open at this point. His speech began to slow, and his breathing became shallow. "You were a dream come true for me and I really wish I could have kissed you more. You're an amazing kisser. I love you. I always will. The time I spent with you was the best of my life. I hope I made you proud." A single flower appeared in front of her. A beautiful red rose in full bloom with a paper wrapped around it.

She leaned down and kissed him. "I love you too. Yes, I am so proud of you." She wiped away her tears and looked down at him. He wasn't breathing. "Justice?" He didn't respond. "JUSTICE?" Tears poured from every eye in the room. She glanced at the rose and saw it dying before her eyes. Then an explosion occurred, blasting away the outer wall of the room. The sky grew dark with a huge moon in the background. A shadow entered the room. The Reaper had returned. "Please, please. Don't take him. He saved us all. His whole life was spent saving others, protecting others, he deserves to live."

He reached out and took the souls of the bodies in the room. He reached into Draco's pile of burnt flesh and retrieved the Resurrection Stone. He listened to her words then moved her aside and scooped Justice up in his arms. "Take me instead. He died saving me. It should be me going with you."

He turned away and Jade was standing before him with the 10-inch knife in her hand. "Take me in his place. I have no redeeming qualities." She raised the knife then plunged it toward her stomach. But the Reaper stopped it before it penetrated her skin. He touched the blade and it melted and dripped to the floor. He waved a finger indicating it wasn't her time. Justice disappeared.

"NO!!!" Hermione screamed. She ran to The Reaper and grabbed his cloak. He spun to face her, and a powerful gust of wind forced her and the others back. He faced her and looked into her eyes. The wind settled and The Reaper reached out a bony hand toward them. He pulled them to him then, one by one, he looked into each of their faces. Jade, Charista, Demetria, Stormy, Mallory, Rochelle, Dani, Professor

Chapter 43 – Draco the Dark Lord

McGonagall and back to Hermione. He backed outside amongst the debris and sprouted wings.

Then, just like that, it was over.

Chapter 44 – Moving on

Charista, Hermione and Ron gathered around Harry who had begun to stir. He reached for Hermione's hand.

"Harry!" Hermione shouted.

"Oh, thank heavens." said McGonagall.

"I'm sorry about Justice." Harry began, "He was a good guy. I can't believe it's over." From the grip he had on her hand she could tell he was feeling better. They inspected his wounds, and they were healing rapidly. McGonagall went to send an owl off to Filch in Little Hangleton. Dani sat with her head in her hands crying. She hadn't made the deal that cost Justice his life, but she felt guilty that her life was being spared at his expense. Cam, Freddy, Jade and Demetria sat around her. They now knew the truth about her and the Elders and, while they knew Justice wouldn't want them to hold a grudge, it was difficult for them to forgive so soon.

Neville held Stormy tight, consoling her. Reggie, Dean Blaise and Seamus sat together, and Mallory told Robyn how sorry she was about Emmerick. When McGonagall came back, she told them that she was going to ensure that Justice got a sendoff worthy of his greatness.

Rochelle sat down beside Hermione. She placed her hand on Hermione's shoulder. "I won't begin to tell you that you'll get over him, or life goes on. We're alive because of him. Life will never be the same for us. I loved him too, but not like you do, and he never felt for me the way he did for you. I am so sorry for your loss. If there is anything I can ever do to help you deal with it, please, don't hesitate."

"What are you going to do now?"

"I don't know. This is new territory for me. Eventually there will be someone who steps up on the Dark side. This won't last forever, but I've never known a time when all the known threats are gone. An offset really doesn't have a purpose without a Dark enemy. Quidditch is over and I have no family. I honestly don't know what to do."

"You're welcome to stay here. Practically all Slytherin house is going away. I'm sure the American coven would love to have you. It would be nice to have you around to help Harry. You two are still tied together."

"I suppose it would be easy enough to transfer, but are you sure it wouldn't prolong your grieving? Knowing that Harry and I represent the same thing that he did?"

"I don't want to forget him. I want to remember him for as long as I can. It would be nice to have a new friend."

Even her beautiful, brave smile couldn't conceal her pain. Rochelle saw through it. "I'll consider it if you'll teach me that magic you did when you cast the spell through another solid object."

"It's called Focus Energy Targeting. I've only done it twice, but I haven't got the hang of it yet."

"You executed it perfectly earlier."

She thought about it, "I guess I did."

Harry called Mallory and Charista over to him and said, "I know now is not the best time for this, but I stumbled across something that I think you should know. Charista, would you do the honors?" He held Mallory's hand and Christa took their free hand. The vision he'd seen in the pensive transferred to Mallory through Charista. The vision was of Aberforth hiding the Elder Wand. He hid it at the Hogs Head. Peeves was right, Aberforth had taken it off the campus and hid it in the leg of one of the bar stools. All they had to do was go pick it up. Aberforth had in fact intended for it to be left to Mallory in his will, but until now, no one knew where it was.

"That reminds me." Neville pulled out a rolled-up piece of parchment. "Aberforth gave this to me to give to you." He handed her his note. It turned out to be his actual will. She could safely possess it now, since Harry was its last master having won it from Voldemort, and with The Reaper having reclaimed the Resurrection Stone, the three Hallows would never again be possessed by one person.

Neville meanwhile walked up to Hermione and pulled her aside. "Justice gave me something to give to you in the event this happened. I don't even know when he did it, but he asked me to give you this." Neville handed her his wand.

The staff and students returned to the school. With the help of the Americans, Hagrid and Filch rebuilt the perimeter and repaired the damage to the interior. Rochelle transferred to Hogwarts and was fittingly sorted into Hufflepuff house. A monument was built to honor Justice, Dobby and Emmerick and it was placed on the island beside the Dumbledore's. Everyone attended the services. Viktor Krum, Fred and George Weasley, Gabrielle and Fleur Delacour-Weasley, even Krysta Marie Madison was in attendance. Somehow everything in the Forbidden Forest was aware of what was going on. As the students, staff and guests sat in attendance you could see animals lining the shore. The Nundu was spotted lying atop a rock. The Centaurs were lined up saluting the fallen warriors. The Chimera came to the water to take a drink. Fawkes, Albus, Buckbeak and the Griffin all soared high in the sky.

At one-point Hermione could have sworn she saw Blaze, Bolt and Blizzard peering out from tree line. But that was impossible. One by one the staff and students took turns speaking. They honored each of them with heartfelt speeches and recall of specific events. Hermione stepped up to the podium and acknowledged Emmerick then recalled when she first met Dobby in the Hogwarts kitchen in her second year. Dobby had always been a true friend to Harry Potter and had always been kind to Hermione after she began making clothes and leaving them around the Gryffindor Common Room to free house elves by presenting them with the garments. He'd saved them many times and was always there for them when they needed him.

When she began to speak of Justice she became understandably choked up. She had nothing but fond memories of him and honored him that day by wearing the Quinashe gown he'd given her. She looked amazing. She told them that Justice gave her a note on the day of his passing, and she wanted to share it with them since its words were fitting for the circumstances. "The words really mean something special to me since these are the kinds of things, he would say to me all the time. He had a real knack for saying the perfect thing at the right time and he loved to sing." She pulled out the piece of parchment and it quickly folded itself into a mouth and began to sing.

"If your lonely, and need a friend
And troubles seem like they never end
Just remember to keep the faith
A love will be there to light the way

Anytime you need a friend, I will be here
Never be alone again, so don't you fear
Even if you're miles away, I'm by your side
So don't you ever be lonely, love will make it alright

Chapter 44 - Moving on

When the shadows, are closin' in
And you spirit deminisin'
Just remember, you're not alone
And love will be there yeah, to guide you home

Anytime you need a friend, I will be here
Never be alone again, so don't you fear
Even if you're miles away, I'm by your side
So don't you ever be lonely, love will make it alright

If you just believe in me
I will love you endlessly
Take my hand. Take me into your heart
I'll be there forever baby
I won't let go, I'll never let go

Anytime you need a friend, I will be here
Never be alone again. No, no, don't worry, don't fear
Yes, I'm with you, wherever you are
So don't you ever be lonely, it's alright
It's alright
It's alright
Yes, you know it's alright
Don't ever fear
Oh, I'm by your side
Don't you ever be lonely
Anytime"

Tears flowed freely from everyone in attendance. It wasn't until later that evening that Mallory and Rochelle came to Hermione and told her that they had never seen a bewitched note fold itself and broadcast a message like that for anyone after they had passed. For the first time since they'd each open their Hogwarts acceptance letters, they were able to have an uneventful winter and spring session at school. Graduation approached and everyone was healthy, everyone was happy. Well, almost everyone. Hermione still cried herself to sleep most nights. There was no threat, no impending danger looming. Things were calm and everyone was able to relax and enjoy the preceding's. They were looking forward to graduating but were nervous too. Some of them were finally going to be leaving Hogwarts for the last time. Some were offered positions at the school, some at the Ministry. Some would be working in Hogsmeade and some in Diagon Alley. Most would be returning to their families, but many would now be on their own. The boys had gone to Gladrags Wizardwear and gotten their Tuxedos. The young ladies had gowns made, shoes imported, multiple fitting appointments. The school was abuzz with excitement of what was to come. Jade offered to do Hermione's hair. Hermione was the Valedictorian, and no one was seemingly prouder than Harry. She purchased a gown, but nervously fussed over how it fit and appeared. Jade couldn't help but laugh at her.

She just didn't seem to be able to settle down and enjoy the situation. Charista was the first to complement her on her choice, but in the end, she wanted more than anything to once

Chapter 44 – Moving on

again wear the gown Justice had gotten her. Time was passing and she wasn't close to being ready. She was alone in the prefect's bathroom when there was a knock on the door.

"Come in," she told them. No one came in. She walked over to the door and opened it. There was no one there. She looked up and down the hall but didn't see anyone. She glanced down and there, on the ground was a box with a bow. She picked it up and on the box was a note with her name typed on it. She opened it and it was an order request dated the day before Justice died. She opened the box and inside was an exquisite Quinashe original gown. It was sleeveless and perfectly tailored. It was gold silk. There were shoes as well. She put it on and looked stunning. The note enclosed with the gown was in Justice's handwriting.

"For the lady who asks for nothing yet deserves everything.
I hope you like it."

She began to cry, "After all this time you choose today to ruin my make up?" She chuckled to herself.

"Well, we can't have that." said Charista. She was joined by Mallory, Rochelle, Stormy, Robyn, Dani and Jade.

"The Hermione Jean Granger project is now underway, and we're gonna need as much time as we can get." Jade said with a grin. The note folded itself into mouth and began to sing.

"Another day has gone
I'm still all alone
How could this be
You're not here with me
You never said goodbye

Anthony Wright

Someone tell me why
Did you have to go
And leave my world so cold
Every day I sit and ask myself
How did love slip away
Something whispers in my ear and says
That you are not alone
For I am here to stay
Though you're far away
I am here to stay
You are not alone
For I am here with you
Though we're far apart
You're always in my heart
You are not alone
All alone
Why, alone
Just the other night
I thought I heard you cry
Asking me to come
And hold you in my arms
I can hear your prayers
Your burdens I will bear
But first I need your hand
Then forever can begin
Every day I sit and ask myself
How did love slip away
Something whispers in my ear and says
That you are not alone
For I am here to stay
Though you're far away
I am here to stay
You are not alone, I am here with you
Though we're far apart, You're always in my heart
You are not alone
Ohhhh

Chapter 44 – Moving on

Whisper three words and I'll come runnin'
And girl you know that I'll be there, I'll be there
You are not alone, For I am here with you
Though we're far apart, You're always in my heart
You are not alone
You are not alone, For I am here with you
Though we're far away, You're always in my heart
You are not alone"

They finished her up and everyone took a step back. "Wow. guess you do clean up well." Jade admitted.

"Thank you. Thank you all, so much."

"Stop it. You're gonna make me cry and I just finished putting on my make up." said Charista.

They walked her out of the loo and when they got to the front steps of the school, there was a car waiting to take her to the ceremony. Once they all arrived at the ceremony Professor Hunt gathered them together for a quick picture. "Everyone get in close." she requested.

Hagrid and Flitwick had decorated the pitch for the event. Demetria was taking the events of the day extremely hard. She looked lovely but chose to stay away from the group to gather herself.

Chapter 44 – Moving on

Hermione put on as brave a face as she could. She waited near the stage for her cue. She looked elegant and when she took the stage every girl there was envious. She gave the speech to end all speeches and received a standing ovation. She congratulated the staff and seniors and waded through the crowd but was clearly distracted.

She was stopped by McGonagall and introduced to several people she called 'The Panel'. She continued into one of the many tented refreshment rooms and a woman, covered in an elaborate cloak, that concealed her face, stepped up and congratulated her.

"Thank you very much." She didn't recognize the woman's voice straight away, "I'm sorry, have we met before?"

"No dear, we just have a common acquaintance."

"Oh really, who's that?"

"Justice Cain. He's an extraordinary Warlock. He thinks the world of you. Is he here? I owe him a thank you."

"Justice passed away several months ago."

"Really? I'm sorry. I must have been given inaccurate information. I apologize."

"It's okay. I didn't catch your name."

"Nicole. Nicole Tattenger-Westerfield." The woman walked off and with just one person passing between them Hermione lost sight of her. The name rang a bell and she tried to follow her but was stopped by Fred and George. Nicole glanced back at Hermione one last time.

"You broke into our shop Granger." said Fred.

"No one else would have paid for what they took with exact change." said George. He extended his hand and placed four Knuts and two Sickles in hers. "You forgot your family and friends' discount." She smiled. She found Neville and gave him a hug. His Gram was standing beside him looking so proud when someone tapped him on the shoulder.

"We'd like to congratulate you too." He turned slowly and nearly fainted when he saw his parents standing there.

"***Mum***? ***Dad***? How did? Where did? I don't understand."

"We're still s bit shaky on the details too, but from what we were told you had a hand in it. A new medication was delivered to St. Mongo's with explicit instructions of how much and how often to administer it and it worked." his dad said.

"And with continued treatments, we can come home and be a family again." said his mum.

He looked sad. "The batch I created was all there was. I had no way to test it, so I didn't make more, and the ingredients don't exist anymore. The last of it was destroyed."

"Well, someone must have found more. The hospital had plenty of it. They gave us a year's worth when we left to come here." his dad clarified.

"But how? Who?" Neville's voice trailed off and he began to look around the crowd. "Hermione!" he shouted, and she turned back and joined him. "Hermione, this is my Mum and Dad."

"Why Hermione Granger, we've heard so much about you. Congratulations dear."

"Thank you. Neville, that's so wonderful your parents were able to make it."

"Yeah, they're better from the antidote I made."

"That's fantastic."

"The antidote I gave to Justice." he whispered.

She looked him in the eyes, "Neville, how is that possible?"

"I don't know."

Professor Hunt walked up to Hermione and hugged her. "Hermione dear, I am so proud of you. You were a sheer delight to have in class this year. It really was the highlight of my career to be able to teach my best friend's daughter. Your parents are so proud they can barely contain themselves."

"Yes, I'm sure they would be. I wish they could have been here to see me today."

Dani stepped aside and standing not ten feet away were Hermione's parents.

Anthony Wright

Her father stretched out his arms to her disbelief. She covered her mouth and her eyes widened. "How is the possible?"

"Hermione, my beautiful daughter. We've missed you so." said her mother.

"Mum, Dad, I love you." She ran to them and grabbed them. "How did you get here? How did you find me?"

"We opened a practice in Edinburgh and a young man came in one day and we began talking, and one thing led to another. He was such a charming lad." her dad began.

"And he had such a nice smile." her mother cut across him.

"We ended up at dinner and during the night he caught us up on all that's gone on this year. We couldn't believe how quickly the year went by. It seemed like it was just the other day that you got your invitation to Beauxbatons. How did you end up back here?" her father asked.

"That's not important honey, she chose to come back here where all of her friends were. We're just glad the year went by without all the usual drama. We just got mixed up with opening the new business. She obviously made the right choice. She's Valedictorian and Dani was here to help her every step of the way." said her mum.

"And then he told us…" said her dad.

"Who, told you what?"

"That he wanted to ask you a question, here, today." said her mum.

Hermione was leery. "Mum, dad, when was this?"

"Last week."

"That's not possible." she said then a bouquet of Lilacs and Orchids appeared in every woman's hand in attendance.

"Actually…" said a familiar voice from behind her. Tears sprang from her eyes before she even turned around. "I guess it kind of depends on who you know. I had a very interesting rehabilitation from my injuries."

Justice was dressed in a black suit jacket and black slacks with a black silk tie. She threw her arms around him and squeezed him as tight as she could. "Ow, Ow, careful. I've just starting walking again."

"It is him! It's Justice, he's back!" shouted Dean. The

whole group rushed him and hugged and patted him and kissed him and shook his hands.

"How is this possible?" Demetria asked.

"It's a long story."

"Give us the short version." said Jade.

"My new ***friend*** and I came to an agreement. He realized he didn't have much of an interest in my kind. He doesn't get many Alphas. He did express that he was very tempted by both of your generous offers." He gestured to Hermione and Jade. "The bottom line is, he's a businessman and business is booming in large part to me being ***here***, rather than ***there***."

"But what about the deal made by the coven elders?" Dani asked.

"Yeah, I thought once you'd been touched your death was just hinging on you fulfilling your commitment to him?" Hermione added.

"That's the thing. I was never touched. The deal I made was to deliver the soul of the Dark Lord, of whom I was the offset."

"Right, Alucard." said Ron.

"I thought that too as he was explaining things to me, but as it turns out, Rochelle and the others were offsets of Alucard. I was the offset to Draco. I delivered both so he considered that payment enough. When he took me, I was still alive, albeit just. He healed me and asked me why so many people throughout my life were willing to give their life for me? I didn't have an answer for him, but he then went on to tell me that he was impressed by how many times I had in turn been so willing to give my life for so many others. He was amused by the conundrum."

"So, does that mean you work for him now?" asked Reggie as he slowly took a step back.

"Let's just say, he and I will likely be doing more business in the future, but it won't involve anyone here. I'll gladly tell you more at the graduation party later. Right now, I need to do something I've wanted to do ever since my vision returned." He stepped to Hermione and spun her around once. "I just wanted to look at you one more time. Now, that I have, I know for sure."

"Know what?" she asked through tears.

"That I want to look at you every day for the rest of my life. Which I've been assured, by a very reliable source, will be a very long time." He knelt down on one knee.

"YEAH!" shouted the twins, Fred and George simultaneously.

"Hermione Jean Granger, will you marry me?"

"Yes." she said in a shaky voice. "Oh yes." He opened a ring box and in it was a ring with a red heart shaped stone.

Harry took one look at the stone and asked Ron, "Is that?"

The crowd erupted with cheers. Harry, Ron and Charista were the first to hug them and congratulate them. As Hermione was being hugged by her parents, Justice was being hugged by Dani, Mallory, Rochelle, Stormy and Demetria.

Jade stepped up to Hermione and said, "This really isn't helping me like you any better." She paused, "But, making me a bridesmaid would be a pretty good start." She smiled and hugged her. "Oh, one more thing." Jade reached into her pocket and pulled out Hermione's Time Turner. "Try hanging on to your things."

"Thank you," she paused, "But why don't you hang on to it. With all we've been through, I've seen enough of the past. Now," She looked at Justice and her parents, "I'm only interested in the future." She turned to Justice, "By the way, since we seem to be giving misplaced things back to their rightful owners," She reached into her beaded bag and pulled out his wand. "This belongs to you."

He took it from her then said, "Not exactly." He turned to Cam and said, "You, my friend, are my choice for the new Alpha One. The coven may have disbanded, but the students, our friends, still need a protector. And since you have a built in right and left hand, in Freddy and Jade, I know you're ready."

Chapter 44 – Moving on

"I don't know what to say." Cam said as he wiped away a tear. "I could never fill your shoes, but I'll try to make you proud." They hugged each other.

Headmistress McGonagall stepped up and hugged them both. "I don't know how this is possible, but I am so glad it is. The two of you make a lovely couple and while either of you are intelligent enough to accept a high-level Ministry position tomorrow, I just want to be the first make the offer. We still need a Librarian and a Quidditch instructor."

"Thank you, Headmistress. I actually thought about Jean and I opening a new coven in America, right after we watch the Star Wars series." He smiled. "We'll think about it and let you know right after the honeymoon."

"Speaking of moons, check out Peeves." said Seamus.

"PEEVES!!!"

The end

Hermione Jean Granger – AKA – Jean – House; Gryffindor
Age 17
Highly intelligent, logical, loyal, strong, powerful, muggleborn, kind
Notable skill; Quick learner, exceptional intelligent, adaptable

Justice Cain - AKA - Just Ice - House; Hufflepuff
Age 17
Alpha One, powerful, fearless, leader, strategic, brave, kind, heightened senses, exceptional intelligence.
Notable skill: Absorbs powers of opponents, uses opponent's strengths against them, can transfer powers, can apparate and vaporize, illusionist, harbors a secret, can cast a patronus, can make himself invisible without a cloak, can make large things vanish, can do magic without a wand

Quidditch Seeker

Alucard Penhold - AKA - Alucard - AKA - The One True Dark Lord

Age – Nearly 1000 years old

Vampire, Former head of the Death Eaters, Former Dark Lord, unlimited power, cunning, cruel, killer, driven to the point of obsession, seeking the Deathly Hallows, made a deal with Death to be granted true immortality while being restored to his youthful prime in exchange for one million souls, has multiple children, is being hunted by the four remaining Ranger/Offsets born in 1995 specifically to find and kill him, twin brother of Kalick Penhold – the Oracle.

Notable skill: Lack of remorse, shape shifter, sucks the blood of pureblood wizards to restore years and function to his form.

Uses Draco Malfoy as his apprentice.

Charista McDonald - AKA - Tabby - House; Ravenclaw
Elf Age - 34, Human age - 17
Elf with a permanent human form after taking a self-brewed potion three separate times to appear as the same image. Daughter of Dobby, the elf. Extraordinary magical abilities, recuperative powers, loyal competitive, good natured.
Notable skill: Ability to recall and broadcast other's memories, inducing nose bleeds and a drain of physical energy.
Came to Hogwarts at Hermione's request.

Quidditch Chaser

Jade Malone – AKA – Jade – House; Slytherin
Age 17
Aggressive, powerful, fiercely territorial, antagonistic, Foster child found by Justice near death and nursed back to health, suspended Alpha protector, being controlled after a head trauma.
Notable skills; Competitive, manipulative, driven, fearless, athletic
Special skill; Ferocious fighter, stealth

Quidditch Keeper

Danielle Hunt - AKA - Dani - Head of Gryffindor House
Age 36
Professor of Muggle Studies - Member of Alpha Selection Committee
Friend of the Granger's - Studied in Scotland with Hermione's parents. Found Justice, Demetria and Marcus. Member of the American Panel of Coven Elders.

Demetria Sanders – aka - Lil' Squirt. House; Gryffindor
Age 16
Highly Intelligent, enthusiastic. Parents; Unknown, orphaned – Out to prove herself, talented artist
Notable Skill; When provided with a mental picture or memory transfer, she can draw the exact image

Quidditch Chaser

Mallory Featherstone
Age 20
Graduated from Hedgepeth Academy in Ireland. Goddaughter of Aberforth Dumbledore, exceptional intelligence, powerful witch, Certified as a professor of History of Magic
Notable skills: The power of illusion/bedazzling, takes on the form that is most appealing to the beholder, called to

Hogwarts to replace Aberforth when he went missing

Marcus Reece – House; Gryffindor
Age 15
Solemn, bitter, hot tempered, feels he has a specific purpose, defiant, lives in Justice's shadow
Son of Alucard
Notable skill – Foresight

Kalick Penhold - AKA - The Oracle - Lead member of The Panel
Age Nearly 1000 years old
Twin sister of Alucard
Blind, powerful, old magic, lives in the Room of Requirement.
Made a deal with Death to keep Alucard alive in exchange for her immortality, but now wants to die
Notable skills; Can take on a younger, more appealing form. The gift of foresight.

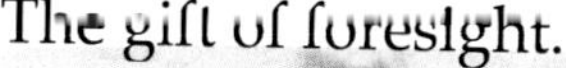

Cameron Tae – AKA – Cam – House; Ravenclaw
Age 17
Loyal, smart, brilliant chemist, levelheaded, helpful, sweet, has a secret crush on Demetria

Quidditch Beater

Alfredo Tejada – AKA – Freddy – House; Ravenclaw
Age 18
Loyal, tough, mechanically inclined, tracker, funny

Quidditch Beater

Stormy Knight – AKA – Stormy – House; Hufflepuff
Age 17
Notable skills: Brave, helpful, has a crush on Neville Longbottom

Quidditch Chaser

Rochelle Maynard
Age 17
Beauxbatons Quidditch team captain
Exceptional speed on a broom, record setting goal scorer, competitive
Notable skills; Ranger/Offset

Quidditch Chaser

Gabrielle Delacour – AKA – Gaby
Age 15
Student Prefect at Beauxbatons
Younger sister of Fleur Delacour

Nicole Tattenger-Westerfield - AKA - Fiona
Age 37
Great-Great-Great Granddaughter of Fiona Tattenger
Descendant of the only Witch to achieve the level of Dark Lord
Notable skill - Possesses the knowledge of a power type of magic called Focus Energy Targeting - The ability to perform magic through a solid object to a specific target.

Reginald Fields - AKA - Reggie - House; Hufflepuff
Age 18
Kind, helpful, strong, funny, thoughtful

Quidditch Beater

Robyn Banks - AKA - Robyn - House; Slytherin
Age 17
Notable skills; Aggressive, eager, skilled flyer, hypnotic eyes

Quidditch Seeker

SOUNDTRACK –

Ain't no mountain high enough
Marvin Gaye & Tammi Terrell
Performed by Justice Cain – Michael Jordan

Like Whoa
Ally & A.J.
Performed by Justice Cain & Jade Malone –
Michael Jordan & Alyson Michalka

Always be my baby
Mariah Carey
Performed by Jade Malone
Alyson Michalka

Unforgettable
Natalie Cole & Nat King Cole
Performed by Justice Cain & Hermione Granger
Michael Jordan & Emma Watson

You're the one that I want
John Travolta & Olivia Newton John
Performed by Justice Cain & Hermione Granger
Michael Jordan & Emma Watson

If you say my eyes are beautiful
Jermaine Jackson & Whitney Houston
Performed by Justice Cain & Hermione Granger
Michael Jordan & Emma Watson

All I want for Christmas
Mariah Carey
Performed by Jade Malone
Alyson Michalka

A moment like this
Kelly Clarkson
Performed by Hermione Granger
Emma Watson

I love you, Goodbye
Celine Dion

Bound to you
Christina Aguilera
Performed by Hermione Granger
Emma Watson

Bonfire
Knife Party

My Immortal
Evanesence

Anytime you need a friend
Mariah Carey

You are not alone
Michael Jackson
Performed by Justice Cain
Michael Jordan

About the author

Anthony lives in Southern California
With his wife Tina and children, Krysta
Madison and Aidan
He writes for the joy and relaxation of it
He writes as a legacy for his children

His other completed works include
"Fury of the T-Rex" – Fiction Thriller
"Harry the Sorcerer" – Fiction Fantasy
"Justice is Served" – Fiction Fantasy
(Feat. original cover art by Krysta Wright)
Look for other upcoming works.
"Ivy-Ambrose" – Fiction Detective Drama
"Creataurs" – Sci-Fi Fantasy
(Feat. all original artwork by Madison Wright)
And others yet to be titled

Made in the USA
Las Vegas, NV
09 March 2024